REAP THE WHIRLWIND

Robert Faulk

Book Three in the Four-Book Series:

THE SONGS OF WAR

REAP *the* WHIRLWIND

"They Have Sown the Wind and They Are Going to
Reap the Whirlwind."

General Arthur 'Bomber' Harris

ROBERT FAULK

Reap the Whirlwind
Copyright © 2023 by Lady's Slipper Books Inc.

Galleon Publishing, Moncton, Canada
www.galleonbooks.ca

ISBN
    Print: 978-1-7750820-9-5
    Ebook: 978-1-7780781-0-1

GALLEON

Table of Contents

Preface

I was born on the edge of a muddy river that drains dry twice daily and then fills itself with forty feet of brown water in less than six hours. A tidal wave rushes up the river to begin the filling process.

There was a narrow, shallow creek between our house and the river, and my father kept a rowboat in it. I fished tommy-cod from the boat when the tide reached it, and, of course, I eventually found a way to get into trouble.

I knew from experience that the fishing was best just before the wave came up the river, but the water was sixty feet down a steep, slippery mud bank. Technically, my mother decreed that I would never go down the bank, which I interpreted to mean that I should not get caught. But whenever I came home covered with mud, my mother considered she had sufficient proof that I had been fishing in the river and punished me appropriately.

The plan I arrived at for the mud problem was to untie the rowboat from the small dock at the edge of the creek, tie a long rope to a post, coil it in the bow, then push the boat over the edge of the steep bank and jump in. I enlisted a brave friend whose legs had been affected by polio, and the plan was to let the rope slide through my hands as the boat slid to the bottom of the empty river while Ken sat in the stern holding onto the fishing gear.

When the boat tipped over the edge, we took off down the wet bank like a bobsled at the Olympics, and everything went well until I ran out of rope before the boat stopped. The end slipped through my rope-burned fingers just before the boat reached the water.

There was no time to find a longer rope; we could see and hear the world-famous 'Tidal Bore' coming, and when the wave hit the boat broadside, we saved the day by diving to the high side and hanging onto the gunwale. We surfed along sideways for a bit, trying to keep the boat upright and keep ourselves in it, then whooped for joy when the wave passed under the keel.

The next emergency to take care of was that we were at the mercy of the substantial current carrying us away from home at an alarming speed. I looked for the oars, thinking we might hold the boat near the creek until the water rose, the current diminished, and later, changed direction. The idea was sound if I hadn't left the oars in the woodshed.

Given the dire situation, there was only one thing to do—wait six hours for the tide to turn and carry us back to the creek. Fortunately, thanks to Ken, we still had the fishing rods, and the cod were so excited they bit on every cast.

I'll tell the rest of the story later… it's enough, for now, to know that Ken and I survived, that I have always had a keen sense of adventure, and for some reason, when I was young, I had difficulty keeping friends.

◇◇◇◇◇◇◇◇◇◇◇◇◇◇◇◇◇◇◇◇◇◇◇◇◇◇◇◇◇◇◇◇◇◇◇◇◇◇◇

I earned my pilot license as soon as I could legally do it and built two airplanes from scratch. A friend, a retired aeronautical engineer who worked for Boeing and became an engineering professor at Washington State, helped me design the second one.

My love of engineering design, flying, the sea, and building things that I could fly, drive or take out on the ocean have been part of me since childhood. At nine, I launched my first boat; I experienced my first shipwreck at twelve and test-flew my first self-built aircraft at twenty-five. My understanding of how mechanical things work helps me understand the intricacies of flying a bomber, firing a cannon, and operating a tank. This passion and love of adventure and all things mechanical produced several situations that should have ended my life. Sometimes, I had to settle for divine intervention as the only explanation for my survival.

But I got to choose whether and when I would take a risk. I calculated the odds—when I had a family, I made sure my life insurance premium was paid—and then did things I shouldn't have gotten away with. In war, people like Juliette in A Song of Sorrow and, in this book, Willie, Erik, Marita, and Norma have no choice. When Willie voluntarily enlisted in the Royal Canadian Air Force, he had no idea he would have better than a fifty percent chance of burning alive in a bomber falling from twenty thousand feet. And when he found out, there was no way out of the "Patriotic duty" trap.

Erik, Willie's nemesis in the air, was dedicated to stopping Willie's RAF lancaster from bombing his homeland. Erik's wife and children were in Bomber Command's line of fire, and Erik saw his night fighter as their only hope.

CHAPTER ONE:

30 March 1944

Theirs not to make reply,
Theirs not to reason why,
Theirs but to do and die,
Into the valley of Death
Rode the six hundred.
Alfred, Lord Tennyson. The Charge Of The Light Brigade

THE RIDE ON THE GRAVEL RUNWAY WAS ROUGH and noisy, but when the thirty-two-ton aircraft had eaten up almost a mile of the packed surface, the vibrations and rattles suddenly ceased. A hundred feet before the hard surface ended, the lancaster gently lifted itself and had eight feet of altitude under its retracting wheels when it crossed the threshold. Twenty missions had accustomed Willie to the slight change in angle when the lancaster tilted upward, and he settled back and rested his feet on the pedals. He released the breath he had held since Pilot Officer Steve White had opened the throttles and watched the lines of runway lights recede. The strings of white dots squeezed together as 'C for Charley' left the safety of the ground behind.

Willie McLaughlin watched the runway disappear in the darkness behind the lancaster with the same foreboding he felt every time he took off on a mission. The sixty-five-thousand-pound overloaded bomber had successfully clawed its way into the air, avoiding the disaster waiting at the end of the runway if one of its four rolls royce Merlin engines coughed. Still, the odds against returning from the mission had barely diminished.

Alone in the dark and safe for the moment, Willie did what he always did at the beginning of a bombing mission; he calculated his odds of surviving his twentieth mission, hoping to find a different solution. But he knew the answer would always be that a rear air gunner on a lancaster had a one-in-ten chance of making it home on every one of twenty consecutive missions. But today, his calculations took on a more sinister meaning—this was Willie's twentieth mission. When the wheels came up, Bomber Command handed him another ticket on a deadly lottery where he calculated that his odds of dying increased exponentially with every trip to Germany. If he survived this one, the odds of surviving the subsequent bombing run over enemy territory would be one in...his mind refused to go there.

The aircraft, loaded far beyond civilian safety limits, climbed to two thousand feet before levelling off under the German radar that searched for it from across the English Channel. The white navigation light mounted on the rear of the lancaster's fuselage lit Willie's turret, and red and green wing lights marked the one-hundred-and-two-foot wingspan of a lancaster flying half a mile behind 'C for Charley.' Forty-eight pistons thrashing in four powerful engines moaned a synchronized monotonic song, pulsing in and out of resonance in a comforting melody. If an engine failed now, the lancaster still had the option of turning around.

If not for the war, all would have been perfect; the clear night and bright moon would have been romantic. But flak guns and night fighters would be hunting for them, and the beautiful night spelled disaster if clear moonlit skies extended to the objective. The forecast was for broken clouds along the route and two layers of scattered clouds over the target. Willie no longer believed that God had any influence in this war, but he lowered his head and said a silent prayer...just in case. Willie prayed for clouds. It was the thirtieth of March 1944, and the flotilla's objective was Nürnberg.

◇◇◇◇◇◇◇◇◇◇◇◇◇◇◇◇◇◇◇◇◇◇◇◇◇◇◇◇◇◇◇◇◇◇◇◇

Willie had removed the perspex from his turret, and although it was now drafty, doing so had eliminated reflection and distortion that could prevent him from seeing a night fighter sneaking up on him. Despite the intense cold, Willie was comfortable in the winter clothes he wore under his electrically-heated coveralls. The heating elements had no thermostat, so Willie usually didn't plug them in until the cold seeped through the layers, and flew most missions without plugging them in. He wore three layers of gloves on his hands and two pairs of socks in his oversized heated boots.

Twice before, night fighters had singled out Willie's lancaster, and twice he had escaped. The fighter's tactic was the same each time: take out the tail gunner, then shoot down the now-defenseless bomber from behind. Tail gunners expected these attacks—they knew their only chance at survival was to see the fighter before he fired. With machine guns against cannons, the lancaster gunner had to wait until the German was close enough for his four brownings to be effective; he had to resist the temptation to fire too soon, but if he fired too late... At long range, the armoured cockpit of a German night fighter was a waste of time and ammunition, but at close range, the four streams of steel bullets would tear a windscreen apart. It was a game of predator and prey, with the predator holding the advantage.

In his first encounter, Willie had seen nothing until the twinkling lights from the fighter's nose cannons coincided with explosions below his feet. The hunter had fired too soon and too low, blasting most of the lower floor out of the turret but leaving Willie alive and petrified. He screamed "corkscrew" into the intercom and hoped that Pilot Officer Stephen White wouldn't take the time to question him.

Before Willie could repeat the word, the plane rolled into a steep left-hand spiral, building speed quickly as sixty-five thousand pounds of bomber, gasoline, and bombs plunged toward the ground. Willie had left his safety harness loose for comfort and held onto the steel handles as he fired a steady stream of tracers into the night despite banging his head on the aluminum window frame. He stopped when he realized that his gun flashes and tracers were laying a trail for the fighter to follow, and the chances of hitting something he couldn't see were minuscule. Pilot Officer Steve White reversed the spiral and spun a complete turn to the right before levelling the aircraft in thick clouds. The fighter was gone.

On the second attack, Willie saw the focke wulf 190's dark silhouette and waited for the range to shorten before he held down the firing buttons on the four browning .303 machine guns, guiding a stream of steel bullets into the nose of the night fighter. The attacker immediately returned Willie's fire, blowing the left-side perspex windows out of Willie's turret. The focke wulf and the tail gunner were caught in a standoff as the fighter's cannons launched their invisible shells, and Willie guided the tracers in his reflector sight straight into the

German's cockpit—forty-eight bullets per second, ten percent of them armour-piercing. The range had closed enough that the impact blew two cylinders off the big radial engine in front of the pilot, then shattered the 190's windshield in thousands of pieces, instantly killing the pilot. The fighter's nose dropped into a terminal dive trailing smoke and debris—and Willie had his first kill. His hands shook, and his voice broke as he said weekly in the intercom, "No need to corkscrew…I got him."

Willie hadn't seen a night fighter since then, but in the past six months, he had watched bombers inexplicably drop out of the sky in flames, most of them with a wing blown off. At two separate briefings, he had reported two flaming bomber incidents but had not gotten an acknowledgment, let alone an explanation.

On his eighteenth mission, Willie discovered what happened to the flaming bombers.

<hr>

A night fighter's shadow appeared between layers of bombers, at least a hundred and fifty feet below Willie's feet. It stalked the lancaster to his right and slightly behind him. Outside Willie's field of fire, the shadow gained on the lancaster but, rather than climb to attack its belly, remained below it. As the fighter came closer, the faint light of stars revealed what looked to Willie like cannon muzzles behind the pilot, pointed almost straight up.

He shouted a warning into the intercom, hoping the radio operator had time to warn the lancaster, but as the fighter passed under the bomber's starboard wing, a streak of flame from the erect muzzles lit up the night. The lancaster's inboard fuel tank exploded, separating two-thirds of the bomber's right wing from the fuselage. It fluttered like a leaf as it fell behind the fighter. The left wingtip lifted to point at heaven—the unsupported fuselage dropped—and a short minute later, the flaming wreck struck the ground in a splash of bright light and a surge of flames that died almost immediately. Willie watched a glow that marked seven men's final resting place fade into the night.

<hr>

When "C for Charlie" landed, Willie reported that a German night fighter had come from behind and below the bomber, crept undetected past the rear gunner, and sent the crew to their afterlife with a burst of cannon fire into the fuel tanks. The squadron leader filed a written report to RAF intelligence, but neither he nor Willie heard anything more about it.

Determined to spot a German night fighter before it slithered under his lancaster, Willie removed every piece of perspex from his turret and hung his goggles on a bolt.

<hr>

Halfway across the black English Channel, Willie used the 'D' handled cable to double-cock his guns, slid the safety back and fired a short burst. He reported "guns ready," and, a few minutes later, felt Steve trim for the climb to their cruise altitude of twenty thousand feet. The white tail light beside Willie's head went out; the red and green wing lights of the planes around Willie's lancaster disappeared, but he could still see their sharply defined shadows and occasionally moonlight bouncing off their wings.

The lancaster climbed slowly, and with every thousand feet, the outside temperature dropped two degrees Celsius. Without perspex, Willie was effectively outside, and twenty-five minutes later, at twenty thousand feet, Willie's porch was a cold minus forty degrees Celsius.

The earth's shadow hid half the nonetheless brilliant moon. The cold front that preceded the raid left clear air in its wake, air that contained very little moisture at twenty thousand feet. Visibility was perfect for anything but a bombing mission, and as Willie watched the earth's curve fall away behind him, he couldn't help but marvel at the peace he felt. He imagined people in their beds in the moonlit houses he could see sliding under his lancaster, and wished they could see this beautiful night from his perch. Reality punched his gut when he realized twenty-five feet from where he sat were eight tons of bombs designed to kill those sleeping people!

<hr>

Willie reluctantly returned to the reason he was sitting in a turret, remembering how badly he needed something to cover that bright moon. He consulted God once more—now that the lancaster was in enemy territory, clouds became the priority.

When Willie finished his prayer, he reasoned that most of the hundreds of bombers in the stream were filled with religious men, all making the same request to the same God. Indeed, if He were listening and on their side, the skies should be covered with clouds thousands of feet deep! Perhaps God had heard their prayers but had decided instead to save the sleeping souls who had prayed for protection in their moonlit houses by guiding the faithful believers in the bombers to their deaths in a clear sky.

If God didn't do something about those missing clouds, he would lose many RAF fans before the night was over. But then, he would almost certainly gain many fans in Nürnberg, the city they were tasked with destroying.

CHAPTER TWO

30 March 1944

Alte Füchse gehen schwer in die Falle.
(Old foxes are hard to catch.)

OBERLEUTNANT ERIK STEPHANIE HAD BEEN FLYING a messerschmitt Bf 110 for three years; first as a day fighter, and then, when the messerschmitt 110 proved to be suicide against hurricanes and spitfires, as a night fighter hunting the British bombers that crossed the English Channel almost every night. Initially, he was as disappointed with the clumsy twin-engine mongrel in the dark as he had been in the daylight, but as radar improved and it became easier to find his prey, Erik's kill tally mounted. He and his navigator accumulated twenty-one kills, five of them lancasters, and Erik expected to increase that number if the British bombers were foolish enough to attack tonight.

Erik stood at the chart table, listening to the squadron intelligence officer as he tried to predict tonight's target. Despite the clear weather, a massive bomber armada was forming over the English Channel, and it looked like it would be the most extensive stream of bombers Erik had seen in a year. He asked himself why the British would send so many men into what could only be a slaughter? What target could be so crucial to them? Erik could think of no city's demise so vital it couldn't wait for a moonless night filled with clouds. There had to be an explanation, but until he found one, he thanked his protestant God for the British generals' idiocy and the opportunity to make the barbaric RAF pay for its brutal attack on German civilians! He closed his prayer with a promise not to waste it.

◇◇◇◇◇◇◇◇◇◇◇◇◇◇◇◇◇◇◇◇◇◇◇◇◇◇◇◇◇◇◇◇

The mappers plotted the usual turn over Belgium and the bombers' most likely course toward the German border. At this point, the intelligence officer could not guess the bombers' destination, but Erik had what he needed—targets—it was time to fly.

He turned toward the door, and Leutnant Michael Gerber, his

navigator, rear gunner, and radar operator, stepped aside to let his commander exit ahead of him. Once outside, Gerber walked to the waiting fighter shoulder-to-shoulder with his friend.

The complicated radar antennae and twin daimler benz engines gave the messerschmitt Bf 110 the appearance of an overgrown dragonfly. Two twenty-millimetre cannon barrels pointed upward from the rear of the long perspex canopy, fixed at a forward slope of fifteen degrees off vertical, an arrangement nicknamed *Schrägemusik*, the German alias for jazz music, by the men who used them. The system devastated the hordes of British aircraft invading German airspace. The messerschmitt 110 night fighter's 30 mm nose cannons and MG 38 machine guns out-gunned the nearly helpless British bombers by a wide margin, but *Schrägemusik* and Lichtenstein radar tipped the scale entirely in favour of the night fighter.

When a crew reached the ten-kill mark, the Luftwaffe allowed them to choose a new plane, and Erik and Michael had chosen well. They asked for and got a messerschmitt Bf 110G-4. The airframe was fitted with a ninety mm thick windscreen instead of the usual seventy-five—the British browning's .303 bullets bounced off that much perspex—and the sides and bottom of the cockpit were protected with 6 mm armour plate, equally impervious to the bombers' machine guns.

The radar, a FuG 220 Lichtenstein SN-2 built by Siemens, could find a lone lancaster at a range of over a hundred kilometres. With this radar, Michael could pick out a single bomber in a screen filled with 'window'—bundles of aluminum strips thrown out of aircraft to confuse German radar. Erik's new Me110's 30 mm nose cannons, when simultaneously fired with the array of four 7.9 mm machine guns, could cut the wing off a lancaster in three seconds. Erik had requested that the fitters rig his Schrägemusik with thirty-millimetre cannons instead of the standard twenty, but was told the ammunition canisters wouldn't fit. However, he did get reflector mirrors so that the pilot or the navigator could operate them.

Erik approached his target from behind and seventy-five metres below, and in five successful kills using this method, no rear gunner had even seen Erik's messerschmitt. As he approached his victims, Erik kept one eye on the rear turret gunner; until now, none had moved. Although German night fighters had been using upward-firing cannons for six months, Erik speculated that Bomber Command still didn't understand, or perhaps wouldn't admit, that he and his comrades were using something as simple as *Schrägemusik* to kill their crews.

◇◇◇◇◇◇◇◇◇◇◇◇◇◇◇◇◇◇◇◇◇◇◇◇◇◇◇

The mechanics had pre-warmed the mercedes 605 engines, and every cylinder instantly roared to life when Erik engaged the bosch starters. Erik's would be the first Bf 110 to take off from runway 27 at Florennes Airfield in Belgium. It was two hundred and fifty kilometres to where he could intercept the bomber stream, and Erik planned to wait from a position above and ahead of them.

On the previous mission, the bomber stream had avoided most of the German night fighters; of those that found and attacked the bombers, twenty percent didn't return. The bomber's gunners seemed keener; they had finally figured out that Schrägemusik was killing them and knew where to look for the German hunters. British escort fighters, the pervasive mosquitos, were becoming an increasingly deadly nuisance. The evidence was overwhelming that the British mosquitos could locate a German night fighter either from its radio transmissions or from the night fighter's radar signals. The Luftwaffe dismissed this as a rumour, but just in case, Erik and Michael maintained radio silence and avoided switching on the radar for longer than a few minutes.

Michael pulled Erik from his reverie when he said, "I will switch on the radar at your order, sir." Erik took that as a reminder that they would not have radar until he ordered Michael to turn it on. They wouldn't need it for a while in any case.

While Erik throttled up the engines to a fast idle and began going through his checklist, Michael took those minutes to go through his pre-flight routine and verify his navigation calculations. Erik finished his ground checks with the magnetos, and when he backed off the throttles, Michael read off his navigation instructions.

"Climb out on a course of eighty degrees; we will reach our hold point twenty-one minutes after liftoff. I'm assuming a southwest tail-wind above two thousand metres."

Erik had seen Michael use radar to locate a single bomber in thick clouds on a pitch-black night. But tonight's visibility was unlimited, and finding this enormous bomber flotilla would be child's play even without radar.

Erik's focus shifted to what was becoming his worst fear. Every intercept brought more pesky, deadly mosquito escorts, every one of them with radar at least as effective as the Lichtenstein set in Erik's messerschmitt. Could it be that the British had sent hundreds of mosquitos to escort the bombers? Was the bomber armada bait for a night fighter trap?

Michael cut in on Erik's pessimistic reflections. "We won't be at six thousand metres until ten minutes after we get to the intercept point," "I'll plan a climbing holding pattern until the bombers arrive."

"That's all satisfactory, but I would like to climb above seven thousand metres, well above the bombers' usual altitude."

"Understood."

Erik taxied to the runway behind a weaving FW 190. With a big radial engine blocking everything directly in front of him, the focke wulf 190 pilot had to weave back and forth so he could see the taxiway ahead of him, slowing his progress and frustrating Erik. Time was a precious commodity at this point.

Finally, the focke wulf pilot lined his plane up on the runway and opened its throttle. The engine produced an air-splitting blat that penetrated Erik's night fighter, drowning out the usual creaks and groans of taxiing and the smooth purr of the mercedes engines. The plane surged ahead, immediately lifting its tail so the pilot could see over the cowling. Erik lined up on the runway when the fighter began its take-off roll, and the Me110 was shaking in its wake when he pushed the throttle levers forward. The messerschmitt accelerated quickly as the agile focke wulf freed itself of gravity's constraints and began its steep climb. Erik's fighter rocked in the twisting air left behind by the big radial engine; and his feet danced on the rudder pedals, keeping the Me110 close to the runway's centreline.

Erik let his mind wander as he gently pulled back on the control stick, lifting his aircraft into its element. Flying was as reflexive to him as breathing, and as he began the turn to the track Michael had given him, the messerschmitt moved out of the fighter's wake into smooth air. His thoughts turned to his wife asleep in their bed in Heilbronn and to his son, the light of their lives. Marita always slept on her back, and Erik imagined her long blond hair covering the pillow behind her head. The focke wulf climbing ahead and to the right of Erik suddenly pitched nose down, dove into the ground and exploded in a ball of flame. In the second it took Erik to process what had happened, a mosquito night fighter zipped past his slow-moving messerschmitt, whose climbing speed was two hundred kilometres an hour slower than the airspeed of the diving mosquito sharply silhouetted against the moonlit sky. mosquitos usually hunted in pairs, and Erik assumed the second mosquito was behind him, lining up his guns. If he did nothing or something the mosquito pilot anticipated, he and Michael would share the burning fighter pilot's fate!

Erik reacted without thinking—he pushed the stick ahead, yanked it to the left, and mashed the left rudder with his foot. The plane jerked left, tried to invert itself, and dove for the ground as a line of tracers passed the starboard wing. Michael breathed a long *"Sheisse!"* as the second mosquito zipped past and disappeared into the darkness.

Erik fought the airplane in the confusing and dimensionless black void—the airspeed increased, the gyro compass heading spun down along with the altitude as the invisible ground approached—he was in a left-hand spiral! Erik used right aileron to level the wings but kept the nose down as he strained to see the jagged black carpet of trees he knew were close. He shouted into the intercom, "Find those mosquitos before they kill us!" Erik was acutely aware that a mosquito had a maximum straight and level speed one hundred kilometres-per-hour faster than his Me110, could easily out-climb it and was infinitely more maneuverable.

Escape from them was impossible unless the mosquitos ran out of gas or made a mistake. There was nowhere to hide except in the darkness close to the ground—and only if it were a perfectly timed and radical departure from the mosquito pilot's expectations. Even then, Erik and Michael's only hope was for the mosquitos to decide that protecting the bombers was more important than sharing a kill.

The trees were suddenly there—Erik pulled the stick to the right, kicked the right rudder, and the plane skimmed along below a ridge of trees, gaining precious speed.

<hr>

An instant before he pushed the firing button on his machine guns, Larry Inman's sure kill suddenly turned hard left and dove. The tracers brushed past the messerschmitt's right wing, and the German fighter dropped below the diving mosquito before he could fire again.

Larry lifted the mosquito's nose and concentrated on avoiding the jagged line of trees that rose from a ridge and filled his windscreen. Using all the power the Merlins had, the mosquito barely cleared the treetops. The mosquito climbed to a thousand feet before Larry kicked in all the left rudder he had and simultaneously cut the left engine. The aircraft obediently flipped on its edge in a beautiful chandelle maneuver and reversed direction as Larry powered up the left engine again.

"Larry said, "Danny, tell Remi to skedaddle to the bombers; we'll catch up after we kill this bastard.!"

"Willco," said Danny and keyed the VHF radio mic.

Larry glanced at the altimeter, then looked back in the moonlight to where the German should be. Danny Powell, the mosquito's radio operator and navigator, found the messerschmitt silhouetted against the black trees. With throttles open in a shallow dive, it took Larry ten seconds to get within range, and the wooden airframe shook as he fired his cannons and machine guns. Again, just as Larry fired, the German disappeared, this time upward, and the mosquito's bullets passed under it. Larry was too low and going too fast to do a steep turn, so he waited until he passed where the Me110 had been.

"Bastard...You fucking lucky bastard!" Larry was working on his cursing habit, but this messerschmitt wasn't helping! He had to raise the nose to stay out of the trees, and when he finally finished his turn and looked for the messerschmitt, the aircraft had disappeared in the darkness. He slammed his hand on the wheel.

∞∞∞∞∞∞∞∞∞∞∞∞∞∞∞∞∞∞∞∞∞∞∞∞∞∞∞∞

Michael had turned in his seat to watch for the mosquito and shouted, "He's right behind us!" just before Erik yanked the plane up and to the left, slamming him against the edge of the canopy's aluminum coaming. Tracers lit the sky below and on the right as Erik pulled up, stomped on the left rudder and jerked the stick against the left aileron stop, banking and climbing as steeply as he could without stalling a wing. The messerschmitt, its wing approaching vertical, soared, then seemed to hover until Erik pushed the stick ahead to prevent the stall. Michael saw the mosquito pass under him and yelled into the intercom, "He went under my feet!"

Erik calculated the mosquito's turn would take about half a minute, and his messerschmitt would need air under it if he were going to outfox the mosquito pilot again.

Erik had less than a minute to think of how he could fool the mosquito again—he couldn't outfly the mosquito, but he might be able to disappear in the dark shadows of the trees. He knew where there was a river, and the river was in a deep valley....

He thought he had more time when another stream of tracers came out of the blackness ahead of him. He pushed hard on the stick with both hands and heard bullets rattling on his windscreen as he shouted, "Scheisse! How did he turn around that fast?" The ME 110 did as ordered; it dove for the ground, and the mosquito turned and zipped past so close Erik glimpsed the pilot and navigator's faces in the glow of their red instrument panel lights!

With his plane falling from the sky, Erik had no time to speculate where the mosquito would turn up next—he only had one chance, and the odds were not good! He cut the left throttle, pulled the stick into the left corner, and straightened his left leg on the rudder. The messerschmitt completed a tight ninety-degree turn, overstressing every rivet and bolt in the airframe, and Erik cleared the tallest black trees by putting the 110's left wing between them. He flattened the aircraft out in a narrow valley with treetops flashing past on both sides, then waited without breathing for the mosquito to pass overhead.

◇◇◇◇◇◇◇◇◇◇◇◇◇◇◇◇◇◇◇◇◇◇◇◇◇◇◇◇◇◇◇◇◇◇

Swearing while concentrating on the chandelle to reverse direction, Larry dove to build up precious airspeed and found the messerschmitt... coming straight at him! He instinctively hit the machine guns' firing button, then turned hard right, praying the messerschmitt didn't do the same!

Danny yelled as they passed the diving messerschmitt so close Larry could identify the pilot, and his hand shook as he climbed to do another one-eighty turn. When he completed it, he was heading for the airfield and the messerschmitt was gone, swallowed into the blackness.

Danny said, "He's not on the screen... I think he may be in the trees, or maybe he's behind us. Either way, the bastard is Houdini!" Larry depressed the nose to increase his speed, hoping to catch him, but with no idea whether he was chasing the night fighter or charging away from him. He said, "Fuck it, we've got to find Remi and protect those bombers. If that bastard wants to fly into the ground, let him do it without me!"

Danny breathed a sigh of relief as the mosquito climbed and turned toward the bomber stream it was supposed to guard.

Flying between and well below two ridges of hills, straight at where he thought the hunter would be finishing his turn, Erik passed the mosquito head-on at a closing speed of seven hundred kilometres an hour but a thousand feet below it. The graceful shape flashed in and out of Erik's vision, blotting out the moon for a split second. Erik flew around the tallest trees, just above the tips of the shorter ones.

"That was too close!" Michael was suddenly hoarse. "Now I remember why I hate flying!"

Erik didn't answer...throttles open, he concentrated on speed, flying as close to the trees as he dared. When the mosquito pilot realized he had been snookered, Erik wanted to be well below him and as far away as possible. He flew away from the airfield in what he hoped was the opposite direction from the mosquito, turning the 'wooden wonder's' high speed to the clumsy messerschmitt one-ten's advantage.

"Are there any fighters back there?" Erik weaved the plane back and forth, eliminating Michael's dead spot.

Michael answered, "All clear back here...let's hope he went elsewhere to hunt."

"We may see him again before this night is over. Is the course still eighty degrees?"

"Eighty is fine, but please climb!"

Erik smiled as trees growing on ridges on both sides of the narrow valley whipped past the fleeing messerschmitt. They flew down a winding river, risky practice in daylight, near suicide in the dark, and Erik chuckled into the intercom as he pulled back on the stick, sending the messerschmitt upward. The new mercedes 605 engines roared at full throttle, drinking precious fuel as fast as it could flow through the lines.

Time and fuel would now be short. When Erik reached the holding point, he would have less than ninety minutes to climb, fight and get back on the ground. He figured it would take half that to find the bombers and most of the rest to reach home.

CHAPTER THREE

30 March 1944

Bedenke, dass du sterben musst.
(Remember that you must die.)

NO 44 RHODESIAN SQUADRON, a gaggle of twenty-four lancasters flying second in an armada of thirty squadrons, was crossing the coast of Holland when the tail of the stream of seven-hundred-and-seventy-nine heavy bombers was still forming over England. The aluminum river occupied over seventy miles of airspace—eight, sometimes ten miles wide, and four thousand feet deep. The stream's organization was the key to keeping over seven hundred heavy aircraft from colliding by making their locations predictable.

In the moonlight, Willie could see dozens of aircraft to his right, his left, and suspended in a geometric river of dark shapes stretching miles behind him. He began counting but stopped when the dark outlines started to overlap.

Willie envisioned himself flying a German night fighter and immediately thought of the bombers as targets and the fighter pilot as a defender of his homeland. He imagined trying to creep under a lancaster in a night fighter and asked himself whether the bright moonlight would be a help or a hindrance.

If the gunner were looking for him, could he avoid detection? Would the moonlight favour the night fighter or the bomber? What about the nearby planes in the formation? If they saw the fighter before he fired, could their guns reach him? Willie's penchant for detail prompted him to list the advantages and weaknesses of each approach, and his analysis led him to conclude that the bright moonlit night gave a talented fighter pilot a distinct advantage, the same as he would have in daylight. The Americans bombed successfully in daylight, but their bombers bristled with guns and had a couple of squadrons of fighter escorts.

Willie's musing evaporated as they neared their cruising altitude in clear air. At the briefing, the Met officer had assured them that the flight would be over broken and occasional scattered high clouds that would protect them, but there were no clouds. To make it worse, Willie watched with increasing concern as trails of frozen condensation began to form behind each wing.

As they climbed, long, slender clouds attached themselves behind the engines, becoming four long silver tails that dissolved into the black background between the bombers flying behind 'C for Charley.' Every plane he could see trailed the same silver slivers, frighteningly visible for miles.

Willie spoke into his mask. "Have you guys seen what we're leaving behind us?" He felt sick—the narrow white clouds shone in the moonlight, a bright road for German night fighters to follow.

"Yes, I see it…" Phillip Carpenter, the flight engineer, had his head in the observation dome… "Every plane has the same problem—a lot of guys aren't going to make it home tonight!"

<hr>

Willie's mind went to Phillip. He was overweight and a few inches over six feet tall, and despite the many exit rehearsals Steve had insisted upon, Phillip couldn't get out of the front escape hatch—the one assigned to the flight engineer—with his parachute on. Finally, after trying a dozen suggestions, Phillip resolved to ride the plane to the ground and take his chances. Captain Steve wouldn't agree to that and threatened to ground him if he couldn't get out of the hatch.

Phillip ate nothing, gave up beer, drank gallons of water, and lost thirty pounds in three weeks but still couldn't get out through the narrow hatch with the parachute. He pleaded with the ground crew to widen the opening, but they nixed that idea, citing necessary structural members on both sides of the hatch. Steve finally grounded Phillip after a mission where two neighbouring bombers fell in flames.

When they landed after the first mission without him, Phillip met Steve after he climbed out of the plane.

"I have decided to shoot myself if you don't let me fly!" Phillip announced his decision in front of the crew.

"You don't have a gun." Steve tried to walk around the big man.

Phillip grabbed Steve's shoulder. "Lend me yours!"

Steve shrugged and handed his pistol to Phillip. "If you shoot yourself, that's your fault, but you will not burn in my plane if there is a chance to get out."

"No one got out of those other planes!"

Steve pushed a finger on Phillip's chest and took his gun back. "Maybe they would have if they had practiced an escape plan!"

Charley McDonald, the navigator, interrupted. "Wa dornt ye gie it withit a parachute an' 'en pit it oan?" His home in the northern Scottish Isles bastardized English with a heavy brogue that made Charley difficult to understand, but the crew had gotten used to his unique way of speaking and now could figure out about half of it. They stopped walking to laugh at the suggestion.

Charley didn't laugh. "I'm serioos, ye boorichie ay unimaginatife turds." For emphasis, he rolled the 'r' in 'turds' more than in 'boorichie.'

Steve shook his head. "That's not a solution, Charley; I said with a parachute. The idea is to use a parachute so that he lives to tell about it!" Steve waited for another suggestion. No one volunteered anything, and he turned to leave.

Charley stopped him again—his black beard wiggled when he spoke. "Sae, ye Sassenach bastards hink we lads frae th' Scottish isles ken naethin' but sheep an' goats? dae ye want tae hear mah idea ur nae, ye croose Sassenach dug?" Charley spun Steve around, using his shoulder as a lever.

Steve laughed with the rest of the crew, brushed Charley's hand from his shoulder, and faced him. He didn't mind being called "Sassenach," abusive Scottish slang for English, but "dug," or dog was more insubordinate than he could allow. "All right, you hairy Scottish bastard, what's the brilliant idea?" He deliberately emphasized Charley's questionable parenthood.

Charley put both hands on his hips and stuck out his bearded chin. "Ance it ay an airplane at twintie thousand feit, there's nae much tae dae fur a minute ur tois, sae wa nae tak' th' time tae pit a parachute oan? ay coorse, ye woods need tae min' tae brin' it wi' ye when ye exited th' hatch, somethin' 'at an Sassenach woods hae difficulty wi', considerin' they can't min' 'at scootlund belongs tae th' Scottish fowk, an' nae tae th' Sassenach invaders."

He held up his hand, and the laughing stopped. "An' althoogh ye main want tae forgit it, ye shoods also min' frae yer history lessons 'at th' Americans kicked th' Sassenach tyrants it ay their coontry an' chased them back athwart th' Atlantic." He put his face against Steve's, put two fingers between them and said, "Twice!"

He stepped back while the crew snickered and waved a hand at Phillip. "Noo, Ah expect 'at a smart yoong Yankee loch Phillip won't forgit tae brin' his parachute wi' heem noo, will he?"

Steve thrust his face against Charley's, hands on his hips, imitating his Scottish accent. "Ye dumb sheepfucker, hoo th' heel dae ye hang ontae th' parachute, lit aloyn pit it oan in a two-hundred-mile-an-hoor win'?"

"I'll shaw ye hoo that's dain afair thes day is it!" Scottish pride was now on the line. "Troost me, ye glaikit Sassenach twit." Charley spit the "t" through his beard, growled for emphasis, and stomped toward the debriefing room, leaving the crew staring after him. They stood silently for a minute or two and then began a serious conversation on their way to the debriefing to figure out how to get the parachute out of the hatch behind Phillip. Once out, he would have to fasten the straps in a fierce wind at forty below zero, where fingers freeze in seconds. Willie shook his head, afraid that Charley had dug his hole too deep... but said nothing.

✧✧✧✧✧✧✧✧✧✧✧✧✧✧✧✧✧✧✧✧✧✧✧

Following the debriefing, the crew met back at the airplane. Steve opened the hatch and pointed at Phillip and Charley.

"Alright, get this over with so we can all go for a Burton." Realizing that he had just taken his words from a ubiquitous billboard advertising a British beer, now a phrase reserved by the RAF for dying in a plane crash, he quickly corrected himself. "I just meant to say we'll go for a beer."

The men looked at one another until all of them were staring at Steve, who had jinxed them for sure. Steve, to try and repair the damage, impulsively said, "If we get this figured out, I'm buying." The men looked at one another, nodded, and smiled at Steve.

Phillip gracefully grasped the edges of the narrow hatch opening and swung his body up and through it. He took his parachute pack from its hook on the fuselage wall and threw it out through the hatch, then followed as athletically as he had entered and stood beside the parachute. Charley was silent—Willie saw a flicker of panic cross his bearded face.

✧✧✧✧✧✧✧✧✧✧✧✧✧✧✧✧✧✧✧✧✧✧✧

Rhodesia sponsored the No 44 squadron, but the aircrews included men from all over the British Commonwealth. In Phillip's case, that included the son of an Idaho potato farmer. Following the latest of many bitter arguments with his father, he crossed the border into Canada at the beginning of the war, renounced his U.S. citizenship, and joined the Royal Canadian Air Force, intending to be a pilot.

He had told his mother not to worry; modern airplanes were safe, and he would be fighting for freedom and helping rid the world of an evil tyrant. But it was clear when she hammered on his chest, screamed, "No, I forbid you to go!" and then bitterly cried as she threw his clothes into his suitcase that she didn't understand why he was going.

Phillip washed out of pilot school during 'unusual attitude' training, and when they gave him a second choice, he picked navigator. Using logic reserved for military organizations and government, the RCAF trained him to be a flight engineer and bomb aimer. When his training was over, he joined up with Steve, and, with the RAF's blessing, they chose their crew.

The crew they picked for 'C for Charley' proved themselves by surviving five missions in a wellington, and their reward was a new lancaster. Every operation they survived made them a more efficient fighting unit while simultaneously creating a generous amount of pessimism. Watching bombers fall in flames and rarely seeing a parachute open underlined the certainty that their turn to burn would come.

◇◇◇◇◇◇◇◇◇◇◇◇◇◇◇◇◇◇◇◇◇◇◇◇◇◇◇◇◇◇◇◇◇◇◇

Steve decided to improve his crew's odds by setting up regular exit practice, and it revealed glaring problems. They found a way to solve them all, except for Phillip's difficulty with the narrow hatch. The big man offered to wait until everyone was out of the forward area and then run to the wide rear fuselage door, but Steve was unwavering—Phillip had to get out of the bomber as quickly as any other crew member.

Every man standing in the morning light hoped that Charley had a solution, but no one believed he did. Ronald Cummins, the mid-upper gunner, spoke up before Charley's embarrassment became acute.

"We can figure this out if we approach it one step at a time." Ronnie, a native Rhodesian with a little this-and-that blood in him, whose family owned a thousand-acre farm in a frontier land, had grown up facing daily problems worse than this one and solved them all. Obstacles on the farm rarely had conventional solutions, and young Ronnie had learned from

19

an early age to look for answers—to avoid preoccupying himself with the problem—and never to give up. Ordinarily quiet, except when he drank, a sober Ronnie only spoke when he had something to say.

He picked up the parachute pack. "First, let's get him out of the plane with the chute attached to his body where he can drag it to his chest and pull the cord. Second, we'll pull out two feet of shrouds so he can drop it out and jump after it, or, if it works better, he can drag the bundle out behind him.

It has to be in a position where he can get it on in less than fifteen seconds, and it must trail in the wind somehow so that he can easily pull it in. If he starts at twenty-thousand feet, he has at least two minutes to pull it in and pull the cord—I can make a cup of tea or skin an antelope in two minutes."

Willie blurted out, "Why not clip it to straps at the front instead of the back...then it will be in front of him when he pulls it in?" The simple solution surprised even him, but his background in the Canadian North Atlantic, fishing from a shallow-draft boat on the roughest ocean in the world, gave him the same survival perspective as Ronnie. A good idea could save your life—a bad one would probably end it.

The radio operator, Jeffrey Conway, grasped the principal instantly and said, "Sure, why not? Let's get to work!"

Steve, Jeffrey and Charley lengthened and rearranged the straps on the parachute bundle until a one-handed pull on them brought it tight to Phillip's chest. The pack was loose enough on the short straps that it would either follow Phillip out the hatch or fall clear of his feet without impeding his exit but would always be close enough that he could pull it in.

While in the aircraft, Phillip would wear the harness, and when Steve yelled "Abracadabra," the protocol command for 'Bail out...now!' Phillip would clip the parachute pack on the harness, drop it through the hatch and jump out. As soon as he was clear, he would draw the parachute bundle back to his chest and pull the ripcord—the silk canopy would then do its thing.

While everyone else went for a beer, Ronnie ran to the shop and talked a mechanic into rigging the clips on Phillip's shrouds. He detoured by the barracks, sloshed down a beer, and the crew returned to the lancaster. Phillip rehearsed the process until Steve was convinced it would work every time, and then every member of the bomber crew tried it. Jake Collier, the bomb-aimer/forward gunner, and Jeff Conway, the radio operator, used the narrow hatch and decided to re-rig their parachutes after trying the 'Phillip' exit.

Amid a chorus of congratulations and backslapping, the crew headed for the mess for coffee, tea, and eggs. Despite the lack of job security, or more likely because of it, the mood was one of hope and exhilaration. Later, at the bar, Steve paid for a round of beer.

While still over Belgium, the bomber behind 'C for Charley' went down in flames, and Willie didn't see any parachutes blossom behind it. In the next five minutes, two more lancasters flying behind the Rhodesian squadron exploded and fell to the ground, trailing fire and debris. Their seven-ton bomb loads spectacularly detonated when they struck, a ball of white light that almost immediately died to become a red glow.

The smouldering red blotches, from four miles overhead resembling a viral disease, marked a tragic trail of funeral pyres strewn behind the bomber stream, but tonight, there were no white parachutes to provide hope and lessen the pain. There had been no flak bursts, and the crews had not seen their executioners, confirming to Willie that German night fighters with vertical-firing cannons were responsible for the carnage.

Willie's eyes followed a scan he had developed from a conglomeration of suggestions he had accumulated from other rear gunners. His technique of thoroughly searching one segment, then another and another in logical sequence grew from the endemic routine fishermen naturally used to search for a lobster trap buoy among thousands of white-capped waves. A night fighter with upward-firing cannons that would target 'C-for-Charley' would have to come from specific areas in Willie's field of view, and his scan concentrated on them.

He searched the blackness behind his aircraft a section at a time, taking no more than a second or two to study each one, and the bomber was approaching the German border when a movement in the lower-left sector caught Willie's attention; he watched a shape grow out of a glint of moonlight in the bottom corner. As it crept forward, the same white arrows trailed behind it as plagued the bombers, and the same moonlight bounced off its aluminum wing.

Keeping his hands on the gun's controls and his fingers on the firing buttons, Willie waited without moving the turret until the range was short enough to assure a kill, and the shadow became a junkers 88 equipped with upward-firing cannons. In one smooth motion, Willie twisted the levers forward, depressing the twin brownings, turned the handlebar, and swivelled the turret until the junkers slid into the reflector sight. Heart pounding, nerves strung tight, his guns sighted slightly ahead of the fighter, Willie pressed the firing button.

The four browning machine guns sent a stream of tracer bullets into the unarmed top of the canopy behind the pilot, instantly killing the rear gunner. Willie led the flashes of light ahead into the pilot as the plane broke right and dove. Willie mercilessly guided four streams of bullets into his disabled victim until the guns could no longer depress enough to hit it. The fighter disappeared, but Willie was sure the hunter's night was over.

"What's all the fuss back there?" Steve's question beat Willie's announcement. Willie resumed his scan before speaking, letting his adrenalin drop, then said without a glitch in his routine, "I nailed a junkers sneaking up under us. It had two cannon barrels sticking straight up from the rear canopy—the perfect setup to shoot cannon shells into bombers' gas tanks. The good news is that we can see their trails just like they can see ours."

"Good show, Willie." There was no hint of excitement, only concern in Steve's voice. "Okay, everyone, it's bright enough to see night fighters, and they have tails. Look for them—find them before they kill us or someone else!" Steve clicked his intercom off for a few seconds, then returned.

"Boys, this will be like shooting rabbits in a pen for the German night fighters, and we've got to be smart or we won't make it home! Phillip, forget the forward guns and get your head in the dome!"

∞∞∞∞∞∞∞∞∞∞∞∞∞∞∞∞∞∞∞∞∞∞∞∞∞

Danny guided Larry to the bomber stream with Remi, their wingman, on station slightly behind and to their right. Radar targets covered Danny's screen, and, at twenty-eight thousand feet, their mosquito was five thousand feet above the stream and above the operational ceiling of most German night fighters.

Danny said, "Turn left to two-ninety degrees."

Larry turned his mosquito, and was speechless for a few seconds. When he recovered from the shocking sight, he shouted, "Jesus Christ... Look at the vapour trails on those lancasters! Contact Remi and ask him if we've got one!"

Danny said, "Cursing is a sign of a lazy mind," as he flipped from intercom to transmit on his VHF. He spoke into his microphone, listened for a few seconds, changed the frequency, and then switched back to intercom.

"Our VHF frequency is being jammed, so I changed to the alternate. Remi says we don't have a tail. It must be too cold and dry at this altitude."

Larry stared at hundreds of bombers, all with vapour trails—a banquet laid out for the German night fighters, complete with the good silver. If he were flying a messerschmitt for the other side, he would have dozens of potential bomber targets in front of him—and he would pick them in a sequence that would get him multiple kills with the least risk.

Larry said, "Danny, every night fighter we shoot down tonight will save at least a couple of bomber crews..."

"Amen to that!" said Danny.

"If I were a messerschmitt pilot, I would work from the outside. The fighters will also have vapour trails, and the moon is shining on them, just like it's shining on the bombers...they won't want to expose themselves from more than one side."

"Right!" said Danny...they will hunt from the outside, like tuna feeding on a school of herring!"

"Yep," said Larry, "Just like that!"

Remi's thick Quebecois accent cut through the static on Danny's radio. Danny listened, confirmed receipt, then relayed the message to Larry. "We have six bogeys between us and the bombers. Remi wants to know what you want to do." Danny said it as though he had found a pearl in his oyster.

Larry didn't have to think about it. "Tell Remi we will take the last two in the pack, then climb like hell and hunt the rest one at a time! I want Remi beside me until I pick a target—tell him to take the one beside mine." Larry pushed the stick forward; Danny relayed the message through a wall of static, and although he didn't get an answer, when he looked sideways, Remi was on station, lining up his kill.

Despite backing off the throttles, Larry's mosquito touched four hundred miles an hour in the dive—barely giving him time to shoot the target before he blew past. He had picked a junkers 88 and sawed the tail off with a short burst from his cannon. Remi passed Larry's mosquito, diverted slightly and downed a messerschmitt 110 with enough time to return to his position as Larry throttled up for the climb.

Larry spoke into the intercom, "Now that they know we're here, they will be more careful. Let's get to the bombers before these vultures do! We will escort the bombers as long as we have ammunition and fuel to get home. After that, God help them!"

Larry approached the bomber stream from high above; a silver tail led to every bomber, but Danny had said there was no vapour trail behind their wingman. Danny asked, "Should I try to tell the bombers to climb to get rid of the tails?"

"Yes, of course…if you can…do it now!" Larry didn't expect Danny to get past the jamming.

Danny tried the bomber frequency and reported, "There is nothing but the usual static. Our frequency isn't much better—Remi doesn't answer—I don't know whether he can hear me, but right now I can't hear him!" Larry didn't reply but made a mental note to avoid friendly fire. In the light of the bright moon, if it had two engines, most gunners wouldn't wait to differentiate between friend and foe.

A bomber on the edge of the stream blew up and fell—Larry immediately dove to where he assumed the shooter had gone, quickly increasing the airspeed to a closing rate of over seven hundred miles an hour. The mosquito crossed a vapour trail that could only be the one he was looking for, and Larry started his turn to end up where the killer would be.

Danny found the fighter on his screen. "Ten degrees more—he'll be dead ahead."

The German pilot, sitting in front of a silver tail, wasn't thinking about mosquitoes as he congratulated himself and his gunner, and when Larry fired, he had no idea what had killed him. Larry had only enough time for a three-second burst, but it was enough for his 20 mm cannon and .303 machine gun shells to rake the aircraft from the rudder to the pilot before he had to pull up to avoid hitting it. The terminally ill fighter dropped its nose, headed for the ground and eternity. Larry didn't bother to confirm the kill; there was no time. Danny kept his eyes on the radar while Larry used the dive's energy and all the power in the twin Merlins to climb, ridding himself of the silver tail he knew he had acquired at this altitude.

Danny said, "Remi is beside us." Larry knew he would be.

CHAPTER FOUR

30 March 1944

Die besten Gedanken kommen allzeit hinterdrein.
(The best ideas always come as hindsight.)

Leutnant Michael Gerber reported, "We're in position forty kilometres inside Germany." He had guided Erik to the exact spot his commander had requested. They had worked together so long that compliments for doing the job right were typically considered redundant, but nonetheless, Oberleutnant Stephanie said, "Good work, Leutnant," with a hint of admiration. "I've decided to climb in a holding pattern with the long side across the bomber track. Keep me over the point unless we hear something different from Deelen."

Michael reported, "There is no Deelen; the English are jamming us again." The VHF was useless…as it had been most nights since late in 1943. The British had developed a sophisticated jamming system against German air defence communications…selected bombers were carrying equipment designed to effectively disable a German fighter's radio communications. Unfortunately for the British, it also inhibited the bombers' conversations with one another and with Bomber Command in England. To counter, Erik and Michael had developed alternative tactics, and sometimes Erik was glad of the freedom it gave him. He had his own Lichtenstein radar to find the target, and he couldn't reconcile the "pack" idea when it came to intercepting bombers. He liked to hunt alone, and a wingman was at the bottom of his list of priorities.

Erik climbed to his aircraft's operational limit, levelling off at seven thousand metres, then turned the sluggish plane to the intercept course.

"Have the British lost their minds?" Erik looked at Michael in the mirror and saw the same astonishment. Michael said, "Perhaps it's a trap... maybe they have a new weapon that can see us and shoot us down— something we won't see coming until it's too late." Hundreds of bombers stretched so far, and the visibility was so good that the line visibly bent with the earth's curvature. The tight formation glinted in the moonlight, and silver contrails streamed for kilometres behind them.

Erik voiced his fear, "…or they've got a hundred mosquitos waiting for us somewhere!" He thought, if he were the British General Harris, he would have at least a hundred mosquitos with the bombers every night!

Over two hundred German night fighters waited to strike against no more than a couple of squadrons of mosquitos, and, for a brief moment, Erik felt a twinge of sympathy for the dozens of crews who would die tonight.

He cut the throttles slightly, lowered the nose, and steered to a point behind and outside the lead formation. Erik concentrated on flying; he spoke to Michael automatically, "We are as visible as the bombers… we'll attack the plane at the rear and on the outside."

"Understood… Guns loaded and cocked."

Assuming his messerschmitt Bf 110 would glint in the moonlight and leave the same silver tail the bombers did, Erik decided to stay out of the lancaster gunners' visual range for as long as possible. He circled and timed his turn so he would not have to engage in a long chase. The messerschmitt finished its teardrop-shaped swing parallel to his target and a hundred metres below it. He edged toward the lancaster, gaining altitude until he was fifty metres below and two hundred metres behind it, hoping the gunners wouldn't see his dark shape or the engines' white tails.

Erik eased ahead, and as he opened his mouth to tell Michael to get ready, the lancaster's right wing parted between the engines in a blast of flame and debris. Ahead and above Erik's messerschmitt, the bomber's left wing rose until it was vertical, and the lancaster began its long dive to the ground. The separated wing flipped past Erik's plane.

Michael announced irritably, "A junkers 88 beat us to it!"

"And damned near killed us!" Erik's voice held a hint of surprise. He had never observed the devastation of a night fighter attack from such close quarters and was embarrassed that he hadn't seen the attacker thirty metres to his right and a hundred metres ahead.

The victorious night fighter peeled away from the bombers, and before Erik turned his concentration away from it, two mosquitos zipped past, their attention focused on the junkers. The lead mosquito passed Erik's messerschmitt, fired a quick burst, and the centre of the junkers erupted in a shower of debris. It pointed straight at the ground, exploding in a colourful pool of burning avgas.

Erik knew they had to become invisible as soon as they could. He said, "Verdammte mosquitos—we'll hide in the bomber stream."

Michael didn't confirm, telling Erik his navigator was either worried or angry, likely the former.

There were hundreds of targets, but if Erik were going to land his messerschmitt in Florennes, he had less than another half-hour of fighting fuel. He dropped back, looking for an enemy aircraft he wouldn't have to chase.

Erik let his messerschmitt bounce around in the white wake of a halifax bomber, merging the messerschmitt's silver tail with the heavy bomber's until he was sure the mosquitos were hunting elsewhere.

When no mosquitos appeared, Erik worked his fighter under and behind the last aircraft in a flight of eight. He crept ahead, staying seventy metres below the bomber until the upward-firing cannons were under its wing, flying in the vapour trail of another halifax bomber below and ahead of his intended victim. Erik gambled that his victim wouldn't see his messerschmitt or its vapour trail until too late. The rear gunner hadn't moved, and if Erik's luck held, seven men would plunge to a flaming death in the next few seconds.

"I'm setting up between the fuselage and the inboard engine. Use minimum ammunition—we're going to need it all tonight." There were two gun sights for the rear upward-shooting cannons in Erik's fighter, one via mirrors in the pilot's cockpit and a more direct one in front of the navigator. Watching the sighting mirror, Erik knew when Michael would fire. Seconds before, he lowered his eyelids to slits, then closed them when the cross found the halifax's wing.

The cannons spit a dozen explosive shells into the halifax's fuel tanks in a two-second burst, exploding the tank and wrapping the plane in flames. A burning human figure dropped from the hatch, followed by a second—Erik opened the throttles, pushed the nose down and turned away from the wreckage.

Usually, Erik felt no regret when a bomber crew died. Almost a year ago, he flew over Hamburg during the firebombing that killed thirty thousand civilians, most of whom were women and children. Without a glimmer of remorse, Erik had happily shot down two British aircraft that July night, and so it had been for twelve kills since then. But the flaming men disturbed him.

Larry moved his mosquito toward the rear of the bomber stream so Danny's radar could pick up any night fighters flying outside or between the packed bombers. He kept the aircraft above the level where frozen vapour from the rolls royce engines would leave a silver trail. His wingman had stationed himself a thousand feet above him, a mile behind, and a mile to his right; distances that meant nothing to a mosquito but doubled their coverage.

"They got another one!" Danny watched a halifax drop between two other bombers, narrowly missing one of them. His eyes followed the burning wreck until it splashed in a blaze of light that faded into a puddle of flame. "If we're going to find those bastards, we need to get into the stream. I can't separate friend from foe up here."

Larry knew Danny was right. "In that case, a wingman won't help. Tell Remi what we're doing, and we'll see him either in England or in Hell."

Danny did as directed, receiving what he took for acknowledgment through the static, and Larry dove into the flotilla of bombers below them. He parked the bouncing mosquito in a vapour trail and waited for Danny to find a target.

Erik moved away from the river of bombers and descended to where an alert rear gunner couldn't see his messerschmitt or its long tail. He picked out another halifax farther ahead in the formation, slowly climbed into a vapour trail, and approached 'von hinten unten,' 'from behind and below.' As before, the gunner didn't see the messerschmitt creeping up on it like a cat on a sleeping mouse—the turret remained motionless.

When Michael fired, the result was more devastating than the first kill—the explosion blew the left wing clear of the fuselage, just missing Erik's head as it flipped end over end past him. The burning fuselage dropped sickeningly on its side, twisting into a vertical dive that put survivors out of the question.

Five miles ahead of Larry and Danny, a falling halifax sent Danny on a search of unaccounted-for-bogeys, but he couldn't find the perpetrator in the mess of blips on his screen.

Danny vented his frustration through the intercom, "It's useless, Larry. I can't identify a single bogey in this mess. Let's try it on top again...and maybe a little closer."

Larry said, "Alright, a lancaster is climbing out of formation, and the bad guys will try to shoot it down. We'll follow it up."

Bombers fell in flames all over the formation, most of them a victim of an exploding fuel tank; the upward-firing cannons took a devastating toll. Ten burning lancasters and Erik's two halifax bomber kills marked the bomber stream's progress over the forty-five miles before they crossed the Rhine. The flotilla's orders were to employ no evasion tactics, and they were cursed with a clear night and contrails that marked the targets for German night fighters. The slaughter would continue until the German fighters ran out of gas or ammunition or the remnants of the bomber force returned to the English Channel.

Erik had no sympathy for the RAF. Bomber Command loaded every aircraft with incendiaries designed to burn people and buildings, and they put delay fuses on blast bombs so they would burrow into civilian cellars and shelters before exploding. He looked down on the eerie panorama of white lines leading to dark shapes glinting in the bright moonlight and felt no pity...he coaxed his messerschmitt up to seven thousand metres to pick another victim out of the hundreds below him. In the less than two minutes that he watched, two more bombers in the massive formation fell in flames.

"Michael, do we have a tail?" Erik synchronized an 'S' turn so Michael could see behind.

"No, I've been watching...It disappeared five hundred metres above the bombers."

"This is madness." Erik was surprised at his anger—at the conflict in his mind. These men were his enemies, but somehow, he felt it wasn't a fair fight. "If they climbed a thousand metres, we would need to use our radar, and they would save dozens of crews!" Erik's anger flared when another bomber fell—he was angry with himself for his sympathy and furious with the British commanders for their stupidity.

The common bond between men who risk their lives to break the pull of earth and venture where mistakes are not forgiven dulled his eagerness to kill these men, and he had to force himself to search for his next victim. He had less than ten minutes before 'critical fuel;' after that, he wouldn't make it home—he would have to land in Germany.

Erik's next target appeared in front of him like a gift at Christmas, and his reluctance disappeared as he said to Michael, "A lancaster is climbing out of the formation straight ahead. We will take the starboard wing tanks. Fire as soon as you're sure of a kill—do not hit the fuselage—it's full of bombs. Understood?"

"*Verstanden, Oberleutnant.*" Michael used Erik's formal rank to send a message to his boss—he knew damned well where bombers carried their bombs and resented being treated like a beginner.

Erik chuckled into the intercom.

Steve White, captain of the 'C for Charley' lancaster, decided to leave the main bomber stream, blatantly countermanding specific orders not to do so except in an emergency. He told himself that the white trail leading to his airplane met his definition of an emergency and decided to climb, hoping to lose it.

He pushed the throttles forward, intentionally neglecting to inform the crew, and the nose rose slightly without any other input. The lancaster eased upward, becoming a lone fish outside the school—drawing the attention of every predator in the vicinity—its white tails bent upward as it ruined the formation's perfect geometry.

He asked into the intercom, "Ronnie and Willie...How do you read?" Captain White knew the intercom worked flawlessly but wanted to be clear that only the gunners were to talk to him.

"Loud and clear," Ronnie answered from his sling in the waist turret.

"Five by five." Willie knew something was up—he had noticed the slight change in angle and that the bombers around him were slowly falling away.

Steve broke a serious protocol by leaving the formation with an undamaged aircraft, and the words he used would be examined in the investigation—if they made it home. He chose them carefully.

"I want you to keep an eye on our vapour trails and let me know if anything changes. Confirm that you understand."

"Roger, understood," both gunners answered, stepping on one another's transmission.

The lancaster climbed almost imperceptibly, but the two hundred feet-per-minute climb was evident to the aircraft around it, particularly to the squadron commander, Wing Commander John Leech. He waited a few minutes to see what Captain White was up to before telling his radio operator to call 'C for Charley.' The radio operator tried but reported nothing but static—Leech cursed and asked the bright moon, "What in hell is Steve White thinking?"

Willie, convinced that he could see the trails becoming thinner and beginning further astern, opened his mouth to speak, but Ronnie's voice in the intercom interrupted him.

"Captain, the trail is half what it was," Ronnie reported from the turret on top of the fuselage.

"Roger. Out." Sober and in the air, Steve White was a man of few words.

Willie hadn't stopped his scan during the conversation, giving each segment equal scrutiny, moving his head smoothly across and down through the blackness behind him. The reward for his diligence came when he spotted propellers glinting in the moonlight before the inevitable gun flashes.

Willie said evenly into the intercom, "Steve...I've got a German night fighter coming into my sights, but he's still below and too far behind us for me to knock him down. He's gaining fast—get ready to corkscrew if I miss." The "corkscrew" usually shook the most talented night fighter pilot loose, but the prerequisites were discovering the fighter before it attacked and timing the maneuver perfectly. And even then, they would be corkscrewing down through a formation of bombers. Willie had filled the first requirement; the rest would be up to Captain Steve.

Willie waited for the shot he must not miss. The angle to the fighter slowly approached forty-five degrees downward, where Willie's four .303 browning machine guns were already pointed. What he recognized as an Me110 inched into the sight until Willie only had to move the barrels slightly before squeezing the firing buttons.

Two pairs of browning machine guns spat four continuous steel lines into the messerschmitt's nose, then moved to the left engine as the fighter dropped its right wing and dove away.

The gunner had outfoxed him. Erik had watched the motionless guns—the turret hadn't moved until his messerschmitt flew into the gunner's sights, and when the rear gunner fired, there was no time to react. The fox had cleverly set a trap, and Erik had jumped in like a stupid rabbit!

"Sheisse" was all he had time to say before the wind blew black oil along the nacelle of the left engine—Erik shut off the fuel and feathered the propeller, then spoke into the intercom, "We're done for tonight. Let's go home."

Busy with the sick airplane, Erik didn't see the mosquito slicing through the night from his starboard side, and cannon shells exploding behind his seat confused him. When the mosquito passed within ten feet of his canopy, Erik instinctively pushed the stick ahead, but nothing happened, and for the first time in his flying career, he panicked.

The bright moonlight silhouetted the mosquito as it flipped on its edge in a steep turn. Desperately, Erik kicked the useless left rudder, pushed the stick against his left knee, and was surprised when the left wing dropped. But the plane moved too slow and too late—the mosquito had the top of the messerschmitt's naked fuselage to shoot at.

The ninety-millimetre windscreen was impervious to .303 machine gun bullets, even the steady rain of them that had come from the lancaster, and it had saved Erik's life. But the mosquito's stream of bullets and cannon shells shattered the perspex behind the cockpit into thousands of tiny pieces, then destroyed everything back to the tail.

Erik instinctively pushed the limp stick forward again, but its cables were severed from the elevators. The plane was helpless as the mosquito hit it again, tearing the rear cannons from their mounts, cutting the fuselage almost in two, and starting a fire in the starboard engine. He unfastened his belts, pulled the right throttle back, jammed the ailerons hard to the right and held them there. He hadn't dared hope that the ailerons would work, but the aircraft rolled until it inverted and fell toward the ground, upside down, in an inverted spin. The move saved Erik's life. Cannon shells hit the plane, but the wing and its engine protected him. The messerschmitt's death throes left a trail of fire and debris as it disintegrated.

Erik was disoriented as his body fell from the dying airplane. The wind speed increased to a howl—he reached for the ripcord but came to his senses soon enough to wait until he was well below the bombers and clear of his burning fighter. In the darkness, with only the howling wind to indicate where down should be, Erik pulled the brass ring, instigating a mighty yank on his crotch and armpits. And then he was hanging from the shrouds in the peaceful darkness. Despite the silly mandatory films, there was no training for this—the assumption being that the urgency of falling toward the ground at three hundred kilometres per hour would motivate anyone to open a parachute. Gravity would take care of the rest.

Although he had no idea what was below him, Erik reasoned it couldn't be worse than the chaos he had escaped. He looked up at the white canopy, then at the bombers above it, droning onward to the fate that RAF Bomber Command had made inevitable. A sense of relief swept over him as he swung peacefully in the arms of the shrouds, the sounds of war fading as he fell into a black void.

Erik thought of Michael and the wife his navigator had married on his last furlough. She lived in Stuttgart, and Erik vowed to visit her—if he survived. He was confident he could tell her that Michael had died instantly.

Erik turned his thoughts to Marita and Walther, waiting for him in Heilbronn, but the appearance of shadows below him yanked him back to his fight for survival. The landing would not be smooth; he was falling into houses, trees, and power lines—a jumbled mess with a thousand ways to kill him. He began to experiment with steering, wishing he had done it sooner.

CHAPTER FIVE:

30 March 1944

Man soll den Tag nicht vor dem Abend loben.
(Don't boast about the day until the evening has arrived.)

NOT A GLIMMER OF LIGHT FLICKERED on the ground, but the German penchant for detail was not what Erik needed right now. The moonlight revealed buildings and trees, but he had no idea when his feet, or other perhaps more sensitive areas, would hit something like a live wire, a nasty tree, or the top of a pole. Tension grew as the inevitable collision with something approached, but Erik landed on his feet and rolled in a soft backyard, just like in the lousy training films. He stood up quickly, ecstatic, without a scratch or a bruise, and congratulated himself on his good luck when he saw that he had narrowly missed a very mean-looking apple tree—the lower branches had even snagged the parachute so the wind couldn't drag him, giving Erik all the time in the world to remove the harness.

Erik laughed, releasing all of his fear in a burst of joy. "Okay, God, I must admit that was good work...better than I had a right to expect." Despite allowing himself to think of Michael, he was unsuccessful in his attempt to feel sad. He looked up and said, "Thank you for getting me out of that mess." He hoped God was listening but somehow doubted Erik Stephanie, night fighter pilot and killer of bomber crews, was that important. With all the souls this war sent to Him each day, he couldn't see how even God would have time to care for anything so trivial as where Erik Stephanie landed. Smiling in spite of himself, he liked to think God might have a plan for him, as long as it included his family surviving the war.

A white-haired woman emerged from the house that belonged to the garden, her white nightdress dragging on the ground, and ran to him. She wrapped her arms around him as though he were a long-lost friend coming to visit, and didn't release him until he stepped back and introduced himself.

"Oberleutnant Erik Stephanie at your service." He half-bowed and removed his flying helmet.

She smiled, and the moonlight reflected off a set of perfect teeth. "I am Karla Schultz, and this is my house. You are welcome to come in and use my telephone..." And then, in a burst of patriotism... "free of charge!"

Erik returned her smile. "The Luftwaffe will pay for the call and send a car for me, but I will need to impose on your hospitality for a few hours." The friendly woman nodded her head and smiled like a schoolgirl.

Karla led the way inside the house, put a kettle of water on the gas stove, and prepared black tea in an ornate china teapot. Erik asked her, "Where should I say that I am?

"You are in Hürth, Hermülheimerstrasse 207."

Erik called the base, the conversation was short—it would be morning before a car picked him up.

He called home and lingered for half an hour with his wife and sleepy nine-year-old son. When he hung up, his mind was clear, and he had his reason to fly again. Fear and doubt retreated to their hiding place.

When Erik returned to the kitchen, the look of distress on the white-haired woman's face was almost amusing—it disappeared when he said, "Thank you," and pressed twenty reichsmarks into her hand.

Karla had set two places on the table with matching cups and saucers...the steaming teapot sat on a copper rack with a lit candle under it. When she sat down, he sat opposite her.

She said, putting her finger over her mouth in a "shh" sign, "We need to be quiet so we don't wake the children." And almost immediately, a sleepy young woman entered the kitchen.

"This is my daughter, Petra Kraus." The woman with the white hair used a tone that sounded like disappointment. "She and my two grandchildren are living with me until we win the war."

Petra looked at Erik, her expression making it clear that she was not glad to see him. He quickly rose to his feet and stretched his hand to her. She stifled a yawn, took his hand and said, "Yes, Karla is my mother, and my children are asleep. Now, tell me why you are here?"

Erik towered over both women, and it was clear that his square chin, blonde hair, and broad, high forehead impressed the older woman.

He thought he likely was her vision of Hitler's "master race." From her actions, he assumed she agreed with Hitler on everything. Petra was just as obviously unimpressed and not likely a Hitler fan.

"I was shot down and had to use my parachute. It wasn't by choice that I landed in your garden."

Petra pulled the blackout curtain back just enough that she could look into the yard.

"Then, I assume the parachute hanging from our apple tree is yours." Petra smiled, deliberately turned on her considerable charm, and carefully repositioned the blackout curtain. "May I have it? The children need undergarments..."

Erik nodded. "We only use them once."

"So...it's a deal?" Petra stretched out her hand to Erik, and he took it in his, clicking his heels smartly and half-bowing to her with a grin fixed on his face and said, "It's a deal."

She took her hand back, pulled a cup and saucer out of the cupboard, and sat next to Erik and opposite her mother. Karla gave her a look that could have killed her daughter, and Erik thought he had gotten good value out of used Luftwaffe property.

Erik's euphoria at surviving a desperate situation was gone, the memory of his conversation with Marita faded into the background, and his mood plunged as he thought of Michael. Sorrow for his friend seeped through the cracks in his mind, drifting upward to the surface of his consciousness. Too much had happened to Erik and the people around him for his faith in God to survive. He had learned to hate—the war, the Nazis, Hitler, the British bombers, his job—he hated them all! And now his best friend was dead, his country was being systematically destroyed, and his family was in the line of fire!

As his depression deepened, he sipped his tea reflexively, his mind elsewhere, and when Karla asked him a question, it took a few seconds for Erik to return to her kitchen.

"Do you believe that we can win this war?" Karla began as though she only had time for one question. Her face was full of hope.

Erik's thoughts wandered back a year; the Russians had destroyed the mighty Sixth Army at Stalingrad, beginning their relentless march to Hitler's Berlin lair. As the Sixth Army died, Churchill demanded the impossible—Germany's unconditional surrender—otherwise, he promised, the Allies would 'annihilate' Germany. Germany's logical and only possible response was Goebbel's declaration of 'Total War.' Churchill responded with a 'campaign of fire,' coordinated with the Russian advance. The RAF under "Bomber" Harris began a clearly-stated campaign to level and burn every German city! The Germans also faced the reality that the British and Americans were defeating the undefeatable Rommel in North Africa.

There was nothing Erik wanted to discuss with these women—he held no hope for his country. A lunatic had set fire to Walhalla, and the death of the teutonic Gods was near!

The fighter crews did their duty every night, abandoning their families and controlling their fear as they flew into the teeth of ever-increasing numbers of British bombers—knowing in their hearts that the armadas would keep growing in size and ferocity until Germany was a wasteland. The fighter crews substituted schnapps and beer for intelligent, honest conversation, talking about women and battle tactics while avoiding any discussion of war politics. Nazi Party policies, in particular, were never mentioned except for the occasional Goebbels, Göring or Hitler joke, whispered or drawn anonymously on a piece of ubiquitous paper and passed surreptitiously from hand to hand.

Almost every night, Erik and his comrades flew over devastated and burning cities—over terrifying firestorms set by incendiary bombs. Thousands of women and children, young and old, perished in terrible fires or were blown to unidentifiable bits. Nameless bodies of neighbours and friends were buried in mass graves while factories continued to churn out war machines, roads and bridges remained untouched, and the trains ran on time.

But in their hearts, they knew of an evil so great that even close friends of victims didn't dare speak of it. When the crews went home on leave, they talked about family and friends. But ignoring rumours of atrocities in Poland and Russia became increasingly difficult, and it became impossible to dismiss tales of extermination camps when trainloads of Jews and 'undesirables' passed through railway stations. People who spoke openly of such things disappeared—the Gestapo was everywhere—even in the barracks among the soldiers and airmen. Brave men fighting for their country avoided conversations that came close to the subject, forcing themselves to dismiss the rumours as nothing more than that, but knowing in their hearts that some part of the horrifying story had to be true!

Erik had seen too much; he feared that the war had blackened his soul.

◇◇◇◇◇◇◇◇◇◇◇◇◇◇◇◇◇◇◇◇◇◇◇◇◇◇◇◇◇◇◇◇

Erik shook his head and kept his eyes on his hands wrapped around his teacup. "I don't want to discuss what I believe—belief has nothing to do with the outcome of this war. I fly my fighter against well-armed British bombers sent to kill German civilians—my family—and I must shoot them down!

He looked at the heavy blackout curtain as though he could see into the garden. "I fight for my wife and son." Erik's voice decreased in volume as he spoke; his right hand began to shake; he felt wetness filling his eyes. He blinked to clear his vision, then used his finger to wipe a tear that threatened to slide down his cheek.

Petra waited, watching Erik closely. He caught her looking at his hand and grasped it, forcing it to be still.

"How many British bombers have you shot down?" Karla was oblivious to Erik's deepening depression, but Petra put her hand on Erik's, and the shaking stopped. Erik looked at her, and she removed it.

"Tonight, I shot down two, and that makes twenty-three. I've killed over a hundred men, and my best friend died tonight because I made a beginner mistake. Tonight, hundreds of airmen on both sides will die..." He paused... "and thousands of German families will die in their homes when the bombers drop their loads."

Petra looked at Erik sympathetically. "I understand how you feel, but I need to hear you say how and when you think this will end. The sirens wake us almost every night. We run to the Keller; sometimes the bombs fall very close, sometimes farther away, in Köln, and I am frightened for my children! I don't believe Goebbels' propaganda."

She looked at the blackout curtain where Erik had focused his eyes. "I lost a wonderful husband in Stalingrad, and every day I work loading machine gun belts—I have to feed my two children and my mother. Even with money, the ration cards don't let me have enough milk for the children and barely enough bread for the family."

Petra put both of her hands on Erik's. "I've heard rumours that our country is murdering Jewish women and children, and I want to know the truth—will you tell me if that's true?"

39

Karla's shrill voice interrupted before Erik could speak. "The Jewish banks ruined your father's business and caused his heart attack! What do you care if our soldiers kill them?" She wagged her finger at her daughter. "But I don't believe any of those rumours! They are lies spread by Jews and Communists to make us turn against the Führer!" Karla spit her words, leaned toward her daughter and shouted at her, "The Führer won't stand for this kind of talk, and this fine soldier represents him! I won't allow you to make a fool of this household in front of Oberleutnant Stephanie!"

Erik couldn't answer Petra's question without his face giving him away. Finally, when he stood up and didn't answer, Petra faced her mother.

"But what if it's true? The Americans and the British will not stop until we have nothing left! Our cities will be in ruins; our men will be dead! We are not fighting to save Germany—Germany is already beyond saving—we are fighting to save Hitler and his thugs!"

Erik waited, gathered his thoughts, then looked down at Karla. She stared defiantly back at him, then at her daughter with an expression that had to be hate.

He said quietly, "I fight for Germany and love my country. I understand how you feel, but the Sturmabteilung, the brownshirts, took my wife's best friend away from her children, and, as far as we know, they took her to a work camp. Her crime is that she is half-Jewish, but her aryan husband fought and died in a tank in Belgium in 1940." Karla's face reddened. There was no sympathy there.

Erik continued, "We care for her children, who may be safe because they are only one-quarter Jewish, and we love them as our own. I don't believe that Germans are systematically murdering Jews like my wife's friend, but I can't confidently say that we aren't!" Erik paused, looked from one woman to the other as he said, "I am helpless to end this war; what I am fighting for now is to protect my family—do you understand?"

Petra raised her head and brushed her long dark hair back from her face. "Yes, I understand, but it's not enough." She looked directly into his eyes with a look so intense Erik was afraid she could read his mind. "I want to trust you, but I have learned to be afraid of every German in a uniform!"

He shook his head, laid his hands on the back of her chair and leaned over, his voice adopting a sympathetic fatherly tone as he said quietly into her ear, "You are right; you can't trust me or anyone else, least of all someone in a uniform."

Her answer was almost inaudible. "But, I must trust you—I must know what will happen—I can't live like this anymore."

Erik walked across the room. Karla sat motionless at the table.

"If you trust me, you must promise never to discuss anything like this again...not even in this house. In today's Germany, you can trust no one."

"Yes, I promise, but—" Petra closed her mouth when Erik's expression frightened her. He turned to face Karla. She had a scowl on her face as she drank her tea. Finally, when Erik waited, refusing to go on, Karla raised her head.

"All right, I also promise, but only because you come from the Führer. And surely you know that Adolph Hitler has a plan to destroy the English and the Russians!" Karla lowered her voice and pointed her finger at Erik. "I have a friend who knows someone in Berlin, and we will soon have a bomb that will destroy an entire city! He says we only need to destroy one or two cities before the English dogs surrender! And don't forget that one of those bombs can kill an entire Russian army! How long will the Bolshevik criminals last if we do that?" Karla's eyes lit up at the thought.

Karla fetched the whistling kettle from the stove and poured boiling water on a new round of tea leaves. Erik sliced the cheese and bread that Petra gave him and slid the plate to the middle of the table. He was not looking forward to dodging around these women for the next few hours.

CHAPTER SIX

30–31 March 1944

Wenn strafen will die Gotteshand, so nimmt sie einem den Verstand.
(When God wants to punish a man, he first takes away his sanity.)

THE DIRECT ROUTE THE BOMBERS FLEW, without diversions or planned evasion tactics, was part of a deliberate plan concocted by General 'Bomber' Harris, the boss of Bomber Command. General Harris decided to test his theory that an unexpected absence of evasion or diversion would fool the Germans—a concept bordering on insanity!

When the Luftwaffe scrambled their fighters, they sent them to a location projected from existing information, and if a combination of evasion tactics and 'window,' aluminum chaff that confused German radar, were used, at least some of the night fighters wound up in the wrong place. When Harris restricted the bomber stream to a predictable course and altitude, three hundred night fighters found them where Deelen ground control predicted they would be, condemning five thousand men to run a gauntlet that would kill hundreds of them and send hundreds more to German prison camps.

<hr>

The armada stopped its radio jamming long enough to allow the bombers to receive what turned out to be a confusing weather report. Steve took the opportunity to update Wing Commander Leech on his disappearing silver tail.

John Leech had won the Victoria Cross when his was the only plane to survive a mission to bomb the M.A.N. engine factory in Augsburg. Leech had lost many friends in what he considered bureaucratic folly and, at the award ceremony for his Victoria Cross, silently vowed never again to allow men under his command to face such a situation. This mission was shaping up to be an equivalent disaster, and when 'C for Charley,' flying three thousand feet above the bomber stream, informed Leech of the absence of a vapour trail, the Wing Commander threw away the rule book and switched his objective to that of No 44 squadron's survival. He immediately ordered his charges to leave their assigned altitude and follow him in a full-throttle climb.

The climb took ten minutes, and when the squadron joined Steve's bomber, 'C for Charley' again found itself on the inside corner of the starboard diamond. The crew's tension eased in the protection of their friends. From his catbird seat, Willie could see almost a hundred of the main formation's seven hundred bombers spread out below him. No 44 squadron had no tails, but the lancasters below Willie still flew at the front end of straight white shafts.

As he watched the bomber stream, Willie thought about how the formation resembled a school of herring. In a school of fish, it was not good to be on the outside or at the rear, where predators could pick you off. Herring shared the risk, continually rotating the outside and inside positions. However, the most vulnerable bombers in an armada had to stay at their assigned station until they landed or a night fighter picked them off.

The clear night and vapour trails added another horrifying dimension. The airmen of No 44 squadron watched burning aircraft fall out of the formation below them. In the time it had taken Leech's squadron to climb three thousand feet to join Steve White's black sheep, sixteen bombers had fallen from the main stream, with only a handful of parachutes visible behind them.

Willie reported the location of the burning wreckage he saw to Jeffrey Conway, the radio operator, and Jeffrey added them to his growing list. But with over seven hundred clearly marked targets drawing the night fighters away from No 44 squadron, they flew in peace.

Willie kept a rough tally in his head. According to Jeffrey, over sixty bombers had fallen in two hours...one every two minutes. It was over an hour to the target, then two more hours back to England—many more would become crematoriums! The number Willie arrived at stunned him. He recalculated, with the same result—if nothing changed, a thousand men would die tonight!

<hr>

"Corkscrew! Corkscrew!" Ronnie's voice had no hint of panic, but the urgency of his tone told everyone in the airplane what would happen next. Simultaneously, Ronnie fired his browning machine guns until the lancaster's vicious left-hand spiral twisted the diving focke wulf 190 out of his field of fire and into Willie's. Willie got off a short burst before it disappeared behind him and kept searching for the fighter as Steve squared the wings and pulled the column back, pinning him in his seat.

The moon glinted on something above Willie and behind him; he tried to elevate his guns as he yelled, "Ronnie, he's above you!" Ronnie pressed the firing button on his brownings—Willie watched the cone of fire hit the FW190 on its right wing root, then move to the fuel tanks—exploding three hundred litres of gasoline, scattering bits of the airplane in all directions!

Unaware that the danger had passed, Steve pushed the column ahead and twisted the wheel to the right, throwing the lancaster into a violent spin in the opposite direction!

Ronnie yelled, "I got him! I got him! For God's sake, pull out before you tear the wings off!" His voice hinted at annoyance as he tried to dampen the whip of his canvas seat by holding onto the turret coaming. In normal circumstances, he hated the tarpaulin strip that the crew called his diaper, but he particularly hated it in 'unusual attitudes,' and the 'corkscrew' certainly qualified as unusual.

Steve chuckled into the intercom, Phillip "hee-hawed" like a mule, and Willie said, "Good shooting partner!" Steve restored the lancaster to its original course, climbing at full boost to rid it of the four silver tails it had acquired, enjoying the good-natured banter that was the hallmark of a happy crew. He said, "Congratulations, lads, but be careful—keep your eyes peeled for fighters…we haven't gotten them all yet!"

The world went back to what passed for normal in a bomber stream.

The corkscrew maneuver had taken them down through the main stream, and Willie could see dozens of bombers above them, all with streaks of silver trailing behind them. Seconds apart, two more flaming wrecks fell away—their bomb loads exploding in a brilliant flash, and he willed 'C for Charley' to climb faster, knowing it wouldn't help.

Willie and Ronnie, aware of the lancaster's vulnerability in a climb, angled their brownings ten degrees above horizontal. Willie broke the rule and concentrated his scan on the most probable area—behind and above. He wasn't surprised when Ronnie said, "Willie, can you cover the bottom quadrants?—I will concentrate on a diving attack from behind. Phillip or Jake, can you cover the rest? Jake, who had his head in the observation bubble, said, "We're going to have company—I can feel the bastard coming!"

Willie smiled. "Roger—will prepare to welcome the bastard."

Climbing in the bright moonlight behind the stream gave 'C for Charley' a life expectancy measured in minutes. The tension sharpened Willie's senses; the excitement was exhilarating! He was the Toreador; the German night fighter was the bull!

Steve said, "If he comes from above and behind, a corkscrew will turn us into his cannons. Shout, "Dive!" and I will dive straight ahead. If he follows, he will come into Ronnie and Willie's line of fire. If they miss, I'll turn hard left, then hard right—that should keep him in their fields of fire but give him a moving target. We've got to get him before I have to climb. After that, if the bastard is still alive, we're screwed!

Willie and Ronnie tried to imagine and plan for every conceivable fight scenario while the surging drone of the synchronized propellers underscored their concentration. The sound compressed time, tightening the tension.

◇◇◇◇◇◇◇◇◇◇◇◇◇◇◇◇◇◇◇◇◇◇◇◇◇◇◇◇◇◇◇◇◇◇◇◇◇◇◇

A junkers 88 chugged along behind the bomber stream. It had just shot down one of the trailing lancasters, its second kill of the night, and had lost several miles and a thousand metres of altitude. With less than a forty-kilometre-per-hour advantage over the bomber stream, he would run out of fuel before he caught and lined up another victim.

He couldn't believe his good fortune when he spotted a gift ahead and below him—a climbing lancaster, glinting in the moonlight, trailing four long silver shafts. The junkers pilot immediately dropped the nose, adjusted his shallow dive to aim his cannons into the top of the lancaster's wing tanks, and lined up his third kill. He hadn't used the nose cannons yet, and their magazines were full—this kill would make him an ace and get him the Iron Cross!

◇◇◇◇◇◇◇◇◇◇◇◇◇◇◇◇◇◇◇◇◇◇◇◇◇◇◇◇◇◇◇◇◇◇◇◇◇◇◇

Simultaneously, Ronnie picked up the moonlight on the junkers propellers, and Willie, whose night vision was legendary, saw its shadow on the moon out of the corner of his eye. Ronnie and Willie shouted, "Dive!" at the same instant. The angle was too high for Willie but perfect for Ronnie—he didn't need to move—the junkers 88 flew straight into a river of .303 bullets.

46

The junkers pilot pressed his firing button at the instant the top turret of his intended victim came alive with flashes. He watched the browning's tracers come together at a spot in front of his windscreen, then spread slightly, beating against the reinforced nose and perspex that protected him. His forward-shooting cannons intentionally had no tracer shells loaded, making it more difficult for the bomber gunners to find the Ju88. However, it had the disadvantage of inhibiting the pilot from adjusting the path of his shells into the target, and when the Ju88 pilot saw no flashes indicating hits, he raised the nose slightly.

At that instant, the lancaster pitched downward at a steep angle, and a fraction of a second later, the night fighter followed the heavily loaded bomber, dropping like an anvil in front of him. Too slow in his correction, he missed the next move of the dark shape he was trying to kill, and it disappeared in the darkness. The German pilot found the lancaster's vapour trail just as the bomber's guns sent a stream of tracers arcing into the side of his cockpit. He died instantly, and two seconds later, his navigator met the same fate.

Steve had turned left, opening Ronnie's firing angle, putting the moon that had been the German's accomplice in killing other British flyers behind the doomed aircraft. Ronnie fired a long necklace of tracers into the side of the junkers, raking it from nose to tail, igniting the fuel in its left wing. The left engine caught fire, but no one was alive to pull the fire extinguisher, and the exploding fuel tank sealed the fighter's fate.

Willie announced, "Ronnie got him," and felt his body relax.

Steve pulled out of the diving left turn into a steady maximum-effort climb, less than five hundred feet below the altitude they had reached before the action. The lancaster was still more than three thousand feet below the formation and at least three miles behind, officially a straggler with a short life expectancy.

Steve climbed for over ten minutes before the altimeter finally passed twenty thousand feet, and he asked, hopefully, "Do you see any improvement in the contrails, boys?"

"It's about half of what it was." Willie exaggerated to the positive.

Pilot Officer Steve White smiled, whispered, "So far, so good," then checked that all his gauges were in the green.

Steve eventually coaxed the loaded plane to twenty-three thousand feet, levelled off, and the indicated airspeed gradually climbed to almost twenty mph faster than the speed ordered at the briefing.

Steve asked, "Charley, what's our true airspeed?" Charley had an altimeter, outside air temperature, and airspeed indicator in front of him. It was his job to keep the true airspeed and ground speed updated, and he replied immediately.

"True airspeed tois fifty-one—ground speed estimate at thee hunder usin' th' guff win' numbers we waur given. However, judgin' frae th' fixes I've taken, ah ken 'at th' briefin' numbers waur Limey garbage. Mah calculations make th' win' less than those imbeciles predicted, an' mair easterly. If we fly oan th' briefin' coorse, we will be west ay th' turnin' point at Fulda, an' abit ten miles cuttie. Ah am ay coorse correct, but ye can dae whit ye limeys aye dae, an' ignair yer wiser Scottish betters."

Steve ignored Charley's barbs but decided that since they were out of the stream anyway, they might as well make the turn where Charley reckoned was the correct time and place.

"OK, Scotty, give me a course and tell me when to turn. You know I can't do math, being an English gentleman with servants to do such mundane things."

Charley gave him the course; Steve turned eight degrees to starboard, set the directional gyro to the compass and engaged the autopilot. Eight degrees would make a lot of difference this far from the turning point.

The next time the jamming stopped for another inaccurate weather report, Steve radioed Wing Commander John Leech and stated his intentions. Jeffrey Conway transmitted, "'C for Charley' to squadron leader: We are ten miles behind the squadron and will navigate to the target using our fixes—they suggest that the Met winds are not usable."

Leech's radio operator came back, "Understood, 'C for Charley.' Out." Five minutes later, Commander Leech turned the squadron to the course that Charley had given Steve.

CHAPTER SEVEN

31 March 1944

Nur tote Fische schwimmen mit dem Strom.
(Only dead fish swim with the current.)

As 'C for Charley' flew the last fifty miles to the turning point at Fulda, Jeffrey and Charley marked ten more spots where bombers had burned holes in the ground. As the unfolding disaster's dimensions began to sink in, they sensed their work would be crucial in documenting the historical event. Emotionally torn between sympathy for their lost comrades and thankfulness that their lancaster wasn't among the fallen, they crowded their survivor's guilt into the background by keeping themselves busy.

No 44 squadron's gunners saw no more fighters after climbing above the main bomber stream, but the swarm continued to attack the formation below, attracted to the silver tails like bugs to a bright light.

At a quarter to one, the arrival time at Fulda predicted using the Met winds, the relationship between moisture content and air temperature changed, and the vapour trails disappeared. The main bomber stream swung right on what they thought was the course to the target, and, as Charley had predicted, they had turned when they were too far north. The British crews had finally gotten their clouds, just in time to obscure the turning point at Fulda, making confirmation of the error impossible.

However, No 44 squadron turned precisely over Fulda, and some trailing aircraft below them followed, scattering the attack.

Willie watched British bombers continue to fall from the sky, becoming flashes of white light, then splashes of orange and red in the carpet of clouds under him. Concentrating on his rhythmic search pattern, Willie had lost count of downed bombers when he asked into the intercom, "Jeff, how many have we lost so far?"

Jeff gave Steve time to interrupt, and when he didn't, Jeff said, "The total is seventy-nine and still counting."

Willie calculated four hundred potential fatalities so far, and they still had to deal with radar-controlled flak and the trip home.

An unhappy Steve came on the intercom. "There are two marked targets ahead of us, separated by over ten miles—it's your call, Charley!"

"Whit th' heel is thes bullshit? Those limey bastards ur tint! They cooldna fin' a sheep in a phain booth!" Charley yelled over the intercom, "Drap th' goddamned bombs oan th' faded markers—there's naethin' but cows under th' other ones!"

Flak exploded well below their lancaster, and no fighters had engaged them since they had shaken their vapour trail. Steve flew toward the now barely discernible markers. He radioed his intentions to the squadron leader and received a simple "Understood, out" in return. The entire squadron dropped their bombs on the faded target markers.

Flying five miles behind the squadron, Phillip, 'C for Charley's' bomb aimer, steered Steve to the target. The aircraft pitched upward when the weight of bombs left it, and Phillip announced, "Bombs gone." The flak continued to be short of their altitude, and Steve had no problem holding his course until the camera took pictures of the damage. Buildings on the ground were already burning from the squadron's main attack, and most of the images would only show a glow through the clouds, but a few would record burning buildings visible through scattered breaks.

Steve banked the plane away from the flak and turned the lancaster toward England. 'C for Charley' was flying by itself, and Steve said, "All right, boys, we're going it alone—the bomber group is all over the sky, and I'm going to stay clear of them." He closed the mike switch, then opened it again, "Jeff, call Leech and tell him we are going home solo."

Steve keyed his mike again. "OK, boys, Charley says the lower we are, the better the winds for us—I'm going to fly home at ten thousand feet, below the vapour trail layer and the other bombers, as fast as rolls royce will take us! Give me a course, Charley." Charley handed Steve a piece of paper.

Willie felt the angle shift as the plane nosed into a shallow dive and heard the wind noise increase as the speed built to the aircraft's structural limit. The course changed slightly to match Charley's instructions, and in ten minutes, the lancaster levelled off at ten thousand feet, covering ground at almost two hundred and sixty mph.

They would find out at the debriefing that they had made a wise choice; the headwind at twenty thousand feet was over forty knots but less than ten at ten thousand. 'C for Charley' hadn't made a wrong choice all night, and every man in the aircraft knew that if only one of the decisions had been a mistake, it would probably have killed them all.

When 'C for Charley' touched down at Dunholme Lodge and rolled into the parking area, it was the squadron's first arrival—Steve's crew was already walking toward the sergeant's mess when the next plane touched down.

Steve dreaded the debriefing—he had technically and blatantly disobeyed orders. And squadron Leader Leech, an excellent officer whose heart was always with his men, had one unwavering rule: he would not tolerate insubordination. The expectation of punishment filled Steve with apprehension, but he had no regrets. His aircraft was undamaged, his crew was alive, the dawn at the east end of runway 27/09 promised a beautiful spring day, and he and his men had lived to see it. Nothing could spoil that.

At the time of the debriefing, no exact numbers were available, but it was clear that the men in the room had been party to a catastrophe for RAF Group Five. Having received and read the pilot reports, the station commander, Group Captain Saunders, described the tragedy in graphic terms. Over a hundred bombers had failed to return, and seven hundred men would never see their homes again!

Willie looked around the room; he could account for all the No 44 squadron crews but one. The squadron had lost one lancaster, less than four percent—the average for Five Group was several times that. Charley had marked the location of over eighty burning aircraft in his log, shot down by night fighters or flak, none of them from No 44 squadron—the missing bomber had gone down on the homeward leg. The fuel tanks would have been nearly empty, so there was a good chance the crew got out safely.

Group Captain Saunders finished his sad report with the statistics as of that moment, handed to him by his second. "We have lost one hundred and eight bombers..." He looked up from the sheet of paper, his broken heart etched in the expression on his face... "And seven-hundred-and-fifty-six men are missing in action."

The men in the room knew there was still time for a straggler or two to make it home, but only those who believed in Santa Claus held onto any hope that there would be more. The Group Captain asked for a moment of silence and a prayer for the missing men, then turned the stage over to Wing Commander Leech.

Leech walked to the front, cleared his throat loudly, and the airmen became silent. He had no notes and stood in front and to the side of the small podium.

"Will 'C for Charley's' crew please come to the front?"

Steve feared the worst as he waited in the aisle until the last man, Jake Collier, passed him, then reluctantly followed him to where Leech waited for them. They gathered in a group on the raised platform in front of a blackboard.

Commander Leech began, "I want to thank these men for saving dozens of our lives. They have three destroyed fighters and a probable, and it's now clear from their report and others that German night fighters are shooting us down with upward-firing cannons. They sneak up, park under the wing, blast a hole in the fuel tanks, and the explosion usually blows the wing off. The only chance we have is to see them coming, so I'm ordering the entire squadron to take the perspex out of the center panel in all rear turrets. It will be cold, but ask Sergeant William McLaughlin how he keeps warm. We must see these fighters before they get under our lancasters! Is that clear to everyone?"

Mumbled approvals echoed throughout the room, followed by discussions between neighbours. Wing Commander Leech cleared his throat and got the silence he needed.

"And now, I can't tell you how much it hurts me to do this, but I would like to say a word to their navigator. I would rather eat shit, but here goes..." Leech looked at Charley and forced his words through gritted teeth. "...Thanks, Charley." The room broke out in laughter. When it died, Leech said, "Charley was the reason No 44 squadron was the only one to hit the objective. We followed his navigation to the turning point and, from there, to the correct markers. Thanks to him, 'C for Charley' made us all proud!"

A round of applause died when Wing Commander Leech turned to Pilot Officer Stephen White.

"Pilot officer White has shown initiative and intelligence. His discovery that our vapour trails disappeared at a higher altitude saved at least two or three bomber losses in our squadron. If not for him and this crew, I am certain that twenty men would not be sitting here!" Applause quickly followed, and the entire room stood, stamped their feet and shouted, "Well done...Good show, boys," and other more colourful congratulations.

While the room cheered, Leech shook the hand of each of 'C for Charley's' crew members—Charley pumped Leech's arm particularly hard, hanging onto his hand as though he were drowning.

Leech struggled, got his hand back and said, "I will recommend that Sergeants Ronald Cummins and William McLaughlin receive a King's commission and a promotion to pilot officer. If I have my way, they will receive the Distinguished Flying Cross for their initiative and bravery." The room roared approval, and Leech had to quiet them down before he could go on.

"It is not usual to announce such things before going up the line, but group commander Saunders and I have discussed this, and we feel that now is the time and here is the place." The room roared again. "Now, get out of here, all of you!" The Wing Commander herded the lancaster crew into the waiting arms of their comrades. The crowd pummeled and back-slapped them until they were outside the building in the early morning air, where the fading dawn promised a clear, bright day without a single cloud.

The roar of American Eighth Air Force B17 bombers climbing on their way to Germany disturbed the celebrations. Some of the men removed their hats, waved them over their heads and shouted, "Go get 'em, Yanks!" Willie watched passively, then turned toward his hut where his steel-framed army bed awaited him. He had never been so tired in his life.

CHAPTER EIGHT

31 March 1944

Survival is a matchless aphrodisiac.

WILLIE BLINKED, HOPING HE WAS DREAMING, but the voice repeated, "Wake up, Willie! It's time to celebrate!" Willie's brain sent move commands to his muscles, but nothing happened. "Come on; we've got a bus and a driver for the night...Let's go!" Ronnie's face slowly came into focus. Charley and Jake stood on both sides of him, laughing, each with a bottle of beer in his hand. Willie wanted to kill them. He pushed Ronnie away. "No! I don't want to—I'm too tired—ask me when I wake up in a few days!"

Willie refused to touch alcohol—not a drop had ever crossed his lips. He had watched it destroy his father, and then his family, and he was terrified that he would one day walk in his father's footsteps. Donald McLaughlin was a lobster fisherman, fit and strong from almost daily lifting a hundred and fifty seventy-pound traps. He dragged them over the side of his rolling, pitching boat, emptied them of lobsters, baited them and slid them over the 'washboard' into the cold green Bay of Fundy water. The image of his strong, drunk father beating his mother invaded Willie's sleep almost every night.

Without alcohol, there was no better father or husband in the world, but add liquor to the equation, and Willie's father became a monster. Afterward, when he was sober, his father was always ashamed of what he had done, but as soon as he could beg, borrow, or steal enough money to get drunk, the cycle repeated itself.

Little Willie and his younger sister Meg cringed in a corner when their father drank, forced to watch their mother take her beating, knowing they would be next. Neither Willie nor Meg cried during their punishment for imagined transgressions—they knew how their mother's heart broke when they did—but they screamed and pleaded when their father pounded on their mother. He paid no attention to them until his wife lay sobbing on the floor.

Willie vividly remembered his mother wrapping her arms around his father's legs, pleading with him to leave her children alone, to hit her instead. He remembered his father kicking his mother in the face before returning to beat Willie and his sister.

Willie hated the sight of a drunk and wished them all dead, including his father, and he didn't want to watch his friends join that group. The surest way to do that was to stay out of the pubs. He rolled over onto his stomach and pulled his pillow over his head.

Ronnie threw the blankets off the bed; Phillip scooped Willie off the mattress and tossed him over his shoulder like a sack of wheat. Willie had been so tired he had removed only his coat and boots, and Ronnie gathered them up and trotted behind Phillip, who laughed but held onto his kicking and complaining load.

The over-sized American dropped him into the back seat of a red bus while Ronnie and Jake cut off his escape. In a gesture of surrender, Willie asked for his boots and coat, and Ronnie handed them over. Still furious and planning his escape, Willie put them on without speaking.

When the bus started to roll, Willie asked, "All right, guys, where are you taking me?" He forced a laugh when they didn't answer. "Okay, boys, I'll have you charged with kidnapping if you don't buy me the best meal I've ever eaten!" He faked good humour while he planned his escape.

Phillip chuckled, "We're going to the Blue Bell Inn in Tattershall, and we're going to hear Vera Lynn!" Willie shook his head. "No, I don't believe we'll hear Vera Lynn in Tattershall."

"Well, not exactly Vera Lynn, but Wing Commander Leech says the woman who sings there is better than the original. The drinks are on the squadron, which is no big deal for you, but for the rest of us, it means we will have a lot of fun until closing time!" Phillip smacked his lips, and Willie groaned.

The big man liked beer more than anything else in his life. No matter how much he drank, he could pace himself, keeping his inebriation level at a constant happy. No one had seen him pass out since he joined the squadron over a year ago, and he was often the only man who could remember every detail of the night.

The bus ride wasn't long, but it was punishing. They covered the twenty-eight miles in fifty minutes, bouncing along on a non-existent suspension, shaking Willie's bladder so he could legitimately beg the driver to stop and let him piss. Unfortunately, Phillip accompanied him to the bushes on the roadside, negating Willie's escape plan.

The last thing Willie wanted to hear was a Vera Lynn imitator...he didn't even like the original!

The Blue Bell Inn is a squat white building built close to the B1192 road in Tattershall Thorpe, a small village in the middle of nowhere, about twenty miles south of Lincoln. The building—a plaque beside the door said that it was built in 1257—oozed history from every corner. A sign over the angled bar claimed that King James had slept in the inn and gotten drunk at the bar. RAF personnel from the surrounding Lincolnshire airfields visited the Blue Bell, filling it every night, and Norma Collette Stanfield played no small part in that choice: every man who entered the room fell in love with her.

Willie stopped at the door—he despised any building that sold alcohol but stood in awe when he looked around the beautiful room. And then, he spotted the most beautiful woman he had ever seen!

Norma noticed the little RAF flyer stop at the door to gaze at the black oak beams that supported the plastered ceiling and was curious. He was the first man she had seen stop before he reached the bar. Despite, or perhaps because of, its familiarity, Norma was still in love with the room and thought it the most beautiful she had ever seen. She was surprised that the man in the doorway appeared to share her fascination.

The intimate setting felt like home to her. The subdued lighting radiating from floor lamps and one small shaded candle in the center of each table created a comforting atmosphere in the hope that it would calm the high-strung RAF crews. Wood was everywhere, from the floor to the dark oak tables and chairs to the posts supporting the blackened oak ceiling beams. As the little aviator and Norma stared at one another, she decided to learn more about him.

RAF aircrews and maintenance personnel from the nearby aerodromes filled the room. Officers and noncoms mingled with no regard to rank. Some sat at tables; others leaned against the old bar.

Large mirrors lined the wall behind the bartender; smaller ones hung strategically around the room. Anyone standing behind the bar could see every corner of the room and keep track of who looked like trouble and who didn't. A cheerful fire burned in the fireplace, and Norma pretended to be interested in it as she covertly watched the little man still blocking the doorway.

She looked straight into his eyes for a long moment, turned, opened the door behind the bar, and disappeared. She was on in 15 minutes, and a corner of the storage room doubled as her dressing room.

"Come on, Willie, you're blocking thirsty customers. That's the girl we told you about, and she doesn't talk to bums like us." Ronnie pushed Willie into the room, keeping his hand on his back until he had propelled him to the bar. The entire crew followed.

"Pardon me, gentlemen, may I show you to a table?" The sweetness of the voice behind them very nearly hid her intent, and Steve, being a little more civilized than the rabble he commanded, took the hint and herded the men behind the barmaid as she led them to a round table in a corner.

They slid along the half-circle padded bench until the entire crew had surrounded the table. The arrangement trapped three men relegated to the center of the half-circle. Steve and Phillip took the outside chairs, leaving the bench's ends for Jake and Willie. No one thought it was a coincidence that the table sat seven, the crew of a lancaster.

"Now, what can I get you gentlemen to drink?" The shapely barmaid smiled; her gaze swept the table slow enough to memorize each face and size up the potential for trouble. The 'C for Charley' crew was not from the neighbouring 'Woodhall Spa' aerodrome, so she was seeing them for the first time. Willie decided the expression on her face was probably pity but could also be distrust.

The crew, except for Willie, ordered beer and ale—he ordered an apple juice and a glass of ice water. When he placed his order, Willie thought he detected sympathy in the barmaid's smile but then, when he looked more closely, decided it was scorn. She left without writing anything down.

Jeffrey whined, "Why can't we go to the bar? I don't like to sit down until I can't stand up," but no one agreed, so he argued that "Waitresses are too slow," crossed his legs under the table, and kicked Steve in the shin.

Steve laughed at his radio operator's discomfort and said, "You colonials are primitive bastards, living in the desert with kangaroos and wild dogs as you do, but if the war lasts long enough, you may yet become civilized." He said it with enough fun in his voice that the sober Australian didn't take it personally. "We will be allowed to go to the bar once we've proven that we're not a bunch of Philistines...Behave for an hour or so, then she'll let you out."

◇◇◇◇◇◇◇◇◇◇◇◇◇◇◇◇◇◇◇◇◇◇◇◇◇◇◇◇◇◇◇

When he wasn't fighting a war, Jeffrey Conway's home was in the Australian Outback near Alice Springs, where his family owned a thousand-acre sheep ranch. A few days after the war began, at dinner, where he hoped his mother would prevent his father from killing him, eighteen-year-old Jeffrey nervously told his parents he had volunteered for the Royal Australian Air Force.

Jeffrey Conway was as wild as his red hair, blue eyes, and freckles promised he would be. He did well enough in school, graduating in the top half of his class despite his frequent absences and a penchant for chasing girls like a nervous border collie near a bitch in heat. He loved to drink and fight and rode horses like a lunatic. His father had given up hope that his son would live to see twenty.

When Joseph Conway rose and came around the table to where he sat, Jeffrey stood up, ready for a fight, but his father put his hand on his shoulder, looked into his eyes, and said, "Son, you might as well kill yourself one way as another. Maybe they'll even figure out how to get you through the next few years alive! If you stay here, you'll die for sure, either on a horse or when some girl's dad shoots you. Go, son, with my blessing." Jeffrey was too happy to be embarrassed.

Jeffrey trained to be a pilot in the RAAF and, throughout training, was above average in every way, including alcohol consumption. Unfortunately, he flunked out of pilot training by crashing his second Tiger Moth when he snapped a rudder cable doing forbidden low-level acrobatics. Over his protests, the RAAF shipped him to England, where they happily gave him to the RAF as a radio operator...the Royal Air Force needed radio operators more than pilots who pranged airplanes.

◇◇◇◇◇◇◇◇◇◇◇◇◇◇◇◇◇◇◇◇◇◇◇◇◇◇◇◇◇◇◇

The waitress returned with tankards and glasses on a large tray, but Willie's juice and ice water were conspicuously missing. She set the tray on the edge of the table and distributed the drinks precisely as ordered.

59

Jeffrey stood, reached for his ale, and she slapped his hand so hard that Willie winced. Jeff winked at her, sat down, and waited until she ceremoniously handed his beer across the table, showing her ample breasts to him as she did. Then she pulled out a fat black purse fastened to her belt with a chain and, looking around the table, waited patiently. Steve put up his hand when his men began looking for their money.

"I've got this." He fished a bundle of folded pound notes out of his pocket. "The squadron is paying for as much as we can drink." Everyone but Willie roared.

The waitress touched Willie's arm and whispered, "I'll be right back with your juice."

The teasing began as soon as she left, but Willie didn't react, so the conversation turned to flying. Every man in the crew, except Willie, had enlisted to become a pilot. Willie tried to appear interested, but his mind kept returning to the angel in the room behind the bar. He got his apple juice a minute later, drank half, topped the glass with ice water, and returned to his dream.

"When Irish Eyes are Smiling" tinkled from the piano, and the beauty of the familiar theme stopped the low murmur of conversation. The aviators were quiet for the first run-through, then began to chat with ever-increasing enthusiasm.

When the piano finished the theme for the second time, familiarity had bred contempt, and the pianist modulated through three or four chords to another key. The melody slipped almost unnoticed into the introduction to "The white cliffs of Dover," the most popular Vera Lynn song of the day. When the men who had seen Norma before recognized her theme, they clapped and whistled.

Willie's interest was piqued when the beautiful woman he had seen came into the room from the door behind the bar. Barely five feet tall, with coal-black hair, she had a light mediterranean brown complexion accentuating her Latin features. Her eyes were black pools designed by her maker to draw men into them. She timed sliding her tongue over her perfectly shaped lips for maximum effect, and Willie's brain immediately told him she was out of his league.

She opened her mouth, beautiful sounds filled the room, and Willie's heart was lost—he fell in love for the first time in his life. Looking around the room, he realized he was not alone in that.

Norma moved gracefully across the floor from one table to the next, singing her way from one awe-struck man to another. She began the final verse as she passed 'C for Charley's' table and stopped beside Willie. She placed her hand on his head and straightened his unruly mousey-brown hair as she trailed the final note to a beautiful diminuendo. Willie looked steadily at his juice glass, not daring to lift his eyes but desperately wanting to.

Willie was twenty-two and had served in the RCAF for three years. Acne scars marked his face, a curse from his teenage years exacerbated by the daily tension his father inserted into the family. Willie had inherited delicate facial features from his mother—a small nose, mouth, and soft, soothing brown eyes—made one almost forget the scars. The essential elements of his intelligent-looking face were attractive. Still, the acne offset the boyish quality that would typically have attracted women, and he considered himself out of luck in that department.

Willie had never seriously dated a girl, let alone had an affair. No girl, let alone an angel, had ever crossed a room to talk to him. When the men in the room hooted and laughed, his brain told him she was teasing him, but his heart wouldn't listen.

The song ended, and Norma strolled over to the piano, leaving Willie to drown in unrequited love.

◇◇◇◇◇◇◇◇◇◇◇◇◇◇◇◇◇◇◇◇◇◇◇◇◇◇◇◇◇◇◇◇◇

Marlene Dietrich was the unlikely heroine in two popular American western films and a darling among the Allied forces. Marlene was German-born but energetically anti-Nazi and became an American citizen in 1939. The OSS, the British army's radio propaganda division, asked her to make recordings they hoped would demoralize the German troops, and she quickly agreed.

The idea backfired—despite the fact the Nazis had set up their German Forces radio stations all over the territory they had conquered, Wehrmacht soldiers preferred Marlene Dietrich on OSS. Fighting men on both sides claimed her for their own.

The rehabilitated Marlene Dietrich raised more money in war bonds than any Hollywood star, including superstar Bob Hope. As Willie was falling in love with Norma, Marlene Dietrich was completing a British bases tour, entertaining Allied troops and RAF bomber personnel.

Marlene Dietrich's interpretation of "Lili Marlene," broadcast by OSS Allied radio, captured the hearts of soldiers on both sides in both languages, and Norma began the song to a roar of applause, followed by absolute silence as she softly began the first verse unaccompanied.

"Far across the ocean, far across the sea; someone is waiting, waiting just for me…."

The piano softly began at the second line, and before the verse was over, men who faced death almost every night sat with shiny, wet eyes, thinking of loved ones whose faces they struggled to remember. She stood beside Willie, her hand on his shoulder, and the room was as quiet as a tomb except for the sweet vibrations that resonated from the white plaster, warmed by the dark wood. Willie's heart filled with hope, and he forgot every bad thing that had ever happened to him.

◇◇◇◇◇◇◇◇◇◇◇◇◇◇◇◇◇◇◇◇◇◇◇◇◇◇◇◇◇◇◇

Norma had agonized over whether she should sing the last verse a second time, but in German. Marlene Dietrich had recorded the song in both languages, and the original recording of 'Lili Marlen' by Lale Anderson had sold a million copies in her native Germany, despite Goebbels having forbidden Germans to play it.

Norma was not sure what the reaction would be. Her Jewish German vocal teacher had warned her not to sing it in German in front of British airmen, but she disagreed, and it was important to her to test the hypothesis. She began the last verse again, this time in German, singing the words of a German soldier speaking from his grave. The dead soldier promised Lili his spirit would return to join her every night under the lamppost.

The room remained as quiet as before. Norma sang her heart out, still standing beside Willie. When she began the last verse for the second time, the pianist stopped playing and sat quietly with his hands on his knees. Without the intrusion of the piano, her clear, resonant tones magnified the mood. and the emotion Norma felt went directly to the heart of every man in the room, but none more than Willie's.

She finished the song, ever slower to the end, and then encouraged the men to sing the English chorus with her. Caught off-guard, they sang in weak tones at first, but Norma repeated it, and they sang beautifully. She then taught them the chorus in German, and they learned it enthusiastically, singing it with as much energy as they had the English version.

Finally, Norma taught them to sing it softly, with the same sad feeling she felt—and the beautiful sound of the spontaneous men's chorus brought tears to her eyes and theirs.

She blew kisses around the room, leaned over to Willie's upturned face, and, before he could move, touched her soft lips to his. The room stood up as one and smashed their hands together until she raised her arms in good-bye. She left as she had come, leaving Willie soaked in rapture. There was no teasing in her kiss; every man in the room knew it, and they hated him.

As she opened the door behind the bar, she said, "So much for hating Germans," quietly to herself.

Ronnie's bladder called, and he tried to get Willie's attention in the middle of "When they sound the last all-clear…," but Willie ignored him. Ronnie persisted, and Willie threatened to kill him with a fork. Just in time, Charley, Jake, and Jeffrey cleared a path for Ronnie to get out on the other side of the table.

The room became hushed whenever Norma sang, and the enchanted men stopped drinking. Management quickly caught on to the fact that they sold no drinks when she was singing but made up for it when she stopped; consequently, they restricted her to two songs before a break, and Willie hated them for it.

Every night, Norma sang to a packed bar and dining room that overflowed into two adjacent rooms. RAF uniforms were everywhere; officers and crews together, slapping backs, shaking hands as they made new friends and greeted old ones. Most importantly, they bought drinks for their friends. And then, every fifteen minutes, a hundred homesick men stopped talking and drinking so they could listen to Norma sing. Willie spent the evening going from ecstacy to mourning and back.

Norma sang her last song, "I'm in the mood for love," to raucous cheers and applause. She waved to her "boys," lifted her long skirt, playfully kicked her leg in the air, and exited into the storage room behind the bar.

◇◇◇◇◇◇◇◇◇◇◇◇◇◇◇◇◇◇◇◇◇◇◇◇◇◇◇◇◇◇◇◇◇

Before she went to the Blue Bell that night, Norma resolved that chastity was not the antidote to the pain of losing her husband that she thought it would be. She had tried it for a year, and the pain in her heart hadn't diminished a whit. She suspected that, without her realizing it, the

63

longing for her husband had become a desire for a man, and it was time to find out.

A year ago, her husband, Brian, had died in a lancaster blowing up dams somewhere in the Ruhr River Valley. He had been the lancaster's rear air gunner, and a night fighter had killed him. The rest of the crew survived and brought the plane back on two engines, ripped to shreds, with Brian's body still in his turret, torn apart by the fighter's machine gun.

Norma lifted her eyes, looked at her sadness reflected in the mirror and made a decision. She wiped her tears, vowed they would be the last she would shed for Brian, and finished taking off her makeup. She returned to the barroom and headed straight for Willie!

"Get up and walk me home. Your friends will wait for you." Her tone ruled out any other option for Willie or his friends. The scrawny little airman looked up but couldn't speak. She took his hand from his third glass of juice and pulled him to his feet.

The entire bar became silent. Every man in the room had heard via bar talk that the little man Norma had chosen was a rear gunner on a lancaster, and they were stunned when the woman they all lusted for decided to go home with this skinny pipsqueak of a rear gunner with a face cratered like the moon!

Rear gunners had the shortest life expectancy of any member of a bomber crew. With phenomenal luck, Willie would live a couple of months but had close to no chance at all of completing his tour. A few men in the room remembered Brian, a rear gunner like Willie, and they shook their heads in bewilderment.

Norma dragged him by the arm until she had him standing outside the door, where she looked straight into his eyes. "It's a half-hour walk to the Petwood Hotel, where I have a room, and that's how long you've got to convince me that you are worth keeping!"

"I can't talk you into anything," he replied anxiously, "I don't know what you want!"

She shook her head and said, "Don't assume anything—I don't know what I want—I just know I need someone with me tonight, and for some reason, I think you are the one I need." She grabbed his hand and pulled him across the yard to the road.

They walked for a few minutes in silence until finally, Willie said self-consciously, "I don't know anything about music. I only like western hillbilly music, especially yodelling." He looked at the ground and shuffled his feet. "I like Jimmie Rogers. He's dead now, but he sure could yodel!"

"They yodel in Canada?"

"How do you know I'm Canadian?" Willie skipped ahead and then, walking backwards, turned to face Norma.

Norma stopped. "One of your pals told the waitress... She's my spy."

He shrugged, picked up a stone and threw it over a wall into a field.

"Only the cowboy singers yodel, like Jimmy Rogers and Wilf Carter. Wilf Carter was born about a hundred miles from Digby, where my parents live. I'm a fisherman, so I don't know how to yodel."

She smiled; he looked at her, and she said thoughtfully, "Then it's probably a good thing that my plan doesn't include having you yodel for me tonight." She tucked her arm under his and pulled him close, laughing as she did. He had to walk with her.

Willie said, "Thank God for that, but I can't sing much either, although I wish I could when I listen to you." He relaxed slightly. "I sure like your singing!"

"I'll take that as a compliment." She paused, and Willie waited. "Do you know that I sang the last song for you?"

"You did?"

"Oh, yes, I did," she quietly spoke as they walked. "I always close with 'Praise the Lord and pass the ammunition!' But tonight, I'm in the mood for love. I lost my husband a year ago today, and I've been a good girl since then." She pulled his arm so that he stopped and faced her. "I want you to corrupt me tonight."

"Oh darn!" He whispered, "I was afraid of that!"

Norma pulled him to walk again, almost dragging him. Then she changed tactic, let go and started running, hoping he would chase her. He couldn't bear to let her go, so he ran but wasn't sure that was what she wanted him to do, so his effort wasn't entirely animated.

At first, Willie tried to keep up by walking fast but soon realized he would need to break into a jog to catch her, and then had to run flat out when she increased her speed. He ran after her until she stopped at a narrow lane on the right-hand side of the road. She kept Willie a few steps behind until she stopped so he could catch her in front of a beautiful Tudor-style building with a dozen chimneys sticking out of its complicated red roof.

Norma pointed at it. "That's where I stay when I sing here. I will show you where my room is, and you'll crawl in the window when I open it."

She grinned, and Willie's legs turned to rubber.

"The woman who sits at the entrance desk knows my mother, and I don't know what the woman will do if I take you in with me. She might tell my mother, kick you out, or both."

She caught his arm as he tried to turn. "Don't worry—I'm not going to hurt you."

"I think I should return to the pub so they won't leave without me." He didn't know whether to stand there or run, but she pulled him down a narrow lane toward the hotel before he could decide. Fifty yards down the driveway, Norma left the gravel and led him across the grass to a bay window, and he found himself looking into a dark room. "That's my room—stay here until I let you in!"

She put her finger on his chest, then disappeared around the hotel. A minute later, light suddenly flooded the room as Norma switched it on and opened the blackout curtain. She threw her coat on the bed and tried to open the latch, but it was stuck, and Willie began to think about running.

Norma looked up at him, and he half-turned, ready to bolt, but the window picked that instant to give in to her. He looked at her, terrified but spellbound. Whatever she wanted, 'no' would not be an option.

Norma took Willie's hand and carefully guided him over the sill into the centre of the room. She closed the window, drew the blackout curtains, and lit a single candle. When she turned off the light and pointed at his boots, he knew he was lost and sat on the bed, loosened the laces, and pulled them off. Without encouragement, he removed his coat and stared at her.

Norma returned his stare as she said, "Take off your clothes…you don't want to miss your bus." She was afraid he would leave if she gave Willie time to think.

When Willie stood up, hardly able to breathe, he got no sympathy from Norma. She devilishly smiled as she pointed at the buttons on his shirt and said, "Start with the shirt."

He sighed loudly but unbuttoned his shirt, and Norma's heart leapt— she felt he had passed the point of no return. When he finished with the buttons, she leaned against him, pressing her small breasts against his chest while tugging his shirt out of his pants. When she helped him pull the shirt off his arms, she leaned her hip against him and felt his hard penis. She had chosen wisely; he would do nicely, but the waitress had said he was likely a virgin, and the timing would be critical.

Before he could stop her, Norma grabbed his belt, unbuckled it and whipped it through the loops in one swift motion. His face burned red; she thought he might fall down or cry or both. She quickly unbuttoned the top two buttons of his fly, and his pants slid to his ankles.

She stared at his bright red face, changed her mind about her next move, and said, "You can finish. I'm going to be too busy to help you anymore." He reached down, obviously intending to pull up his pants.

Norma quickly stepped over to him. "Oh no, you don't!" She pushed him back onto the bed, grasped the cuffs of his pants in both hands and leaned back to get the leverage she needed. They yielded. She threw them against the wall, whipped her skirt over her head and unbuttoned her blouse so fast that Willie gasped. Her bra fell to the floor, and her panties followed almost before it came to rest.

With something that lay somewhere between fascination, lust, and paralyzing fear, Willie said, "Oh, my God!"

She laughed at him, "He is not going to help you...He is on my side! Now, get the rest of your clothes off! You can leave the socks if you want to."

◇◇◇◇◇◇◇◇◇◇◇◇◇◇◇◇◇◇◇◇◇◇◇◇◇◇◇◇◇◇◇◇

Willie had never made love to a woman in his life, not even close. He had no idea what he should do, either to please her or, in Norma's case, to defend himself. Terrified, Willie sat on the bed, slid his underwear down, and removed his socks. Norma leaned over and kissed him, tenderly at first, then passionately as she pushed him down on the bed.

Norma took Willie to a place he hadn't imagined, and when she finished with him, he knew he could never leave it.

"You can go to your pals now." She turned over, turning her back to him. He swung his feet over the side of the bed, hesitated, then stood up on shaky legs. He looked back at Norma, his eyes filled with tears. "I love you," he said.

"What have I done?" She laughed gently, turning to him.

"You've ruined me...I can't live without you." He reached for his clothes and began to put them on; he started with his shirt and got the buttons wrong.

Norma smiled at him. "Go to your friends, but come back on Saturday. We can do this again if you like."

Willie panicked, "What if we have a mission, and I can't come?... He tried to find a solution... "I'll send word if that happens!"

Norma shrugged, "If you're not here..." She thought for a second, then pouted, "I'll just have to find someone else, won't I?" Willie sensed a note of playfulness, but he wasn't sure, so he blurted, "Oh, please don't!" And she laughed, her musical voice filling the room.

Willie left through the window and walked back to the pub, sometimes weaving back and forth on the road like a drunk. It was past closing when he arrived; the Blue Bell Inn was dark, and the bus's diesel engine clattered at a slow idle. They had waited for him, and Willie gratefully climbed in and sat alone in the front passenger seat. He looked silently out the window, ignoring the string of good-natured comments.

CHAPTER NINE

1–2 April 1944

Das Haus steht nicht auf der Erde, sondern auf dem Weib.
(It is not the earth that supports a home; it is the woman.)

IT WAS LUFTWAFFE POLICY to grant time off to crew members who survived a bailout. Erik mildly protested that his regular leave was in another month anyway, and he would prefer to wait. He lied when he expressed a desire to return to battle as soon as possible. His C/O wisely disagreed and ordered Erik to take a two-week leave now, combining the week of scheduled time with the stress leave due in a month. The Luftwaffe gave Erik rail passes to Heilbronn and back, and his chief mechanic, Sergeant Fritz Hagerman, drove him to the Charleroi station in Erik's old mercedes.

Eight hours and three train changes later, Erik stood on the platform in Heilbronn, holding his wife in his arms. His nine-year-old son, Walther, waited patiently until his father turned and wrapped his arms around him.

Erik knelt in front of Walther, his hands on the boy's shoulders. "Have you left any work in the house for me to do?"

"No, Vati, you'll have lots of time to spend with me and Mutti. I finished planting the vegetable garden, and we've weeded all the flowers." He excitedly hugged his father again. "I'm sure glad you're home!"

Erik waited for his son to ask what he'd brought for him, but Walther didn't do it. He ruffled his son's hair, stood up, pulled a gift-wrapped box out of his pack and handed it to Marita. She removed the fancy paper, folded it and put it in her pocket. Crouching in front of Walther so her son could see the contents before she did, Marita lifted the cover slowly. Erik squatted beside his son as he peeked under it, and the pink dawn light revealed handmade Belgian chocolates individually wrapped in white tissue paper.

"Oh, Mutti!" Walther touched the tissue paper in awe. "Would you let me have one when we get home?" He pulled his hand back but continued to stare at the box. "Thank you, Vati, for giving Mutti such a beautiful present!" His eyes shone. Erik hugged him again, stood up, and took his son's hand.

The family covered the two-kilometre walk from the station to Wacksstrasse 21 in twenty minutes. Progress was slow at first—Walther insisted on carrying his father's small bag, too much load for his child's frame, and gave it up gladly when Marita found an excuse to take it from him. The pace quickened, and Walther had to skip to keep up.

Marita's mother, Annalisa, met them at the door. She put her arms around Erik in an affectionate, atypical mother-in-law hug. Tall, like her daughter, but more delicately built, she had brown hair and hazel eyes, contrasting Marita's blue eyes and blonde hair.

Erik and Annalisa Müller had formed a special bond following her husband's death early in the war. Georg Müller, a major in the Luftwaffe, had mentored Erik from the beginning of his training in 1939 until, in late 1941, a British night fighter had shot his bomber down over London.

Following Georg's death, Annalisa moved in with Erik and Marita, drawing Walther and the two little girls they had embraced into their family under her wing. Annalisa and Marita rotated the children's care as they worked alternating shifts at a small motorcycle factory converted to manufacture tank parts.

When Erik entered the foyer, two squealing girls ran down the hall from their bedroom. The younger, Elke, dark-complexioned with black hair and brown eyes, was four; the older, Brigitte, was six years old and blonde, with blue eyes. They squealed in delight as they hugged their unofficially adopted father. Hugs over, he kissed them and picked them up, one on each arm.

When he headed for the sofa, Annalisa directed him to the kitchen, where she had prepared a breakfast of hard-boiled eggs, fresh Brötchen, and sliced Wurst.

Marita said, "Walther, you must eat quickly; you've already missed your first class." She shelled an egg and began cutting it into small pieces on his plate.

Walther pushed his mother away, "I can do that myself, Mutti! You've forgotten I'm nine years old now!" and finished cutting the egg while sneaking peeks at his father. Marita said, "Yes, I forgot," and winked at her husband. Erik smiled—the war receded—he was home.

The family sat down, and Annalisa put the girls on either side of her… Erik filled Marita's cup with fake coffee. He put a finger up, stopping Marita before she could drink the brew, and retrieved a package of beet sugar from his pack. The girls shrieked in delight. Marita looked at the cup when he added a generous teaspoonful to her ersatz coffee, smiled sweetly at him, and Erik added another. She widened the smile—he dug the spoon into the bag for a third, and she pulled his head down, kissed him and whispered, "I have something sweet for you later!"

Erik winked at Annalisa. "Maybe we can talk Oma into baking a Torte with the sugar. I have two more packages in my big bag, and we can have some every day while I'm home."

Walther turned to his grandmother. "Will you make a rhubarb torte, Oma?" and then applied nine-year-old logic, "The rhubarb is ready; I will cut some when I get home from school."

Walther looked after the garden, refusing his mother's help. When he went to war, his father gave him that assignment, and Walther would not let anyone else touch it. He permitted his mother to give advice, but Walther forbade her to touch his gardening tools. Despite that, Marita did some of the heaviest digging when Walther was sleeping or away at school, but her son wisely ignored that intrusion.

An amused Annalisa said, "I was counting on you suggesting that, Walther. How about taking a vote? Rhubarb takes much more sugar than strawberries—maybe I should make a strawberry torte."

Walther shouted, "Make a rhubarb and a strawberry torte!"

"Yes, make a rhubarb and a strawberry torte!" It was unanimous around the table.

Walther told Oma, "Don't forget to leave some sugar for Mutti's coffee!" His mood shifted, "…my strawberries aren't ready yet."

Marita said, "They will be ripe before your father returns to his squadron. Meanwhile, we'll bake a rhubarb Torte."

Erik said, "The strawberries will have time to ripen. The Luftwaffe gave me two weeks' leave; I got the extra week for making a mistake!"

A Wave of guilt suddenly swept over Erik. He thought bitterly, *I got an extra week because I lost an airplane, got my best friend killed, and survived.* Erik laid his fork down and looked silently at his plate. *It's a strange world when we reward such stupid mistakes.*

Marita took his hand. As usual, she had read his mind.

"Erik, you didn't start the war that killed Michael. I'm thankful you're alive, and I'm grateful for the extra week."

Annalisa said, "Yes, I know you did everything you could to save Michael, and the truth is, I'm thankful it wasn't you. You should also know that while you are home, Bertha and I have arranged to fill in for Marita at the factory so she can spend more time with you and the children." Annalisa looked into the distance. "I wish I had spent more time with my husband!"

Marita took her mother's hand. "Thank you for the offer, but you can't work more than you do—you are already doing far too much!"

"Don't worry about me; I'm only taking one extra twelve-hour shift; Bertha is taking the rest. She needs the extra money and is happy to get away from her husband. He's a mean drunk, and they fight like Italian cats! I'm sure it would surprise his comrades in the SS to learn that he can't beat his wife in a fair fight!" She laughed and angrily went on. "He drinks most of his pay, and every day, it becomes harder for Bertha to feed her children—she can't pay the rent without working extra hours and hiding the money. When this is over, I hope our men appreciate what we're doing to keep their damned war going!"

Marita said softly, looking at her plate, "And what if there aren't any men left?"

Erik thought of Michael as he looked out the window, and Walther broke the silence by getting out of his chair and wrapping his arms around his father. "Someone is coming to our school tomorrow to talk about flying. Would you like to come with me, Vati?"

"Yes, I'll be coming." Erik messed with Walther's hair. "As a matter of fact, I'm the one who's going to talk to you and your classmates. The Heilbronn Schuldirector has invited me to talk about night flying, and you'll be in the Harmonie Halle with children from the other schools."

Erik tried to hide the dread he felt. Speaking in front of children terrified him more than strapping into his night fighter and stalking a bomber bristling with machine guns.

Walther shouted, "Wow, that's wonderful—I can't wait to tell Otto!" He let go of his father and ran toward the door.

"I've never seen him so eager to go to school!" Marita laughed as her son skidded around the corner and out the front door, leaving it open in his hurry. She followed him out and shut it, then turned to Erik, who had followed her. She laughed as she said, "How do you feel about talking to hundreds of children like Walther?" He reached out with his arms, and she hugged him.

"I know they're just children, but I'm scared to death!" He laughed nervously as she let him go. "I have no idea what to say." Marita went around him, and he followed her to the kitchen.

Annalisa raised her hand. "I'll help you write something."

"If you help me, I will be grateful. My commanding officer gave me a standard speech outline, but it's so political and adult I can't use it in front of children. I can't say what I know and believe, but I want to help these children understand what it means to fight a war; otherwise, they will repeat our mistakes."

Erik winced as he thought of the speech. "If I say what I want to say, I'll wind up on the Russian front, or worse, in the Gestapo's cellar!"

Annalisa cynically laughed, saying, "I think I understand your problem, and we'll work something out."

<hr>

The Neckar River flows through the heart of Heilbronn, and after breakfast, Annalisa took the girls for a walk to feed the ducks that called the river their home. The girls kissed Erik goodbye. "We'll be back real soon!" said Brigitte, but Annalisa quickly interrupted, pushing the little girl's hair back. "Not soon; we're going to try and find new shoes for both of you." She smiled naughtily and turned to Marita. "We won't be back for hours—for sure not before Mittagspause." Marita returned her smile.

Erik turned his back so his wife and mother-in-law wouldn't see his expression, busying himself, clearing the table and putting the dishes in the sink. He caught Marita mouthing a "thank you!" to her mother.

Annalisa herded the children out, Marita closed the door, and Erik heard the click when she turned the key in the lock. A few seconds later, she appeared in the kitchen, where he had begun washing the dishes.

"There's no need to do the dishes now," she said sweetly, "you've been up all night travelling, and you must be tired—why don't you go take your clothes off and get into bed? I'll come in a few minutes to tuck you in." She pulled him away from the sink and kissed him, a little more adult than the welcoming kiss on the platform.

"Yes, dear," he replied, suddenly out of breath. "What did you say about clothes?"

Marita smiled and pushed him through the kitchen door. "Go into the bedroom and take them off—I'll be there in a minute to show you what to do after that."

His breathing became ragged. Erik had never had a woman other than his wife, preferring to wait rather than suffer the guilt of cheating. While away, Erik absorbed himself in his flying, letting the pressure build until he saw Marita again. Running four kilometres every morning and evening, playing chess with anyone who would play with him, and taking cold showers had been enough to suppress his need for the past eight months. He never accompanied the other flying crews on their frequent trips to the local bars and brothels, and Erik's self-discipline with alcohol and women was legendary.

Although a complete klutz with tools, to kill time, Erik often 'worked' on his fighter with the maintenance crew, deluding himself that he knew how to fix an aircraft.

Erik's flying skill and dedication had earned him the Iron Cross two years ago, and his recent victories and surviving the loss of his messerschmitt 110 had earned him the Oak Leaves. Erik's mechanical skills were also legendary, but for the opposite reason—his chief mechanic would not allow him near the aircraft unless he was there to supervise.

When Marita said she wanted him in the bedroom, the heroic flying ace became a pile of mush. Discipline disappeared; he left his uniform in a heap on the floor, undressed in seconds, and pulled the feather comforter over his naked body. When Marita entered, lighting up the room with her mischievous smile, the eagerness on her face was enough to cause Eric's penis to rise out of its long sleep, removing all traces of heroism.

Marita was tall and blonde; her blue eyes twinkled, and naughty wrinkles turned up from the corners of her slightly open mouth. Erik's heart pounded as she undressed—his breath caught as she pulled the comforter to the floor.

The double bed was built in two sections, with a board on its edge separating the mattresses. Only half the bed was available for lovemaking, and the narrow single-width on each side left little room for wandering or splayed limbs. Marita lay on her side next to Erik, her back very near the edge. He rolled on his side to face her, and she stroked him gently.

His voice cracked, "Too much of that, and you'll have to wait until tonight!"

Marita pulled him on top and helped him slide into her. He groaned and moved, pressed her down on the bed, pushing himself into her as far as he could. He lasted less than half a minute—she held him against her as he shuddered.

He asked, "Are you OK?" He doubted that she had an orgasm—she still seemed eager when his penis went soft.

She kissed him gently. "Yes, darling, I'm fine."

"I can't believe you're all right…"

"Well, it was so good for me," she said coquettishly, "that I would like to do it again tonight—so, rest now so you'll be ready, my handsome prince!"

Erik closed his eyes… Thirty seconds later, he was asleep, breathing quietly.

Marita waited another five minutes until his breathing slowed and deepened. He never snored, but his breath came in surges when he was soundly asleep. She got up and went to the bathroom.

When she returned to bed, Erik reached out in his sleep and wrapped his arms around her. His hand found one of her breasts, and Marita rolled over to lay with her back against his flat belly, her bum against his limp penis. She pulled his hand away and kissed it, then replaced it before she closed her eyes. She went to sleep almost immediately.

CHAPTER TEN

2 April 1944

Wenn die Buben Soldaten spielen, so gibt's Krieg.
(When boys play soldier, war follows.)

WALTHER THREW THE FRONT DOOR OPEN against the doorstop that Erik had bolted to the floor for that particular purpose and shouted, "Mutti, Vati, I'm home!" Annalisa sat in the living room playing a board game with the girls—she sat on the end of the sofa where she could cut him off when he slowed down to throw his coat on the floor and kick his boots into a corner.

"They're sleeping," Brigitte moaned, "and we're not allowed to bother them until they come out." She spread her hands in frustration. "We're not even allowed to use the bathroom!"

Elke wiggled and jumped up and down. "I can't hold it much longer!"

Just in time, Marita shouted from the hall, "Okay, the bathroom's free!" and Elke and Brigitte took off in a race for the toilet. Elke bullied her way in front of Brigitte, and Brigitte let her younger sister go but issued a warning... "You better not take very long, or you'll have to wash my panties!" Elke swung around the door frame into the bathroom, and Brigitte added, "...and the floor, too!"

Erik came out of the bedroom, tucking in his shirt. "What's the commotion?" He wore a broad smile. "Have we inconvenienced our young ladies?" He rubbed the top of Brigitte's head; she folded her arms and turned away from him.

"I'm six. I don't like that anymore, and I need to go to the toilet!"

"Okay," said Erik, "it's been a long time since I've seen you, and it may take a few days before I get used to you growing up so fast." She smiled at him, taking her eyes off the bathroom door for the first time.

The door opened, Elke ran to the living room, and Brigitte streaked inside without stopping to close the door. The whole family heard her say, "I made it!"

Erik laughed, and Elke pushed him. He purposely fell—she jumped on his stomach and tickled him. They rolled on the floor, laughing while Walther folded his arms in disgust. Marita saved the day by entering the living room and saying, "Come on, Walther, I want you to cut some rhubarb; we're going to bake a torte!" Walther quickly forgot his silly father.

Thirty minutes later, Marita announced dinner, starting a stampede to the kitchen. Walther shouted, "No dirty hands allowed at the table," as he tried unsuccessfully to cut the girls off before they got to the bathroom ahead of him. Three minutes later, all three children sat at the table, ostensibly with their hands washed.

Annalisa put ersatz coffee on the table for the adults and glasses of fresh milk in front of the children. Most of Germany did without whole milk, drinking a sterilized skimmed version that tasted like it had spoiled. Over time, children became accustomed to the sour taste, but their taste buds jumped when fresh milk hit them. They laughed and asked for more, and Annalisa tried to slow them down by filling their glasses with ever-decreasing amounts.

The torte cooled while the family ate a Mittagessen of pork and sauerkraut. When the main meal was over, Annalisa cut the pastry and passed it around. Everyone ate quickly, but Walther easily won the race and held out his plate to his mother, spitting crumbs on the table as he said, "Bitte! I want some more,"

Marita smiled as she rubbed the top of his head. "No, Walther, I'm sorry, but we mustn't eat it all today; we should leave some for tomorrow and the next day."

Walther stood up and shouted, "I've got lots more rhubarb! I'll cut some tomorrow before I go to school, and Oma and I will help you bake another torte!"

Erik opened his mouth, but Annalisa broke in to rescue Marita. "Yes, but where do we get the sugar and flour? If we eat a torte every day, we'll soon use up all the sugar, and I'll get fat!"

Walther pushed his plate in front of Marita. She stood but didn't take it from him. He said, a sense of desperation in his voice, "Vati will come home sooner next time, and he'll bring more sugar!" He looked at Erik for confirmation. "Or, he can send us more sugar in the post!" Walther slapped the table with his free hand, emphasizing satisfaction with his excellent idea.

Erik stepped into the fray. "If I could decide when to come home, I would never leave!" He decided to soften the blow for Walther. "I'll try to send some sugar, but it's rationed and hard to find." He pleaded with his son, "I think we should make the bags we have last as long as we can—do you understand that, Walther?"

"No," Walther stamped his foot, "I want more torte now! You must let me have more torte!" He held the plate out to his mother while looking at his father.

Erik waited, giving his son time to back down. Tears formed in Walther's eyes, and when it was evident that his son would not see reason, Erik said quietly, "I don't want you to speak to anyone like that, least of all your mother and me. You must go to your room until you can apologize to us."

Walther turned to his father, smashed his plate on the floor, saluted with a stiff outstretched arm, and shouted, "Jawohl, Herr Oberleutnant! Heil Hitler!" He turned expertly on his heel, marched to his bedroom and slammed the door. Erik sat still for a moment, then turned to Marita.

"Did he learn that in Pimpfe?"

"Yes," Annalisa answered as she bowed her head. "He practices the salute with his friends. He has Pimpfe this afternoon from four until six." She said sarcastically, "He is now a 'block boy,' and his goal is to win a gold medal before he graduates to the 'Jungfolk' next year!"

Erik intended to follow his son, but Marita took his hand and pulled him to her. He looked toward Walther's room, trying to decide what to do, and she said, "Don't be too hard on him; he's only a little boy."

"Yes, but he could become a very dangerous little boy! I will let him cool off, and then I will talk to him." He looked at Marita, "When the time comes, I want you to come with me—you must hear what I have to say—he has to see that we are united."

Annalisa busied herself with clearing the table and washing the dishes while Erik and Marita sat down and discussed what to do about Walther. When she was halfway through the pile, she left it and sat opposite Erik. Marita went to the sink and started washing the remaining dishes, leaving her mother to continue the discussion with her husband.

Annalisa twisted the wedding ring she still wore back and forth on her finger. "We ran into Reverend Matthias on our walk. He was going to the Zwangsarbiter barracks with food and told me he had heard a rumour that Monica Lindenbaum had died. Have you heard anything about that?"

Erik nodded, "Yes, I was waiting for the right moment to tell you. The day after I lost my plane, I called Jacques, our friend in Brussels, and he told me he had unofficially heard that she died last winter in the Ravensberg work camp near Berlin, probably of typhoid fever. He also told me that the Gestapo in Amiens captured Juliette, and the Maquis rescued her. Juliette and Marcel are now members of the fighting arm of the Résistance."

Marita heard the conversation, left the dishes and sat beside Erik. "I've known somehow that Monica was dead." She put her hand on his. "You said 'unofficially'…is Jacques sure?"

Erik nodded. "I told my commanding officer I would quit flying if they didn't find out what happened to her. Major Fischer made a few calls… the Ravensberg camp had a typhus epidemic last winter, killing more than half the inmates. The prison officials said they tried to save them, but the disease spread too fast. They confirmed that Monica was one of the dead."

Annalisa asked through clenched teeth, "Did they say how many guards died?" She got up, went to the sink, and began energetically washing the plates.

Erik had no answer to her question but believed he could make a close guess.

Monica had been Marita's close friend since childhood, and Marita had been there when the SA took her away. If the 'brownshirts' had come just a few hours later, their friends from Belgium would have gotten Monica and her children out of the country. The incident had broken Marita's heart. Until now, she had hoped that Jacques would perform a miracle and Monica would return.

Annalisa put a plate in the rack and picked up another, talking as she worked, "I've heard that trains full of Jews are going through the station at night, on their way to camps in the east, just like Marcel and Juliette told you the last time they were here." She finished with the last plate, wiping her hands as she turned to look at Erik. "What more do you know? What else did Jacques tell you?"

80

Erik hesitated and clasped his hands together on the table. Annalisa crossed the floor to stand beside him, "Tell me...I'm not a child!"

Erik slowly shook his head and spoke while looking at his hands. "Jacques confirmed that it's as Marcel and Juliette told us. We don't speak of this on the base because the walls have ears, but I will tell you another story I've heard. A French guard on one of the trains that stopped in Florennes told Michael that trains take carloads of Belgian and French Jews east to camps in Poland and perhaps Ukraine. He said that he has heard reliable rumours that they kill them in the camps by the thousands."

He looked at Marita. "Whether that is true or not, we must protect Elke and Brigitte. Hitler is desperate to finish dealing with the Jews and hide the evidence before the Allies finish him off—he is genuinely insane, but the people around him are in so deep they don't dare oppose him."

Annalisa supported herself with both hands on the back of a chair. Her shoulders shook.

Marita cried, "Why are you fighting for these people? Why can't we leave here?"

Erik tried to keep his voice calm. "We can't leave; there's nowhere to go. The English, Americans, and Russians are determined to keep killing Germans until they get to Hitler or run out of Germans to kill, and I must save as many lives as possible by destroying British bombers. Hitler's insanity has spread to the other side—to stop Hitler, they have become his mirror image, and they have the German people caught in the jaws of a vise between the Russians and the Western Allies. Every day, they turn the screw tighter!"

Erik had talked himself into a corner. He said, "We must all do our job as well as we can. The men who drive the tanks you help build are fighting to keep the Russians from taking revenge on Germany's women and children. The ultimate goal of the bombers I shoot down is to rid the world of a madman, and in the process of doing my job, I am actually protecting the Führer. It's all goddamned absurd! Forget about winning—how do we survive?"

When Erik stopped talking, he felt he could cut the tension. It was time to insert something positive, so he said, "I haven't told you yet, but as soon as I get back to the base, I'm receiving the Oak Leaves to my

Ritterkreuz…" He paused, then went on without giving anyone time to congratulate him.

"A direct representative of the Führer contacted me regarding the ceremony. He is high enough in the Nazi circles to have a certain amount of power, so I asked whether he could help us adopt Elke and Brigitte. He agreed to try, but I wasn't sure what he could or would do. I had to tell him the reason, so there was some risk that he would react badly."

He saw a flicker of fear cross Marita's face and quickly added, "He called back the next day and told me we should go to the Bürgeramt as soon as possible. He said we don't have to worry—they will help us." The look on Marita's face made Erik's heart jump. "I know I took a risk trusting him, but I didn't know what else to do. We have an appointment tomorrow morning at eight o'clock, and I want to try."

"Oh, God, do you think it will work? It's not too late?" Marita stood up, too excited to stay in her chair. She faced her mother, and Annalisa smiled, but her expression still held doubt, and she expressed it, "Did you tell him the children were one-quarter Jewish?"

"Yes, I did, and he confirmed that if we adopt them, the girls will be safe. In fact, he verbally guaranteed it."

Walther came into the kitchen and apologized to the family in a monotonic rehearsed speech, then left for Pimpfe. He returned at six, silently ate black bread and cheese, then went to his room. Erik, worried, followed him, but Walther turned on his bed and faced the wall. He didn't answer when his father tried to talk to him, and when Annalisa and Marita came to the room, he squeezed himself against the wall and said nothing.

Finally, the adults retreated to the living room and tried to play cards, but the mood was abysmal, and Marita went to bed early. Annalisa and Erik stayed up to work on his presentation to the schoolchildren.

Annalisa read the speech prepared by Erik's advisor and immediately dismissed that possibility. She suggested a completely different approach—one that would keep him out of jail yet satisfy Erik's desire to teach the children the truth about what he and other night fighter pilots faced and why.

◇◇◇◇◇◇◇◇◇◇◇◇◇◇◇◇◇◇◇◇◇◇◇◇◇◇◇◇◇◇◇◇◇◇◇◇◇◇◇

Marita was asleep when Erik went to bed, and he tossed and turned until the wail of the air raid siren at four o'clock. The household dressed quickly, met in the living room, and walked along the dark streets to the closest shelter, the General Wever Turm, named after General Walther Wever, head of the Luftwaffe until he died in an airplane crash in 1936. Walther, who liked to think he had been named after the famous general, ran ahead of the family.

While they sat comfortably on blankets spread over benches, Walther wandered around the massive room, avoiding the family as obviously as he could. Several bombs exploded across the river, but none was close, and the all-clear siren sounded after an hour in the shelter.

British mosquitos often made nuisance raids at night, irritating and discouraging the city's inhabitants and upsetting infrastructure. Erik's familiarity with those effective and elusive fighter-bombers caused him to wonder why the Allies used anything else. As he sat and listened to their bombs fall, he silently wished for a squadron of those 'wooden wonders.'

It was daylight and time for breakfast when they arrived home, but Walther tried to avoid coming to the table. Erik insisted, and the boy sat down, ate his usual boiled egg and buns without speaking, and went to his room to wait until it was time to go to school. School started at eight, but Walther left the house early. Marita coaxed a hug from him at the door, but he avoided his mother's kiss.

Annalisa said, "Never mind, he'll come around once he gets to school."

Erik said, "I'm not so sure…perhaps that's where all this is coming from." He and Marita were due to visit the Bürgeramt, so he went to the bedroom to dress for what he feared would be a battle against Nazi bureaucracy.

He came out of the bedroom dressed impeccably in his formal Luftwaffe uniform. Bars sewn over his left breast represented his decorations and rank; most prominent was the Knight's Cross on the Iron Cross, received when he shot down his tenth bomber. Typically, the medal resided in a drawer at the base, but Erik had brought it with him for his stage debut in front of school children. He decided it wouldn't hurt to wear it in front of the German bureaucracy at the Bürgeramt.

Marita put on her black leather coat, carried matching leather gloves and wore black leather shoes with moderate heels. Her blond hair spilled out from under her hat, a peaked version with a long yellow feather that barely cleared the door frame.

Annalisa opened the door for them and said with an encouraging smile, "I would hate to get in your way!" Erik touched the brim of his hat and saluted smartly.

They walked quickly without speaking, and Marita could not bridle her excitement as she smiled at her imposing husband. He never dressed in his full uniform at home, and she had forgotten how imposing he could be when all the paraphernalia was added to his dress uniform. She turned her head and smiled at him several times before they reached the building that housed Heilbronn's Nazi officialdom.

The Bürgeramt was on the second floor; they climbed the wide oak stairway and marched in as if they owned the building. Erik discreetly waited until Marita picked her seat and sat beside her. He held his officer's cap in both hands and sat as stiffly as he could manage. The man sitting beside him looked down, folded his hands on his knees, and hunched his shoulders.

Marita cut an imposing figure with her leather coat and stylish feathered hat perched cockily on her head à la Marlene Dietrich. German women either didn't know or refused to acknowledge that Marlene had switched sides. Perhaps they didn't care. Two women who sat behind a long counter dealing with distraught clients stared at Marita when she breezed into the room, freezing their mouths in mid-sentence.

A moment later, the door to an adjoining office opened, and a large woman with a sterile smile came over to greet them. Erik immediately stood up to face her, clicked his heels, and extended his hand, bending with a perfectly straight back from his waist to his head. She shook it and introduced herself as Frau Director Hoffmann.

Erik turned to Marita. "Frau Director Hoffmann, may I introduce my wife, Marita Stephanie?" The Director nodded and shook Marita's hand with a stiffness that women reserve for their competition.

Marita said sweetly, "Thank you for your prompt attention."

Frau Director Hoffmann nodded slightly and swept her arm, indicating to Marita that she should precede her through the open office door. Erik insisted Frau Hoffmann enter ahead of him, then closed the door. Marita and Erik sat on two hard wooden chairs on the client's side of a plain wooden desk, everything clearly designed to keep the rabble in their place.

Frau Hoffmann, who had lost the meaningless smile, leaned forward in her leather office chair and said to Erik, "Anticipating your visit, I have already prepared the necessary papers for you and your wife to sign. My office has verified the death of the children's parents. Their father died fighting for the Führer, and their mother died of typhus while working for the Reichswehr. You must closely examine the sections where I filled in details. Please press hard—there are three copies."

Erik examined the papers and noted that Frau Hoffmann had prepared the forms precisely as they should be, with the client information already filled in.

As he read, Erik wondered what was going on...this was not how German bureaucracy worked! In a typical official administration, Frau Director Hoffmann would grill them, then make an appointment to meet again after verifying the information they had given her. A week later, she would question them again, ask for papers she hadn't mentioned in their first meeting, and, after at least three sessions and frustration that bordered on insanity, she would formally decide whether they had succeeded or, more likely, not.

Erik corrected a minor spelling error in his mother's maiden name and signed the forms. Marita slid her signed copies across the desk with his. Frau Director Hoffmann took a rubber stamp from a small metal case, opened an ink pad, and, with a flourish, slammed the rubber stamp on the ink pad. Her hand was a blur as it flew from pad to paper and back. When every sheet was correctly stamped, Frau Hoffmann slid a copy of each page to Erik and Marita.

"Congratulations!" She smiled warmly and spoke pleasantly and freely, starkly contrasting to any bureaucrat Erik had ever met. "You are now officially Elke and Brigitte's mother and father. I wish things were this easy for everyone, but these are distressing times." Her face articulated what appeared to be a genuine concern, and the smile remained.

The Frau Director escorted them to the door. "You have a friend in a very high place," She continued to smile pleasantly, "and that made my job easier. In the present circumstances, I don't have many good days." Her smile gradually disappeared.

Erik had his answer and decided to throw her a bone. "I thank you for your attention to this matter, and I will be sure to inform the person concerned of your cooperation." He wasn't sure who to inform but planned to find out.

Walking home, Erik took Marita's arm. They were as happy as they had been for a long time.

Marita asked, "Erik, did you notice that the children's religious affiliation was not on the forms? Monica's religion was Evangelisch, and her race designation was aryan, the same as her husband."

"I did, and I don't think my contact could or would have done that. The children are now Protestants like us—and just as aryan." Erik paused, then said, "Someone else, probably here in Heilbronn, has gotten involved, and I don't think we should say anything until we are certain who it is."

They approached the house, and Erik's heart sank when he saw a grey Gestapo sedan parked at the curb. He looked at Marita—her eyes didn't leave the car.

Erik said, "I'll see what's going on…stay behind me!" He felt for his luger's holster…it was there.

Erik took the four steps up the stairs to the front door in two bounds, putting distance between himself and Marita, and found the door unlocked. He checked that Marita was staying back, entered the house with the flap on his leather holster unfastened and stopped in the foyer to listen. Hearing worry in Annalisa's voice coming from the living room, Erik pulled his P08 Luger out of its holster and racked a shell into the barrel. He flicked the safety lever up to the gesichert position, put the pistol back in its nest and rested his hand lightly on the top of the butt. He entered the living room, prepared for a confrontation.

A young Gestapo officer sat on the sofa opposite Annalisa. He stood up and saluted Erik, a perfectly straight arm Hitler salute with fingers as tightly together as he could press them. Erik outranked the young man by a wide margin and did not return the salute, forcing him to hold the position. Erik used the seconds to assess the situation.

The Gestapo was a civilian police organization under Himmler's jurisdiction and usually avoided business with Hermann Göring's Luftwaffe. The Gestapo Police didn't wear uniforms in Germany as a rule and rarely saluted, let alone using the Heil Hitler straight arm. The young man was obviously trying to impress Erik—a good sign.

Erik said tersely, "At ease, young man. State your name, and tell me your business here!" Erik's demeanour left no doubt he wanted the Gestapo out of his house.

The awkward young man lowered his arm and stood stiffly at attention, trying not to look ridiculous in his dark suit and tie. "I am Sturmmann Schmidt, and Kriminaldirektor Richter requests that you accompany me to his office at your discretion, sir. I am to wait at your convenience." He saluted conventionally, and again, Erik ignored it.

Erik had been an officer long enough to know how to impress his authority on others. He asked abruptly, "What is the nature of his business with me?"

"Herr Oberleutnant, my instructions are only to request that you meet with him. I...I don't know the reason." Sturmmann Schmidt stammered; he was beginning to sweat.

Erik let him worry for half a minute, looked out the window, then turned to him and said, "My wife will accompany me...I am going to assume that Major Richter will have no objection." Erik suspected this informal meeting had something to do with his speech, so he had hit the ball into the young man's court, using the Wehrmacht equivalent of his boss's Gestapo rank.

"I...I...don't know, sir." He stammered again, then quickly thought of an alternative. "If you want, I could telephone him, sir." He didn't salute this time, and more beads of sweat became visible on the young man's smooth face. Erik was sure the boy hadn't yet needed to use a razor.

"No, that won't be necessary... " Erik dismissed the suggestion with a wave... "She will come with us, and I will take responsibility." The relief on the young Sturmmann's face was pitiful to the point of comical. Erik used a warm smile to dismantle the rest of the young man's fear. As he waved the boy toward the door, he said, "As you can see, we are already appropriately dressed—shall we go now?" Sturmmann Schmidt looked at Erik's unbuttoned holster; Erik broadened his smile, checked again that the safety was on, and fastened it.

When Marita reached the car, she stood beside the door, waiting for the Gestapo messenger to open it, but he had already rounded the front bumper to the other side. Realizing his mistake, he dropped his head, braced himself on the fender and skidded as he reversed direction.

The embarrassed boy opened the door quickly, and Marita slid grace-fully into the leather seat. Sturmmann Schmidt remembered to check that her feet were inside before he gently closed the door...a little too gently... only the first latch clicked. He opened it again and closed it a little firmer, but unfortunately, it still didn't latch. Erik watched the embarrassed young Gestapo officer over the car's roof. The boy looked at him; Erik nodded and smiled, and the young man opened the door, then swung it shut with a no-doubter. He looked at Erik; Erik grinned; the young man relaxed and touched the brim of his hat. Erik slid into the rear seat and firmly closed his door.

The Gestapo errand boy quickly climbed into the driver's seat and smoothly drove away—surpringly so, considering Erik was quite sure he was too young to qualify for a civilian driver's license. He pictured Major Richter trying to determine which of his officers would be least likely to upset a war hero and decided Richter had chosen well.

Marita shivered as the young Gestapo officer led them up the stone steps to the entrance to Gestapo headquarters, and Erik squeezed her cold fingers, flashing a grin that said, "Don't worry, I'll take care of this."

They followed the boy to a door at the end of a long hallway with Kriminaldirektor Richter painted in bold Gothic letters on the glass. The building's entire width was devoted to his suite of offices, and the young Sturmmann escorted Erik and Marita directly through the double doors that separated Richter from the lower ranks who served him.

After checking with a seated officer, the young man led them through the waiting room directly into Richter's office, then stepped aside as they entered. Marita walked ahead, and Erik followed, his relaxed right hand close to the butt of his nine-millimetre Luger pistol.

"Are you expecting trouble?" asked a smiling, balding man as he stood up and glanced briefly at Erik's hand. The Kriminaldirektor wore a well-cut dark-grey suit and tie.

"This is a Gestapo office, and I know what you do here. I have no reason to trust you." Erik left his hand where it was—he hated every-thing this man stood for.

Richter shook his head. "I assure you that this is a friendly meeting; you will not need to defend yourself." His tone was gentle, and his smile genuine. Erik took his hand away from the gun.

The Kriminaldirektor extended his hand as he walked around the desk. "I am Kriminaldirektor Helmut Richter, and I consider it a privilege to greet a hero of the Third Reich." He shook Erik's hand vigorously, with a firm grip, then turned to Marita and shook her hand gently, elegantly.

"And, of course, I am equally honoured to meet your beautiful wife; I wasn't expecting her, but it is indeed a pleasure." Marita gave him a cold smile and sat in the upholstered leather chair he indicated. The major pulled up a matching chair for Erik before returning to his desk. Erik waited for the major to sit before he seated himself.

"I trust that everything at the Bürgeramt was satisfactory?"

Erik leaned forward. "Your spies are very efficient." Richter nodded and waited for the answer to his question. Erik continued, "Before we talk about anything, I want you to tell me why you frightened my wife and my neighbours by sending a Gestapo car to my house when a telephone call would have been enough?"

"I sent Sturmmann Schmidt, believing he would not intimidate anyone, but I understand your concern. You will understand why I didn't use the telephone when you hear my reason for summoning you here." He lit a cigarette and offered one to his guests. Marita shook her head, and Erik said, "No, thank you...I don't smoke when I'm at home."

Major Richter took a long draw, made a sad face and crushed the cigarette in a crystal ashtray. "I wish I could stop smoking that easily."

Erik looked at Marita. "I didn't say it was easy." Everyone laughed a little, easing the tension, and Erik tapped his finger on the arm of the chair. "I am curious why you asked us to come. I made an assumption that I am beginning to doubt."

Major Richter looked from Erik to Marita. Erik stopped his nervous tapping, and Richter went on.

"Do you know our system of gathering information using the Hitler Jugend organization?"

Erik and Marita nodded, puzzled, and Erik said, "We've heard such rumours but hoped that such abuse of our children wasn't true."

Richter didn't smile. "I am afraid it is true, and the system works as you imagine it would. Information comes to my office from all levels of the Hitler youth, including the Bund Deutscher Mädel, the girl's equivalent of the Jugend.

Throughout the chain, junior officers examine the information these young boys and girls report to their superiors, rejecting what they believe to be unnoteworthy or gross exaggerations. They pass the filtered information to our office, where my people process it, separating the important and realistic items for further examination."

Richter looked from Marita to Erik. "As you no doubt know, it is our job to ferret out traitors to the Reich." He waited for a few seconds. "Do you understand what I'm trying to tell you?"

Erik suddenly feared where this was going. "Perhaps, but I need you to tell me exactly why this concerns us. I assure you that we have no disloyal intentions. We are not traitors to Germany!"

Richter responded patiently, "I understand, but this concerns your son. He shared information with his monitors, and because it concerned you and your wife, it reached me rather quickly. Of course, I have taken no action—the accusations are obviously a product of the boy's imagination, and I wanted to speak with you before this went any further." Richter let his words sink in. Erik looked at Marita; she tried to hide her shock, but her face betrayed her. Richter asked, "Do you want your son here? Should I send Sturmmann Schmidt to his school?"

Marita quickly said, "Yes, please."

Erik thought momentarily of a Gestapo officer marching into the school to get Walther and decided to deal with that later. He nodded; the Direktor lifted the phone and gave the order. His last words were, "Take my personal car."

"We have a few minutes before he brings your son, and he will be discreet. He will take my private automobile for this purpose." He seemed sympathetic. "I understand what you and your wife want to do, and I will help you as much as possible. There will be no repercussions for you or your son—the information I have will not leave this office—indeed, I have already destroyed it, and there is no need to bring it up."

He sat back in his chair and folded his hands in front of his chest. "Since we have a few minutes, I would like to hear how you find and destroy the British bombers. I've been stuck in this wretched office since the war began, listening to our fine German citizens denounce one another, and your adventures would be a breath of fresh air." He leaned ahead, put his folded hands on his desk, and looked earnestly at Erik. I have never seen action, and flying has always fascinated me. Unfortunately, there was no war and no possibility of learning to fly when I joined the Polizei."

Erik doubted that Richter would make a pilot; he couldn't picture him accepting the risks associated with it. While Erik assessed his adversary, Richter continued, "I would appreciate your honest impression of how the war is going—Goebbels' Ministry of Propaganda is not a reliable source of information. There are rumours, of course, and there is the official position, and neither seems to fit the events our state news service is reporting. According to their reports, we are defeating the Russians as we retreat—we are told that we are defeating the Allies in the air while their bombers destroy our cities. None of that makes sense, and these walls are secure—I give you my word that anything you say will stay in this room."

Erik's face betrayed his astonishment. He did not trust Richter's offer of immunity and decided to tread carefully. Something about this made Erik uncomfortable, but somehow, he trusted this man.

"I will take you step by step through my last mission—it might help you resolve the discrepancies. Please understand that everything I tell you is my experience, not my opinion." Erik sat back, comfortable in the soft chair. Richter nodded, and Erik began.

"We took off behind a focke wulf 190 into a clear night with a bright moon and thousands of stars." He leaned toward Richter. "A British mosquito night fighter shot down the focke wulf before the wheels on my messerschmitt were up!" Erik leaned back again, noting the surprise on the Kriminaldirektor's face. "We turned and ran while the mosquito was busy, but there is always a second British fighter, and mosquitos are much faster and more agile than our messerschmitt Bf 110. The second fighter caught us in seconds, but I outmaneuvered him, and he missed us on his first pass.

Richter opened his hands in a gesture of impatience. "Are British fighters allowed to fly unmolested through our airspace? How is this possible?"

Erik observed that Major Richter was skeptical of information contradicting what he had been told, even though he wanted to hear more.

Erik went on, "Herr Kriminaldirektor, you must understand that modern British and American fighters are superior to ours, and they can avoid our defences with their speed and higher altitude capabilities. The mosquito can fly a hundred kilometres per hour faster than my aircraft and three thousand metres higher—it can climb almost twice as fast and turn inside my aircraft. That is how it is, and I don't see how we can change it unless the British sell us a few squadrons of their mosquitos!" Erik waited for the Kriminaldirektor to respond. The head of the Gestapo leaned back in his chair, incredulous.

"Please use the Wehrmacht equivalent of my rank. I prefer the less cumbersome 'Major' Richter."

Erik nodded, then went on. "In the end, we eluded the mosquito with a maneuver he didn't expect, and he left us to search for a less crafty victim. We then climbed on a course we anticipated would intercept the bomber stream. Deelen, our ground control, instructs us to fly to a prescribed beacon, and we use radar to find the bombers from there."

"How can you see the bombers in the dark?" asked Richter, "Does their exhaust glow?" Major Richter's expression indicated he thought he had logically hit on the method.

Erik shook his head, "No, their exhausts have spark arrestors on their exhausts as we have on ours. The engine's exhausts are only visible from directly behind them, and then they are very dim and not visible from more than a few metres."

Erik leaned back. "To find the bombers, we use sophisticated radar made by Siemens. The antenna is eight small tubes on our fighters' nose, and we can identify a bomber a hundred kilometres in front of us. Unfortunately, I am convinced that when we turn our radar on, the British bombers have a system that locates it. Their mosquito night fighters then use that information to shoot us down. Fortunately, the British don't appreciate the mosquitoes' value and haven't built enough of them to catch all of us. We've learned how to avoid them in many circumstances, but sometimes we make a mistake, which usually gets us killed."

Erik had never told Marita anything about his job. When he saw her wringing her hands, he ignored the Kriminaldirektor and spoke directly to her. "The key to survival is experience, and sadly, many crews are killed before they accumulate enough knowledge to keep them alive. Despite that experience, I made a mistake, but I won't make that mistake again!" Erik turned back to Major Richter and settled back in his chair, hoping he could tell the story without Major Richter's interruptions.

"The night was clear, and unusually cold for late March. The moon was only half, but it was very bright due to the lack of moisture in the air. I decided to wait between two beacons instead of at the one recommended by Deelen, and the sight I saw when the bombers approached was the most disturbing I have seen in my life. I was directly in the path of hundreds of bombers approaching me from the west. From the front of the armada, I could see white vapour trails shining in the moonlight, and I knew we would slaughter them. And yet they came, even though they had to know that their losses would be terrible! I suspected a trap... Perhaps squadrons of mosquitos waited above the bombers!"

The major stepped in when Erik paused. "I don't understand—how could you disobey orders to wait at a specific beacon? And I don't understand what a vapour trail is."

Erik couldn't believe that Richter had missed his point, but he decided to answer the irrelevant questions first. "The more experience we have, the more freedom we take until, as I do, we only use ground control to find the main bomber stream. In any case, the British regularly block Deelen ground control's radio frequencies for hours, often sending false instructions using anti-Nazi German people broadcasting from powerful British radio sites." Erik shifted in his chair. "It is amazing how difficult it can be to find five hundred bombers in the dark, especially if they're in clouds." He flicked a piece of lint from his sleeve and remembered the second question.

"The vapour trail is a narrow cloud of frozen moisture particles. A combustion engine's exhaust is mainly condensed moisture and carbon dioxide. If the temperature is low enough and the humidity high enough, the combination creates ice particles that form a long, narrow cloud behind the plane. The tiny ice crystals reflect the faintest light, such as moonlight or even starlight. The bombers' white trails extended back toward England as far as I could see, each pointing to a target."

Erik pointed at the major. "I concluded that if I could see their tails, they could see mine." Erik hesitated and looked into Richter's eyes, but Richter didn't react. "I had to adjust my attack, or I would be a sitting duck for the mosquitoes." Major Richter was now fully immersed in the story and quietly waited while Erik shifted in his chair.

"I flew across the bomber formation and turned at the outside edge, slipping into the stream three hundred metres behind and a hundred metres below a lancaster bomber. That put me in the vapour trail of a bomber ahead of and below my target." Erik stood up and began pacing.

"A modern Luftwaffe night fighter has a pair of twenty or thirty-millimetre cannons fastened to the bulkhead behind the navigator, pointed upward and slightly ahead. The navigator changes magazines and fires the cannons at my order. I approach the bomber from behind and below, then fire the guns from about seventy-five metres under its wing. The British bombers are blind there, and we are outside their field of fire. The fuel tanks in the wings are our targets."

"Why not target the fuselage where the men are? Wouldn't that be more effective?"

Erik smiled. "Effective, yes, but no, not a good idea because that's where the bombs are. A lancaster or a halifax bomber carries five-to-seven thousand kilograms of high-explosive bombs and incendiaries. If a twenty-millimetre cannon shell detonates one bomb, the entire load explodes, killing the night fighter with the bomber. We aim at the fuel tanks, guaranteeing a kill, and it all happens so fast that very few British airmen escape the fire."

Marita was horrified. "You mean, those poor men burn to death?"

"Yes, they do," Erik turned to Marita and spoke without sympathy, "It takes at least two minutes for an aircraft to fall to the ground from six kilometres above it, and two minutes in a gasoline fire is a very long time."

Marita became pale. Major Richter waited, and Erik thought he saw a twinge of sympathy for the airmen but decided he was mistaken. He stood and went to Marita's chair.

"Those poor men you feel sorry for cheered when they saw my fighter fall in flames! If they reach their target, they drop bombs designed to burn a city and the women and children who live there! War is not a game we play with a trophy for the winner. When we win, the only trophy we get is our lives for another day." He looked into his wife's eyes, and Marita's look held nothing but pity for him. He added, "It is the same for them."

Erik returned his attention to Major Richter, then began pacing again. "The plane we were stalking blew up before we could fire our guns—the explosion blew the wing off, and it narrowly missed us. Another fighter had hit the lancaster's fuel tanks from the opposite side before we could get into position, and we hadn't seen it." Richter started to open his mouth but stopped, and Erik went on.

"We moved over to a halifax bomber in another group, and this time, we could get under it and fire. It went down quickly, with two crew getting out, but they were burning and didn't deploy their parachutes."

Marita was pale as she stared at Erik, distress in her blue eyes. Erik returned her stare, then briefly looked down.

"After that, Michael and I were busy avoiding the wreckage, the gunners in neighbouring bombers, and a collision. The sky was full of aircraft, headed for what we now know was Nürnberg."

Erik put his hand on Marita's shoulder. "There are seven men in a British lancaster. From a humanity point of view, it is better that they burn in their bombers than leave defenceless women and children to burn in their houses. Every one of those bombers kills dozens if not hundreds of people."

Marita shook her head slowly, and Erik felt he had gone too far. He wished he could take it back, but time was irreversible, so he turned to Major Richter.

"I picked out another halifax, and when Michael fired, the entire wing separated from the fuselage and fluttered down. Again, I saw two shapes fall from the plane, and again, no parachutes." He looked at Marita. "They may have opened them when they were clear of the bombers; I didn't wait to see."

Major Richter rolled a pencil between his palms as he looked up at Erik. "That was the second clean kill in one mission. So now you have twenty-three?" He stood the pencil on its blunt end and tapped it on the desk.

Erik tried to read Richter but couldn't. "Yes, that was number twenty-three. We still had ammunition, so we climbed to get rid of the vapour trail and out of the traffic. Bombers filled the air, and over two hundred of our fighters flew among them—a thousand aircraft flying in the same airspace at night, without lights. The danger of a mid-air collision was at least as great as the danger of being shot down. I wanted to get out of the stream and assess the situation. There were mosquitos—not more than a squadron, but enough that with their radar and speed, they were my biggest worry."

Erik put his hands on the back of Marita's chair and looked over her head at Richter.

"Another factor in my decision was that a messerschmitt 110 is only a little faster than the British bombers, and if my timing were incorrect,

I could spend the entire mission chasing them. I planned to use the extra altitude to build a more significant speed advantage for my next attack. I would pick a bomber, hit it fast and get out of there before the mosquitos found me.

"When I reached sixty-five-hundred metres, a lancaster appeared before me, flying slower because he was climbing with a heavy load...I had to throttle back to keep from catching him too soon. I descended until I was directly behind and about seventy metres below him. There was no chance that the rear gunner could see my exhaust from that position, and the vapour trail was gone at that altitude. I eased up on him, observing his turret—it didn't move. The four machine gun barrels pointed slightly down and to my right—and they didn't move until he fired at me!" Erik leaned ahead with his elbows on his knees.

"Suddenly he fired—bullets bounced off the windscreen, then struck the left engine and propeller. I banked right to escape him and met a mosquito coming straight at me, firing everything he had! Cannon shells hit the fuselage, shaking the plane and tearing everything behind me to pieces, including Michael." Erik paused, remembering his friend, and Richter waited.

"I lost everything in the tail that controlled the aircraft and could only use the ailerons to twist away. Thank God the mosquito had so much speed that he blew past before he killed me. I cut the starboard throttle and applied full aileron, inverting the plane. I didn't have a canopy over me—the mosquito had blasted it away—I unfastened my belt and literally fell out of the burning wreckage!

"The battle passed me on my ride to the earth, and the quiet and the night were strangely beautiful." Erik turned to his wife. "As I hung under the parachute, I thought of you and prayed those bombers were not coming to Heilbronn."

Major Richter said confidently, "I doubt that many bombers would have gotten through with hundreds of fighters shooting them down!"

Erik didn't try to keep the sarcasm out of his voice. "Major Richter, there were more than five hundred bombers, perhaps six hundred, maybe more. I can confidently say that we shot down fewer than a hundred before they reached their target." Erik paused. "If five hundred made it with four tons of bombs in each, two thousand tonnes of bombs dropped on a German city...Nürnberg. But I would bet a year's pay it was more!" Major Richter's face revealed his surprise. It was evident to Erik that the man had never stopped to figure such things out. He put it in terms Richter could understand, "The Wehrmacht's heaviest Lastwagen carries 20 tonnes, so a hundred loads at least, probably more. Another way to look at it is this: two thousand tonnes of British bombs equal eighty thousand of our most powerful artillery shells!"

Richter gasped perceptively. "My God! Are there so many bombers? How often do they come?"

Erik could see that lines were beginning to form and join in Major Richter's brain—a picture of destruction was developing in his mind.

Erik said, as though lecturing a student, "The British drop bombs somewhere almost every night, and the Americans come during the day, two or three times a week, depending on the weather. Again, using artillery shell analogy, the equivalent of about three-hundred thousand 88 mm artillery rounds kill ten thousand civilians weekly and badly injure over fifty thousand. Against this, I have shot down twenty-three bombers since 1940, and I have a medal to prove it!"

Major Richter whispered, "I had no idea; the Propaganda Ministerium does not inform us of this!"

Erik spoke softly, "If I were you, I wouldn't do anything that someone looking at it later could see as a crime. I would advise you to avoid damaging your reputation among the good people of Heilbronn. I am aware of the punishment for saying that we will lose the war, but you must know that if we lose the war, there will be repercussions for criminal acts against innocent people. And remember that the definition of who is a criminal and who are the innocent people will be decided by the army occupying our country."

Erik's smile had nothing to do with pleasure. "Of course, as you are, I am convinced that we will win the war and that our retreating soldiers will defeat the Russians." The expression on the major's face told Erik the man understood what Erik was saying.

"I can confirm that the reports of our cities being ravaged, some of them burned to the ground, are true, and not, as Goebbels says, fake reports from foreign media trying to undermine Hitler and start an uprising against him. I have felt the heat of the fires from six thousand metres above them!"

The look on Richter's face told Erik that Major Richter understood what he was saying and was considering whether he should let him get away with it. Richter stirred, but before he could say or do anything, Erik said, "I will do my job for my country, and I will shoot down as many bombers as I can so that fewer bombs fall on German civilians. That is all I can do, and that does not make me a criminal." Erik then spoke as carefully as he could. "I fight to protect my family and yours, and the threat of death from any source will not change that. Can you say the same?"

Richter nodded. "Yes, I understand you, and my intentions are identical to yours. Your family will have the full protection of this office for as long as I am in this position." He stood and reached across the walnut desk to hold his hand out to Erik. Erik took it, and the Kriminaldirektor held on until he finished talking. "I will guarantee to protect your family with my life if necessary."

Erik got his hand back and stood facing Richter across the desk, his mind racing. He was looking at a man who wanted out, but there was something more. Erik surmised that Richter had been apprehensive before he and Marita had come into his office—Kriminaldirektor Richter knew Germany was doomed and was looking for an ally to help him survive when Armageddon arrived.

Erik said, "Major Richter, are you defending the people of Heilbronn in a way that they know you are their protector?"

The door opened, and Sturmmann Schmidt guided Walther, a terrified little boy, into the room. Marita stood up, looked at Erik, and he shook his head.

Richter walked around his desk, intercepted Walther and steered him toward his parents. "Young man, I've been speaking with your father, and he's been telling me about his last heroic mission. You should be proud of him." Major Richter put the boy between his father and mother. Walther went where the Gestapo officer pointed him but remained silent. He looked at his father, his mother, then at his feet.

Major Richter waited until the boy lifted his head, then said, "I am the Kriminaldirektor for this region, and do you know what could have happened because of your wild tales of your parent's betrayal of their country?" Walther shook his head, lowered it and looked at his feet again. The major glanced at Erik, turned back to the top of Walther's head and went on.

"If I had believed your tale of their treachery against the Führer, I would have taken your parents to prison and possibly shot them for treason. According to your story, I could have had your grandmother and the minister of your church shot as well!" He lifted Walther's chin so he could look into his eyes. "Do you understand? Do you want me to shoot your parents and your Oma?"

Walther said, "Nein, bitte nicht!" He trembled, fought back sobs, and finally gave up, shaking his head and crying on rubbery legs. Richter let his chin go. Walther started to fall, but before he could, Marita knelt and took her son in her arms, holding him as he cried into her shoulder. He couldn't lift his arms to hug her.

Major Richter rounded the desk and looked sympathetically at Erik and Marita. Suddenly, he turned toward the door as though he had just thought of something urgent he must do.

"I believe we have no more to discuss." He shook Erik's hand. "I want to thank you for coming and clarifying this matter. I will see that your family isn't bothered again, and I will speak with the Hitler Jugend unit concerning your son—there will be no problems for you or your friends." Richter held Walther's hand as he said, "And you, Walther, must learn to keep your mouth shut! That medal you want is worth nothing when you know what you must do to get it!"

Erik shook the major's hand as he said, "Major Richter, we thank you for your understanding, and perhaps we will meet again under better circumstances." Erik lifted his son in his arms and carried him out of the room, glad to get away so he could think about what had happened. He was apprehensive as he walked quickly down the hall to the entrance, where he put Walther on his feet. Marita took her son's hand, and they walked down the steps and along the sidewalk toward home. Neither she nor Erik wanted the Gestapo car to drive them, and Major Richter hadn't offered it. Walther walked between his mother and father without saying a word. They walked fast, and sometimes, he had to run to keep up.

"I'm sorry," said Walther with a voice so tiny Erik almost missed it.

Erik slowed down and spoke with a tenderness that warmed Marita's heart. "We don't need to talk about this again, Walther. I want you to understand that this was not your fault. You have done nothing wrong, and I love you more than my own life." He pointed at Gestapo headquarters. "I want you to see that the evil is not in you but in that building."

Walther pulled his father to a stop.

"You mean you forgive me for telling on you and Mutti?"

Erik smiled and shook his head. "Did you lie to someone?"

Walther shook his head slowly. "No, but I told things I shouldn't have."

"Then no, I don't need to forgive you because you did nothing but tell the truth, although you should know that sometimes it is better to say nothing than to say what you believe to be true." Erik knelt and took one of Walther's shoulders in each of his hands. "There is nothing wrong with what we say and do in our home, but there are people who would hurt us for it. The people who need our forgiveness are those who want you to tell them something they could use to hurt others. Those people are wrong, and someday they will change, or they will be gone!"

"But don't you hurt people with your fighter plane?" Walther's innocent face looked up at his father. Erik remained silent for a moment. Marita rescued him.

"Some people want to kill us with bombs, and it's your father's job to stop them."

Walther pressed on. "But, don't we kill people with our bombs, too? Our teacher said…"

Erik looked into Walther's eyes. "Yes, son, it's all wrong, but I don't know how to stop it. Maybe, when you grow up, you can figure it out."

Erik straightened up, Walther walked ahead, beckoned to his parents, yelled, "I'll race you home," and started running. Erik ran after him, and Marita tried, but her 'moderate' heels prevented her from keeping up, so she stopped and laughed at them.

Annalisa was pacing the floor when they arrived. She was already dressed for work in her coat and leather work boots. She waved as she passed them, shouting, "The girls are in the garden. I want to hear all about it when I get back!" She ran down the street to catch the shift bus, passing Marita with a wave.

Erik leaned over, gasping for air, his hands braced on his knees. He looked sideways at his son. "Okay, Walther, find whatever you need for school and see how fast you can get there…I'll see you at the Halle at noon."

Walther disappeared in the house, reappeared a moment later, and ran out the door, slowing to say, "Goodbye, Vati," from the stone steps. As he met his mother, Marita pushed her hand through his hair, and Walther smiled. Erik and Marita watched him run down the street, across the next intersection and out of sight.

Marita took Erik's hand. "What's going to happen to us? How will this end?" The tears in her eyes reflected the light. "When will it end?"

Erik suddenly felt depressed, and his voice gave him away. "I don't have any answers, but I know this will end soon because there's not much left of our country to destroy, and there are no men to replace those who die."

CHAPTER ELEVEN

3 April 1944

Jedes Warum hat seinen Darum.
(Every wherefore has its therefore.)

Erik buttoned his freshly ironed Luftwaffe fliegerbluse over his blue-grey shirt and pants, all without a wrinkle or spot. He checked twice that the epaulets on his shoulders and the bars on his left breast were perfectly square and impeccably arranged and that the wings on his chest were level, positioned precisely according to Luftwaffe regulations. Flawlessly symmetrical, his appearance was precisely as the Wehrmacht manual dictated it should be.

Erik's immaculate uniform contradicted the turmoil in his head. He had never before spoken in public, and Annalisa had rejected the speech the publicity officer had outlined. The words exalted Erik's victories and the glorious Führer, but he and Annalisa had made other, distinctly different plans.

Heilbronn had four elementary schools spread strategically throughout the city so all children could walk to a school. On special occasions, the students from these schools gathered at the Harmonie Halle, a venue for concerts and special political events.

A Wehrmacht mercedes drove Erik to the front of the Halle and stopped at the bottom of a set of wide steps. Erik stepped out without waiting for the driver to open his door.

As he walked up to the impressive oak entrance doors, the Gestapo car that had driven Erik and Marita to police headquarters pulled up. Erik waited for Major Richter to get out and approach him.

Major Richter offered his hand. "I'm pleased to meet you again so soon. I hope you don't mind if I listen to your talk today on the glories of our war." His smile was friendly, but Erik understood the underlying message.

He released the Gestapo officer's hand. "No, I don't mind at all, and I trust you will find it as enlightening as you seemed to find my story this morning."

The Gestapo major hesitated, measuring his words.

"This morning was 'under four eyes,' not for the public. This occasion is different; you must remember that I am the Gestapo Officer responsible for everything that happens in this city." He paused, Erik waited. "Do I make myself clear?"

A switch flipped in Erik's mind—he decided to test a theory he had construed following the morning meeting. Kriminaldirektor Richter had understood the implications of Erik's narrative long before he heard Erik's story, and Erik believed the major would not arrest him unless he crossed a line. The only question for Erik was, "Where was the line? How far could Richter let him go?"

"Have you brought handcuffs, or do you want me to surrender now?" He looked straight into Richter's eyes, "I will not be giving a speech that you would officially approve of beforehand. You can prevent me from corrupting those children by arresting me here, or you can wait until I've convicted myself. Please decide before I have to face them." Erik was committed to Annalisa's plan, but if their theory were wrong, his arrest was inevitable, and, in that case, he would prefer to avoid the terror of public speaking, especially to an audience of children.

Major Richter interrupted Erik's thought, "You are intelligent enough to tell your story without destroying yourself and me. We both have much more at stake than we can afford to lose, and I think you know where officialdom's limits are. I ask you to be realistic and consider the consequences. Any gain you achieve by openly fighting the bureaucratic system will be negligible. You know how to avoid incriminating yourself without compromising the truth as you and I know it to be." He put his hand on Erik's arm. "I am better informed than you think, and I will not have you arrested under any circumstances. I will write a report concerning what happens here today and leave anything beyond that to others. Oberleutnant, I am telling you that your boldness may cost me as much as it costs you!" He took his hand away. "I love my wife as you love yours, and I would like to die with her at a time very far in the future."

Erik said, "I have an additional concern. My wife and I have three children. We have a boy, and we adopted two girls this morning. We love all of them, and we worry what will happen to them." He looked into Major Richter's eyes. "Do you have any children, Major Richter?"

"I regret to say that my wife and I cannot have children...the doctors say it has something to do with me, but I congratulate you on the additions to your family. I am sure you have made the children's mother happy."

Erik answered bitterly, "She died in Ravensberg last winter. She was a Zwangsarbiterin."

"You refer to Monica Lindenbaum... Yes, I know she died of typhoid—it's a pity. The Gestapo had nothing to do with her arrest. I knew Monica was a fine Christian woman and didn't belong there, but the SS and SA don't answer to me!" He paused, then said, "I was referring to Marita as the children's mother."

Major Richter had confirmed Erik's theory when he referred to Monica as Christian. Richter was not who he seemed to be. But what did he want from Erik?

An SS officer held the massive door open, waving his hand to urge the two officers to hurry. Major Richter, who outranked him, put up his hand; the officer nodded and closed the door. Richter pulled Erik away from the SS officer and waited for Erik to speak.

Erik spoke quietly. "I don't know exactly how this will go, but I will do it without crossing your line—you have my word."

Major Richter returned a warm smile. "I am going to trust you, Oberleutnant, and I look forward to working with you in the future...I am not as far from your ideals as you think." Erik's surprise at his response held him mute and momentarily still. When Major Richter turned to the entrance, Erik followed him.

The SS officer opened the door, and the two men entered. The officer clicked his heels, stretched a stiff arm in a perfect sixty-degree salute and issued a loud "Heil Hitler." Erik and Major Richter grunted, touched their caps in acknowledgment and stepped past him.

<hr>

The Heilbronn Schuldirector introduced Oberleutnant Stephanie, reciting the medals and actions that qualified Erik as a "Hero of the Third Reich." He followed the introduction with a neat "Heil Hitler" salute, impressing Erik with his rehearsed but relaxed precision. Erik began his dissent with a smartly executed Luftwaffe side salute, then walked over to the oak lectern.

A large round microphone fastened to the sloped top was connected to an invisible sound system, and Erik suspected it was also likely linked to a modern recording or listening device. A switch on the microphone activated it, and Erik turned it off, confident his strong baritone would carry throughout the small theatre. In any case, Erik did not intend to remain behind the podium.

The SS officer coached the children by clapping, and they vigorously took the hint. Erik gave them a few seconds, then raised his arms, halting the applause.

The Schuldirector left the stage, and four hundred children aged six to twelve years sat perfectly still. As Erik let his eyes wander throughout the auditorium, he appreciated that his presence represented their hopes and aspirations. He was a hero to these children, and most of them would remember every word he said for the rest of their lives, repeating them to their children and grandchildren. He laid the bundle of papers that his commanding officer had given him on the podium, stepped down from the padded step, and crossed to the center of the stage to the sound of intense silence. Erik broke it with a question.

"How many of you think I'm a hero?"

Four hundred little hands shot in the air.

"When I finish talking to you," he said, letting his gaze roam across the auditorium, "some of you might not think I'm a hero, and when I ask the question later, I want you to be truthful."

The confused children slowly lowered their hands.

The children listened to tank commanders, fighter pilots, submarine captains, and infantry officers every month, all presented to these children as heroes. Their teachers had told them of the night fighter pilot's glorious victories and told them exaggerated stories of air battles in the dark. They waited expectantly to hear exciting stories of how he had accomplished such heroic deeds for the Führer.

◇◇◇◇◇◇◇◇◇◇◇◇◇◇◇◇◇◇◇◇◇◇◇◇◇◇◇◇◇◇◇

Erik began, following the script Annalisa had designed. "I will tell you who I am and what I do. I will explain how my airplane works, how I find the enemy, and how I kill him."

He stepped to the edge of the stage and faced the children. "This is how we will proceed. I will tell you about my last mission, and then I will answer all your questions as honestly as I can."

The children looked at one another and whispered, and Erik realized

106

that he had introduced a concept the children had never seen…asking questions of an adult and getting a straight answer. He put his hands out in a signal for quiet and said, "It's simple…just raise your hand if you have a question. If I choose you, you can ask me your question, but only one. I will answer all of you clearly and honestly. As you listen to me answer someone else's question, I want you to think about what you want to ask, and you should say whatever comes into your head. There are no wrong questions—no bad questions. It is only wrong if you don't ask." Erik looked around the room. Is that understood?"

At first, the children reacted tentatively, deciding whether or not to trust this man, but Erik encouraged them again and received a "Jawohl!" from the majority."

He began the rehearsed opening dialogue Annalisa had put together for him. He was tense and unsure…but then he thought: *These are only children…how bad can it be?* And began, scared to death!

"I am not alone in the plane when I hunt for English bombers; I always have another man with me, my navigator. He uses radio signals, a compass, and maps to guide me to the target and back to the base. He also uses radar signals to find the enemy and fires one of the guns. I've only had one navigator all the years I've been flying a night fighter. His name was Michael, and he was my best friend." Erik fought the grief he hadn't yet dealt with as he thought about Michael and the last evening they had spent together before the British bombers interrupted them.

Erik looked at a little girl sitting in the fourth row, and his voice cracked as he said, "Last Thursday night, I made a mistake when I was attacking a bomber, and my friend died. It was the last mission I flew before coming home on leave." He paused as he suddenly felt hot tears on his cheeks. Erik looked at the little faces and saw shock in those close enough to see his tears. They silently waited as he wiped his eyes with his sleeve.

"A gunner in a British bomber and a British mosquito fighter shot our airplane down, and the bullets killed my friend before he could get out of the plane. I was luckier; I escaped from my burning fighter to tell you why and how these things happen, and why I'm going back to fight against the *Englander*."

He waited, head lowered, and the auditorium was as silent as the grave when he began again. Erik paced slowly back and forth as he told the children in simple terms how the airplane operated in the dark, how his navigator found the British bombers with radar and the help of controllers on the ground. He became more relaxed as he explained how a night fighter lined up its target. And then Erik explained how, in the dark, they could find the airfield they had left. Erik told them about the marauding British fighters waiting there for them to return, and he explained how he avoided them.

The talk lasted twenty minutes, and the children were so still that Erik found it challenging to keep his concentration. He paused several times, waiting for his attention to return before he could go on, and every time, the children sat in silence.

When Erik finished, he shifted his gaze from child to child. He said, "At this point, I would like each of you to think of your question for me, and I will answer it if I can. Put up your hand, I will point to you, and you can ask one question—if another child asks your question, then please don't ask it again." The children waited for Erik to signal the beginning.

Erik said, "All right, if you have a question, put up your hand," and at least a hundred hands shot up.

Expecting three or four, he exclaimed, "Wow! All right, I'm going to start at the front." He pointed at the little girl in the fourth row. "You don't need to tell me your name if you don't want to. Just ask the question."

She surprised him. "When you shoot at the bomber, does it blow up?"

Erik knelt on the edge of the stage so he was close to the little girl. "Sometimes, it does. We aim at the fuel tanks so that we're sure it will crash and not reach a city where it would drop its bombs." She started to open her mouth to ask another question, but his smile told her that her turn was over. He straightened, and dozens of hands shot up again. He picked a little boy sitting close to the girl.

"If it's dark, how can you tell if you're shooting down an Englander plane and not one of ours?"

Erik answered immediately, "No German bombers fly over Germany at night, and none of ours have four engines. Our fighters are much smaller than their bombers, and even at night, we can see their shape and the four engines they all have."

The children were getting the hang of it now, and hands shot up as soon as he finished. He chose another little girl, this one in the third row.

"When the other airplane explodes and burns, what happens to the people inside?"

Erik had expected the question. He said, "Sometimes, the men in the airplane jump out and parachute to the ground where our army takes them as prisoners. They must wait until the war ends before they can go home. But sometimes they die if they don't have time to get out of the airplane." He watched the little girl slump down in her seat.

She said in a small voice, but one that carried in the perfect acoustics of the theatre, "But can't you wait until they jump out before you shoot it down? You could just tell them on your radio that you're going to shoot, and they better get out!"

She was directly in front of Erik, and her large eyes and innocent expression forced him to hesitate—he tried to think of an answer that would satisfy her.

He answered softly, hopefully lessening the impact by concentrating only on her—but the sound of his resonant voice carried to every child.

"If I told them we were there, they would kill me, and they can't jump out because they must do their duty and fight me. I can't let them kill me because I must shoot their airplane down before it drops its bombs on our cities."

She opened her mouth to ask another question, but the boy next to her jabbed his elbow in her ribs, and she closed it, giving him a reproachful look. He put his hand up.

"All right, what's your question?" Erik hoped that it had nothing to do with killing people. The little boy stood up and asked his question in a loud voice, his arms stiff at his sides.

"How many bombers must you shoot down before they are all gone?" He looked down at the little girl. She pouted at him and crossed her arms.

Erik straightened and spoke loudly to the whole room. "Our enemies—the British, Americans, Australians, Russians, and many other countries—are building bombers every day, and they are building them faster than we can shoot them down." Erik moved his eyes from child to child. They all understood that something was wrong with what he had said.

The little boy sat down slowly, another question in his head, his sense of logic having a problem with Erik's answer. A dozen hands were in the air when Erik chose another little girl, this time an older girl. She stood up.

"Doesn't the Führer know how to shoot all the bombers down? My Mutti says that he can do anything!"

Erik waited for a few seconds—he and Annalisa hadn't found an answer to that question. He began thoughtfully, hoping for divine intervention. None came.

"The Führer hasn't got enough fighter airplanes and pilots to shoot them all down!"

He knew that the next question would begin to close the truth trap.

The one-question rule went out the window when she asked, "Why doesn't he build some more fighter planes and get some more men to shoot the bombers down?" Erik smiled—he had to answer her question. Annalisa was right—these children would get the truth out of him.

"The German people are working hard to build airplanes and everything else we need. Everyone is working as hard as they can. I will shoot down as many bombers as I can...And that is all we can do right now."

Before Erik could choose another child, the SS officer in charge of the presentation stepped on the podium, turned on the microphone and spoke, his imposing voice booming through the speakers. The intimacy and trust Erik had carefully built evaporated; the children shrank back in their seats.

"Oberleutnant Stephanie has used up all of his available time. It is now Mittagspause, and some of your parents are outside waiting to take you home. I want you to thank the oberleutnant with your applause."

He waved his arm in Erik's general direction and smiled like a Cheshire cat. Erik turned to the children, and the smattering of applause the SS officer had instigated died immediately.

Erik said to his audience, "I see that some hands remain raised. Would you please put them down?"

The hands went down. Erik ignored the uncomfortable SS officer waiting behind the podium.

"If you want me to continue answering your questions, I want you to raise your hand."

The room was suddenly full of raised hands.

"Just to be fair, how many of you want to stop now and go home?"

Fewer than a dozen hands went up. Erik thought he probably

should ask how many of those just wanted to go to the bathroom but decided to keep that to himself.

Erik looked at his watch. "Okay, those of you who want to can go home now. The rest of you can stay and talk to me for a few minutes longer." The SS officer reluctantly stepped back from the stage and quickly exited through the wings. Erik walked to the podium, switched off the microphone and turned to the children.

Hands shot up, and the questioning began again.

A boy, not more than eight years old, stood up and asked in a loud voice, "Why don't we talk to the Englander and ask them to stop sending the bombers over to kill us?"

Erik concentrated on him when he answered, "Herr Hitler is our Führer, and he is the only one permitted to speak to them. Your next question would be, "Why doesn't he talk to them?" but I don't know the answer to that." Erik pointed to a little girl, and the boy slowly sat down.

She stood and asked, "Is it true that we have a 'wonder weapon' that can destroy a whole city and that we will destroy London with it? My parents say we have one, but it is so awful that Herr Hitler will only use it if he has to." She waited for him to answer.

Erik had expected the question earlier. The *Wunderwaffe* was the country's last thread of hope, and many Germans believed that such a weapon existed. He said, "I have heard people say that there is such a thing, and perhaps the Führer plans to destroy British cities with it, but no one I know has seen proof that it exists." Erik quickly pointed to another child.

He wasn't quick enough—the little girl said, "A bomb killed my Opa and Oma in Nürnberg when it blew up their house. My Mutti is afraid that the bombers will soon come to Heilbronn and kill all of us. Is that true? Are they going to kill us?" She sat down and waited.

Erik hesitated and searched for inspiration but found only despair. Annalisa had told him that when he was stuck, and all he had was the truth, he had to try it.

"I don't know the answer to that question. But the bombers are only attacking the big cities where the factories are, and Heilbronn only has the railroad and a few small factories at the edge of the city. They will likely leave us alone, except for a few bombs aimed at the factories or the railway yards, as they do now." Erik wanted to leave the stage and hug the little girl, but he had to go on—there were still a few hands. He pointed to another girl. She shot to her feet and stood at attention.

"My mother works in the motorcycle factory. Vati died in the army and can't come home anymore, and I'm scared that Mutti will die when they bomb the factory. Why can't she stop working there and come home?"

Erik sobbed inside, but he had committed himself. He had to answer with the truth.

"My wife works in that factory, and so does her mother. They work during the day, and the bombers come mostly at night. There is a bomb shelter near the factory, and my Marita and your mother will be safe there if the bombers come." The little girl sat down and hung her head. Clearly, his answer hadn't helped.

Only one hand was up, and it was Walther's.

"I want to know if you are afraid the gunners will kill you in your fighter. They shot your plane down once—won't they try to shoot it down again?" He stood, waiting. Erik spoke to him as though they were alone in the room.

"I can't answer that question, Walther, because I don't think about it. I get in my airplane every night and hunt for bombers to shoot down because I must do that to protect all of our families. I'm fighting to protect your mother, your sisters, our country, and you. If they kill me, I hope you will understand that I did my best, as I know you will do your best to take my place. I'm sorry, but I can't guarantee anything. War, like the rest of life, has no guarantees."

Walther sat down, and no more hands appeared. The silent room was full of bright little eyes focused on Erik.

"It's time to go home now, but there is still the question I asked you when we started." He folded his hands together in front of him. "How many of you still think that I am a hero?" A few unenthusiastic hands went up. He smiled at the children and waited until they lowered them.

"You are right; we do what we must do, and the same is true of everyone—those who fight and those who work at home. Either we are all heroes, or there are no heroes. We must all have courage, but most of all, our children must be brave. You will grow up in the world we leave to you, and it will be your job to fix what we have ruined." He pointed to one child after another. "I know that you will all make me proud!"

The SS officer returned to the stage, standing beside Erik until he turned and walked to the wings.

The children filed out of the auditorium in silence. Not one child clapped, cheered, or laughed, and Erik had never felt so sad in his life.

✧✧✧✧✧✧✧✧✧✧✧✧✧✧✧✧✧✧✧✧✧✧✧✧✧✧✧✧✧

Erik stayed in a small room behind the stage until all the children had gone, and when he followed the adjutant assigned to escort him out to his waiting car, Walther was waiting with Major Richter. Erik took his son's hand and asked Richter, smiling, "Are you here to arrest me?"

The major shook his head and looked at the brick pattern under his feet. He lifted his head and said, "No, Oberleutnant, but you've had your last speaking engagement in Heilbronn. I feel honoured to have been present, and I wish you the best in the future, but I would also appreciate your discretion. Lives, perhaps even ours, depend on it." He held out his hand, and Erik shook it.

Erik said, "I appreciate your arranging for this to be my last speaking engagement—I would rather face a clever gunner than those children! As for discretion, I will say whatever you need me to say. Otherwise, I will keep this day entirely between us. I trust Heilbronn can sleep well, knowing it has a sympathetic Gestapo Kriminaldirektor?"

"Yes, and you can rest assured that no one will bother you or your family while I am alive." He released Erik's hand. "We can't end the war for Germany, but perhaps we can make it more bearable for Heilbronn."

Walther was already in the car when Erik slid in beside him and slammed the door a little too hard. The mercedes accelerated away from the major. Erik turned in his seat and watched him get into the back seat of the grey Gestapo car.

Erik decided that Richter was doing his best to survive. Many forces had aligned against him, and Erik couldn't see how the head of the Gestapo could get through the minefield he had constructed unscathed.

He was surprised when he realized that he wished the leader of the Gestapo in Heilbronn well.

CHAPTER TWELVE

4 April 1944

Die Familie ist der Stamm, die Kinder sind die Blüten.
(The family is the trunk, the children are the blossoms.)

THE DAY WAS STILL SUNNY AND WARM when Marita and Erik took the girls down to the river for a walk along the hiking path. The city had set up clothing bins on the way there, where those with surplus clothes could help those less fortunate, and once a month, Marita forced Walther and the girls to give away a piece of clothing they liked. Today was the day, and the girls agonized over what it should be. They settled on a skirt and blouse and reluctantly slid them into the bins.

Brigitte and Elke ran ahead to the riverbank to feed the ducks stale bread as they did several times a week. Erik and Marita were fortunate to have enough money for everything they wanted and, despite rationing, could find enough of the staples to satisfy their family's needs.

The ducks gathered around the girls, quacking and pushing to be closest to the food source. Marita talked while watching them fight for position—only the strongest made it to the girls' feet, and Elke rewarded the winners by dropping pieces of bread in front of them. Brigitte threw her bread over their heads to the less aggressive ducks swimming anxiously around the outside.

Maria said, "Every day, more forced-labour people work in our factory. Some live in barracks on-site, but many come in *Lastwagen* or walk from the camp in Buchendorf. I don't think the camp feeds them enough to keep them alive—they are so thin I can count their bones." She grabbed Erik's arm. "Those people are starving! Everyone knows that many of them die just because they don't have enough food!" Marita passed the last of the bread to Elke.

"The SS guards forbid the *Zwangsarbiter* to speak to us—they will kill them if they try—and, of course, feeding them is *Verboten*!" She watched the ducks crowd around Elke, taking pieces of bread out of her hand. Marita choked back sobs as she watched the ducks fight over the scraps of bread. "And we have enough to feed *verdammten* ducks!"

Marita picked up a stone and looked across the river as though she intended to throw it that far.

"My heart can't stand watching those people shuffle to their section of the factory. They have only one layer of clothing—their prison uniform—They shiver when it's cold, even when they're working hard!" She threw the stone into the water, and the ducks scattered but quickly regrouped around Elke.

The girls, temporarily distracted by the splash, looked at their mother, checked with their father, decided everything was alright, and resumed throwing bread to the growing flock of ducks. A determined Marita faced Erik. "I want you to get Major Richter to help us feed and clothe those people! The people will help if the guards will let us."

Erik shook his head. "Major Richter can't help—the Gestapo has nothing to do with the *Zwangsarbiter* camps. Major Richter's responsibility is controlling the people of Heilbronn—the SS is in charge of the *Zwangsarbiter*, and, at the moment, they have no reason to help them."

Erik looked up and down the river—no one else was on the riverbank. A family of newly hatched ducklings swam back and forth at the children's feet, quacking and flapping their wings. He counted thirteen tiny ducks following their mother as she gobbled the bread Brigitte threw in the water in front of her nose.

The ducklings tried to eat the smaller bits, but even those were too big for them, so Marita took a piece from Elke and showed her how to break it into smaller morsels.

Marita straightened, and Erik knew she was waiting for him to stop looking across the river. He faced her, and she asked, "What do you mean by 'at the moment?' We must fix this now...The people in that camp are dying, and it won't get better unless we help them!"

Erik shifted his gaze back to the railway yards on the other side of the Neckar River. A pile of broken and bent tracks testified to the accuracy of the mosquitos' bombing. A bulldozer graded and trimmed the roadbed while a crew of men installed new rails. Locomotives shunted strings of cars back and forth on most of the yard.

He asked, "When did the bombers last hit the railway yards?"

Marita followed his eyes to the railway yards and showed her frustration with her tone. "You weren't listening to me, were you?" Erik looked at her with his undivided attention.

She said, "They bombed the yards four days ago, and the trains were going again in two days. They work on the tracks daily, and the bombers ruin them as soon as they get them fixed." She put her hand on his cheek and turned his head to face her.

"Now, what about those people who work in the factory? We must do something..."

Erik took her hand from his cheek and held it between his.

"Marita, this is important too!" He looked across the river... "If they keep fixing those tracks, it's only a matter of time before the Allies bomb the city and put an end to it!"

Frustrated, he turned to Marita. He needed her to understand the situation Germany was in, and especially what it wpuld mean to her and the children.

"The Allies have more equipment in England ready to cross the channel than everything we have available on all fronts. The British and Americans bomb German cities almost every day, and the Russians will cross Poland in the next few months. It's a race between the Allies from the west and the Russians from the east, and the German people have nowhere to hide."

Marita opened her mouth to speak, but he touched her lips.

"When they arrive, the Allies will find those who have committed crimes against the Jews in that camp and the Zwangsarbiter at the factory, and they will punish them. Think about what that means! Perhaps we can use it to help those people."

Marita threw a piece of bread in front of the mother duck's beak as she listened to Erik.

"I wonder if the people guarding those slave workers so diligently realize what is coming at them? What if someone reminded them? Wouldn't they want to get rid of that responsibility?"

Marita stared across the river as she said thoughtfully, "Do you think if they knew what you know, they would try to save themselves by feeding the prisoners? What if Major Richter spoke to the SS?"

Erik smiled at her, bent over, picked up a stone and threw it far out in the river, where it created a half-dozen perfect concentric circles.

Marita shook her head and said, "I don't understand why boys like to throw stones."

He turned to her. "I promise to do what I can about the Zwangsarbiter, but you must leave it with me. Richter is my only avenue, and I don't know whether he will do what I have in mind. Meanwhile, my priority is for you and the children to survive! Heilbronn will be bombed to rubble if this war continues, and it could happen any day or night." Erik stroked her blonde hair. "You and the children must leave the city and move to the country. It will be difficult because your income will only be what I earn, but you will be safe."

Marita picked up a stone. Erik smiled as he watched her consider whether to throw it, but she simply rolled it from one hand to the other.

"We have the General Wever Turm," she said, "and the shelter near the factory. The Wehrmacht engineers say they will withstand any bombs the British and Americans have, so I feel safe here with our friends." Marita paused, then continued, "I would rather keep the children here." She looked at her husband. "What's in Heilbronn that the British and Americans would waste bombs on?"

Erik lowered his head and kicked the dirt with his polished leather boot. "I understand, but my gut tells me you should go. Hitler has nothing to gain by surrendering and everything to lose; the same is true of his followers. Himmler has been the head of the SS, the SD, and the Gestapo for so long that it is certain if Germany surrenders, his life expectancy would be a few days if not hours.

Those bastards know the consequences of surrender; they have nothing to gain by negotiating and nothing to lose by fighting to the last German child! There are no voices of reason in Berlin!"

He picked up a flat stone and threw it, trying to make it skip. It landed on its edge and sank.

"The Americans and British on the west and the Russians on the east will take revenge on our country, and they have made it clear that they intend to annihilate us. The power aligned against us is more than we can ever defeat."

He faced Marita. "Perhaps you are right. When the end comes, maybe the best place to hide will be in the cities where there are many people and lots of work. I understand your logic, and despite my hunches, it is probably better if you do what you think is best. You must follow a plan you believe in—I must return to my squadron. I won't see you for another six months."

He threw his last stone in the river, not bothering with the skip. It skipped, nonetheless. "The war might be over before then."

Erik took Marita's arm and said, "Let's go to the General Wever Turm—I know what British bombs can do, and I would like to look at it up close."

The ducks had figured out that the children had no more bread and swam toward an elderly couple walking along the path with a promising brown bag in their hands.

◇◇◇◇◇◇◇◇◇◇◇◇◇◇◇◇◇◇◇◇◇◇◇◇◇◇◇◇

Erik and Marita strolled along the river trail arm in arm, enjoying the close contact while the girls ran cheerfully back and forth, hovering around them like flies. The pathway to the tower branched off the river trail and went up the hill a hundred metres to the entrance. When they reached the open door, the girls ran inside, their shrill voices bouncing off the concrete walls. A soldier guarding the door saluted Erik.

The ground-level lower chamber was a large round room with a square air vent opposite the door. Stairs led down to the machinery room, and the only pieces of furniture were benches lined against the curved walls and straight rows of them in the rest of the available space. Erik judged the room to be about ten metres in diameter, and he estimated the thickness of the reinforced concrete walls at a metre-and-a-half. Unlike the upper layers that shared an entrance, the lower chamber had its own.

He examined the steel door, checking the thickness with his fingers. "This room looks like a good place to go in a raid. The door leads directly outside, so you won't be caught in a stampede to escape." He motioned to the main entrance at the top of an outside stairway. "Let's look at the upper chambers."

Erik led the way out the door to the lower chamber and up the outside stairs. At the top, they went through an identical door to the one below it and entered a small foyer with an entry into another round room, much smaller than the lower chamber. A narrow sloped hallway circled between the one-and-a-half-metre-thick outside wall of the tower and the thinner chamber walls. The steady slope functioned as a circular ramp corkscrewing upward to the six upper levels, replacing what would typically be stairs.

119

All the levels were connected to the power ventilation system, backed up by a generator. The only light came from bulbs in the ceiling, protected by wire cages. There were benches to sit on and a tiled coal-fired heater in each room for cold winter days and nights.

Erik decided the upper floors would be traps if anything went wrong. He could see nothing combustible in the tower but was none-theless apprehensive.

He said to Marita, "The lower chamber will be the coldest and the noisiest with the generator under the floor. For those reasons, it will always be the last to fill, and access shouldn't be a problem."

Erik warned Marita to "Stay out of the upper rooms. The cone-shaped roof's design will deflect bombs, but I don't like the feel of you following that many people out if escape is necessary. Panic would turn an evacuation into something I don't want to think about!" Erik looked at her. "Please promise that you will stay in the lower room." He waited for her answer.

She smiled at his concern and said, "Yes, of course, I promise," then took his hand and led him outside—it was apparent she hated the confined space of the shelter as much as he did.

She pulled on his arm. "Let's go home; I hate this place; it gives me the heebie-jeebies. Walther will be home at noon today, and I've got something special planned for Mittagessen..." Erik went where she led him... "How about sauerbraten and red potatoes?"

"And rhubarb torte?" Elke chimed in, pulling her mother's hand and looking up at her. Marita leaned over and gently pinched her cheek.

"Yes, and rhubarb torte for the children."

"Don't forget the father of your children—he likes torte too." Erik feigned a broken heart.

Marita growled like a cat. "I've got something sweet for you, too, but it will have to wait until the children go to play at their friend's house. Walther has soccer practice, and we will have the afternoon to ourselves."

Erik chuckled and followed Marita out of the tower. The girls looked curiously at their mother.

◇◇◇◇◇◇◇◇◇◇◇◇◇◇◇◇◇◇◇◇◇◇◇◇◇◇◇◇◇◇◇◇◇◇

Two days of soaking in vinegar and pickle spices had made the piece of tough beef that Annalisa's butcher friend had put aside for her as tender as butter. Meat of any kind was seldom available, and the family loved it.

Not the most eager meat-eater, Walther liked sauerbraten because it came with peeled potatoes cut into small pieces and carrots from the cold cellar cut lengthways, all browned in a big iron pot with the meat. When everything was brown, Marita submerged the vegetables in spicy gravy made using some of the marinade liquid.

Walther grew the carrots and potatoes in his garden, harvested them the previous fall, and Marita had put them between layers of newspaper in the cold cellar. He had also raised the cucumbers and onions that made the sweet pickles that were Annalisa's specialty.

Erik looked around the table. "I want to propose a toast to the persons responsible for this delicious meal, beginning with the vegetables grown by Gartenmeister Walther."

Erik lifted his glass of cranberry juice, squeezed from berries that grew in a small marsh along the Neckar River, pointed it toward his son and said, "Thank you, Gartenmeister Walther."

The girls and Marita chorused, "Prost!" and Walther's face turned red.

Erik turned to his wife, a twinkle in his eyes, his glass held high. "And congratulations to you, Frau Stephanie."

"Prost!" chorused the girls and Walther, laughing as they raised glasses of milk.

Despite Marita's promise of other delights, she gave Erik a square of rhubarb torte—the largest piece. Walther and the girls protested, and Erik cut a sliver from one edge and split it with the children. They complained that it was still unfair, but Erik ate the remainder fast enough that there was no question of measuring. They complained so loudly that Marita gave the children seconds.

"More please," asked Erik, holding out his plate.

Marita slapped his hand. "No, you can't have more. You cheated the children. Bad Vati, bad!"

Erik whined, "That will teach them not to complain!"

Marita countered, "Maybe they could stay home this afternoon so you could teach them some manners!"

Marita's eyes twinkled, and the girls protested loudly. Erik smiled with relief as they ran to the door before anyone could change their mind. Marita stopped the girls before they could get out without putting on their coats, and she watched them from the open door until they reached the neighbour's house a few doors down the street. As they went inside, Marita exchanged waves with their friend's mother.

Walther played in a local football club, and the season opener was on Saturday, in two days. He looked up as he jammed his feet into his tied shoes and said, "Vati, why don't you come to Fussball practice with me?"

Marita put on a deadpan face. "I have some important work for him—he'll come to the game on Saturday."

She spoke so innocently that Erik decided he would never believe her again.

She looked at Erik for confirmation—he nodded and said, "I'm sorry, Walther, I really would like to come, but I need to help your mother this afternoon. You must practice hard so you will play well on Saturday. I promise we will go to the game." Marita nodded when he finished.

Erik turned his head away and coughed, but recovered quickly to bid his son goodbye. Marita tried to button Walther's jacket, but he fastened the buttons himself before she could do it. Marita smiled and straightened his collar.

"Goodbye, Walther. Work hard so you can make us proud on Saturday." She tried to kiss his cheek, but he turned his head and ran out the door. Marita watched him until he disappeared and followed Erik to the living room, where he had picked up the newspaper from the coffee table and opened it as he sat on the sofa.

"Our little boy is growing up; I'm afraid he doesn't need his Mutti anymore." She entered the living room, swinging her hips as her husband watched her cross the room.

Erik threw the newspaper in a pile on the table and stood up.

"That's true for some things, but he will always need his Mutti for what's important." Erik welcomed her into his arms. "Just as I will always need you."

Marita pulled his head down and kissed him, gently at first and then with serious passion. She put her hand down and rubbed his crotch; he was so surprised he became disoriented. He began to fall over but stepped sideways just in time to catch himself. She released him, turned away, and he followed her crooked finger into the bedroom.

Erik had unfastened his pants and was helping Marita with her bra when the air-raid alarm sounded. She looked at Erik standing with his pants around his ankles and laughed. He sadly handed her the sweater he had helped her remove and pulled up his pants, muttering, "Verdammte Englander," as he did.

◇◇◇◇◇◇◇◇◇◇◇◇◇◇◇◇◇◇◇◇◇◇◇◇◇◇◇◇◇◇◇◇◇◇

Erik was out the door ahead of Marita, trotting down the sidewalk toward the house where Elke and Brigitte were playing, when he met the girls and their friend Gertraud and her mother on the street. The girls skipped ahead, the siren wailed, and Marita calmly joined women coming out of their houses, chatting and laughing as they made their way to the tower, a five-minute walk.

Erik had seen what a flotilla of bombers could do, and he was baffled by the people's *laissez-faire* attitude toward the reality he knew. Erik had expected the scene to be dramatic, with people running to the shelters, but it was anything but that. He concluded they had done it so often that it had become a social event, part of daily life. They were unintentionally nullifying the British and American efforts to terrorize them.

The British occasionally sent a pair of mosquito fighters over the city, one to take photographs and the other as an escort. Consequently, many sirens were false alarms. When planes came to bomb, the damage was in the industrial area, usually when the workers were at home, or in the railway yards where very few people worked on the tracks that were the target.

Bombs had hit a few houses, but residents were in shelters, and the bombs hadn't caused many casualties. When the dust settled, the luckier neighbours housed and fed the victims while the neighbourhood helped rebuild or repair the unlucky victim's house.

As they walked to the shelter, Erik observed that a unified German resistance against the hated Englander was the only plant that grew from the seeds of terror planted by British bombers.

In the city's center, the Stadtmitte, residents fortified their cellars, cutting doorways through common walls to connect houses—partly as escape routes, but also so they could socialize with their neighbours until the 'all-clear' sounded. Engineers designed heavy bracing and posts to reinforce the floors to support the entire house if it fell, and residents stored candles, lanterns, canned food and water in their cellars.

The *Luftschutzdienst* published a list of recommended emergency supplies and checked the home shelters to see that windows were sealed, floors were adequately braced, and there was an emergency exit.

123

Germans were comfortable in their homemade refuges with their makeshift toilets and fully equipped kitchens. They stocked their Hütte, their weekend 'hut,' with Schnapps and beer, then gathered in the best-equipped cellar and celebrated a "Bombenfest" …proof that defiant people can turn anything into a party.

Erik had inspected some of these homemade shelters and decided against building one in their cellar. He did add walls and posts to reinforce the floors and boarded up the cellar windows, just in case, but insisted that Marita take the children to the General Wever Turm for every alarm, without exception.

Marita, tempted to stay home for this one, had seen no daylight raids for months and assumed this was another false alarm. However, Erik insisted there could be no exceptions, so there was no discussion.

At home in the tower, the girls and their friend Gertraud were already sitting on their usual bench when Marita, Erik, and Gertraud's mother, Beata, entered the shelter. Everyone in the room chattered and laughed, the siren wailed, and the people had to raise their voices ever louder to be heard over the rising volume of the vivid cacophony. Sounds bounced off the concrete walls, making it impossible to separate them.

The generator started, Marita introduced her friend to Erik, and, after a round of shouting at one another, he figured out that her name was Beata and her little girl's name was Gertraud. Marita said something else, probably Beata's last name, and Erik smiled and nodded as though he had heard her over the siren's wail.

Erik and Marita sat on a bench with Beata. An elderly man and woman came from the opposite direction and sat on the bench with them. They attempted to introduce themselves and explain where they lived but eventually gave up trying to talk over the bedlam. They finally just sat there, looking at the opposite wall.

The door clanged shut, and a soldier, presumably there to keep the peace, closed the steel shutters on the vents. The closed door and vents muffled the siren's sound, and after a few minutes, it stopped. The generator stopped its initial cold-diesel clatter, settled into a smooth purr, and the people in the room started talking, laughing at one another's tales.

Erik took the time to look around. There were a few children, but the room held primarily women of all ages. There was only one man close to Erik's age, and he was in the uniform of the Waffen SS, with skull badges sewn on his sleeves. He wore a tank regiment's insignia on his shirt collar, and Erik would like to have spoken with him, but he was on the other side of the now-crowded room.

The first bombs surprised Erik. He hadn't heard the bombers and could barely hear the bombs' soft krump, but he felt they were close. The chatter stopped, and the room listened to an older man dressed in a suit as he leaned ahead, his hands on the top of a silver-handled cane, and said, "Railway yards!" A few heads nodded in agreement, and a steady rain of bombs followed, all at about the same distance and direction. Sharp explosions shook the shelter, and the old man said, "Close, very close."

The sounds inside the chamber were reduced to whispers, as though a bomb aimer might hear them, but the conversation Erik could pick out was still about children, fashion, and recipes. Bombs were not the topic du jour.

A hammer blow above them shook the building, followed seconds later by a very close explosion. The old man pointed up with his index finger, "Bounced off the roof! It's good that it had a delay fuse!"

That was enough to stop the conversation, and Erik, suddenly nervous, asked Marita, "Where is Walther?" Walther was supposed to be in a shelter on the other side of the city, but Erik wanted more information.

Before Marita could answer, the conversation resumed at full volume, and she spoke over the clamour into Erik's ear, "He is at the shelter at Kaiser Friedrich Platz—the sports field is near there." Marita didn't appear to be concerned. Erik suddenly wanted to yell at her—their son was alone and in danger. As he opened his mouth, Marita said in his ear, "Don't worry, he'll be alright; our son is with good people who will take care of him, and Walther can take care of himself if he needs to."

Marita seemed confident, and Erik relaxed slightly, but flying seemed less dangerous than this. He wished for a control stick in his hands.

He said in her ear, "It seems you know the routine here, but I find it worse than flying a fighter at night!" Marita squeezed his arm and spoke to him as though comforting a frightened child. "Don't worry, Liebling, it will all be over soon." Erik looked at Brigitte and Elke feeding a rag doll and felt his face burning.

Fifteen minutes later, the 'all clear' sounded, and the old Luftschutzdienst soldier opened the door. The citizens, accustomed to the routine, greeted and thanked the veteran of the Great War as they filed out into the crisp air, still chattering. They became silent when they reached the daylight outside; the sight that greeted them brought any thoughts of gossip or recipe exchanges to an abrupt halt.

Less than thirty metres from the entrance, in the middle of Theresienstrasse, was a crater ten metres wide and two metres deep. Next to the river were two more holes of similar dimensions—one less than ten metres from the shelter. Erik looked up at the cone-shaped roof and saw the damage where a bomb had struck the edge of the tower and deflected off it. It undoubtedly was the bomb responsible for the nearest crater. Four bomb impact points, beginning at the crater on Therienstrasse, led down to the water, a line pointing at the marshalling yards across the river—a mosquito had dropped its load too soon.

The damage to the yards was visible from the tower, a distance of a thousand metres. A few railroad rails pointed skyward, indicating the source of the bombs. Silhouettes of piles of dirt that appeared to touch one another marked the craters.

Repair crews already moved toward the damaged yard—a rail-mounted crane belched smoke and steam as it crossed the undamaged railway bridge. Lastwagen, loaded with gravel, ready for the next attack, and bulldozers puffing black smoke appeared from nowhere. Dozens of men joined them, and Erik reckoned the yards would likely be operational within forty-eight hours.

He could see no damage to buildings and assumed this had been a low-level mosquito raid, targeting only the railway yards. Erik silently wondered why the British didn't build thousands of mosquito bombers and forget massive attacks on the inner cities with heavy and expensive lancasters. Assessing the damage he could see, Erik thought that one mosquito could have put the railway bridge in the river, crippling rail traffic for months. He asked himself why they hadn't targeted the bridge and couldn't find the answer.

His mind was still on the mosquitos as he walked home with Marita and the girls. Marita and Beata walked behind him, incessantly talking while the noisy girls buzzed around them. Erik saw no bomb damage on the way home, and the houses were as they had left them.

Luftschutzdienst soldiers patrolled the streets during air raids to prevent looting, with orders to shoot looters on the spot—but disappeared when the residents returned. The soldiers' presence eliminated the temptation to stay in their houses to protect the only assets most of them possessed.

Elke and Brigitte begged to stay with Gertraud, and although it was almost time for the evening meal, Marita and Beata agreed. Erik feigned resistance, and Marita laughed, sharing a wink with Beata. He took Marita's hand and led her away as she continued to assure Beata that she should send the girls home before the evening meal at six. That gave them an hour, and Erik planned to make the most of it. Beata shouted after them, "I will send them home after Abendessen at about seven."

"That gives us two hours." Erik turned and waved. "I think I like your friend."

"Make sure you use all of it!" Marita laughed, and Erik felt the heat rising from his collar.

Marita unlocked the door and ran playfully ahead of Erik, bouncing into the living room like a little girl. Erik chased her, laughing, reaching for her flapping coat. When she abruptly stopped, he ran into her, barely catching her before she fell.

<hr>

Standing in the hall outside his bedroom, Walther laughed, pointed at his mother and father and said, "What's going on with you guys? Why are you acting so silly?"

"Oh, we're just happy that the bombing's over and no one got hurt," Marita replied, smoothly changing gears. "How was Fussball practice?"

Walther waved his hands in disgust. "It was too short to get anything done. The coach showed us what he wanted us to do, and we had just started shooting at the goalie when the siren started. We didn't want to go to the shelter, but he made us, and it was boring as usual…no bombs fell anywhere near us!" He spread his hands, frustrated. "We could hardly hear the explosions, and the coach wouldn't even let us go outside!"

"I'm glad to hear that; you have a wise coach." Marita went into the kitchen. "Does anyone want something to eat? I've got Vollkornbrot und Käse."

Erik said, "I was hoping for something sweeter, but I guess that will have to do." He turned on his heel and went to the radio. It was time for the evening news, although he knew it wouldn't be accurate or helpful. All news reports came from or were approved by Goebbels' Propaganda Ministerium and, therefore, were entirely political propaganda; any resemblance to the truth was coincidental and imperceptible.

Sure enough, the local news flash claimed that the British had bombed the Neckar River in Heilbronn, with the loss of two British bombers, shot down by the city's heroic flak batteries.

Erik was familiar with the light flak guns employed in defence of Heilbronn—they couldn't hit a high-flying mosquito if it were stationary, and it would be cruising at 300 knots. Their altitude limit was below six thousand metres, and the mosquitos would have been at seven or eight thousand, above the operational ceiling of most German fighters, which in the spring of 1944 were a rare sight.

All the mosquitos would have returned to their base, barring a mechanical failure or running out of gas. According to the broadcast, the damage repair crews would have the trains running by tomorrow—probably as close to the truth as German Radio ever got.

The National news followed the local report and was, as usual, contradictory and confusing. As the Russians advanced, heroic German soldiers destroyed hundreds of their tanks, killing and capturing thousands of Russian soldiers while suffering only a few casualties. The announcer opined that it would be a few weeks before the Germans would drive the Russians out of Poland.

Marita sent Walther to cut rhubarb and dig radishes, then went into the living room to sit beside Erik. "No need to be sad—we'll go to bed early, and you can have your dessert then." She kissed him on the cheek.

"I'm looking forward to it, but that's not why I'm depressed." Military music vibrated the Volksempfanger speaker, always a preliminary to an official speech, so Erik turned the receiver off.

"I don't see how we will get through this." Erik leaned forward on his elbows, his eyes focused far away. "I don't see a future for us or our children. British and American bombers will destroy our cities, and the men who could rebuild them are dying in a futile battle to save Hitler."

Marita sat beside him, putting one hand on his leg and the other on his shoulder. He lifted his head and looked at her, his eyes wet.

"That egotistical megalomaniac is determined to sacrifice my family and me—Hitler will allow the Allies to destroy our cities and take our lives. And all because he can't admit he is wrong! No matter how many bombers I shoot down, the Russians are on our doorstep, and Germany cannot survive! How can I save my family from this insanity?"

Marita put her head on his shoulder. "We will survive...I don't know how we will do it, but somehow, we will—as a family and a country. We will have grandchildren, and they will build a better country for their children than we've built for ours." She put her hand on his cheek and forced him to look at her. "Our son, our daughters, and their children will rebuild what we cannot."

"But will we live to see it?" Erik struggled to remain depressed, but Marita was winning.

She smiled and put her arms around his neck. "I don't know, and neither do you. Life goes on until it doesn't, and living it as though we were dead already makes no sense. We have many things to do, and among them are things that create a great deal of pleasure." She kissed him, pulled him to his feet and pushed him toward the front door. Erik tried not to smile as. Marita handed him his coat. "Put it on...we're going to get the girls."

They walked hand in hand to Beata's house, and Marita talked about her friend. "Beata's husband has been missing since the disaster in Stalingrad. He was a *Feldwebel* in the Sixth Army when the Russians wiped it out—she has no idea whether he's alive or dead!"

"You're telling me this so I'll stop feeling sorry for myself and feel lucky to be here?" Erik smiled at his beautiful wife.

She returned it and pulled him close to her. "No, I'm telling you this so you'll know how lucky I am and why I'm so happy."

When they reached the house, Marita lifted the knocker, let it drop against the door, and Beata was in the open doorway in less than ten seconds. Beautiful blonde Dutch braids surrounded her rosy cheeks.

"My, that was a quickie!" Beata giggled. "If you're not too tired, why don't you stay and share our pot of borscht? I've got lots, and there are twenty more bottles of cabbage in the cellar."

Marita tried not to look disappointed when she said, "Walther was home when we got there."

Erik sensed that she felt guilty having a husband, while Beata didn't know whether to mourn, move on, or hold onto hope and wait for her husband to return from a Russian prison camp.

The girls tried to escape down the hallway to Gertraud's room, but Beata ran after them, laughing and teasing them about how she was "coming to get them." Elke and Brigitte reversed directions and ran out the door, then up the street ahead of Erik and Marita. They were full of fun and life, as little girls are supposed to be, and Erik forgot the war as he watched them jump from block to block on the sidewalk, never stepping on a bad luck crack.

◇◇◇◇◇◇◇◇◇◇◇◇◇◇◇◇◇◇◇◇◇◇◇◇◇◇◇◇◇◇◇

The children tolerated the black bread and cheese evening meal and loudly expressed their misery when there was no dessert. Marita promised to make another torte tomorrow, and the girls shrieked in anticipation. Walther went to his room to do his homework. Erik followed him, but Walther kicked him out, wanting no help from his father, who always wanted to expand on the lessons. Erik wandered back to the kitchen, where he found Marita cutting rhubarb into small pieces for the morning.

"Do you still have the 'Lili Marlen' recording?" He watched her scoop his precious sugar over the rhubarb.

She laughed, "You're not going to tell on me, are you?"

Erik said, "Everyone in Germany who owns a phonograph bought that recording, and Goebbels' decree against playing it is a joke! But I still might tell on you if you're not nice to me!"

She looked at him and winked. "You hold up your end, and I'll be good." Erik blushed—he went to the living room to lick his wounds and read the local paper.

Ten minutes later, Marita came into the room and pulled the record from behind books on a tower of shelves.

She turned on the phonograph, carefully laid the irreplaceable disc on the turntable, and placed the needle on the starting edge. There was a brief soft scraping sound, a hint of static, and then, the lilting sound of Lala Anderson's heart-wrenching song filled the room.

Walther entered the room with the girls, already in their nightdresses and ready for bed. The children waited until the song had ended before Walther said, "Good Night, Mutti und Vati..." He faked a yawn... "I'm tired, and I want to go to bed."

Marita nestled against Erik while she looked curiously at her son. Erik

130

motioned for Walther to sit down beside him and his mother. Walther sauntered across the room to them, and the girls tentatively followed.

Erik looked at each of them in turn, "Now, tell us, why are you so anxious to go to bed?"

"Oh, just because of all the excitement of the air raid, I guess." Walther had always been a lousy liar, and Erik could see that he hadn't improved recently.

Marita took over. "Now, you and I know that isn't the reason. I'll bet it has something to do with school." She was fishing.

"No, no...school's fine... I'm just a little tired." Walther pushed out another simulated yawn and stretched his arms.

Brigitte, dancing back and forth from one foot to the other, couldn't keep it in any longer. "Walther told us that you need privacy from us kids!" She smiled a sweet, toothless smile. Both front teeth had fallen out in the same week and netted her two Groschen—a fortune.

Marita laughed. "We will get all the privacy we need once Annalisa is home and has supper. It's sweet of you to think of us, but we love to see you as much as we can, and your father wants to be with you as much as he can before he has to go back—he will only be here for a few more days."

"How about a game of Skat?" Erik was one of the best Skat players in his squadron, and Marita knew it, so she joined her children in a moan. She said, "No, no, that's too easy for you and too hard for us...I want you to lose!"

Marita's eyes twinkled. She knew how she and the children could beat Erik, and so did he. She said, "Let's play memory!" Marita shouted, and the children cheered. Erik knew he couldn't win against the girls, let alone Walther.

Groaning and complaining while shuffling the cards, Erik mumbled about the tyranny of the majority as he spread them face down on the coffee table.

He invited Brigitte, sitting to his left, to begin. She turned over two cards and nailed two sevens but turned over a queen and an eight on her second try. Elke was next—she missed a pair by one spot.

As they went around the table for the fourth time, it became apparent that either the best memory or the best luck belonged to Elke, and she slaughtered them. The game lasted a half-hour; Erik insisted on a rematch, so they played another. This time, Walther almost beat Elke, but she won by a pair. Erik came in a distant last with only two pairs.

The laughing and teasing finally ended when the mechanical clock on the bookshelf chimed nine o'clock. Marita took Brigitte's hand, and Erik picked up Elke, slinging her over his shoulder to shrieks of delight. They went to the bedroom to get their toothbrushes and then to the bathroom for the ritual brushing. The squealing girls, snug in their beds, prayed for everyone in the world and got kisses from their Mutti and Vati. Marita and Erik went in to say goodnight to Walther.

"Vati, I don't want you to go back to the war." Walther squeezed so hard that his small bones bit into his father's neck.

"I must go—no matter how much I want to stay with you, I must do my job."

Marita turned away.

"Can't you just say no?" pleaded Walther. "You could hide in the cellar until the war is over—please, Vati, don't go!"

"Then who would stop the bombers from coming to Heilbronn?" Erik spoke quietly. "I have to do it, just like all the men in my squadron do. Circumstances sometimes force you to do things you don't want to, and you must remember that your family is why you will do it." Erik sat on the bed and pulled the blankets up to Walther's chin.

He leaned close to his son. "A wise woman once told me we shouldn't ruin today by worrying about tomorrow. There are things we can't change; we must accept the life we have right now. I love my life today and will think of you when I'm away. I will look forward to coming back to you."

Marita turned away, put her hand up to her face, and Erik caught it.

"Now, go to sleep, and I will see you in the morning. I love you, son."

"Good night, Vati...I love you too." Walther let Erik kiss him on the cheek, then reached up and pulled his father's head down so that he could kiss him.

Marita replaced Erik on the edge of the bed, and for the first time in weeks, Walther let her kiss him, returning the kiss as he had done with Erik. She rose from the bed, looked back at him as she left the room, then silently closed the door.

She embraced Erik, holding him for a long time.

CHAPTER THIRTEEN

5 April 1944

Behind every great man, there is a greater woman.

Annalisa clomped into the front hall at ten-thirty, and Marita helped her mother with her coat and boots. Shoulders slumped, Annalisa shuffled to the kitchen.

Erik poured a cup of ersatz coffee for her and held up a teaspoon of beet sugar. She held up three fingers, and he added three heaping teaspoons. She sat down and took the hot cup in both hands. Marita set down a steaming plate of sauerbraten and potatoes; Erik perched a piece of grey semmel bread layered with butter on the edge of her plate.

Annalisa speared the meat, cut it into small pieces, then picked up her large spoon and ate. She said nothing as she spooned the hot food into her mouth as fast as she could chew and swallow.

Marita sat beside her mother while Erik cut a piece of the freshly baked torte, put it on a small plate and placed it in front of her. Sitting opposite his mother-in-law, he said, "Annalisa, I think you should cut down on the hours you're working." She lowered her spoon, put her elbows on the table and rested her chin on her folded hands.

"Then who will do the work I do? The Zwangsarbiter? People with no food, no shoes, and no proper clothes?" She was upset, close to tears. She sat back, dabbed her eyes with a napkin, and Marita took her hand.

"What's wrong, mother? What happened?"

Annalisa waved her hands, frustrated. "I tried to get permission from the SS guards to bring shoes and clothes for those poor slave workers. I told them that dozens of townspeople want to help—all they need to do is let them. But the guards said if I spoke to any of them or tried to communicate in any way, they would shoot the worker on the spot. They said, "It is *Verboten* for German civilians to interfere with the discipline of the zwangsarbiter!" She squeezed Marita's hand. "Marita, you know they are dying of starvation and exposure...surely God will punish us if we don't do something!"

Erik slowly shook his head as he walked across the kitchen and stared at the thick black cloth covering the window. He stood there for a moment, then returned to the table and Annalisa. "It's time for you to quit working at the factory. I'll find a way to get you released; I'll say you must stay home to look after your grandchildren so that Marita can work."

Annalisa responded almost before he had finished, "If I don't work, the slave workers will do my job, and when those die, they'll bring more from Poland or one of the Jew camps in Czechoslovakia, and they will work those slaves to death. How many will I kill if I do the easy thing?"

Erik threw up his hands in frustration. "My God, Annalisa, you're not young enough to work so hard—you can't do it all! Please consider your family; your grandchildren need you now, and they will need you in the future. If you continue to work this hard, I'm worried you will have no future!" Erik looked desperately to Marita for help.

Marita took over. "Mother, I beg you to take Erik's advice."

"I'll do what I damned well like!" She stuffed a piece of torte in her mouth.

The air raid siren wailed as if to put an exclamation mark on her statement.

"Sheiiiissssee!" A frustrated Erik headed for the girls' room, and Marita went to get Walther. Despite the screaming siren, the children were fast asleep when Marita and Erik woke them up and dressed them. They hurried to the front door where Annalisa was waiting, chewing the last piece of her torte and carrying her coffee cup. She slurped the last drop, set it on the floor and followed the family out the door and down the street.

◇◇◇◇◇◇◇◇◇◇◇◇◇◇◇◇◇◇◇◇◇◇◇◇◇◇◇◇◇◇◇◇◇◇◇

The lower chamber was almost fully occupied when the Stephanie family arrived; the old man with the cane sat in his usual place, and their empty bench waited for them. Erik was amazed at the impromptu organization of what logic told him should be a chaotic event.

Although the noise level was not nearly as high as it had been in the afternoon, Erik turned his head so his mouth would be close to Marita's ear and he could speak without shouting.

"Is this always your bench?"

A small elderly woman on the bench behind them had excellent hearing and answered his question.

"Yes, it is their bench, and someone will find them if they don't show up. When you return to your unit, you don't have to worry—we care for one another.—we have to take care of one another…our government has no time for us! Our Luftwaffe sits on the ground while we sit in shelters, waiting to be killed like lambs." She wagged her finger at Erik, nodded her head vigorously, and then turned to her neighbour, who nodded her head in agreement. She concluded with, "There is a conspiracy in our Luftwaffe to make the Führer look bad!" She nodded like a hen pecking at her food and Erik acknowledged her by touching his hat."

Erik turned to Walther, and the girls stretched out on blankets Marita had spread on the concrete floor. The girls had curled up and fallen asleep, but Walther still fought to keep his eyes open.

People were quiet—they didn't try to talk over the wailing siren—and when the soldier closed the door, the siren's scream was no longer intrusive. Only the clattering diesel interfered.

The explosions began ten minutes after they entered the shelter, but the sound was far away. *"Industriegebiet,"* said the old man with the cane. Erik was willing to bet he was right, having heard his accurate assessment in the afternoon, and the industrial area was a reasonable target. The old man looked at Erik and nodded to show his respect for the Luftwaffe officer.

Erik asked Marita, "Do you know who that man with the cane is?" and turned his head in the old man's direction. "He seems to know everyone in the room."

"Yes," Marita said, "that's Herr Kuhlmann. He fought in the four-teen-eighteen war and earned the Knight's Cross with diamonds, and it cost him his right leg. Herr Kuhlmann works as a warden in the *Luftschutzdienst*, finding help for people with problems—mostly women who can't fix their blackout curtains or get their children to the shelter alone. He also finds somewhere for families who lose their homes to live. He knows everyone in Heilbronn, and everyone listens to him, although he has no official power." Erik looked at the man again, seeing much more than he had in the afternoon.

The cross with diamonds was Germany's highest award for bravery. Only true heroes got them, and usually posthumously.

The bombs stopped after less than half an hour, and the "all clear" sounded fifteen minutes later. Erik carried Elke, and Walther, whom Erik had trusted with the lantern, helped Brigitte find her way back in the dark. Erik looked over Elke's head at the fires in the industrial area a couple of kilometres north of them. He said nothing, but the direction seemed very close to NSU Motorenwerke AG, the motorcycle factory converted to manufacture tank parts where Marita and Annalisa worked.

◇◇◇◇◇◇◇◇◇◇◇◇◇◇◇◇◇◇◇◇◇◇◇◇◇◇◇◇◇◇

When they had tucked the children in, Annalisa called from the living room, "I've been thinking about what you both want me to do, and I've decided that you are right; I must do something. Marita and the children need me, and I can't do anything for them or you if I'm dead! The bombing tonight was near the factory, and I would have been there if they had come an hour earlier!" She smiled at Erik as he reached the sofa. "I want to talk it over with Herr Schneider—he owns the place, and I will need his permission for whatever arrangement I can live with. We are 'sort of' friends, and I know he won't be pleased—so, if you don't mind, I would like you to accompany me—it will help me get a better deal." She put her hand out to him, and he pulled her to her feet.

Erik laughed. "What's to negotiate?... If you want to quit, he has to give you permission. Perhaps we could drop Major Richter's name if he shows reluctance—the Gestapo still has a certain amount of influence. Of course, I will go with you. I'm so glad you've decided to do this!" He hugged her tightly.

Marita took three long-stemmed glasses from the cupboard, handed them to Erik, went to the cellar, and returned with a bottle of Riesling. They drank a toast to Annalisa, to each of the children, to Erik and the new airplane he would have when he returned to his base. Then to Marita and the torte, and then... a bottle of Riesling was empty.

Marita announced, with a slight slur, "It's one in the morning, and I'm going to take my husband to bed." She took Erik's hand and carefully set her glass on the coffee table. Erik put his glass beside it and followed her. Annalisa raised hers toward them, "I'll be asleep in ten minutes." She winked, set her glass beside theirs, turned off the light, and left the room behind them.

◇◇◇◇◇◇◇◇◇◇◇◇◇◇◇◇◇◇◇◇◇◇◇◇◇◇◇◇◇◇

There were no more alarms that night, and life returned to normal in

136

the morning. Marita woke Walther at eight for school, an hour later than usual because of the bombing, and went to the kitchen to prepare his oatmeal porridge and boiled eggs. He would have fresh milk and brown sugar for his porridge; Annalisa had brought home the milk and a bag of raw beet sugar she had gotten from her secret source the night before. This morning, Marita's family could have all the sweetness they wanted. As she worked, she hummed a pretty Beethoven love song titled "Ich Liebe Dich."

Annalisa entered the kitchen an hour earlier than usual, and as she put the kettle on the stove, she said, "I hear you had a good night." She took the coffee funnel down, slid a Melitta filter in it, took out the measuring spoon and ladled ersatz coffee into it.

"Now, how would you know that?" Marita laughed as she stirred the rolling, boiling oatmeal.

Annalisa chuckled. "I haven't been sleeping very well lately."

"Why don't you drink a glass of warm milk, Oma? That's what you give me when I can't sleep," Walther advised as he entered the kitchen with his school bag.

Annalisa chuckled, "Good morning, young man. No, milk won't help—I've decided I need a man to help me sleep."

Marita set a bowl of porridge on the table in front of Walther and put a bowl of raw sugar and a pitcher of fresh whole milk beside him. As she had hoped, his attention shifted to the porridge.

"Wow, porridge with brown sugar! How much sugar can I use, Mutti?"

"Be reasonable... " She ran her fingers through his hair... "but if it were me, I would want two or three big spoonfuls." She stooped to give him a quick kiss on the cheek. He rubbed the spot and dipped the spoon deep into the sugar bowl. He spread it on the oatmeal with his finger, waited for the brown to melt in puddles, then added two more. When the sugar became a molten layer covering the porridge, Walther slowly poured milk on the brown blanket, and coffee-coloured fingers crept through the white liquid.

He looked up at his mother, smiling from ear to ear, his spoon poised, and said, "Thank you, Mutti," making nine years of nurturing worthwhile.

"What's all the noise—can't a Luftwaffe hero sleep in?" Erik entered the room with a smile as wide as his face would allow. He pecked Annalisa on the cheek, then spun his wife away from the counter and kissed her.

"Oh, Vati, that's too much!" Walther made a face.

"What do you think, mother? Was it too much?" Erik patted Marita's back and pecked her on the cheek.

She returned the peck. "No, it was just right. Now, sit down and eat your porridge." She placed a large bowl in front of Erik and slid the sugar bowl over. "Your mother-in-law has a secret sugar daddy."

"My, you two seem to have been bitten by the love bug!" Annalisa didn't try to hide her pleasure.

"I can't think of when I've been as happy!" Marita winked at her mother. Erik was pleased at the exchange between Marita and her mother. His wife's happiness was at the top of the list of his objectives in life.

Erik decided to stop that conversation. "Annalisa, whenever you are ready, I'll go with you to talk to your boss." Annalisa opened her mouth to reply, but Erik continued, "But only if you want me there."

"I was about to say I could do this myself, but since you insist on being such a gentleman, I won't refuse your help. Just stay out of my way until you see that I'm in trouble—then you can try talking some sense into him!" She gave Marita a secret smile and rounded the corner from the kitchen to the front hall.

Walther went to school, and the girls begged for more sugar on their oatmeal. Marita put another spoonful on their porridge, poured on more milk, then buried everything in her large bowl under a layer of sugar. Erik looked pointedly at the entombed porridge, shook his head and kissed her goodbye. He had to run to catch Annalisa and finally caught up to her on the path beside the Neckar River.

✦✦✦

Before he spoke, Erik knew he was going where no man should, but they were alone, a rare occasion, and he felt the time was right.

Erik bravely asked, "Annalisa, why don't you find a man?" He added the sugared pill, "You are a beautiful woman like your daughter; you are still young, and even if he's not perfect, you could train him—as your daughter trains me." He smiled a mischievous smile, further cutting the odds of getting slapped.

Annalisa took Erik's arm and pulled him close. Erik, feeling happy to be alive, walked arm-in-arm with her along the river. He had given up on getting a response when she said, "You know, Erik, I've heard of bad relationships between mothers-in-law and their daughter's husbands, but in my case, I think I love you as much as my daughter does. Thank you for being a good husband to her, and especially, thank you for how you treat me. But, dear Erik, I don't need your advice regarding men!" She affectionately tightened her grip on his arm and marched him down the path.

It was a thirty-minute walk along the river to the Industriegebiet, where Annalisa and Marita worked. They crossed under the tracks on the river path, and a faint odour of smoke polluted the clear morning air. Erik's senses sharpened as they walked across the narrow island, then uphill from the East branch of the Neckar River onto the high ground of Weipertstrasse. The smell strengthened, becoming acrid as they approached Industrieplatz, then dramatically increased as they neared the factory.

The motorcycle factory was located on the west side of the road just before the intersection with Salzstrasse, and the entrance to one of Europe's largest salt mines was only a few hundred metres down that road. But the smell seemed to originate much closer than the salt mines.

The factory buildings were not visible until Erik and Annalisa were almost opposite them, and the extent of the damage didn't become apparent until they walked through the gates.

The two-storey company offices were close to Weipertstrasse, and the long, high factory building was twenty metres behind them. Bomb blasts had broken windows located high on the brick walls, and half the roof was scattered over the yard or collapsed into the working space. But a large section of the building appeared undamaged.

Farther from the street, behind the factory building, were the smouldering remains of a smaller building that had burned to the ground. Firefighters still pumped water on hot spots where tiny plumes of smoke rose from small piles of ashes.

Annalisa put her hands over her mouth. "Oh my God, Erik, that was the Zwangsarbiter barracks!" She began to cry and leaned on Erik for support.

Erik put his arm around her. He had seen his share of death, but this… there was no chance that anyone in the building had escaped.

Annalisa shrieked, "What kind of animals lock people in a building when bombs are falling? They knew that this factory would someday be a target! What would have been the harm to our *Tausandjähriges Reich* if someone had taken them to the shelter?"

Erik put his hand on Annalisa's shoulder. "We can't help them now. Do you still want to go to the office?"

"Hell, yes!" She took Erik's arm and pulled him toward the main entrance to the office building as fast as she could walk without running. She released him at the door and stomped up the broad steps to the second floor. The first door she came to on her left was the one she wanted, and she yanked it open fast enough that anyone on the other side would know that trouble was on its way!

She impatiently waited for her embarrassed son-in-law to go meekly past, then slammed it so hard Erik was surprised the glass window built into the door survived.

"I want to speak to Herr Schneider!" She said it loud enough to get her point across, then leaned over the receptionist's desk to emphasize it with a loud "Now!"

"*Es tut mir Leid,* Frau Mueller, but at the moment, he is not available." The receptionist smiled condescendingly, as though she had been through this before. Erik imagined that disgruntled employees sometimes tried to get to the boss.

Annalisa looked at her for a short two seconds, then went to the door with Jonas Schneider, Director, painted in black letters on the glass window.

"Unauthorized entry is *verboten*!" The receptionist shouted at Annalisa, but she was too late.

◇◇◇◇◇◇◇◇◇◇◇◇◇◇◇◇◇◇◇◇◇◇◇◇◇◇◇◇◇◇◇◇◇◇◇◇◇◇

When Erik tried to follow her, Annalisa slammed the door in his face. He looked at the receptionist—she shrugged and examined her nails.

He asked her, "What in hell just happened?"

With a wave of her hand toward the door, the receptionist answered, "Herr Director Schneider won't throw *her* out." Erik noted the receptionist's name, Fräulein Baumann, on the brass nameplate sitting on her desk. She smiled as though she knew something Erik didn't, and Erik decided to find out what it was.

140

"Fräulein Baumann... " he began, but he could immediately see that she wasn't in the mood to tell him anything.

"She is upset about the *Zwangsarbiter.* "

"Why?" Fräulein Baumann seemed genuinely curious.

Erik couldn't believe the callousness of this woman. "Those poor people...such a terrible tragedy... Don't you feel anything?"

"It could have been much worse. The factory is reparable." She spread her hands. "A few weeks and..."

Erik interrupted—this woman couldn't be as callous as she seemed!

"But what about the *Zwangsarbiter...* doesn't that upset you?" Erik's voice rose.

"Oh, I've never been there, but I've heard it's not so bad in the mine, and Herr Schneider will begin building a new barracks immediately." She waved her free hand around. "He'll build a much better barracks with private bathing, private toilets, and only four workers in a room. Men and women will have separate facilities. I'm certain they will be much better off in the new barrack." She looked at him, puzzled. "You know, Herr Schneider was going to tear that old building down anyway."

Erik understood and smiled. "Ah, the Zwangsarbiter were in the salt mine last night?"

"Of course. Herr Schneider insisted that they spend the night there. He has felt for some time that the British would attack the factory and has insisted for the past couple of weeks that the workers sleep in the mine—and it appears he was correct."

"Did my mother-in-law know that? I mean, about the workers sleeping in the mine for the last couple of weeks?"

It was Fräulein Baumann's turn to smile. "I don't think so—they haven't been together... But, of course, I wouldn't know for sure." She cupped a hand over her ear and leaned toward the office door. "But, I believe Herr Schneider has told her since she entered his office." The shouting had stopped.

"Well, I'll be damned." Erik sat down in a comfortable leather chair, chuckling to himself. Annalisa's voice had softened until he couldn't hear it anymore. Perhaps neither of them was talking.

Fifteen minutes later, a balding man who appeared to be in his late fifties followed Annalisa out of the office, and both were smiling.

Herr Schneider offered his hand. "Oberleutnant Stephanie, I'm honoured to meet you. Annalisa has spoken about you in glowing terms." Erik caught the familiar use of Annalisa's name.

Herr Schneider had a firm grip—Erik could barely match it. The director was in excellent physical shape and as tall and muscular as Erik. His face was pleasant, and he seemed in a good mood for a man recently attacked by an angry woman—especially one like Annalisa.

"I was just telling your mother-in-law that last night, the guards moved the workers to the salt mines so they would be safe from British bombs. Many small factories are already in those mines, and more are moving there every month. The Zwangsarbiter are safe and can return to work when the Organization Todt engineers decide whether to repair the factory or move it underground.

"The bombers struck us quite badly, and they tell me that we will be out of operation for at least two weeks." He looked at Annalisa, then back at Erik. "Annalisa and I would like to discuss the Zwangsarbiter situation with you if you would stay for lunch with us—she thinks you could help us with some ideas we have."

Erik looked at his mother-in-law; she had an intentionally non-committal smile plastered on her face. He said, "You want me to have lunch with you and Annalisa?... To discuss the Zwangsarbiter?" Erik's tone was more incredulous than he intended, and when he saw Annalisa vigorously nodding her head behind Herr Schneider, he quickly added, "Why yes, of course, I will do that."

<hr>

The factory had its own workers' cafeteria, the Menza, undamaged by the attack, and Erik sat in a corner with Annalisa on his right and Schneider on his left. He looked from one to the other and asked, "Are you two something more than boss and worker?" He pointed at both of them.

Herr Schneider looked at Annalisa, and she moved her head to indicate a 'yes.' He turned back to Erik with a self-satisfied grin.

"Yes, we are more than worker and boss and more than good friends." Herr Schneider touched Annalisa's hand. "Apparently, everyone but you knows it. I have asked this woman to marry me, but she hasn't taken the bait yet. On the other hand, she hasn't said no, so all hope has not died. Perhaps you could help me with that."

"I don't want to call you Herr Schneider all night, so could you give me something shorter I could use?"

"Jonas is my first name, and that will do fine. May I call you Erik?" Jonas used the familiar du form.

Erik shook his hand again and said, "I'm very pleased to meet you, Jonas, and Erik will do fine. Now, what do we have to discuss?" He also switched to the personal du.

Jonas looked at Annalisa; she nodded, and he returned to Erik.

"Annalisa is trying to improve our treatment of the workers, particularly the slave workers, but the SS guards are getting in her way. It is basic decency that we feed them as we feed our citizens and that they have comfortable shoes and warm clothing. Annalisa plans to ask the people of Heilbronn for clothes and shoes, and the factory will supply the food. She has promised to help me by organizing the people in St. Kilian's Church, where you worship, and I will organize the catholic parish. Together, we will help them if we can get the permission of the SS guards."

"That's great, but how do you expect me to help? I go back to my squadron in six days."

"Annalisa tells me you've tamed Kriminaldirektor Richter, and perhaps you could get him on our side."

Erik opened his mouth to explain, but Jonas raised his hand."

"I understand that he hasn't got any official authority where the Zwangsarbiter are concerned, but he could contact the SS for us and find out what is possible."

Erik said, "So, you want me to talk to Major Richter and find out if he will risk his career, and perhaps his life, by asking the most vicious people in Germany to be merciful and kind..." He leaned ahead... "It might surprise you, but I'm going to be honest; the members of the SS are not merciful and kind people! Himmler actually chooses them for the opposite qualities!"

Annalisa put her hand over Erik's. "Until you try, you won't know what Richter will do." He understood now why Annalisa had seated him between Jonas and herself—he was meat in their sandwich.

Jonas took his turn. "I hear you talked Major Richter into emptying the basement cells at Gestapo headquarters. I'm hearing the people in town say he is a changed man, and Annalisa says you are responsible." He hesitated before he added, "I am sure you know that there are people, worse than the SS, who would like to stop us from doing this. Those people are not Major Richter's friends; they hate him because they think he has gotten soft."

Jonas lowered his voice, looking around the empty room before he went on, "But we have to do this. These people are dying as we talk about trying to save them. They are imprisoned in a salt mine and a work camp with little or nothing to eat. This inhumanity has to stop, or we won't be able to live with ourselves when this war is over! They are human beings like us, and we must work together, or we shall certainly perish together."

Erik lifted both hands in front of him as a gesture of surrender and said, "All right, I'll do what I can. The major appears to be a reasonable man, now that he is terrified of hanging if, or, more likely when we lose the war. I'll appeal to his survival instincts, and perhaps he will use similar tactics with the SS."

Annalisa looked down at the table, her voice uncharacteristically soft. "The problem is that most of these men have so much blood on their hands now that no amount of goodwill will save them once the British and Americans see what they've done. The Allies may hang the whole country—after a fair trial, of course."

She looked at Erik, then at Jonas. Despite her negative outlook, Erik could still detect an optimistic glint in her eye.

A quarter-litre of local beer arrived, accompanied by Jägerschnitzel, peeled potatoes and a side dish of sauerkraut. They ate enthusiastically, and when they finished, the waiter brought a carafe of real coffee and a small plate of rhubarb torte. The workers' Menza had no issues with rationing.

Erik spoke as he looked into a space outside the room, "Have you been married before, Jonas?"

He had unintentionally inferred that marriage was in Jonas's immediate future and intended to correct that, but Jonas spoke too quickly.

"Yes, I had a happy marriage to a beautiful and caring woman. She gave me three children—a son and two daughters." He looked at Erik sadly. "My son died in a messerschmitt 109 over England when he was eighteen, and my daughters live in Berlin with their husbands. My wife died of cancer a little over a year ago. I was devastated for months and still suffer from bouts of depression, but Annalisa and Marita have come to my rescue. I've fallen in love with your mother-in-law, but this lady believes I need more time."

"Jonas, that's not what I said!" Annalisa wagged her head. "I said I needed more time, and I did."

"Did?" Jonas's face lit up as he leaned across Erik. "What if I asked you to marry me right now...?"

Erik, feeling like a giant wart on a small frog, suddenly thought the situation was going according to Annalisa's secret plan. He was trapped—feeling like an intruder and suspecting that was what Annalisa wanted.

Annalisa leaned in front of Erik and spoke to Jonas, speculatively, "I would say yes, but I have to stay with Marita and help care for the children. As a matter of fact, I came here this morning to tell you that I intended to quit!"

Erik wanted to say that Marita could handle that without her, but he couldn't think of how she could. He was quite sure that if she married Jonas, Annalisa would be going somewhere else to live.

Annalisa returned to her natural sitting position, and Jonas emphatically laid his hand on the table in front of Erik. He put his arm across Erik's chest and pointed at Annalisa. "You can't quit! I'll hire someone to take care of all the workers' children. You and Marita have been discussing a children's care center for all the workers—I'll find a place for it in this building and let Marita run it if she wants to!"

Jonas sounded very accommodating, but Erik knew from experience that Annalisa typically started negotiations small and then raised her bid exponentially.

Annalisa smiled, and Jonas backed off Erik's chest. She continued, relaxed—a warning for Jonas—but would he see it in time? She issued her subsequent demand, masked as a speculative suggestion.

"What if Marita and the children want to come and live with us in your house? You've got a large house that's much too big for two people."

Erik wondered how she knew that. Jonas smiled as though he knew he had her; reeling in the line, Jonas mistakenly believed he was the fisherman and she was the fish at the edge of the boat.

"They are welcome to live with us." And then, in his naïve eagerness, he added, "I will put that, and anything else you want, in writing! Marry me, and you get anything you want—I love you, Annalisa."

Erik discarded his belief that businessmen knew anything about negotiating.

Annalisa grabbed it and said, "Yes... " Erik smiled so broadly he had to look down to hide it—he could hear Annalisa's silent 'gotcha'... "I will want it in writing. And make it clear that when you marry me, you get my grandchildren!"

And then she surprised Erik and threw Jonas a bone.

"Marita and the children won't be coming to live with us unless circumstances force it, but the children will be sleeping over whenever I want them to—I do love them dearly."

And then, another condition. Erik felt sorry for Jonas…a sheep against a wolf.

"Of course, I assume you would have no problem helping Marita financially, should the need arise?" She leaned over and covered Jonas's hands with hers.

"I love you and want you to be the most important thing in my life, but Marita and my grandchildren are part of me!"

Erik noted that she hadn't included him in that group. Jonas immediately replied without thinking,

"Of course they are, and I will love them as though they were my own, and Marita can count on my support. It's a deal!" He grasped her hand over Erik's chest and, shaking it in both of his, said, "Thank you, Annalisa, thank you so very much!"

Erik decided that if he ever had a business, he would hire women to do his negotiating, preferably his mother-in-law. And somehow, he suspected she wasn't done with Jonas yet.

Jonas stood; Erik pushed his chair back, got to his feet and shook the pushover's hand. Erik had no idea what he had done, but the man was happy, and Erik was delighted to be out of the space between the dickering pair. Annalisa was also pleased—that was unmistakable and, Erik thought, understandable.

He momentarily considered the episode, realizing Annalisa had probably set him up. She had used him to get the best deal possible out of the man she was going to marry anyway, deal or no deal. Somehow, as he looked from Annalisa to Jonas, he knew there would be more before she finished with him.

CHAPTER FOURTEEN

7 April 1944

Those who have no fear often don't understand the situation.

Erik telephoned Kriminaldirektor Richter, and the major surprised him when he seemed to expect and welcome his call. He told Erik to come to his office as soon as possible.

Jonas offered his car, a new mercedes, and when he and Annalisa entered Richter's office, smelled real coffee, and found a pile of Belgian chocolates on the small table, Erik tried to imagine what the man had up his sleeve.

"Kriminaldirektor Richter, I would like to introduce my mother-in-law, Annalisa Mueller." Erik stepped aside. "She's convinced me to bring her here, and I think you should listen to what we have to say!"

Major Richter took Annalisa's outstretched hand, shook it gently, and ignored the hostility that she made no attempt to hide. He said, "It pleases me to meet you, Frau Müller," smoothly overlooking her attitude.

She looked at the chocolates, smiled, and took her hand back. "I will reserve my decision on whether or not I am pleased to meet you, Herr Kriminaldirektor. I have heard disturbing stories about what you do here."

Erik cringed, but the major said pleasantly, "I trust you will judge me on what you see and not on what you hear from others."

"I am not a Nazi, Kriminaldirektor Richter—you can depend on my judging you by what you do."

Erik expected Richter to kick them out, but his expression was of admiration. He paused for a few seconds, gave Annalisa a smile that said, 'touché,' and then graciously motioned them to sit on the sofa behind the table. They obliged, and he pulled up a plush leather chair and sat opposite them.

"Now, what can I do for you?" He poured a cup of coffee and slid it in front of Annalisa, then did the same for Erik. The coffee aroma was intoxicating.

Major Richter watched Annalisa shovel three heaping teaspoons of sugar into her coffee before he said, "Frau Müller, I assure you that I am not the villain that some people imagine me to be."

Annalisa gave him no quarter. "I should hope not! But you cannot be a Kriminaldirektor in the Gestapo without having some villain in you—it's a prerequisite for the job."

Erik liked his coffee black, without sugar. He sipped it quietly while Annalisa annoyed the major, thinking this was not a good start. He decided to interrupt.

"Major Richter, I will get to the point. Annalisa works at the NSU motorcycle factory, where the SS separates the slave workers from the company workers. She wants to help the Zwangsarbiter, but the guards refuse to allow her even to speak to them!"

<hr />

Richter spoke as he filled his cup. "I am aware that we have slave labourers in our factories; it may surprise you that there are over eight thousand of them in Heilbronn. They are, for the most part, prisoners taken from countries that have resisted us. The SS says they separate them from the German workers for their protection."

He crossed his legs, sipped his coffee, and continued. "As I have told Herr Schneider as late as this morning, I have nothing to do with these people, and if your request has anything to do with them, I'm afraid we are wasting our time. I suggest we enjoy the company, the coffee, and the chocolates. On your way out the door, you may take as many chocolates for your children as you wish."

Annalisa started to rise from her seat, but Erik took her hand and gently pulled her down. He said to Richter, "You know who we need to see, and you are aware that this situation can't continue. Slave labour violates the laws of human decency, and whether you are personally responsible or not, you are at the top of the organization that will carry the blame."

Major Richter looked at Erik for a few seconds before replying.

"Yes, of course, I know who is in charge of the Zwangsarbiter, but I am certain you would not want to meet with him. He truly does not qualify as a member of the human race as you know it, and he will have you both for his dinner. You cannot influence these people, and I am sure you do not want them looking into certain details of your life!"

Erik felt apprehension creeping in as he said, "That's why we're here. We need you to help us in any way you can."

Richter opened the door a crack. "I assure you there is nothing I can do, but before I send you home, please tell me what you imagine I can do."

Annalisa looked at Erik—he nodded. She then described the slave labourers' conditions, ending with the present situation in the salt mine. Major Richter listened while occasionally sipping his coffee. He sat back, comfortable in his chair, silently watching Annalisa as she talked.

When she finished, Erik waited a few seconds while Annalisa and the major stared at one another like two alley cats claiming the same territory, then took the ball from Annalisa.

"Although we believe they should be freed, we are not asking for the prisoners' release; we are more realistic than that." Erik put down his coffee and leaned across the table. "We are asking the SS to allow us to treat the slave labourers as human beings, thereby perhaps saving those SS from the hangman. The citizens of Heilbronn want to help them with food and clothing—they want them housed in heated and sanitary housing. We only ask them to step aside so the people of Heilbronn can do this."

He threw in the bait. "I believe we can increase production if we give them food, clothing, and a reason to hope. If the factory has that, it will gladly share that increased profit with the party." And then he threw in the poison. "But, if we go away empty-handed, I'm afraid that you and your friends in the SS will be on record as having refused an opportunity to help save lives."

Richter set his cup on the table and passed the plate of chocolates to Annalisa. She took one and noisily peeled off the wrapping, noting the Belgian stamp. He set the plate down and took his fourth.

"I understand what you want, but I cannot give you any encouragement. I am not in a position to help. Contrary to your assumption, the people in charge of those workers are not friends of mine. They are dangerous people, even to a Gestapo Kriminaldirektor."

"All right... " Erik put his coffee down and leaned back. "I'm going to give you some facts that may be useful in your attempts to help the Zwangsarbiter."

Richter sat back in his chair with a neutral expression on his face. Erik began his pitch.

"I've shot down twenty-three bombers in three years as a night-fighter pilot. On a good night, we have approximately three hundred fighters to attack the British bombers and about a thousand fighters to meet the American Eighth Air Force during their daylight raids. The day fighters are no match for the American mustang and British spitfire escorts, and even if we could eliminate the Allied fighters, the American bombers have formidable defences. We are losing fighters faster than we can replace them and their pilots. During the British night raids, including the planes downed by anti-aircraft batteries, we destroy an average of fifteen bombers. There are three hundred lancaster and halifax bombers in a small raid and up to a thousand on a big one."

Erik looked at Major Richter as he put his cup down. "They have accurate electronic navigation and destroy a city and kill thousands of civilians on every raid—in nineteen-forty-four, their targeting is so good they never miss their target! The English General Harris has promised to eradicate our cities one by one, and he is succeeding at a breathtaking rate, and Heilbronn's name will top the list before the end of this year!"

Major Richter put his elbows on the arms of his chair and slid his fingers together on his chest.

"Yes, you told me this at our first meeting, and I was impressed. But since then, I have asked some questions. Those bombers are not as accurate as you would have me believe. Sometimes, they kill more cows than people, although I will admit they are German cows and represent a considerable loss for the farmer." He smiled.

Erik put his hands in his lap so he wouldn't take more chocolates.

"The farmers have lost no cows for at least a year, and I assure you that the British can hit a city, even a small one like Heilbronn, every time, with every bomb. They have improved their navigation in the past year to the point where pathfinders, usually mosquitos, drop their target markers exactly on whatever objective Bomber Command assigns them...in the dark...from above the clouds. Hamburg was an example of what General Harris and his British Bomber Command can do, and they get better results with every raid."

Richter took a pipe out of his shirt pocket, tapped it upside down on an ashtray in front of him, and stuffed it with tobacco from an orange packet. He waved the unlit pipe and said, "I will believe that in part, but I am not a fool that you can deceive. Keep talking, but be very careful!" He scratched a match on the side of the small box it had been in and lit his pipe. Erik noted that Annalisa made a face, but Richter didn't acknowledge her discomfort.

'Careful' was a luxury Erik could not afford, not with his irate mother-in-law sitting beside him.

He took a deep breath and began, knowing he was walking through a minefield.

◇◇◇◇◇◇◇◇◇◇◇◇◇◇◇◇◇◇◇◇◇◇◇◇◇◇◇◇◇◇◇◇

"The British and Americans are building bombers at many times the rate we can destroy them, and there is no limit to their capacity to build fighters to defend them. In every bomber stream, mosquitos hide among the bombers, trying to catch a night fighter in the act. On my last mission, my best friend paid the ultimate price when I didn't see one of them."

Major Richter sucked on his pipe and blew the smoke well away from Annalisa, but she still made a face at him. Erik tried to ignore her obvious discomfort.

"The bombers they are building are bigger, faster, and carry more bombs than the ones we shoot down—I could make a case that we technically do them a favour when we destroy their old technology. Our capacity to build fighters and train competent crews is becoming more critical every time they destroy another factory or shoot down a fighter. I am not trying to deceive you—I face this reality on every mission. Do your information sources have such first-hand knowledge, or are they quoting Goebbels?"

Richter remained stoic, but Erik sensed a crack and leaned forward. "In another six months, we will not have one intact city; most of our factories will be closed or destroyed, and you will search a long time before you find a family that has not lost loved ones. When this is over, those who have lost the most will judge those who are responsible!"

Erik watched Major Richter's complexion change. Red stripes spread from his starched collar upward. Erik had expected Richter to stop his rant and was surprised when the major allowed him to continue.

151

"The next problem, and perhaps the most dangerous, is the Russian Army. Today, they are in Poland, across the river from Warsaw. The Russians have destroyed three armies since they destroyed the Sixth Army at Stalingrad, killing or capturing a million German men, but who's counting? Certainly not Goebbels! And you should note that two of those armies were elite Panzer armies—Waffen SS—the best we've got!"

Richter held his pipe before him, shaking it as he said, "This is treason, and I should have you arrested!" Richter slammed his fist on the arm of his chair, then picked out another chocolate with his free hand.

Erik decided the fist-slamming was bait and forged ahead. "Treason?—Those are events reported by our state Propaganda Ministerium; Goebbels has personally reported these facts. I hear it on Hitler's radio station every night at six o'clock!"

Major Richter said, "Go on, finish what you have to say...I have work to do," then sucked hard on his pipe.

Erik did not like how this was going and came close to leaving. The look Annalisa gave him said that he should keep trying. He shrugged and went on.

"Russian tanks and artillery now outnumber ours at least four to one, and it's getting worse daily. Russian factories run unfettered, day and night, and a steady stream of U.S. parts and equipment flows to the Russians through the Arctic Ocean. The Americans are building tanks and planes for the Russians—and we can't bomb those factories because we can't reach them!"

Erik lowered his voice. "Of course, you must understand that I am not saying that Germany will lose the war—I believe in miracles! In fact, I pray for a Hitler miracle." He looked for a reaction, but Richter had interrogated too many people to expose his thoughts on his face.

Major Richter moved to stand, but Erik motioned him to stay in his chair. Richter said, "We should end this interview before you go too far!"

Erik looked at Annalisa, and her expression egged him on—she wasn't concerned about the potential cost—Erik was on a roll.

As he took another chocolate, he said, "There is a joke among the reconnaissance pilots that the island England occupies would sink if not for the air defence balloons holding it up! Tanks, British and American lorries, artillery, and men from all over the globe cover the island from north to south and east to west. The harbours are plugged with landing barges and ships ready to transport this war equipment to France. The Allies control the skies over England and France, leaving us no way to stop them when they decide it's time to cross the channel. We avoid airspace west of the German border, and there are plans to move my squadron out of Belgium into Germany." He popped the chocolate into his mouth.

Major Richter waited, expressionless. Erik sipped coffee and let it absorb the chocolate before he swallowed. He went on, "You know very well that they will soon cross the channel, and once they are on the beach, they will send ships in a line stretching to the horizon, bringing thousands of tons of guns, tanks, and fuel. Hundreds of thousands of men—at least a million are waiting—will keep coming until the sheer weight of their numbers overwhelms our Western army!"

It was Erik's turn to wait. Richter looked at the wall and said evenly, "You might as well go on... You are in too deep to stop now."

"They will attack our men and tanks with a thousand ground-attack fighters and bombers, swarming over our armies like bees. Aircraft cover the grass on every airfield in England...parked arrogantly in rows because we don't have the aircraft or pilots to attack them. They are waiting for the word to strike.

"Six months after the invasion, the Allies will be in Germany! That is a prediction Goebbels will not make publicly, but he knows it is inevitable!"

Major Richter's face was red, his eyes wide. He said, far too loudly, "That is not the intelligence that I have! Where do you get your information?"

◇◇◇◇◇◇◇◇◇◇◇◇◇◇◇◇◇◇◇◇◇◇◇◇◇◇◇◇◇◇◇◇◇◇◇◇◇

Erik spoke softly to lessen the impact but kept the sternness, knowing Richter's talent for discerning the truth. "There are reconnaissance aircraft on every Luftwaffe base, flying almost every day. The pilots eat and sleep with us, and they see everything the camera sees. There is no such thing as a secret in the barracks, and we all know the truth...that we are fighting to buy the time to get a better surrender deal. Everyone hopes that we can prevent the destruction of our country and save our loved ones, but few believe it is possible." His tone was now sad and quiet. "Now, you must decide whether to arrest me or work with us to save those Zwangsarbiter. If you work with us, perhaps you can save yourself and the SS officers who are now responsible for them."

Major Richter sat with his hands together in his lap. He ignored the implications of what Erik said and asked, "What about the new wonder weapons? Are you saying that the Führer is lying?"

Erik couldn't believe Richter was stupid, so he played it straight.

<hr>

"You are not a fool! You know he has lied since the beginning; why would you believe him now? If we have a wonder weapon, where is it? We have messerschmitt jet fighters. Our Führer says it is the fastest plane in the world, but we keep them hidden because American mustangs and the new British spitfires can catch them and shoot them down. There are rumours that we have a bomb that could destroy a city, but why not use it to destroy a Russian Army? The Russians would surely return to Moscow and beg for peace if we used such a weapon on their army! If such a bomb existed, don't you think the Americans and the British would be the first to have it? Our best scientists and physicists now live in the United States of America. Reason dictates that the Americans will find something for them to do!"

Erik was tempted to leave it there, but Richter seemed to be weakening.

"When was the last time a German bomber flew over England? France? Our unguided rockets and drones are little more than a nuisance to the British—they kill British cows and sheep by the dozen but mean nothing to the Americans and Russians. Katya rockets are far more effective, and the Russians have hundreds of thousands of them!"

The blood in Major Richter's red face slowly drained until his normal colour returned. His face betrayed him before he spoke—Erik knew he was winning.

"If you are right, why wouldn't Hitler make peace long before the Allies reach our borders? Perhaps he is waiting for them to fight us where we can hurt them most. Surely, our enemies would negotiate to save the thousands of Allied lives they would sacrifice in a house-to-house battle on German soil!"

While Richter filled Erik's cup, Erik, now completely off the wagon, took another chocolate. He picked up the cup, added coffee to the sweetness in his mouth and swallowed while holding it in his cheek.

"Major Richter, you know why Hitler, Himmler, Göring and the rest of that gang can't make peace. Their carefully documented crimes guarantee that they are dead men in every scenario. The Allies will correctly claim what they've done to be beyond murder, deserving of death—and their public trial and execution is a certainty! But more powerful than that is Hitler's ego! He cannot, and he will not admit defeat!" Erik waited, but Richter was deep in thought. Erik got his attention by passing him a chocolate, then took care of the second point.

"Why would the Allies fight house-to-house? If a German dares to shoot at them from a building, it will be a pile of rubble within minutes, covering the German soldier's and any other person's body in or near the flattened building!"

Richter tried again, "The Allies are sane people, and they would surely make a deal to save many thousands of lives on both sides... Don't you agree?"

<hr>

Erik patiently started again, "Do you think the British or the Russians would give Hitler immunity for peace now that they are on his doorstep? They won't lose thousands of men—they will knock down every house with their bombs and guns before they sacrifice their men by fighting their way through towns and villages. They will flatten and burn city after German city until nothing is left! Genghis Khan was a mouse compared with Stalin and Churchill! The more we resist, the more we lose. They can fight us until the last German dies, and no brick sits on top of another! We invaded Russia and murdered its people: probably, when the truth is known, we've murdered millions of Russian civilians. They will have revenge— they will laugh at an apology!"

"You paint a bleak picture, but no one can tell the future, least of all a mere pilot." He looked at Annalisa. "Do you believe this treasonous talk? Are you willing to wager with your life?"

Annalisa smiled sweetly. "Maybe you should ask yourself that question, Major Richter. If Erik is right, and you do nothing, you will hang for your crimes—thousands will witness against you! The SS leadership will suffer the same or a worse fate. When the Allies knock on a door... any door in Heilbronn, they will find a witness. No one will admit they supported the Nazis! The National Socialists will disappear and leave you and your SS friends standing naked before your accusers!"

Erik talked before Richter could comment. He had one last important point he wanted to leave with Richter. He said calmly, "You cannot dismiss the reality that Western governments are heavily influenced and financed by Jewish money. The people who finance politics control them, and Jews control the most influential companies and banks in the Western world. They are not the complacent 'lambs to the slaughter' that Hitler thinks they are. The Jewish people are intelligent and hardworking and will fight, given the opportunity and tools. Do not underestimate their determination! When this is over, they will not rest until the people responsible for the torture and murder of their people swing from a rope or die from a Jewish bullet! And I will wager that more than half the Zwangsarbiter in Heilbronn are Jews!" Erik used his fingers to illustrate the coup de grâce.

"I don't know for certain what happened to the Jews in Heilbronn, but my wife's best friend and the mother of the children we adopted died in a work camp in Berlin. She has a mother, a father and other relatives living in America—relatives who left shortly before the *Kristallnacht* horror, and they will turn over every rock in their search for her! Millions of Jews from all over the world will use their power and money to find their families, and they will appropriately punish everyone who had even the smallest role in this horrible thing you and I know the Nazis are doing. What do you think will be the fate of those at the top of this ladder? How far down the ladder will they go before their lust for revenge is satisfied? Can they ever forgive any of us? Why would they forgive any German who stood by while this happened?" Richter sat frozen to his chair, motionless—his pipe had gone out, and he chewed on the stem. Erik said, "You must give them a good reason to forgive you—an apology won't do!"

Major Richter spoke like a beaten man, "My God, this is treason, and I am a traitor for listening to you. We are all traitors!"

Erik said, "Are we? Does a traitor want what is best for our country, and isn't that the measure of loyalty? Or do you think loyalty to our country means blind obedience to a lunatic even as he destroys that country?"

Major Richter rose from his chair and paced the floor. Erik looked up at him. His coffee was cold.

Erik said, "Hitler may say it's treason, but when the Allies are in Heilbronn, the National Socialist Party will have nothing to say about it—they won't exist! A new government will determine whether you are a traitor or a patriot. I am suggesting that you and the people who control the fate of the Zwangsarbiter have a chance to save yourselves, and if you don't take it, you are betting your life that Germany will defeat Russia, England, and America. If you kill me, you will gain nothing and lose what might be your last opportunity to save yourself."

Major Richter sat down and leaned toward Erik. "You want me to help you with the Zwangsarbiter, but I can't defy the SD or the SS. They will kill me just as the Allies will, but sooner and more painfully."

Erik felt a twinge of sympathy for the man, but it passed quickly... "You need witnesses who will protect you when the Allies come. Most of the people in Heilbronn, who are not true Nazis, want to help the workers living in those terrible conditions. If you can find a way to permit these good Samaritans to help, you will be a hero to them. Who better to witness for you than the Zwangsarbiter and the good people of Heilbronn?"

⬦⬦⬦⬦⬦⬦⬦⬦⬦⬦⬦⬦⬦⬦⬦⬦⬦⬦⬦⬦⬦⬦⬦⬦⬦⬦⬦⬦⬦⬦⬦⬦⬦⬦

Major Richter stood up and began pacing, head bowed, hands behind his back. Erik and Annalisa waited, and he finally stopped, looked at Erik, then at Annalisa. "You know that I know about your Belgian friends, including the beautiful opera singer, Juliette—and I know what your church minister has been up to." He spoke confidently, and Erik believed him. He and Annalisa could not hide their shock.

The major smiled. "I see that you didn't know that—this is the reason for the chocolates; they are Belgian, as is my last bit of real coffee... clues you didn't see." He swept his hand across the little table. He looked at Annalisa. "Perhaps I can talk to the SD in private...I know some of them through our frequent meetings, and I could feel them out under four eyes. They are intelligent, brutal men, and, in their hearts, they all suspect, as I do, that what you are saying is true. When the Russians didn't slow down at the Polish border, we realized they would not stop at Germany's."

When Annalisa opened her mouth to speak, Major Richter put his

157

hands in a 'stop' position. "I will try, and I might succeed, but there is no guarantee."

Annalisa said, "I understand, but failure will worsen things."

Erik said, "We all understand the problems, but if you can do this, it will count heavily in your favour if the worst happens. And if the worst doesn't happen, what have you lost?"

Major Richter slumped back in his chair and looked from Erik to Annalisa as he spoke. "If I can do this, many innocent people will benefit, and later, when I need help, I want you to consider that." He put his hands together, his elbows on his knees, and looked at the floor. Erik and Annalisa waited. He lifted his head and said, "If you could speak to your Belgian friends on my behalf, I would be most grateful. Monsieur Durand and I have certain interests in common, interests that could influence my situation in the future."

◇◇◇◇◇◇◇◇◇◇◇◇◇◇◇◇◇◇◇◇◇◇◇◇◇◇

Erik rose from the sofa and took four chocolates "for the children."

Major Richter rose with him and took his hand. They shook slowly; the major laid his left hand on Erik's. "I'm afraid you are right, but I am also afraid it might be too late. Hitler has no way out except to die in battle. We all know he is mad, and limiting the damage may not be possible." He released a confused Erik's hand. "I will contact you soon."

Richter faced Annalisa, and she stood up to reluctantly shake his hand. He cupped his hands and dipped them in the chocolates, getting almost half of them. Annalisa opened her handbag, and Richter dumped them in. He emptied the plate into the bag, and the smile on Annalisa's face showed Erik that Richter had just scored a goal.

The mercedes engine purred quietly in the background as they drove back to the factory. Annalisa looked over at Erik as he held the steering wheel, deep in thought, and asked, "What are you thinking—will he help us?"

Erik felt confident that Major Richter would do his best but was not optimistic that the SD or the SS would agree to anything. He stared at the road as he said, "I think he will try. At least, that is his intention, or we would both be in his cellar having our fingernails extracted. He knows I am right; he has seen too many things that disprove the government's official line. Every day, a few more Germans understand that peace will not come before the destruction of the country, and

158

those who believe that the heads of the Gestapo and SS will not roll for their crimes might as well believe in fairies! Major Richter is openly terrified, as he was even before we clarified the situation. His fear will be contagious when he speaks with his friends in the SD and SS. The level of power in the room will be high enough that those men can openly speak to one another about things we can't."

Erik drove slowly. "My worry now is that our family won't survive. I feel I have no control over what happens. Whether I shoot down a dozen bombers more or less doesn't make any difference—the power of the Allied bombs is something that wakes me in a cold sweat. I have seen entire cities on fire—it's enough to terrify Lucifer!"

Erik glanced at Annalisa, then took his eyes back to the road. "Heilbronn has been very lucky because it is small, but that will end... Heilbronn's number will come up. Allied Armadas are destroying city after city, and if the war goes on long enough, they will run out of larger targets and come for Heilbronn."

Annalisa was silent as Erik pulled into the factory yard. Erik decided to change the subject. "Do you want help telling Marita that you're getting married?"

Annalisa shook her head as the car stopped. "Oh, she knows I'm going to marry Jonas. We've discussed it, and she knew I would try and get the best deal I could."

Erik made no move to get out of the car. He grinned as he said, "So, I believe I've been the unwitting accomplice in a conspiracy. Why don't you open your purse and compensate me for that!"

"You would steal candy from your children?" she asked as she opened her purse.

CHAPTER FIFTEEN

8–13 April 1944

Einem Menschen verzeihen, der nicht bereut, ist wie Zeichnen im Wasser.
(To forgive a man who doesn't repent is to draw a picture on the surface
of the water.)

THE NIGHT PASSED WITHOUT AN AIR RAID, and the following day
dawned cold and bright, perfect for an American attack, but none
came. A mosquito Erik assumed was a reconnaissance aircraft flew
over the city at low altitude and high speed, and two Me109 fighters
crossed the city a few minutes behind it. Erik knew from experience
they wouldn't catch it.

The anti-aircraft batteries had no warning that the mosquito was
coming, and it passed overhead so quickly the gunners had no chance
to sight on it. As he watched the aircraft fly unchallenged, a thousand
kilometres from its base, Erik again wished he could fly a mosquito into
battle. To him, the mosquito symbolized the hopelessness of his job.

Late in the afternoon, Annalisa and Erik walked to the factory. The
weather was warm for late April, and the sun was powerful. They took
a leisurely pace, and Annalisa used the time to bring Erik up to speed
on her negotiations with Jonas.

"Jonas is not just the director of the factory where we work; his
family owns it and other small businesses in Bayern. Jonas has a house
near Weinsberg, and I will move in with him." She changed her tone.
"Today, I would like to discuss Marita, her job in the factory, and the
children. I want this settled before you go back to your squadron."

Erik dismissed the issue with a wave of his hand. "Those problems
belong to Marita and me; you and Jonas shouldn't worry about it." Erik
had considered those obstacles, but he and Marita would find a solution.
They had some money put away, and his pay was enough without Marita
working, but only barely.

He owned a car at the base, and if he sold it... Annalisa interrupted
his thoughts when she stopped and looked toward the river. A child

played at the water's edge, splashing with a piece of wood, getting himself and his sister soaking wet. His mother took the board and whacked his bum with it.

"I didn't put that the way I intended. I want the girls to live with me as much as Marita will let them. Walther can take care of himself and is in school most of the day, so Marita can work if she chooses. I say "chooses" because I will have it in writing that Jonas will help with the finances so that she doesn't need to."

"That's very generous, Annalisa, and perhaps Marita will be happy with that arrangement, but I am learning that she is happier when she does things her way. I've also learned that I am happier when she is happy."

She started walking again, "I guess all that matters is that you and Marita are happy, but I will see that the offer stands for as long as I do."

◇◇◇◇◇◇◇◇◇◇◇◇◇◇◇◇◇◇◇◇◇◇◇◇◇◇◇◇◇◇◇◇

Fräulein Baumann smiled sweetly as Annalisa pointed at Jonas's door on her way past. Erik followed her into the room, feeling uncomfortable. Jonas stood and blushed when Annalisa kissed his lips. He shook hands with Erik, then said, "I have good news for you—the Zwangsarbiter are out of the mine today and temporarily living in a military barracks in Neckarsulm."

"Wonderful!" Annalisa clapped once. "Do you think that Major Richter had a hand in this?"

"I have no idea, but there is more. Wehrmacht soldiers are now guarding the workers—the SS has turned over control to the regular army. I have met with the officer in charge, and he has told me they will build a new barracks for them and the Jewish prisoners, with showers, proper toilets, and heat. During air raids, the guards will take the workers into the salt mines."

Erik almost jumped for joy. "Oh, I smell Richter in this all right—I had no idea he had this much power!"

He waited for a response; Jonas put a hand on Erik's shoulder, squeezed it and asked, "What did you promise him?"

"I think you should ask your bride-to-be what we both promised."

Annalisa said, "Erik and I promised we would help him when the Allies take over the country and begin punishing the Nazi leaders."

Jonas stood with his back against the desk, both hands supporting him as he leaned back.

162

"I've listened to you two talk about defeat—you even have our leaders in jail or hung as criminals—but there is an old saying... "Man plans, and God laughs.""

Erik looked into Jonas's eyes; he couldn't read him. He said, "Believe me, Jonas, within a year, maximum two, many Nazi leaders will be dead or in jail. I know the forces aligned against us; their power is endless and relentless. There is no chance that Hitler will negotiate because he is dead in any scenario. But until he dies, no one else can negotiate for Germany. If someone or something doesn't kill Hitler, we will fight until Germany's Armageddon."

Jonas sat down.

"In your mind, would I be guilty of something? Slaves are working in my factory, although I have no control over them. If the miracle you and Annalisa appear to have accomplished turns out to be real, there will be a significant change in their conditions, but they will continue to be prisoners. There will be additional problems for us now because we have some control over their welfare and must share the responsibility."

"Then you had better do your best for them." Erik decided to go further. "I would put their pay in a Swiss franc account, as you likely do with your own money. When this is over, any new government will force every company profiting from slave labour to spend fortunes searching for those slaves. When the government finds them or their families, those companies will be forced to pay compensation. If you take care of that now, the new government will not treat you as harshly as those who don't. Show goodwill, and you will receive it."

Jonas appeared embarrassed. "The amount of money we make from this war is obscene, contradicting Hitler's claim that he is behind the working man. He is behind Krupp, Mercedes, Messerschmitt, Telefunken, AG Farben and every other big company in Germany. The Nazis charge next to nothing for slave labour, but because of war demand, companies receive high prices for their products!

"I promise you the money will be there for them as soon as there is an administration to handle the transaction, and we will keep track of every worker we can. Of course, I will convert as much as possible to Swiss francs and keep it in Switzerland; the Reichsmark is doomed if Germany loses the war."

Jonas took a deep breath, looked at his bride-to-be, then Erik. "Now, what can I do for you and your family?"

Erik had agreed to walk to the factory to discuss Marita's problem continuing to work there, but he could not think of a solution other than Marita quitting her job.

Erik glanced at his mother-in-law as he said, "As Annalisa predicted, Marita will have a problem when her mother moves out of our house. Weinsberg is too far from us for Annalisa to be of any help to her. Marita wants to keep working but doesn't want to give up seeing her children every day, even if they are with her mother. We have no one else to help with them, and they are far too young to be left alone while Marita works."

Annalisa stood up, walked around Jonas's desk, and sat on it, facing him.

"I told Erik you would sign a contract that we would help out in any way we can, including financially. You're not going to disappoint me, are you?"

Jonas leaned back in his chair, and Erik jumped in.

"We don't need your financial help if Marita can work. I see the job as the problem, not money."

Jonas laughed uneasily as he looked at his betrothed. "Of course, I would never disappoint you..." Erik could hear the hesitation in Jonas's voice. "I've had enough experience with you to know better than that! But how can I resolve this problem with money?"

Jonas suddenly cheered up. "Why don't Erik and I let you and Marita solve the problem? However, you must remember that half the world is trying to destroy our factory, the source of most of my money. If you and Erik are right about the world ending in a few months, we must make contingency plans founded on a worst-case scenario!"

As Erik anticipated, Annalisa had her solution ready. "I know there are a lot of women in Heilbronn with children who would gladly work here if they could bring them with them. Some women working here have young ones at home alone or running around the neighbourhood with no supervision. They would work longer hours every week if they had a solution."

Jonas jumped in.

"Yes, I already agreed that you and Marita can have space in this building to set up a care center for our employees' children. We agreed that the two of you would organize it."

He looked at her, hoping the discussion was over. "Will there be anything else?"

Annalisa leaned over and gave him a sincere "thank you" kiss. "There is just one more teeny-tiny thing. Marita and I think fourteen hours is too long for women to work. We will find more employees if we can offer a place for their children, but we will also need to reduce their work hours each shift. We think that eight hours should be the maximum."

Jonas broke in, waving his arms. "No, no, you promised me longer hours—shorter hours won't work. The factory has to run fourteen hours, preferably more, now that the Allies are pressuring us!" Erik could see from the expression on Jonas's face that this was a bridge too far. The man's face expressed dread at drawing a line between himself and his future bride.

Annalisa's smile was not a sign of defeat or victory. She was obviously very pleased with herself as she said, "We think you should run the factory sixteen hours a day and split the shifts into four-hour segments—only a man would come up with a fourteen-hour day! The Zwangsarbiter will use the same four-hour shifts, and we want them to work alongside and among us. There are children in the Jewish camp, and we would care for them along with ours. Furthermore," —Jonas cringed—"I would like to change the terms of their employment. First, they will be called Gastarbiter, guest workers, from now on—second, you will suggest what you think they should earn, and you must get them to agree. Of course, since you would pay for their upkeep and supply their living quarters, you would stop paying three marks an hour to the bastards in the Party."

Jonas got up, shoulders rounded, took three steps to a cupboard with glass doors, pulled out what looked like Scotch Whiskey and filled three shot glasses.

"I don't think the Nazi party will go that far, even with Major Richter's help. In any case, I propose a toast to the new management team. I know when I'm beaten."

Despite his good nature, Jonas seemed nervous. His labour costs had doubled since his future wife and son-in-law had come to visit.

Resigned to his fate, he said, "Oh well...If you are right about the war, this will be of no consequence in a few months when the Allies shut our factory." He raised his glass. "In the meantime, I will raise prices to cover the cost. Live today—tomorrow?... Who knows?"

They raised their glasses in a resounding "Prost" and downed the scotch. Jonas and Erik coughed, but Annalisa wiped her mouth and smiled like a spider who found a fat fly in her web.

The evening meal was on the table when Erik walked into the kitchen. The girls ran to greet him and wrapped their arms around him until he kissed each of them. Walther waved from his chair, said, "Hi, Vati," and went back to staring at a heaping plate of pork hocks and sauerkraut. It was his favourite meal, and, for now, it had his full attention. He used his fingers to pick at stray strings of sauerkraut as he waited impatiently for his father and mother to seat themselves. Erik sat at the head of the table, the family joined hands, and he thanked God for the food, his family, and Major Richter's help.

"Where's Oma?" asked Brigitte.

"Yes, where's Oma?" Walther repeated the question as if that would guarantee a truthful answer.

Marita said, "She and Herr Schneider are making wedding plans tonight...uh... She won't be home until tomorrow."

Marita looked at Erik—he shrugged, wore a grin that said, "You're on your own," then clapped his hands.

"I think I can win a game of memory tonight. Is there anyone here who thinks they can beat me?" The children shrieked for joy.

Erik shuffled the cards while Marita put a recording of folk songs on the turntable. When she sat down, Erik and the children had the cards messed up on the small table between the sofa and a kitchen chair that was reserved for her. Erik sat at one end of the table, Walther on the other, and everyone agreed that Marita should go first. She flipped over a king and a Jack. Erik flipped up a king and tried to decide which card was the king Marita had turned over. He guessed wrong; a ten of hearts grinned back at him.

Elke flipped over a Jack and immediately found the one her mother had unearthed.

For the parents, to the children's delight, things went downhill from there. When the table was almost empty, Erik, who was in last place with one pair, said, "Now I know what they mean when they call someone, "Cannon-fodder."

"What does that mean?" Elke didn't look at her father as she flipped over three pairs, two of which he had exposed, making her pile at least half the deck.

The first game of memory was almost over when the air raid siren began its annoying wail, but they left the cards on the table, gathered blankets and pillows, and started the journey to the shelter. No one complained; each had their job and did it automatically as a routine. The girls' responsibility was jackets and pillows; Walther took care of the lunch basket, and Erik carried the regulation battery lantern that gave almost no light.

The walk to the tower was short and dark. The girls chattered, rehashing the memory game, and Marita and Erik walked hand in hand. There was no moon or illumination beyond the small round pools spilled on the ground by the lights people carried.

The lanterns had metal cones above the light source to prevent the brightness from escaping upward, and they had long wire handles, so the yellow glow was close to the ground to better show the way. They converged from side streets on their way to the General Wever Turm— yellow pools shining on feet shuffling to the tower amidst the murmur of low voices coming from invisible bodies.

Walther walked behind his family, throwing stones at imaginary targets in the dark street, hitting God knows what—until Erik reminded his son that not everyone had a lantern. The siren still wailed as they reached the shelter and entered the lower chamber.

The girls raced ahead to their regular bench with Walther close behind, but they slowed, then stopped when they found it occupied. Erik caught up and paused when he recognized Major Richter and a woman he assumed to be his wife sitting on the bench customarily occupied by the Stephanie family.

◇◇◇◇◇◇◇◇◇◇◇◇◇◇◇◇◇◇◇◇◇◇◇◇◇◇◇◇◇◇◇◇◇◇◇◇

They seemed out of place, dressed as though the raid had interrupted a formal occasion. The major's expensive suit, shirt, and dark red bow tie were starkly out of place. The obviously uncomfortable woman sitting beside him was equally conspicuous, dressed in a

167

stylish leather jacket, feathered hat, and long dark blue skirt. Her eyes darted around the room as if expecting an attack, and her efforts at hiding her discomfort only intensified the impression. Erik, ahead of Marita, walked directly to them and shook the major's hand as he stood up. Marita sat beside Major Richter's wife, laying one of the blankets she carried over her knees before she could object. Every eye in the room was on them, and the uncomfortable silence communicated the intense dislike and fear most of the people of Heilbronn had for the head of the Gestapo.

The siren stopped, the guard closed the door, and Erik addressed Major Richter as he would a friend, "Good evening, Kriminaldirektor Richter; it's good to see you again. I want to thank you for what you've done for the Zwangsarbiter—Annalisa and Jonas are making plans for the townspeople to help them." The room had acquired all the ambience of a tomb.

"Please call me Helmut." The major swung his hand toward his wife. "And I would like to introduce my wife, Frieda."

Erik acknowledged her with a smile, graciously shook her hand and continued, "I'm glad you've decided to come to the shelter. No cellar is safe with the bombs the British are now using!"

"Yes, I agree. I had a Luftschutz Ingenieur look at my cellar and others in the vicinity, and he said that if a delay-fuse bomb hit the house, it would not protect us at all. He also confirmed that most of the British bombs have delay fuses." Helmut looked around the concrete room. "The engineer told me that nothing could harm us here."

The silence continued for a few more minutes as their neighbours digested what they had witnessed, and then, gradually, habitual talking regained momentum.

Walther and the girls made their nests on the floor and immediately fell asleep. The night chatter became a low murmur, and a few bombs exploded—none close enough to wake the children or pause the chatter.

When the old man with the cane announced that it was the railway yard again, Erik realized he had no sense of direction in the round room and could not accurately guess the distance to the bomb blasts. He wondered how many bombs it would take before he could do that, but had no real desire to find out.

The all-clear sounded two hours after they had entered the shelter, and people filed out, still chatting as though what they had to say was so important it couldn't wait. Helmut carried the sleeping Brigitte in his arms, and Erik took Elke, walking side by side, while Marita and Frieda chattered behind them.

"You have done a good thing with the Zwangsarbiter problem." Erik stepped over a brick he knew was higher than its neighbours. "I had no idea you could do it at all, let alone in two days."

"I'm not done yet. The first step was to get the Wehrmacht to take control so I would have at least some authority."

"So, if you would tell me how you accomplished that, I would be very interested."

Helmut seemed eager to go on, "You are not the only Heilbronn officer home on leave. I know of a few officers serving in the Waffen SS who write confidential and truthful reports from our Panzer armies in Russia, which tend to circulate. The information that the SS in Heilbronn receives indicates that our losses on the Russian front are unsustainable, and Russian losses are tolerable compared with their ability to replace them—all contrary to the news from the Goebbels' Propaganda Ministerium."

Erik waited for him to continue, but Helmut seemed lost in thought, so Erik filled in a blank, "So, I suppose you used the Waffen SS information to convince your SD and SS counterparts to get out of the Zwangsarbiter business?"

Helmut recovered from his reverie and smiled. "It was more a question of giving them the opportunity."

Again, there were no details, but Erik already had more information than he had a right to... So he was surprised when Helmut went on.

"I made several phone calls following your recent visit, beginning with Jacques Durand, and the people he directed me to were men in positions of real power. They are convinced, and they convinced me, that the invasion of the lands we occupy in the west is now a certainty, and only Hitler believes that we can stop the Allies once they have a foothold on French ground. The Allied air forces rule the skies with low-level ground-attack fighters and high-level bombers. When the British and Americans turn their lancasters, B17s, and thousands of fighters on our armies instead of our cities, it is childish to believe they will not annihilate those armies."

Erik asked softly, for Helmut's ears only, "Do you believe you can escape?" And wished he hadn't asked the question as soon as it was out of his mouth.

Helmut lowered his voice to match Erik's. "No, I don't think that's possible. No matter what good deeds I do, my defence will be weak and will likely come too late. Unfortunately, I have known for years what is happening in Arbeit camps like Dachau and am indirectly responsible for some of it. I will get credit for the death of more than a few inmates."

Erik had no answer for what sounded like an acknowledgment of Helmut's fate. He walked in silence, adjusted the little girl sleeping in his arms, raising her head onto his shoulder—she flopped into her new position like a rag doll.

Helmut said, "I do have a request for you," then waited for Erik to ask the obvious question, but Erik didn't do it. Helmut made the request anyway.

"We have no children. Frieda and I weren't blessed in that manner. She bears no responsibility for what I've done and does not deserve to share my fate."

He paused, but Erik waited. It was less than a hundred metres to Wacksstrasse 21.

Helmut said, a little louder, "I have no one to protect Frieda when I am gone. You and I haven't known one another for long, and you cannot see into my heart, but I think I have proven I will protect your family as long as possible. Will you and your family protect my Frieda if the unimaginable happens?"

Erik looked at Marita, and she answered Richter's question. "Yes, Helmut, we will, and I know that Annalisa and her husband will do it if we can't. I promise you that we will protect Frieda."

Frieda squeezed Marita's hand and said, "Thank you, Marita. Only a fool would not be terrified of what will almost certainly happen, and I only ask that we survive!"

They shook hands at the bottom of Erik and Marita's steps, and Marita took Brigitte in her arms. She and Erik watched Helmut and Frieda disappear in the darkness—two pools of light and four feet.

◇◇◇◇◇◇◇◇◇◇◇◇◇◇◇◇◇◇◇◇◇◇◇◇◇◇◇

When Marita and Erik had the children in their beds, they went to the living room. Marita said as she went to the bookshelf, "I have always pictured Kriminaldirektor Richter as a monster, but perhaps I was wrong... he may yet save himself. If not in this world, perhaps in the next."

She dug out the forbidden recording of Lili Marlen, put it on the phonograph, and they listened in silence as Lale Andersen sang her bittersweet lyrics accompanied by a melancholy men's chorus. The last verse was the motive for banning the song. The propaganda ministry assumed the soldier's request, made from his grave, for Lili to meet him under the streetlight would have a demoralizing influence on German soldiers and their wives, mothers, and sweethearts who waited at home for them to return. His ban resulted in the record becoming the most popular of the time, and eventually, he changed his mind.

While the song played, Erik thought of the many men he had killed, men he didn't know, men who were doing their job. He thought of the politicians and generals who ordered the murders, men who would never kick at the end of a rope. History would celebrate some of them as heroes, others as goats, but they would survive while the soldier in the song could only look forward to his ghostly meeting with his lover under the streetlight.

The needle slid into the inside groove and circled soundlessly. Erik reached across Marita, lifted the arm onto its cradle and moved to close the cover—and Marita stopped him with her hand. He put his arm over her shoulder, smelled her hair, leaned back and said, "I am not convinced that Major Richter has anything in his heart but to save his own skin. What puzzles me is that Richter knows what Matthias has been up to... And he knows about Marcel and Juliette. Why hasn't he arrested them?"

Marita said thoughtfully, "Helmut has been playing a dangerous game, and there is something else there...I can't put my finger on it, but perhaps he isn't all bad. Frieda stays with him, so he must have some good in him."

"Do you regret agreeing to protect Frieda?" Marita snuggled against Erik's shoulder.

"No, it's the least we can do. We're committed to those workers and need Helmut on our side."

Marita moved the needle to the beginning. While the record played, Erik thought about Marita's change in attitude toward Richter and decided that, even though a glimmer of good flickered in Helmut, the world would never forgive him. Like all good bureaucrats, he would have documented his brutality, and no one on earth could redeem him for that kind of crime. Erik decided to continue to take advantage of Helmut's newfound humanity and keep Marita's promise to protect his wife. Still, he could never forgive what the major and his Gestapo stood for!

◇◇◇◇◇◇◇◇◇◇◇◇◇◇◇◇◇◇◇◇◇◇◇◇◇◇◇◇◇◇

Marita read his mind. She said, "I am not so sure that he is as evil as you think. I know what he has done is horrible, but his redemption is still possible. Remember, even as he died, Jesus forgave the people who crucified him!" She rested her case with, "Frieda is a good woman, and she would not stay married to a monster!"

Erik was surprised at Marita's willingness to forgive Richter but knew better than to argue—it wasn't the first time she had read his mind, and it wouldn't be the last. Erik was almost convinced she was right…almost.

◇◇◇◇◇◇◇◇◇◇◇◇◇◇◇◇◇◇◇◇◇◇◇◇◇◇◇◇◇◇

The night was warm and romantic, but Erik and Marita had too much on their minds for physical love and fell asleep in one another's arms. Marita woke an hour later, her arm numb from Erik's weight, and slipped over to her side of the split bed to massage it. Erik stirred, mumbled something, and Marita leaned over to hear what he was trying to say.

He said, *"Ich liebe dich,"* and, immediately awake, pulled her on top of him. She slept naked on warm nights, and he slept naked whenever his urges reached a boiling point—his idea of a subtle hint. She slipped off him and lay against his side, stroking him with her hand.

Their lovemaking was tender and sweet, but Marita's climax was anything but… Afterward, they slept until Walther banged on their door at eight.

There were only six days and nights before Erik had to return to his squadron.

CHAPTER SIXTEEN

15 April 1944

Ja, man muß seinen Feinden verzeihen, aber nicht eher, als bis sie gehängt worden.
(Yes, one must forgive his enemies, but not before they hang.)
Heinrich Heine

WALTHER LEFT FOR SCHOOL AT EIGHT-THIRTY, and Marita dressed the girls to feed ducks in the river. She and Erik walked behind them as they ran, laughing and singing a Brahms folk song Annalisa had taught them. When they found two parallel lines of square sidewalk blocks, the girls stopped to play Hopse. Erik and Marita watched as they threw a stone to a spot, hopped to it, picked it up, turned 180 degrees while standing on one foot, then bounced back to home.

While watching the children, Erik picked up a stone and asked, "What do you think of Jonas's plan to start caring for children at the factory?" He lobbed it at the bottom of a lamppost and missed.

"It's not Jonas's plan," Marita answered. "Annalisa and I have been planning that for weeks, and the poor schmuck has nothing to say about it if he wants to marry my mother."

Marita was silent for a moment before she spoke again, and she chose her words carefully. "I do like Annalisa's idea; she will make the plant more productive. The paid workers are eighty percent women and twenty percent older men, and Annalisa knows how to handle both. If we have a safe place for the women's children, close to their mothers, more women will want to come there to work. More happy workers equals higher production. The sixteen-hour day can be split into four-hour shifts connected so it's convenient for the workers. The hours can be flexible for everyone.

Six fourteen-hour days a week is too much for anyone. We are losing workers because they can't stand hard physical work for that long. Add to that the fact that most factory women have children, and sometimes older parents to care for, and that schedule is impossible for them, so they stay home."

Erik smiled, pleased with himself as he hit the post on his second try. He said, "Poor Jonas is gaining a wife and losing his business." The third was a glancing blow, but nonetheless, a hit.

Marita shook her head. "I don't think of it that way. He's gaining a partner in his business and his life. My mother is fantastic in both roles."

Marita and Erik watched Elke lose her balance and step on a line. She pouted as she gave the stone to her sister. Brigitte said, "You'll get it next time," and threw the stone underhand to her next block, missing it by a hair. Elke laughed as her sister passed the rock to her, then threw it to the exact centre of her next target.

Erik found another stone that suited his purpose. "I agree, your mother is fantastic, but does Jonas want a business partner or an affectionate wife? The jury is out on whether Annalisa can manage a business…what if he changes his mind when the reality hits?"

Marita laughed at him. "This morning, he knows she's an affectionate wife, and he'll soon see about the management part. She loves him, and he loves her, and they are both intelligent, unselfish people—those types of individuals always make things work!"

Marita took the stone from Erik's hand and threw it at the post, hitting it squarely. Erik laughed, but not happily. He couldn't hide his dented ego as he said, "I suppose you won't need my advice in all this… It certainly seems that you and Annalisa have everything worked out."

He decided to challenge their preparations. "What if the American Eighth Air Force comes during the day when you are at work? How are you going to get the children to the shelter?"

"Annalisa and I will teach the children to follow us to the shelter by having regular drills. The older ones will be responsible for the younger ones."

"All right," said Erik, "I surrender. They will probably be safer with you than at home." He looked at his wife's confident smile and hated that he had to leave. "Damn the war!" He took her hand.

"Yes, damn the war!" She kissed his cheek. "Don't worry; it will be over soon."

"Hopefully, soon enough." He looked into her eyes and stroked her hair.

The children finished their game and ran ahead.

Erik asked, "Did you see who won?"

"Does it matter?" Marita took his arm, Erik shrugged, and they followed the children.

The week ended with another air raid on Saturday night, again hitting the railway yards, and Major Richter and his wife Frieda joined the Stephanie family on their way to the tower. In the shelter, Frieda and Marita chatted while bombs fell on the other side of the river while Helmut obsessively talked to Erik about the consequences of an Allied victory. His obsession with Allied, primarily Jewish retribution, triggered Erik to ask himself what terrible things Helmut had done that would cause him so much apprehension. Erik had no desire to know the details, so he steered the conversation to his favourite topic… mosquitos.

An hour later, the mosquitos had done their duty, and the children were back in their beds. Marita caught Erik before he took off his clothes and took him to the sofa in the living room. She put Lale Andersen's "Lili Marlen" on the phonograph and snuggled up to him. A few seconds later, she said, "I invited Frieda to church with us. What do you think?"

Erik laughed, "I'm surprised you would ask my permission."

"Oh, I'm not asking your permission," She squeezed his hand. "I've already asked her to come, and I just wanted to know how you feel about it."

"What about Helmut—did you ask him?"

"I asked Frieda about Helmut, but she said he doesn't believe in God or the Devil right now. In his case, I suppose it would be inconvenient to believe in God and terrifying to believe in hell and the devil."

Erik thought he detected pity for Major Richter in Marita's voice but decided not to mention it.

"Yes, I will happily escort you and Frieda to church on Sunday morning. Afterward, Frieda can have a late breakfast with us if she wants to—I don't mind doing the cooking."

The song was over. Erik got up and picked the first movement of a Mozart piano concerto from their collection. He laid the needle carefully on the beginning grooves, and the joyous, sweet sounds of the first of Mozart's C Major piano concertos filled the room with romance. Erik snuggled beside Marita. She took his hand and laid it on her breast, and Erik silently wished someone would invent a phonograph that would play longer than three minutes. Later, Marita was in the mood for a long and tender affair.

They woke in the daylight, still on one side of the bed and sweating where their bodies had been touching all night, not wanting to let go. They silently lamented how quickly the days had gone by. Tomorrow, Erik would board the train and leave his family to defend them with his night fighter. He silently worried that he might not come back.

◇◇◇◇◇◇◇◇◇◇◇◇◇◇◇◇◇◇◇◇◇◇◇◇◇◇◇◇◇◇◇◇◇◇◇◇

Pastor Matthias Bergman welcomed his flock at St. Kilian's Church's wide-open door, shaking hands and chatting with them as they entered. At forty-five, he was young to have such a large and prestigious congregation, and he was brave, even heroic, in his beliefs. Pastor Matthias disapproved of Nazi doctrine and many times had risked trips to Gestapo headquarters to speak on behalf of the prisoners. He fought Major Richter to the brink of arrest for the Jews in the community, and his congregation correctly suspected he was responsible for many Jews escaping the Nazis.

Matthias recognized Frieda when she walked up the steps alongside his favourite parishioners but quickly extinguished his initial shock.

Marita shook her pastor's hand and motioned to Frieda. "Pastor Bergman, I would like to introduce our friend, Frieda Richter." The pastor shook Frieda's hand warmly.

"Welcome, Frau Richter, welcome..." Pastor Bergman hesitated, choosing his words. "I am so glad to see you here. I know your husband well, and I would like you to also extend my welcome to him."

Erik noted that Matthias's friendly greeting had surprised Frieda but that she had almost immediately collected herself.

She said graciously, "I will do that, Pastor Bergman, and thank you for your hospitality."

Marita led her up the steps, gently tugging on Frieda's arm when she glanced back at the pastor and half-stumbled on the edge of the door sill. Erik caught her and held on until she regained her balance. He looked back at Matthias, whose mind seemed to be stuck on the wife of the most dangerous man in Heilbronn. His next parishioner got only a tentative handshake—Matthias bowed his head as if praying for help.

Pastor Bergman always planned his sermons carefully, devoting much of his week to fashioning the message to suit everyone's needs and limitations. Consequently, the well-thought-out package was meticu-

176

lous, and when Matthias changed his routine by pointedly pushing his notes to the side before he began his sermon, the congregation restlessly shifted in their seats. Every one of them knew that the wife of the head of the Gestapo was sitting in the congregation.

Pastor Bergman was tall and thin, with a sparse beard and sparkling blue eyes. He combed his hair back, accentuating a receding hairline he could just as easily have hidden for a few more years. Every eye was on him, and the church was silent when he began to speak.

"My sermon today is from my heart," he began, grasping both sides of the pulpit. "And I will say things that will disturb some of you." He laid his hand on the large leather-bound Bible lying open on the pulpit.

He went on without looking down.

"Matthew 26, verses 52 to 54. 'Then, Jesus said to him. Put your sword back into its place. For all who take the sword will perish by the sword.'"

He looked from one parishioner to another, picking his targets, then continued, "I cannot quote the remaining verses from memory, but Jesus goes on to remind His disciples that He had the power through His Father to avoid his fate, but that He must sacrifice himself, that they may live."

Pastor Bergman let the words of the Bible sink in, and Erik dreaded where he was going.

"It is no secret that I have devoted the last five years of my life to helping people who were and are victimized by the Nazi regime, and it is no secret to all of you that I continue my quest. I disagree with Nazi policies, and I abhor their actions. I have spent more time in Nazi offices, cellars and prisons pleading for mercy and reason than I have in this church!"

Erik looked at Frieda; she stared at Matthias without wavering. He would have given much more than a penny for her thoughts.

"Every night, I wait for the knock on my door that will mean my death at the hands of the Gestapo, and it may come tonight. I have no idea why they have not come for me before now. I can only believe God has given me an angel to look after me."

He paused again, looking down at the congregation facing him. He found Erik's eyes, and Erik shook his head slightly, hoping Matthias would steer his sermon in another direction.

Pastor Bergman wrenched his eyes away, sweeping his gaze across the congregation without pausing on individuals.

◇◇◇◇◇◇◇◇◇◇◇◇◇◇◇◇◇◇◇◇◇◇◇◇◇◇◇◇

"Today, my question is whether I should worship with those who may be my enemies."

Erik felt Frieda shift in her seat.

"If Hitler came to this church, would I welcome him? Would I change my sermon to avoid hostility toward him?" He looked at the shocked faces in his congregation, pausing for a meaningful second at Frieda.

"The answer is..." He held his hand up... "I would welcome him..." and half the congregation became restless. The others leaned forward in their seats, and Pastor Bergman went on. "But I cannot forgive him!"

He let the audible gasps from the congregation die into silence before he said, "That is not my right. All I can do is lead our Führer to the One who can. I will ask Herr Hitler to put down his sword before even God cannot forgive him!"

It was evident to Erik and everyone else in the church that Matthias did not intend to even try to save himself from the hole he seemed determined to dig.

"I am not going to ask who would salute the Führer—who would support him in continuing this senseless war that Germany cannot win—you all know who you are. Those of you who would salute and fight on are in need of the Lord's help. Surely, we have had enough idol worship and hate—we know their awful power! If we don't put down our swords and choose love over hate, the power directed against us will annihilate our country!"

A murmur rippled through the church. Angry faces turned red, terrified faces turned white—few were indifferent.

Erik dared not take his eyes off the pastor. Matthias was signing his death warrant. He had said Germany could not win, that Hitler should surrender to the Allies so that God would forgive him for the evil he had done. The woman sitting between him and Marita was the wife of the head of the Gestapo! She sat quietly, unflinchingly, her hands twisted together on her lap. Erik closed his eyes and silently prayed that Pastor Bergman would invoke a neutral blessing to take the edge off condemning Hitler to hell, and God answered Erik's prayer, but in the negative. Matthias seemed determined to tell the truth...suicide in Germany.

"Jesus pleaded to His disciples to accept His fate, as God compelled Him to endure it. He bore no ill will to those who would kill Him and refused to allow his followers to take up the sword. Jesus was the last hope of the Jewish people; he was the one God had chosen to lead them out of servitude to the Romans. But, rather than fight the Romans, Jesus chose peace and martyrdom. With His last breath, our Saviour forgave the Romans and the Jews who had betrayed him."

The congregation was silent. No one coughed, and as far as Erik could tell, no one breathed. Matthias stepped back and waited. A couple stood up and walked down the wide aisle toward the door, then another, and then a dozen people crowded the exit. A few stood, looked at their neighbours and then sat down. Matthias stepped to the front of the pulpit.

"Our enemies' leaders follow the direction of the loudest voices, as does our Führer. Churchill and Roosevelt are destroying our beautiful cities and murdering our women and children because the English and American people demand it from them. In plain, clear language, they have told us their objective is the German people's annihilation unless our Führer agrees to surrender. Adolph Hitler chooses to fight to the death because his supporters demand it of him, and surrender means death for him and his supporters. No one has a choice, from the men carrying rifles on the Russian front to the man who releases the bombs that fall on our cities. Once the cycle of hate begins, events force events, and catastrophe breeds catastrophe in a never-ending circle until everything is destroyed, or the participants become exhausted." He paused.

"I am pleading with you to break the circle today in this holy building. Together, we, the people of Germany, united in our determination to survive, are the only ones who can stop this insanity! If we refuse to fight the people we hate...if we turn to love, or at least tolerance, instead of this insane hatred, the Allies will see that we want peace. Only the people can change this church, Heilbronn, and Germany. We must form a new circle—one of love. Turn to your neighbour, shake his hand and wish him well! Pledge to stop this insanity!"

Erik tried to find a glimmer of hope for Matthias. Seated in an aisle seat, he turned around to shake the hand of the man seated behind him, but although a few people looked sideways at their neighbour, he was only one of four or five who shook hands.

The prayer was longer than usual, and the congregation wiggled impatiently in their seats until Pastor Bergman ended it with a quiet "Amen."

A third of the congregation headed straight for the exit, trying to reach the warm spring sunshine before their pastor could stop them at the top of the stone steps. Matthias watched the stampede from the pulpit, then walked down the aisle, shaking the hands of embarrassed, frightened people who avoided his eyes by looking at the floor.

✧✧✧✧✧✧✧✧✧✧✧✧✧✧✧✧✧✧✧✧✧✧

As usual, the Sunday service ended with Kaffeeklatch, 'conversation, sweets, and coffee,' in the outer room. What had been before the war a warm, inviting place to worship was now sterile and empty. The altar, the stained glass windows, and the carved figures had all been transported to Austria for safekeeping. The only furniture in the outer room was a plain stone table that had stood along the wall for centuries and was too heavy to move. The women of the congregation had covered it with coffee urns, bread, cheese, and exceptional wartime sweets. Friendly conversation and sweets usually attracted a mingling, hungry crowd, but today, there was no joy in the few who remained.

Most Sundays, the chatter in the room resonated loudly off the stone walls, but today, the volume was muted, and no one dared to mention the sermon. Most of those who stayed loved Pastor Bergman like a family member, and they feared his death was inevitable because he dared speak the truth. The topic left no room for anything else in their minds, so most people said nothing; in the shadow of impending doom, they had already begun the grieving process.

Pastor Bergman circulated through the room as he did every Sunday. His wife, Maria, who most Sundays took care of half the room for him, was ignored. When they turned their backs on her, she turned to Marita.

"I'm afraid Matthias has gone too far this time." Her hand shook as she sipped her ersatz coffee. "It's one thing to help people in need and to pray for peace, but another thing entirely to compare our government to the Romans who crucified Jesus and to condemn Hitler to eternal damnation if he doesn't surrender! And he did it in front of the wife of the man who will arrest him!"

Marita feared her friend was right but couldn't face that logic, so she tried to soften the rhetoric.

180

"I am convinced that Kriminaldirektor Richter is a changed man. He is helping the Zwangsarbiter, and I am sure there will be no repercussions from him. In fact, Erik and I believe that Helmut had something to do with our adoption of Elke and Brigitte. He knows what your husband knows and agrees in principle with what Matthias preaches. You will feel better about it if you speak with Frieda."

Pastor Bergman joined Marita and Maria. He asked Marita, his voice normal and cheerful, "Where is Annalisa this morning? I've heard pleasant rumours that she's in love."

"Yes, she is." Marita put her cup back on her saucer and turned her attention to him. "She and Jonas Schneider have informally 'pledged their troth,' and I trust they will see you shortly about their wedding plans."

"Do you think I will be losing a member of our Sunday morning meetings or gaining one?"

Marita shrugged her shoulders. "You know Annalisa; she will go to church every Sunday as usual and drag Jonas with her. The problem is that they live near Weinsberg, and the church they choose will probably be closer to home. Today, she is in Weinsberg with Jonas, and our children are home alone, hopefully not tearing the house down." Marita had been apprehensive about leaving the children, but it was only for a couple of hours, and Walther knew to take the girls to the shelter if the alarm sounded.

"Does that mean she's living in sin right now?" Matthias whispered, laughing.

Marita whispered in his ear, "Yes, if loving one another before marriage is a sin, but no if it isn't." Her eyes twinkled as she sipped her coffee. She leaned toward him, her mouth close to his ear. "Of course, if they sin, God will have chosen their path for them, and they will bear no blame."

Matthias, smiling, replied quickly, "I know Annalisa will only sin if she has to, and God will forgive her."

Erik and Frieda had joined the group, and while Erik laughed, Frieda attentively watched the play between Marita and her pastor.

Maria kept her attention on Frieda, the wife of the man who held her husband's life in his hand, assessing her as only another woman could.

"Matthias, you are as slippery as a snake!" Marita raised her voice jovially, and Matthias turned to Frieda.

"Frau Richter, I hope I didn't embarrass you this morning. I am afraid your presence inspired me to make a point I've wanted to make for a long time."

Frieda looked concerned. "I think everyone got the point you were trying to make, Pastor Bergman, and I will soften it when I relay it to my husband." She took a bite from a piece of Kuchen. "As he has until now, my husband will do everything he can to protect you!"

Pastor Bergman's face registered shock briefly before he regained control. Maria watched Frieda as the pastor answered her.

"Then you missed the point of my sermon, Frau Richter; I don't need or want your protection. I think the evidence shows that we will lose this war, and when the Russians and Americans drive their tanks through our city, I want to be in a position to tell them that I stood on the side of mercy and love. Your husband hardly represents those qualities and..."

Frieda cut him off. "You are talking about martyrdom for yourself and everyone who fights the Third Reich. The idea of peace is always laudable, but fighting the Nazi government will get you killed. There are members of the National Socialists who may not be as willing as my husband to overlook your foolish audacity. Your naiveté and desire for martyrdom may get you and perhaps even your wife and friends killed despite my husband's efforts, not because of them! God will ignore your prayers, as he has the pleas of millions who have gone before you! As they always have, the SS will deal with those who speak as you did this morning, and God will stand by while they do it!"

Frieda paused, but no one filled the silence. In a softer tone, she said, "Reverend, don't talk to me of love and peace—it doesn't exist in this time and place—I truly fear for you, your wife, and the lives of your friends, Erik and Marita." She looked at Erik, then Marita. "There are people in this town who have more power than my husband has, and they have German steel where Helmut has a heart!"

Matthias lowered his voice, looked at Maria, whose eyes pleaded for him to stop, then went on.

"I know those people as well as your husband; I know the methods employed by all of them, and they are not noticeably different from

Kriminaldirektor Richter's. I have been in the Gestapo and SS prisons and cellars and seen what Himmler's minions do to innocent people!"

He became aware that his voice had risen as he spoke and adjusted the volume, speaking softly but full of intensity. "I have cried, begged and prayed for help as the SS loaded families in Lastwagen and took them away to concentration camps. Perhaps there is a difference between the SS and the Gestapo, but we are at the point where it doesn't matter—a higher power will judge them all, in this world or the next!"

He paused and put his hand on Frieda's in a gesture of affection. "Ironically, as frightening as that is, you and your husband are our best hope to survive. I cannot tell you how disappointed I am in God, not in His house. I pray for His guidance, but with all His power, I don't understand how we arrived in this awful place!"

He turned to an old woman with a cane who had been listening to the conversation. She said, looking at Frieda, then at her pastor, "You are a brave man, Matthias, but perhaps your timing could have been better."

Matthias said, "Perhaps, Frau Kehring, but I prefer to think the timing was the Lord's." She shook her head, turned and limped to the doorway, looking back and shaking her head again before bending over and putting her cane on the first step.

Matthias turned to Erik, Marita, and Frieda, touching each of their hands as he said, "Don't worry about me...I'm in God's hands." Maria took his arm and guided him through a door into the rear of the church.

Erik interrupted the heavy silence that lingered with Pastor Bergman and his wife's departure when he said to Marita, "I propose we return home to our children and my surprise breakfast."

Marita took his hand, and Frieda followed. Five minutes into the walk home, Frieda said to Erik and Marita, "I am sorry I made things difficult for your pastor, but I am afraid for him. He is bent on getting himself killed, and I am afraid the same fate may await his beautiful wife. Helmut has protected Pastor Bergman in the past, but there are growing elements of the party that my husband can't control. I am afraid that good man has more courage than sense."

Erik said, "I had no idea Helmut spoke to you about his work."

"I suppose I should be angry that you would assume that, but I try not to advertise my private relationship with my husband."

"I would say you hide it very well," said Marita.

When the late breakfast was over and Frieda had gone home, Annalisa arrived with Jonas in tow. Erik and Marita laughed as she breezed into the house. Marita brushed her mother's hair back and kissed her forehead.

"Mother, you're glowing like a teenager. What have you been up to?"

"I feel like a teenager, my dear. Now I need a preacher to make an honest woman of me!" She pulled Jonas to her side and squeezed him.

Jonas said lovingly, "She's an honest woman, preacher, or no preacher." His grin seemed to be permanent. "We've come to see Erik off."

The room became silent. Erik turned to Marita, wrapped his arms around her, and tenderly kissed her while everyone watched. He said, "I'll be back before you know it. I expect the war won't last much longer, and I promise to be careful."

As soon as the words fell out of his mouth, Erik regretted them. 'Careful' was not a word a soldier used because it was contradictory to doing his duty, and 'promise' was a word for children.

Marita's eyes filled with sadness. "Yes, I know I'm just a foolish worrywart, but these last two weeks have been so wonderful..." She openly wept as she raised Erik's hand to her lips, kissed it, then held it against her cheek.

Walther ran to his father, wrapped his arms around him, squeezed him and pressed his face against his side.

"Don't go, Vati, please don't go!" The boy cried pathetically. Elke and then Brigitte picked up the mood and began to wail. Annalisa went to the girls and wrapped her arms around them while Jonas stood in the middle of the chaos he had caused, looking helpless.

Marita touched Walther's cheek. "Walther, Vati has to go and protect us because he's brave and strong like you are. He's leaving you here to protect the girls and me, and I'm counting on you to be as strong as he is." She leaned down to look into his face. "Can you do that for me?"

Walther turned to his mother and stood as straight and tall as he could.

"Of course, I will protect you, Mutti, and I'll look after my garden too. You and Vati can count on me!" Marita wanted to pick him up and hug him but decided not to. Instead, she brushed his hair back and spoke confidently.

"I'm glad you're here to look after us; I feel safe with you to help me. I love you so much, Walther. Can I kiss you on the cheek?"

He turned his cheek to his mother, and she kissed him firmly, holding his head in her hands. When he'd had enough, he wiggled away and gathered his sisters from Annalisa.

Walther grabbed Elke's hand and steered her toward the hall. "Come on, Elke, you and Brigitte can help me with Vati's things so he won't miss the train." The girls ran behind Walther into the bedroom. They tried to lift Erik's suitcase and duffle bag, then decided to carry his small bag, one on each side. Walther dragged the heavy suitcase and duffle bag to the living room, where the adults had gathered over another ersatz coffee.

"Come on, Vati, or the train will leave without you!" Walther carried the big suitcase toward the door.

Erik checked his pocket watch. "Ah, you're right. But why don't I carry the suitcase, and you take care of the duffle bag?" Walther gladly gave up the tightly packed suitcase and picked up the duffle bag, slinging the long strap over his shoulder. The bag touched the floor, so Erik shortened the strap. He showed Walther how to sling it over his head, hanging it from the opposite shoulder so he could carry it comfortably bent around his body. Walther smiled up at his dad and covertly touched his hand.

Jonas and Annalisa took the girls and the luggage in the mercedes, and Erik, Marita, and Walther walked to the station, ten minutes away. The sunny, cool day and the fresh spring air lifted their spirits. As expected, the train wasn't there when they arrived, and Walther ran to check the schedule. It was conveniently fastened to a wide gray post under a large round clock on the platform. He verified the arrival time, then announced the news to the gathered family. "The train will be here in eight minutes and thirty seconds and leaves three minutes later."

Marita said, "Thank you, Walther; we'll wait here until the train pulls in." Marita held Erik's hand and pulled him close to her. "If it's OK with you, I want the last few minutes alone with your father."

"Yes, Mutti, but I want to say goodbye too." Walther sulked but left his mother and father alone, joining Annalisa, Jonas, and the girls. Marita pulled Erik down to sit beside her on a bench.

The children gravitated to an old man turning the crank of his organ grinder, playing a cheerful alpine song. His monkey pulled on its leash, trying to get the children's attention. The girls immediately became friends with the monkey, but Walther remained aloof. The old man's hat lay on the platform with a few Groschen in it, and Jonas added a five-Mark note, bringing a broad smile to the man's wrinkled face. Walther sat down on a bench where the monkey could reach him if it wanted to, and it jumped on his lap and curled up, looking at Walther with a "pet me" expression. He rubbed the monkey's head and stroked its back and side in a long, fluid motion. The girls came over to join the petting but soon returned to Annalisa and Jonas, who stood arm in arm, watching Erik and Marita say their tearful goodbyes. Annalisa asked, "Why don't you girls pet the monkey?"

"Because Walther's crying," said Elke.

The train arrived a full minute and a half late, barely acceptable by German standards, even in wartime. Therefore, it would leave a minute and a half early, giving the family little time to say goodbye. Walther ran to his father, flung his arms around him without a word, then stood back, tears rolling down his cheeks. The girls joined Walther and received their kisses and hugs from Erik. He turned to Annalisa and Jonas.

"Please take care of Marita and the children; I'm afraid we haven't seen the worst yet. My family must survive!"

Annalisa looked at Jonas, and Jonas responded for both of them. "We'll take care of your family, Erik, and we will all be here when you return."

Eric vigorously shook Jonas's hand. "Jonas, I appreciate your kindness more than I can express."

Marita waited for her final kiss. They had scarcely a minute, and the sweet kiss took half of that. Erik picked up his suitcase, slung the duffle bag, then gripped the small bag in his fingers. He smiled at everyone and stepped through the door three seconds before it closed. The train moved precisely on time.

Marita watched it disappear, tears in her eyes, her arms hanging by her side, her body motionless. Annalisa put her arm around her daughter and steered her toward home. Walther followed his mother, head high, trying to disguise his sobs.

CHAPTER SEVENTEEN

16 April–1 May 1944

Die Menschen haben nur zwei Wünsche: alt zu werden und dabei jung zu bleiben.
(Man has only two wishes: to become old and remain young.)
Old German saying

THE TRAIN LEFT HEILBRONN FOR WIESBADEN in the daylight, and Erik couldn't believe they would reach their destination unscathed, but they did. Where were the mosquitoes? Where were the American and British ground attack fighters? Until the train arrived in Wiesbaden, the occasional bombed-out building was the only sign of war Erik had seen in over two hundred kilometres.

Bombs had damaged Wiesbaden, but not as severely as most other industrial cities. The railway station functioned as though there were no war, and cars drove on the streets. Where bombs had destroyed buildings, the rubble was gone, and everywhere he looked, rebuilding was underway. Darkness fell while Erik waited for his train to Aachen, amazed at how few signs of war he had seen, and he could understand why many Germans still believed in victory for the Third Reich.

It was past midnight when Erik's train stopped at the Charleroi station platform. His young replacement navigator met him, driving his old mercedes.

"Sergeant Becker reporting, sir." He saluted smartly, avoiding the straight arm 'Heil Hitler' salute his boss despised. Erik couldn't believe this boy was old enough to qualify for a driver's license, let alone navigate a fighter in the dark and fire cannons at a bomber. He was trim, lean, and small, with a boy's smooth face. Erik felt a little shabby as he returned the young flyer's smart Wehrmacht salute.

They exchanged pleasantries, and the sergeant picked up the heavy bags and sprinted to the car, carefully placing everything in the back seat. Erik headed for the driver's side, but the young man cut him off. He stood with his hand on the driver's door handle until Erik smiled and stepped around the front of the car to the passenger's side. Erik climbed in, the engine started with a roar, and they drove away. Young Sergeant Becker shifted smoothly through the gears, and neither man spoke until the car stopped in front of Erik's quarters. Becker carried everything into the room they would occupy together.

The young man neatly arranged his possessions on the bedside table that had belonged to Michael and seemed to understand the significance of Erik's sad stare. He asked, "Shall I move to the sergeant's mess, sir?"

"No, Sergeant, my wife can stand my snoring, so perhaps you can too. Let's try it here together and see if it works out." He felt more like a father to the young man than a comrade-in-arms.

Sergeant Becker woke before dawn, and his efforts to be quiet woke Erik, who made a sleepy mental note to explain the house rules to the boy, then drifted into a deep sleep and didn't stir until ten o'clock. His new protégé didn't show up until Erik was showered and ready for a late breakfast, and he discarded the mental note on the way to the dining hall.

The young man fiddled over a cup of coffee and a piece of rye bread while Erik wolfed down his boiled eggs, Brötchen, wurst, apple juice and two cups of coffee. The young man introduced himself as Sergeant Karl Becker from Kiel, the son of a civil engineer and a teacher. Erik pried until he discovered that the young man had finished first in his class in just about everything he had studied, including navigation. Most navigators were flunked pilots, but Karl had chosen the back seat from the beginning.

Karl didn't talk to make conversation; he answered queries succinctly and clearly, and his questions were purposefully and maddeningly direct. The walk to the command building was more like a cross-examination than a conversation, and Erik was glad to reach safety.

Inside, Major Fischer passed Karl's file to Erik, and he sat down in a plush chair to read it. Karl, ignored by the two older men, remained standing.

Erik's new navigator/gunner had graduated from gunnery school two weeks before. He had taken compressed courses in navigation and wireless and had been at the top of his class in every subject. He had flown thirty training flights, ten of them in the dark, and had performed flawlessly.

Erik closed the folder and looked at the young face of his new navigator. Karl held his gaze for a few seconds but lowered his eyes as Erik tried to decide whether he should complain to the commander. As an ace, Erik had a right to expect Michael's replacement to be a navigator with battle experience. Still, perhaps a talented, adaptable rookie would be a better fit than a tired veteran who was solidly stuck in a rigid military rut. A combination of experience, intelligence and flexibility was a scarce item in the unemployed navigator pool, and, in the end, Erik decided to reserve judgment until he had put this intelligent young man through the combat wringer.

Erik handed the file back to Major Fischer. "How long have I got before we go hunting?"

The major almost smiled but controlled himself in time and said, "It's not up to me, but it's not likely there will be a mission tonight—after the Nürnberg disaster, the British seem to have lost their taste for clear nights. You should check out your new ride and prepare for your ceremony tomorrow." Karl audibly let out a breath he had been holding. Major Fischer took Karl's file from Erik and waited for a reaction but got none. "You get your oak leaves tomorrow afternoon, and Michael will receive the Ritterkreuz posthumously. The squadron will assemble for the ceremony at fifteen hundred hours, and it would be nice if you were there."

Erik acknowledged the ceremony with a nod, then asked, "What is the fuel situation? Do we have enough for a flight or two to get used to one another?"

Major Fischer surprised him. "Yes, if the British don't come, you can take a few nights to commission your navigator and the new plane. Fuel is scarcer than when you left, but good pilots and navigators are even harder to find. Make sure you and Karl are ready before you go hunting for real!"

Erik thought the Luftwaffe commander had aged ten years in the two weeks he had been away, and when he struggled to his feet and waved a sloppy salute at his best pilot and friend, Erik knew duty was all that kept him going. An exhausted Major Fischer smiled sadly when Sergeant Becker neatly touched his forehead with a perfect Luftwaffe salute.

◇◇◇◇◇◇◇◇◇◇◇◇◇◇◇◇◇◇◇◇◇◇◇◇◇◇◇◇◇◇◇◇◇◇◇◇

On the long walk to their parked aircraft, Karl stayed a half-step behind Erik. It was identical to the Me110 Michael had died in, a BF 110G-4,

189

equipped with a modern FuG 220 Lichtenstein SN-2 radar and the familiar insect antennae array on the nose. The forward armament was the same, but the Schrägemusik was a pleasant surprise. The gun was a twin-barreled MK108 30mm cannon with one hundred and eighty rounds in ammunition storage barrels on each side of the fuselage. The navigator no longer needed to exchange ammunition canisters; both sides fed into the gun automatically. The night fighter came with factory-fitted mirror reflector sights for both the pilot and navigator, something that Erik and Michael had retrofitted in Erik's ill-fated previous ride. The angle of the gun was seventy-five degrees, precisely as Erik preferred. His chief mechanic had performed this miracle in the two weeks since he had left, and he was anxious to thank him.

"Sir, do you like her?" Karl stood beside his new boss, nervously watching him examine the aircraft.

"Yes, I like her. Do you know who's responsible for the wax?" Erik stroked the bottom of the nose, noting the newly waxed surface.

"Yes, Sir. I arrived here a week after you left, on the same day as the aircraft, and Sergeant Hagerman let me help him. I finished waxing her this morning." He stroked the fuselage skin precisely as Erik had—as if he were caressing a woman—something Erik suspected the boy had never done in his short life.

"Is she ready for battle?" Erik knew the answer, but he wanted the young man to have the pleasure of answering.

"Yes, Sir, she's ready. The tanks are full of fuel, and the magazines are full of ammunition. We ground-tested the engines, and the controls are smooth—will we be taking her up for a spin, Sir?"

Erik was aching to "take her for a spin," but he was still tired from the trip and the strain of leaving his family. He was too tired to be a safe pilot, and unless there was an emergency, he would not fly until he had slept. The young man was technically ready for a mission, but Erik wanted to talk about tactics and work out a few wrinkles in the air before the real thing.

"Karl, I need to rest before I fly, and I will need to get rid of two weeks of rust. Why don't I sleep now, and we can talk about tactics later? We can play with our new toy tomorrow."

He wanted to say more—tell him the pass mark in battle is a hundred percent and failure meant death—but the boy would learn that soon enough. Looking at the beautiful aircraft, he contemplated how much he would enjoy flying it with this young man if there were no war.

◇◇◇◇◇◇◇◇◇◇◇◇◇◇◇◇◇◇◇◇◇◇◇◇◇◇◇◇◇◇◇◇◇

Larry Inman and Danny Powell truly enjoyed a good fight, whether on the ground or in the air. They argued with anyone and everyone about anything and everything and went to the pubs mainly to pick fights. Despite their wealth of experience, they weren't particularly good at fighting, but they were as tenacious as bulldogs.

Flying a mosquito into battle was a sport for them, and the more danger there was, the happier they were. The adrenaline rush of war was intoxicating—they were addicted to it—and a couple of days without the exhilaration of flying in an environment where someone was trying to kill them made them restless and edgy.

It was the middle of the day; the Florennes airfield was their target. The last time they were there, on the night of the Nürnberg fiasco, their wingman had bagged an FW 190 as it was taking off, but this time, they were out to do some real damage in the daylight. The mosquitos avoided radar detection by flying fifty feet above roads that led them to Florennes, reaching the target before the defences had reports of a visual sighting. If their luck held, their first pass would be a complete surprise!

Larry and Danny's mosquito had traded its cannons' magazines for room to carry four delay-fused 500-pound high-explosive bombs in its bomb bay, designed to burrow, then explode underground. The operations plan was to drop them from three thousand feet so they would reach terminal velocity and burrow into the underground fuel tanks marked on a photograph of the aerodrome. If the tanks were where they were supposed to be, there would be a big bang and a lot of fire…and Larry and Danny loved fireworks!

Larry's wingman, Remi, had cannons and machine guns fitted instead of bombs. His job was to eliminate the opposition by disabling the anti-aircraft installations on his first low-level pass. Larry lined up his bombing run, watching for fighters whose pilots felt a patriotic need to try and take off, but none did. Without enemy fighters to distract them, Larry could concentrate on Danny's flying instructions, and Danny could drop the bombs without interference. Both aircraft would then strafe the field until their ammunition was spent.

Two anti-aircraft batteries guarded the airfield, one at each end of the runway, and Remi's mosquito, hopping over the roofs of the buildings in the town at two-hundred-and-fifty miles an hour, flew straight at the distinctive gun-barrels, pointed skyward like pencils.

Larry pulled his mosquito up in a zoom-climb to three thousand feet, lining up his bombing run as Remi's cannons took out the first Anti-Aircraft gun and lined up on the second.

⸭⸭⸭⸭⸭⸭⸭⸭⸭⸭⸭⸭⸭⸭⸭⸭⸭⸭⸭⸭⸭⸭⸭⸭⸭⸭⸭⸭⸭⸭⸭⸭⸭⸭

Erik and Karl strolled to their barracks after an evening meal of black bread, cheese, and onions, washed down with an excellent Belgian beer. Exhausted, tired of Karl's constant questions about every conceivable situation they might encounter, Erik looked forward to his bed. When he heard a familiar sound coming out of the southwest, a sound that he knew meant trouble, any thought of rest vanished. He turned toward the source, knowing what he would see.

He swore, "Scheisse! mosquitos!" grabbed Karl's arm and shouted, "Run!"

Karl ran effortlessly alongside and a little behind Erik, unsure of what was happening or where they were going.

Defence engineering crews had dug strategically placed slit trenches all over the field, and Erik headed for the nearest one. Karl followed his boss into the trench at the same moment a mosquito opened fire on the Anti-Aircraft guns.

Erik held Karl down until the chatter of machine guns and cannons faded, then peeked over the rim of the trench. One AA gun was on its side, the other burning as a mosquito executed a steep climbing turn at the edge of the field, telling Erik it would be back. The attack on the airfield's anti-aircraft defences was only the beginning.

When Karl began to climb out of the hole, complaining about the damned English, Erik caught a handful of his shirt, and Karl landed on the bottom of the trench with a loud expiration of air.

As Karl looked up at him, gasping, Erik said, "That was just the preliminary; he'll be back, and I will bet there's another mosquito with bombs. We'll stay here until they're finished!"

⸭⸭⸭⸭⸭⸭⸭⸭⸭⸭⸭⸭⸭⸭⸭⸭⸭⸭⸭⸭⸭⸭⸭⸭⸭⸭⸭⸭⸭⸭⸭⸭⸭⸭

The aerial photographs Larry and Danny used, taken twenty-four hours ago, showed twenty-one FW 190 fighters, thirty-five messerschmitt Bf 110 night fighters and miscellaneous transports and bombers scattered

192

around the aerodrome. In total, there were seventy-nine prime targets for the British raiders. As he flew the bombing run, Larry looked at the rows of fighters, planning the strafing attack he would execute after the bombs had lightened the aircraft. He had no cannons, but the machine guns were full of ammunition, and without the bomb load, the mosquito moved like a cat.

Larry was at three thousand feet and still flying his bombing run when Remi's mosquito tipped onto its edge and turned over the roofs of the town, lining up for its second attack, this one on the neatly parked fighters. The field had no time to set up a defence or get a fighter to the runway, so Larry's only restriction after dropping his bombs would be Remi, who was lining his mosquito on a string of parked Ju88s. That left Larry with a neat row of parked Me110 fighters for his run.

"They're coming back." Erik stood up in the trench so he could watch Larry's graceful aircraft fly across the field with its bomb bay doors open. He tried, but he couldn't hate the mosquitos.

"The one low on the left will strafe the field again, and it looks like the one on the right will bomb the barracks." He pulled Karl down and peered over the rim of the trench, watching the mosquito drop its bombs in the grass field on the other side of the barracks.

Karl announced incredulously, "He missed!" as the ground exploded in a plume of dirt and a sheet of orange flame that rose over two hundred metres. Erik crouched and covered his head as dirt and rocks fell around them.

"That was our fuel!" he yelled in Karl's ear. "And the other mosquito is going after the Ju88s!"

The fighter roared over their heads and down a line of parked airplanes, firing its cannons and leaving exploding and burning pieces of aircraft behind it.

"It's okay, sir; they're leaving now." Karl started to climb out of the trench, but Erik pulled him back.

"They still aren't finished with us. Wait here until I tell you to go!" Erik felt his temper rising.

The mosquitos returned, and while the one that had destroyed the anti-aircraft guns and four Ju88s lined up on three messerschmitt 110 night fighters, his wingman picked out two FW 190 fighters sitting side by side. Men trying to get to their planes threw themselves on the ground.

The first Bf 110 exploded, and the other two were in flames when the first mosquito finished his pass, kicked the rudder over to coordinate a sweeping turn and lined up two more. The cannons fired for a few seconds, then ran out of ammunition. The .303 machine guns fired for a few seconds more before also quitting. The mosquito bomber shredded the FW 190s with its machine guns and pulled beside the mosquito fighter.

Erik jealously watched the beautiful aircraft climb away at full-throttle in perfect formation and turn west. He judged the climb rate at over a thousand meters per minute at an airspeed of over three hundred kilometres an hour, unimaginable numbers for a messerschmitt 110 pilot! The wingman flew behind the tip of the bomber's port wing as the mosquitos dashed for home. Even if the radar found them, always a question when it came to wooden mosquitos, the Devil couldn't catch them now—light on fuel and with bombs and ammunition gone.

∞∞∞∞∞∞∞∞∞∞∞∞∞∞∞∞∞∞∞∞∞

Erik let a stunned Karl leave the trench. In less than five minutes, two mosquitos had left behind six dead men, two mangled AA guns, twelve destroyed aircraft, and thousands of litres of Avgas rising to heaven on tongues of flame. The heat from the burning benzene had ignited a wooden storage building, and the airfield fire equipment hurried across the field to put it out.

Erik began walking toward his new 110, thankful the mosquito shooting at it had run out of ammunition. Walking alongside his mentor, Karl said, "Sir, why don't we shoot them down before they get here? Why didn't we know they were coming so we could get our fighters in the air? We do have radar and daylight fighters, don't we?"

"It's not that simple."

On the first day of training, every country's armed forces teach new recruits that their equipment is the world's best, and the propaganda department reinforces the myth every day after that. The instructors had told Karl that the Deelen ground radar he would consult could pick out a fly on a manure pile and that German fighter aircraft were superior to Allied aircraft in every respect. And the growing number of German aces confirmed the myth.

Erik decided the truth was the best antidote for the propaganda crap the Luftwaffe training had fed his navigator. "If we could find them, perhaps we could shoot them down, but they build the mosquito of wood, and radar passes through it. And even if I could find it, I could only shoot it down if Hermann Göring bought me a mosquito! I barely escaped from one of those bastards when I took off the night before I went on leave." Erik was prepared to leave it at that, but the young are curious.

"Tell me about it, sir."

"I got away from that mosquito, but when I found the bombers, some kid in a lancaster tail turret teamed up with another fighter; they shot down my plane, killed my friend, and damned near killed me." Erik stopped and faced Karl. "I doubt that the Luftwaffe can live up to your expectations."

"But how could something like that happen? You're an ace... Sir!"

"Anyone who can fly would be an ace if they flew fighters three times a week for four years and survived. I would need to look at my logbook to tell you how many missions I've flown, but it's at least a couple of hundred." He waved his arms.

"Look, Karl, it's simple; I am not a hero. A kid like you outsmarted me and kept shooting until my aircraft was a piece of junk and my navigator was dead! I would classify my escape as 'divine intervention,' and sometimes I think God saved the wrong man." Erik began walking again as he said, "I fucked up! I killed my friend! Don't put me on that fucking pedestal, and for Christ's sake, stop thinking that we can win this fucking war!"

Karl stopped asking questions.

When they reached the messerschmitt, a neat line of holes across the left wing and the engine cowling foretold significant damage. The waxed surface reflected the flames towering above the fuel storage tanks, giving the illusion that the messerschmitt was burning.

"I doubt we'll be flying anytime soon, even if they can find enough avgas to fuel us up." Erik turned away from his plane and began walking toward the command center. "Let's go report the damage."

"What will we do now, sir?" Karl sounded hurt, as though the British fighters had offended him.

"We'll find a soccer ball and kick it around, and then we'll go to a tavern and sing some songs—after we've had a few beers. And, by the way, how's your chess?"

Karl smiled broadly for the first time since Erik had seen him. "Oh, I win once in a while, sir."

Erik and Karl walked to the field headquarters intending to report the damage to their plane, but the place was in an uproar, and they decided to return in the morning.

Erik was tired, and Karl begged off the trip to town, favouring chess with his commander. Erik told himself that fatigue was the reason Karl made him look bad, but a little voice told him this young man would beat him a lot, tired or not. His navigator gave no quarter to his commanding officer, aggressively opening with the Queen's Gambit and, ten minutes later, forcing a humiliated Erik to tip his king. Karl was smart enough to make excuses for Erik, concentrating on his evident exhaustion. Erik cut him off when the boot-licking reached the level of embarrassment.

Morning dawned bright and sunny, and after a typically excellent Luftwaffe breakfast, Erik and Karl went to their aircraft to assess the damage. Sergeant Fritz Hagerman and two helpers already had the cowling off the engine and the inspection plates off the wing. As Erik approached, Hagerman shook his head.

"The left engine is kaput, and the wing spar will need some work. To fix it properly, we need to remove a section of the top skin, and we will do that while we wait for a new engine." He wiped his hands, shook hands with Erik and said, "Welcome back to the war, Erik; sorry for the shitty reception."

Erik motioned toward Karl. "I've got a new navigator, Fritz, and he can beat me at chess. He says he worked with you to get the plane ready, so I'm wondering if there's any chance I will lose him to the maintenance department?" Erik tacked on a "Ha ha."

Sergeant Hagerman cocked his head toward Karl. "Yeah, the boy is a born mechanic—I'll take him on my crew if you scare him bad enough that he won't get in your airplane. That kid can handle wrenches, and he knows how things work. And if he gets tired of beating you, send him over—my chess is better than yours!"

Karl grinned, and his smooth, whiskerless cheeks coloured a little.

"When will we have an airplane to fly?"

The sergeant stroked the edge of a propeller blade. "We have spare engines on the way. Normally, we would have two here, but we lost both of them last Saturday. Unfortunately, some pilots can fly the aircraft but don't know where the engine limits are. They over-boost on the way up and over-rev on the way down—a perfect way to kill any engine, even a mercedes, and something you ignore at your peril."

Erik interrupted, recognizing the signs of another Sergeant Hagerman rant about pilots abusing his beautiful engines. Erik had a thousand hours behind mercedes engines without a failure and didn't need a lecture on how to care for them. mercedes delivered an engine manual with every airplane, and Erik knew every word.

"I will ask the major about a spare aircraft, but I don't expect any help there. How soon can you get me in the air?"

"Sheisse, Erik, do you want to die? The longer it takes me to fix your fighter, the longer you live! Anyway, who the hell do you think I am, a magician? Do you think I can take my magic wand down to the shed, whip it through the air, and a spare engine will appear? If I wave it again, will some nice structural aluminum appear? Yeah, and then I'll work everyone twenty-four hours a day until you have your precious airplane back! Oh, yeah, I shouldn't forget that I will need a third wave of my magic wand to conjure up some fuel for your flying coffin! Would that suit your holiness?" Fritz embellished the last bit with a deep bow.

Erik waited a moment before answering. He outranked his chief mechanic, but his life depended on this man's work. In addition to that, and more importantly, Erik liked and respected him. He put his arm over Sergeant Hagerman's shoulder.

"Fritz, you're the best chief mechanic in the Luftwaffe. I appreciate everything you do, and I know that you will have the plane ready as soon as humanly possible. I didn't mean to pressure you—I was just wondering if I would have enough time to return to my family for a few days."

Fritz cooled down and grinned at Erik. "Didn't you get enough bumsen in two weeks, you lucky bastard? I haven't been home in over a year, even though my patient wife is only a few hours away."

Fritz had refused leave twice since Erik had known him, and he knew that Fritz had a French companion in Florennes. He decided to call his friend's bluff.

"You're right, Fritz; it isn't fair. When I go to report the damage to Major Fischer, I will demand that, when my plane is ready, he give you two weeks' leave to go home and see your wife!" He put his hand on Fritz's shoulder, then turned and headed for Major Fischer's office. Fritz caught him before he'd gone two steps.

"No, no, no need to do that, Erik. I wouldn't be here to check your oil and kick the tires… you…uh…would just go out and get yourself killed! Erik, trust me, I will stay here until you've shot down the last British bomber!" Something clicked, and Fritz figured out that Erik was playing with him. His tone changed. "How long do you figure that'll take you...uh...a month?...maybe two? Oh...and Erik...before you tackle the bombers, maybe you should swat a few of those mosquitos that keep pestering us?" Erik didn't answer soon enough; Fritz put his hands on his hips and said, "Exactly when can I expect you to take care of that so I can go home to my wife?"

"I'll get on it as soon as you've got my damned airplane fixed. Now, when would that be?"

Fritz smiled. "The spares were on their way before you deadbeats let those mosquitos shoot up our airfield, and my spies have told me that they will arrive tomorrow morning. It will take a couple of days to finish up once we have the parts, so I would say Friday, but that depends on many other people who are not as reliable as I am."

Erik squeezed Fritz's shoulder, and Karl followed his boss to the squadron command building.

Fritz called after Erik, "Ah...Erik...please don't bother the major about any time off for me. I have a lot of work here, and I'll let you know when I want to go home." Without turning around, Erik waved his arm in a deliberately ambiguous gesture, denying Fritz the benefit of his mischievous smile.

Erik noted that the banter between the two men amused his navigator, but Karl said nothing about it as he walked shoulder-to-shoulder with him. He asked, "Sir, would you have any objections if I helped remove the engine today? Fritz gave me some coveralls and grubby clothes."

"Of course not. I have paperwork to take care of, and we can meet later today to review tactics. We will need to rehearse everything. During the next few days, we will sit in the plane and run through scenarios until it's as natural as breathing."

Karl brightened. "Yes, Sir, I would like to do that. I have already started a list and will finish it by evening. We could run through it tonight if that suits you."

"You wouldn't rather go into town and have a few beers? We have a few days before the plane is ready."

"No, Sir, not if you will work with me. I would rather take this time to learn as much as possible before we fly a mission."

Erik smiled. So far, he did not regret his decision to adopt the boy, but the continuous stream of 'sirs' was beginning to wear thin.

◇◇◇◇◇◇◇◇◇◇◇◇◇◇◇◇◇◇◇◇◇◇◇◇◇◇◇◇◇◇◇◇

Major Fischer was busy when Erik and Karl arrived, so they waited until a maintenance officer left the office, and the adjutant waved them in. The major was vigorously writing and motioned them to sit without lifting his pen. He continued writing as he spoke.

"I don't have to tell you what a blow that attack was, and there is no reason not to expect them to continue. The Allies appear to have a surplus of mosquitos, fuel and pilots. On the other hand...." He left the sentence hanging, lifted his head and laid his pen on the paper. "We have no idea how they knew where the fuel storage tank was, but we suspect it came from one of the Belgian workers on the field. The SS is questioning them, and I have requested that regular Luftwaffe personnel replace them, but getting them is more faint hope than expectation."

He leaned back and locked his fingers together on his lap. "Meanwhile, I have decided to use wagons and lorries to store and deliver fuel. I will have what I need in a few days and will disperse them around the field, assigning each aircraft a fueling area where the lorries will come to them. There will be no recurrence of this catastrophe!"

Major Fischer stepped around the desk, half-sat, half-leaned on the edge of it. "You can forget the familiarization flights we discussed last night, but I suppose that's a redundant point considering the damage to your plane." The major turned around, picked up a piece of paper from the desk and read from it.

"All defence aircraft are hereby grounded except under specific orders from the Reichsverteidigungs Ministerium..." He wiped spit from his lips... "Hunting patrols are forbidden. Running aircraft engines on the ground to warm or test them is forbidden." He threw the paper on the desk.

"Those are the orders as I received them." He tapped his finger on the document he had been writing. "I am writing to explain the fallacy of doing this, although I know it'll do no good."

Major Fischer looked straight at Erik. "There is no fuel for anything but the most urgent needs. It is in short supply on every airfield, and ammunition is also scarce. You have the only thirty-millimetre cannons on the field, and I have four drums for you, with no idea when I can get more. It isn't any better for those using twenty-millimetre cannon

199

ammunition." He laughed. "The orders on that paper state that you must only fire when a kill is certain."

Erik slumped into a chair. "So, we are to baby our engines, save fuel and ammunition, and only shoot when we are certain of a kill." He grinned. "I guess that's logical to a bureaucrat, and it's precisely what we will do, but tell me, who will shoot down the bombers?"

Major Fischer ignored the sarcasm.

"Erik, I wish I could do more, but the fuel isn't there. Fuel plants need electrical power and coal. Every day, English bombers destroy fuel plants, power plants, rail lines, and railway yards needed to get the coal to the fuel plants. Russia has retaken its oil fields and the Romanian fields. The American industrialists are now betting on the Allies so that source has also dried up. I can't predict when there will be an improvement; until then, we must preserve our fuel. The same goes for ammunition and spare parts."

The two men silently looked at one another for a moment; Karl watched them without moving. Erik stood and saluted; Major Fischer straightened and stood away from the desk, returning Erik's salute with the same sloppy effort. Erik looked at Karl, pointed at the door and followed his young navigator through it, closing it with enough force to show his frustration.

American thunderbolts attacked the train carrying spare engines and parts destined for NJG4, including the material needed to repair Erik's fighter. Replacement parts arrived from the factory in a Lastwagen a week later, and it was Mayday before Erik's messerschmitt was finally ready to fly.

Sergeant Hagerman holed up with his girlfriend in Florennes until the parts arrived, and when he returned to the base, Erik noticed that his mood had dramatically improved. He assembled the plane in 24 hours without griping, and, after running the engine for two hours, contrary to direct orders, he declared the aircraft airworthy.

"She's ready, sir"—Fritz spit tobacco juice on the ground— "and I appreciate your patience and the effusive gratitude you have given us. You can take her up for a test flight now."

Erik hadn't said a thankful word, but he corrected the omission, noisily clearing his throat before he said, "Sergeant, I sincerely and vociferously acknowledge all of your heroic efforts. After deducting your sinful ways, you will receive your just reward in Heaven. I would love to take her up for a test flight, but I have specific instructions not to fly unless British bombers are attacking our homeland."

Fritz growled. "Your effusive gratitude is duly noted and appreciated." He smiled, relaxed and said, "She'll be okay. We double-checked every nut, bolt and screw, and the spar is stronger than a new one." He looked up at his handiwork and stroked the bottom of the cowling. Even the bullet holes were gone. Karl was awkwardly proud as he stood to the side, sharing Sergeant Hagerman's limelight.

Fritz pointed at his protegé. "Oberleutnant Stephanie, I am not exaggerating when I say young Karl is an excellent mechanic—he knows his way around an airplane." Karl's pleasure in doing a good job lit up his face.

Erik said, "We'll soon know about his skills in the air, and I am confident his navigation skills will equal his mechanical gifts. Thank you again, Sergeant. I have confidence that you have her perfectly rigged, as you did my previous ride." Erik shook the hand of every man in the maintenance crew. Finally, he turned to Karl. "Let's get you back to the barracks for clean clothes and a bath. We're going to town for some relaxation as soon as I find out whether we're on for tonight."

Erik found out they were indeed on alert in case the British attacked. The weather wasn't perfect, but not bad enough to ground the lancasters. There were enough clouds to make it an ideal bombing night. The Luftwaffe had stopped wasting valuable fuel chasing mosquitos or small flights of bombers. Erik would only have to fly if a significant armada of heavy bombers formed over Britain. The British, aware of the Luftwaffe's fuel shortage, had begun creating artificial radio chatter, feigning phantom attacks with phantom planes so that the Luftwaffe would scramble their night fighters, wasting fuel trying to intercept ghosts. The British regularly sent a few aircraft across the channel to throw out a load of "window," aluminum chaff that resembled a stream of bombers on German radar, forcing the Luftwaffe to scramble their planes just in case the threat was real.

Karl and Erik started the evening playing chess, but when Karl disgraced him in the first game, Erik decided to call home.

CHAPTER EIGHTEEN

1–3 May 1944

Violence is the weapon of the weak.
Mohandas Karamchand 'Mahatma' Gandhi.

THE PHONE RANG TWICE before Marita's voice came on the line. As clear as though she were next door, she said, "Stephanie," and Erik's heart accelerated.

"Erik here, Liebling.

Marita hesitated, and Erik said, "I know it's only been a few days, but I needed to hear your voice. I'm on duty tonight, but there doesn't seem to be much activity." He could hear Marita take a breath, but she didn't speak. He asked, "How are you and the children?"

They usually kept their calls short only called when they had something to say because of the high cost but Erik desperately wanted to talk to her before he went to war again. Marita's hesitation puzzled him, and her tone frightened him when she said, "Oh, Erik, I've wanted to call you every night since it happened, but I couldn't find the words." Erik held his breath, thinking of the children.

"On Monday night, a group of men hanged Matthias Bergman from the big oak tree in front of his house and then burned the house. The fire department found Maria inside."

Erik couldn't speak.

"Erik?"

He took a breath, swallowed, and asked, "Oh God, why would they kill Maria? And who would do it? Even the Gestapo and SS wouldn't do something so terrible! They would only have arrested him." His voice was soft, but there was no mistaking the bitterness.

"We don't know who did it; no one dares say anything, and the bishop was silent about it at the funeral service. There was talk about the SD and the Gestapo, but I asked Frieda, and she doesn't think the Nazi government had any part in it. She talked to Helmut, and I believe her when she says the Gestapo wouldn't even have interrogated him. Helmut told her it wasn't the SS either. He has an idea who is responsible, but the Berlin authorities, likely Goebbels, will almost certainly protect the guilty party."

Erik interrupted, "There is nothing new about Berlin protecting murderers! But, in this case?...even Goebbels wouldn't..." Erik couldn't imagine who could be that cruel.

"Helmut said Goebbels issued a decree whereby the police will not arrest anyone who kills traitors or enemy airmen. The Gestapo is trying to keep the decree quiet because, Helmut says, the saner local authorities are afraid that if the public knew they could get away with it, they would riot and raid the military prisons for British and American aircrews."

Erik's voice broke, "My God, where does this madness end?"

Marita said, "I've had a few days but still can't sleep. Annalisa comes over every day, and Jonas and Helmut pull all the strings they can, but they hit a wall of silence whenever they get close. Helmut says a radical movement is growing—mostly bullies and thugs who think the official Nazis, including him, are becoming too lenient. Unofficially, they are encouraged by Himmler's department, while officially, the government technically and theoretically opposes their crimes. Kriminaldirektor Richter has orders not to investigate these criminals and is taking a considerable risk when he asks questions."

"So, now we have the SD, the SS, and the Gestapo as the good guys?" Erik felt his exasperation and rage growing. "I can't believe they've found something worse!"

He paused for a few seconds, and Marita waited.

"I pity the poor bastards who jump out of their burning planes only to be murdered by lunatics on the ground!"

◇◇◇◇◇◇◇◇◇◇◇◇◇◇◇◇◇◇◇◇◇◇◇◇◇◇◇◇◇◇◇◇◇◇◇◇

Marita tried to force Erik to move on. "Tell me about your new navigator. You're at the field, so he must be capable of getting you home, and that's all that matters to me."

Erik's mood did change. "You wouldn't believe this kid; he's eighteen, almost thirty. mosquitos raided the field and damaged our plane, and he worked day and night with Fritz and his men to change an engine and repair the wing. Fritz even offered him a job if he didn't work out as my navigator!" Erik laughed half-heartedly. "I haven't had him in the air yet, but we've run through every scenario I can think of, including sitting in the cockpit with the radar on, simulating the search for bombers. I've taught him the attack sequence once we've found them, and he caught on so fast... Karl is the smartest young man I've ever seen; I wish Walther could meet him. Sometimes, I feel a little stupid when he catches me exaggerating or pulling the truth a little." He grinned to himself.

"On the negative side, he consistently beats me at chess; I win about every third game, and I suspect he engineers about half of them. This young man should be in university studying some impossibly difficult technical stuff, not guiding me around the sky in a situation where my mistake could get him killed!"

Marita politely laughed at her husband's enthusiasm. "He must have a weakness. Does he drink too much, or maybe he's got a bad temper—and, at eighteen, surely he's chasing women!" There was a pause while Erik thought about the question.

"He works hard, and he nursed one beer the only evening I could get him into a tavern. He played chess with every player in the room until he had beaten anyone who wanted to play. He didn't look sideways at the women in the place. No, none of those are his weaknesses. I think his biggest problem will be his heart."

"His heart? How did he get past the medical with a weak heart?"

Erik paused, and Marita waited.

"No, not that kind of weakness...I'm afraid he won't be able to watch men burn in their aircraft. I consider myself a bit soft in that department, but this young man has a special spirit. I'm afraid it might break—that such a wonderful young man will become cynical and refuse to do his job." Erik could feel depression raising its head.

Marita sensed her husband's sad mood and steered him back. "You can only try to keep both of you alive until this ends. If he is with you, I don't believe he will lose his humanity any more than you have. Despite the war, you're still the same sweet man I married."

He couldn't see the tears welling up in her eyes, but he heard them in her voice. "I love you, Marita." The call was almost over, and Erik's depression was returning. "It's you and the children who keep me sane and alive. I have to go now. I'm afraid we just blew a week's pay on this call, but I needed to hear your voice."

They wasted ten seconds of silence; Erik swallowed hard, then remembered a good news item.

"I believe I have a sale for the car, and I will send you the money." His voice caught. "Please kiss the children for me."

Marita quickly broke in before he could hang up, "Please, Erik, don't sell the car. Jonas has already deposited more than enough money in our account to take care of us, and he won't take it back. The man is an angel, and he and Annalisa are servants of God sent to look after us. Please, keep the car."

Erik smiled. He couldn't take money from Jonas without sacrificing his luxuries; the car would have to go.

"Fritz and his crew already agreed to buy the car and to lend it to me whenever I need it. The maintenance crew will chip in to pay for it, and they will maintain it. I have the best of both worlds, so don't worry. Anyway, it's just a car."

Erik knew he would never borrow the car, and Marita knew it too. She said, "That sounds like a great arrangement for everyone. It's wonderful to have friends like Fritz, isn't it?"

Erik smiled into the telephone. "Yes, it is. I must go now, so I'm kissing you over the phone. Goodbye, Liebling, and good night." Tears welled in his eyes, and he choked a sob. He thought of Matthias and Maria and imagined the terrible things that could happen to his family. He didn't know how to go on; he only knew that he must.

"Goodbye, Liebling. I'm kissing you back." Marita and Erik, hundreds of kilometres apart, simultaneously laid the phones in their cradles.

◇◇◇◇◇◇◇◇◇◇◇◇◇◇◇◇◇◇◇◇◇◇◇◇◇◇◇

It took two weeks after the mosquito strike for the Florennes field to return to full strength. The field engineers replaced the AA guns, scattered three fuel lorries and four fuel trailers around the airfield, and the ground crews parked them in different spots every time they used them.

Older aircraft replaced the lost fighters—obsolete models set aside because they were technically outdated or worn out. Four replacement night fighters were older Bf 110s with time-expired engines and no upward-firing cannons. Their radars weren't the newest Lichtenstein sets, and if the operator turned it on, a British night fighter immediately saw the signal, limiting the crew's life expectancy to the time it took a mosquito to cover the distance between them.

On May 3, as the sinking sun was still bright in the clear Belgian sky, Erik and Karl finished their final inspection of their aircraft. In his sometimes maddeningly meticulous way, Karl had created an extensive checklist, much more comprehensive than messerschmitt and mercedes' checklists combined. Erik watched him pedantically inspect every item before checking it off. He thought his navigator was going over the edge, especially considering they hadn't yet flown a mission together. But time wasn't a premium item, so Erik did as Karl requested and joined him in inspecting the fighter. Fritz watched them do the fourth inspection since he had officially signed off the aircraft as "airworthy," shook his head and smiled. Erik gave him a look that said, "Leave the boy alone," and Fritz turned away.

Following the mosquito raid, the field services and quarters had been scattered over a wide area, extending the stroll from the aircraft parking spot to the mess to about ten minutes. Erik waved goodbye to Fritz and shrugged his shoulders as he and Karl started walking. Karl stared at his list, for the third time checking that he hadn't forgotten anything.

◇◇◇◇◇◇◇◇◇◇◇◇◇◇◇◇◇◇◇◇◇◇◇◇◇◇◇◇◇◇◇◇◇◇◇◇◇◇◇

When Karl finally put the list away, he pointed at the new AA guns. "Did you ever think about how many anti-aircraft guns there must be in all the airfields, military compounds, and cities in German-held territory?" Erik wondered where Karl was going but didn't actually care. Karl was always coming up with new hypotheses and testing them on him.

"No, but it must be in the thousands." Erik had not stopped to think of that before. Now that he did, he couldn't see the point.

Karl motored on, "It's probably more than you think. This morning, before you got up, I listed all the cities and towns I could think of that would have anti-aircraft protection and, using my home city and this airfield as a benchmark, it would be over a hundred thousand guns. I have calculated how many tons of ammunition that would require, and I came up with a number. How many tons do you think that might be?"

"I haven't thought about it"—Erik was already a little tired of the game—"but probably more than a few."

Karl nodded toward the guns. "I assumed that the 88mm guns we have here are the average, and I asked the gunners—and they told me that each round weighs about ten kilograms. Then, I asked what the reserve for each gun should be, and the crews here confirmed that they have four hundred rounds beside each gun or stored nearby. Make

207

a reasonable guess at the total tons of ammunition available for the anti-aircraft guns in Germany and the occupied countries."

Erik did the math quickly in his head. "Wow, it's forty thousand tons!"

Karl laughed. "No, you've got the decimal point in the wrong place, but not bad for a quick mental calculation. It is well over four hundred thousand tons of ammunition. And during a raid on a major city, the guns fire an average of about two hundred tons of ammunition."

Erik interrupted, hoping that would end the topic, "I'll take your word for that,"

Karl forged on. "A train carries about nine hundred tons of AA ammunition…if it doesn't carry anything else. That ammunition must be loaded on Lastwagen, taken to the train, transferred to rail cars, transported to the city where the guns are, back to a Lastwagen, and finally trucked to ammunition storage facilities. Following a raid, soldiers and Lastwagen replenish the guns' reserves. Each Lastwagen carries five tonnes, so if a city is bombed, a crew of men must load and unload forty Lastwagen."

Erik could think of nothing to say.

Karl looked at him with a quizzical expression that said he had expected more from his mentor. He asked, "Isn't it true that those guns and that ammunition could be on the Russian front or facing the English Channel to stop the inevitable invasion?"

Erik nodded without committing and continued to be silent, but an ember of interest began to glow.

Karl asked, excited now, "Have you thought about how many men it takes to operate those guns?" Erik didn't answer—Karl was in territory Erik had never visited and was gathering momentum without his help.

"If we allow five men per gun, that's five hundred thousand, but there are support personnel who maintain the guns, transport ammunition and parts, build gun fortifications and repair guns damaged in raids. I'm willing to bet there are at least a million intelligent, physically fit men twiddling their thumbs while waiting for British and American bombers that may never hit their city! But they have to be there because the citizens demand protection."

Erik finally spoke, words jumping into his head. "Are you saying that the British and Americans are justified in bombing our cities?" The logic of his conclusion surprised him.

Karl nodded. "Yes, I suppose that, perversely, it is a good strategy to tie up those vital German forces, but perhaps from our point of view, we could defend ourselves better with fewer civilian casualties." He waved his arms, frustrated that the solution was obvious to him but no one else.

"Why don't we evacuate the cities' centers—if we know that is the bombers' target, wouldn't it be cheaper, both in money and lives, to get the people out? Perhaps the British would do something more sensible with their airplanes if there were no people in the city centres."

Erik scratched his head and was going to say, "I've never thought about that," but decided to keep it to himself.

Karl kept going, "The Defense Department evacuated Hamburg the day after the bombers incinerated, according to Goebbels' ministry of lies, close to one hundred thousand people. I admit it could be twice that or half that, but isn't the actual number irrelevant?"

Erik shrugged. "I suppose…if you can make people's lives irrelevant… And I will also admit we could actually do that, just for this discussion."

Karl nodded. "Before fire-bombing Hamburg, the Allies had destroyed the entire Ruhr valley, so wouldn't it have been reasonable to expect them to attack Hamburg, one of the largest German industrial centers and a densely populated city? If we could evacuate the city after the raid, why not evacuate it before?" He waved his hands in frustration, tainted with a hint of arrogance.

Erik sensed that Karl wasn't done yet. He didn't like where the young man was going and silently wished he would shut up. However, he shook his head and encouraged him further by commenting.

"You make it sound like Hitler wants the civilian body count to be as high as possible…" He was stunned when an idea hit him like a blow from nowhere, and suddenly asked, "Do you think Goebbels wants those people to die so he can use their deaths as propaganda against the British?" A tiny ember burning in Erik's brain became a roaring fire.

"Is he fueling hate for the enemy and prolonging the inevitable by letting the British and Americans waste resources killing German civilians!" He felt his excitement growing and tried to contain it. "If you carry the hate theme a little further, isn't that how Hitler came to power? First, we hated the Communists, then the Jews, the Poles, the French, and now…"

Karl interrupted to finish Erik's logic... "the British, the Americans and the Russians. Wouldn't the slaughter of civilians build his popularity through hate for the perpetrators—the British and the Americans?"

Karl chopped the edge of his right hand down into his left palm.

"Now, the important question: you and I can't be the only ones who have thought this through—so, is there a serious flaw in the logic?" Karl asked questions no one ever asked, and Erik was stunned at the depth of the boy's thoughts.

Erik thought of his family—Marita refused to leave Heilbronn. It made no sense to stay, but only an evacuation order would get Marita out of her home!

Erik said, "I believe you are more right than wrong, and the answer may be even more drastic than your picture, but this isn't something we can change. People who live in the cities don't want your solution because they don't want to leave their homes. The English didn't evacuate London when we bombed it—hell, the English King and his family stayed in Buckingham Palace—and they thumbed their noses at Hitler by advertising that King George was there!"

Karl shook his head, reluctantly correcting his boss. "They evacuated their children and many of the women and old people. Only essential workers stayed. Many who left went to work and live on farms outside the city."

Erik thought of Pastor Bergman and stopped walking. Karl stopped to face him. Erik put his hand on the boy's shoulder.

"Karl, you must stop this and never speak of it to anyone else. I want to get us both through the war alive, and fighting the British is tough enough without you bringing the SS and Gestapo into the fight against us." Erik resisted the temptation to tell Karl he was too young and naïve to understand—he wasn't sure enough that Karl was wrong. He glanced at the men smoking on the steps of the mess hall, satisfied they were out of earshot. Erik addressed Karl as he imagined talking to Walther when he was eighteen.

"Karl, you must promise not to speak of such things again!"

Erik saw no fear in Karl's eyes. This young man was concerned with his country's welfare, not his own.

Karl said, "Yes, sir, I promise—I will do my duty, and we will try to survive." Erik heard his own voice in Karl's words.

Erik and Karl were in the middle game of their evening chess match when the Luftwaffe squadron messenger stuck his head in the door. "Bombers up! It's time to go!" Erik nodded, picked his flying jacket from the hook on the wall and headed for the door. When he reached it, Karl was ahead but stepped aside to let his commander exit first. They jogged to their new zero-hour messerschmitt Bf 110G-4, parked five hundred metres from their barracks. Erik was conscious of his navigator trotting slightly behind, a deliberate but delicate accommodation to Erik's relaxed running tempo. Erik deliberately paced himself—time wasted recovering from running hard would be greater than the time saved by running fast. Once a mission began, time became a valuable commodity, especially if the venerable mosquito vultures timed their attack to pick off Erik's messerschmitt before it cleared the runway. When they arrived, Erik hoped to be in the air and far away from the field.

CHAPTER NINETEEN

3 May 1944

There is nothing remarkable about coincidence…it happens all the time.
It only becomes remarkable when we recognize it.
Oscar Wilde

BETWEEN MISSIONS, NORMA TAUGHT WILLIE the art of making love
to her. He gained confidence, fell irredeemably in love—and his
fear of death grew proportionately. Whenever 'C for Charley' had no
mission and Norma sang at the Blue Bell Inn, Willie took the base bus
or hitched a ride in someone's car to spend the evening playing with
her in the hotel room. His dread of flying the next mission grew with
every evening spent with Norma. On the third of May, it had reached
panic proportions.

As usual, 'C for Charley' received its operation orders just before
noon. When the briefing at 20:00 hrs revealed that the target was Mailly
le Camp, eighty miles east of Paris, every man in the room breathed a
sigh of relief.

Mailly le Camp, a training and mustering base for German tanks,
stood separated from the town—and the crews looked forward to bombing a strictly military target. Most of the past month's objectives had been
at least partly military, and the airmen had pushed their feelings of guilt at
intentionally bombing civilians into the background. The new RAF term
for civilian deaths on these missions was "collateral damage," insinuat-
ing that the primary objective was military and civilian casualties were
unavoidable.

The Germans were not as keen to defend the French, exhausting
their crews, ammunition and fuel to protect French civilians. No 44
squadron had lost only one lancaster since the Nürnberg fiasco, and the
crew had survived, albeit in a German prison camp. Consequently, the
first item at the briefing was that the Mailly le Camp operation would
only count for a one-third credit toward the crews' thirty-mission tour,
predicated on intelligence that predicted little resistance. mosquitos

would mark the target using the OBOE navigation system and flares, and the buildings at the tank base would present easy targets in what 'Met' promised would be clear weather.

Despite master bomber Group Captain Cheshire's confident assurances, the bombing approach worried Steve and his crew. The strangely designed bombing route required three hundred and fifty bombers to muster at a yellow marker fifteen miles from the target and wait for instructions to follow a flare path to the tank base. Parachute flares would illuminate the target, but the elaborate procedure the bombers must follow before and during the bombing run depended entirely on the master bomber.

The plan called for the attacking aircraft to stack over the yellow marker, flying in circles separated vertically by one-hundred-foot increments until directed to the target by the master bomber. There was no backup for the man or the communication system.

Checklists finished, the line of lancasters crept toward the end of the runway, and Steve took the opportunity to voice his concerns over the intercom. "Boys, Our intrepid Scots navigator has reckoned how we will fly the circuits around the yellow marker. We will fly in a circle, staying a constant mile from a yellow flare. It's about six miles around the circle, and each layer will have at least a dozen aircraft nose-to-tail. There will be a hundred feet between layers, and the accepted error in an altimeter is thirty feet. Unfortunately, it is nearly impossible to maintain altitude within less than fifty feet in a circular holding pattern where course adjustments are necessarily continuous."

Steve added, more emphatically, "It's dark, we have no navigation lights, and if you want to get home, I need everyone to keep their eyes peeled for friends and enemies. Don't even think about anything else!"

Willie said, "So, what you are telling us is that our friends are as dangerous as enemy fighters. That scares me!"

"Not quite. Don't forget the fighters have guns and are trying to get close enough to use them! It won't take those clever Nazi bastards long to figure out what that yellow flare means, and then we will be sitting ducks in a round barrel. There are a hundred night fighters on bases less than an hour from our target. If the Nazis decide to defend that base, they'll have a turkey shoot, and we'll have a disaster!"

The crew's silence said everything. Ronnie broke it as Steve released the brakes. "Shit, look at that moon! Those bastards have organized another Nürnberg operation!"

"And did ye hink they woods fire th' Sassenach twits jist fur killin' puckle hunder lads?" Charley laughed into his mask. "Dornt ye see, lads? Those lackeys aw got promotions an' noo they're gonnae kill mair lads sae 'at they gie promoted again? Jobby, wee jimmies, they'll aw be generals if they dae it again!" Silence returned.

<hr>

'C for Charley' was scheduled for takeoff at five minutes before ten and received their wave-off on time. The bombing load was high explosives, including a 4,000-pound "Cookie"—no incendiaries. The objective was not far from the base, and the fuel load was light, allowing for a higher bomb payload. The targets were tanks and buildings; high explosives killed tanks and flattened buildings.

As usual, the lancaster barely cleared the low fence at the end of the runway and laboured to reach the planned altitude of twelve-thousand feet in twenty-five minutes of full-throttle climbing. The sky was clear, the three-quarter moon was bright, and Flight Operations predicted no night fighters in the area. The C/O had said, "Get in and get out—easy as pie!" Willie was scared as hell!

The short route to the target had two kinks, the first ten degrees to the left over Dieppe at twelve-thousand feet, the second at the yellow flare. Flak to the yellow marker was as predicted, light to non-existent. No 44 squadron was the first to begin the circling maneuver, and five minutes from their assigned holding point, Steve backed the throttles to descend. He concentrated on the altimeter as he approached his assigned seven-thousand-four-hundred-foot altitude.

The Flight Engineer, Phillip Carpenter, checked the barometer setting on the altimeter during the descent, tweaking it to precisely 29.92, Standard Air Pressure, as assigned at the briefing. At seven-thousand-four-hundred-feet, Steve added just enough throttle to freeze the altimeter needle.

Keeping the marker at the leading edge of his left wingtip, he started the standard rate two-minute left turn specified in the briefing, adjusting the radius with the trim and throttles until the yellow flare remained stationary. With little wind and stable night air, precise flying was easy, but the complicated scenario still required all of Steve's attention.

Halfway around the first circle, the wireless operator, Jeffrey Conway, spoke into the intercom.

"Listen to this, mates...I'm going to feed the radio through the intercom." His voice disappeared, and in its place, an American disc jockey on American Armed Forces Radio announced, "'Deep in the heart of Texas,' for all those guys and gals lonesome for the wide-open spaces." He added a "Yee-Haw!" and the record began.

A couple of bars into the song, Jeff came back. "I hate to be the bearer of bad news, but that's the VHF frequency the master bomber plans to use to give us our bombing instructions!" The intercom went silent for a few seconds, and then Steve asked, "Will we hear him over that racket?"

"Not a chance, skipper; that station has a ton of power, and to answer your next question, no, we don't have an alternate frequency." It was the answer that Steve feared.

A lancaster in the layer below and flying inside them suddenly lost its right wing to a terrific explosion, putting an exclamation mark on Steve's worst fear. There was no time for the crew to escape; the wreck plummeted like an anvil. A thousand feet into its plunge, it sliced the tail off another lancaster and seconds later became a ball of bright light when it struck terra firma, leaving a red glow that immediately began to die. The tailless lancaster tipped nose-down and exploded a few hundred yards from the first. Willie watched the brutal sequence, then spoke into the intercom.

"One of those night fighters with the guns that shoot upward got a twofer—and tell me again—why are we packed like my mom's pickles in her stone crock?"

Willie understood what the German upward-firing guns could do, but some crews still didn't believe him. There was even a ridiculous belief, propagated by officialdom, that the exploding bombers were "scarecrow" explosions caused by shells fired from AA guns and designed to simulate an exploding aircraft, supposedly to ruin the bomber crews' morale. The entire aircrew of 'C for Charley' knew what the explosions were, and their report after the Nürnberg raid had been clear. Somewhere up the line, the information had disappeared or, more likely, been purposely ignored.

Ronnie Cummins sounded nervous, something unusual for him,

when he said, "Remember boys, we have to find those bastards, and we have to watch out for falling lancasters."

The resonance of his words hadn't died when a bomber ahead burst into flames and dove to the ground. The low altitude compressed the time it took for it to fall—twenty seconds from the cannon shells hitting the lancaster's fuel tanks until it struck the ground—no time for the crew to do anything but curse one last time.

Willie tried not to watch the carnage around him, but despite his efforts to concentrate, every plane that went down took his eyes away from his scan. He forced himself to search for propeller reflections, the twinkle of guns firing, a shadow that didn't belong, but he hadn't seen anything in ten missions and was afraid the edge was gone.

A few minutes later, the shape Willie saw was not what he was looking for nor where he expected to find it. Moonlight glinted off a whirling propeller a few feet from his head. A wing, a second propeller, more wing—and then a messerschmitt's cockpit was going to hit his turret!

Willie screamed, "Dive, Steve! Jesus Christ...Dive! A damned messerschmitt is going to ram us!" He corrected, yelled, "Corkscrew!" And, just as he got it right, he found himself staring into the face of the night fighter's pilot. As their eyes locked, he saw the surprise on the German's face, and he saw the pilot's arms stretch to push his control stick forward. Willie was a second too late depressing his guns; his tracers arced over the fighter's elevator, missing the rudder as the hunter disappeared under his feet.

Steve broke into Willie's shock, "What did you say? Say it slower!" The German pilot's face remained—burned into Willie's brain.

"Forget it. A night fighter almost rammed us, but it's gone now—I was too late."

"Yell 'corkscrew' if you want me to dive. That's a command that I can understand when you yell. Whatever else you say when you scream like that is so blurred I can't understand it!"

Ten minutes later, a dark shadow became a lancaster, its outboard propeller inching toward Willie's turret. He said, "Shit!" Yelled, "Corkscrew," into his mask and fired tracers over and in front of the lancaster's fuselage. Steve pushed the column ahead; the elevators lifted Willie above the intruder's wing, and its tip sliced the air under his feet.

Willie said, "Okay, he's turned away from us."

'C for Charley' dove through a cloud of heavy bombers at two thousand feet a minute—and seven men braced for a collision that would end their lives.

Steve announced to his terrified crew, "Don't worry, I'm inside the bombers and heading for the flare. The only safe place is in the middle of this mess!" He levelled the wings and eased back on the column, headed for what he hoped was empty air over the flare.

Steve gained most of the lost altitude as he flew over the flare and joined the circling mixture of aluminum, gasoline, and high explosives on the other side.

Two more bombers hit the ground. Willie talked into his mask, "They're like sharks around a school of herring. They pick off the outside fish. Smart herring go to the inside—why don't we do that?"

Without answering, Steve slowed twenty mph, and when the plane was settled, the two-minute turn put 'C for Charley' well inside the stream of bombers. When he had found his new groove, Steve said into his mask, "Well done, Willie. The Scottish sheepherder tells me we're two hundred yards inside the stream's edge."

Willie's breathing became normal again, and he re-established his scan rhythm. He began to hope he might yet survive another mission.

CHAPTER TWENTY

3 May 1944

Überleben ist ein Beruf, der gelernt werden muß wie jeder andere.
(Survival is a learned skill, like any other.)

FRITZ HAD THE MERCEDES ENGINES PURRING and everything in the green when Erik and Karl arrived at their place of business. Erik hadn't finished locking his harness when he heard Karl identify their messerschmitt to ground control and ask for instructions. The tower immediately came back with taxi clearance, and Erik powered the mercedes engines up, swung out to the taxiway, and headed for the end of runway 'two-five.' He did his mag and carb heat checks as he taxied and barely had the runway lined up in the windscreen when the tower cleared him to take off. Twenty seconds later, they were the first fighter in the air.

Erik heard Karl switch over to Deelen Control, announce their position and altitude and ask for instructions in the clipped, clear diction that his training had taught him.

Erik heard Deelen say, "Climb to six thousand metres and wait at the Alpha beacon."

On the ground for a week with nothing to do, Karl had memorized every beacon's location and plotted courses to them in every kind of wind. Close was, in this case, good enough, and on this night with little wind, Karl came back with his pre-calculated no-wind solution in seconds. "Steer two-sixty degrees and climb to six-thousand metres."

Erik had gone through all the possible scenarios with Karl, including the typical and frequent jamming of Deelen. That would happen at any moment, and Erik reminded Karl, "Ask Deelen where to expect the bombers."

Deelen had chosen Alpha, a beacon on the French-Belgian border, which told Erik that Deelen anticipated an attack west and south of the messerschmitt's position, but he wanted confirmation.

"There's no answer, sir—I'm only getting static." Karl sounded surprised.

Erik decided to let Karl relax and get the feel of the mission. "Forget Deelen, and don't turn on the radar until I tell you. Relax, look out the window for mosquitoes."

Erik reached the beacon while climbing through three thousand metres. He adjusted the trim nose-down, stopping the climb. The airspeed passed three hundred kph.

"I'm levelling off on this course. The location of Alpha is no secret, and mosquito night fighters will be there shortly. When they arrive, we should be somewhere else."

A few minutes later, with the 110 west of the beacon, Erik switched to what Karl had dubbed in his mission list, 'phase two.' He said, "Switch on the radar, and I'll swing the nose across the southwestern horizon as soon as you have a picture. Those bombers aren't far away."

"Switching radar on," Karl replied, and thirty seconds later, the tubes were warm, and the pale green screen came alive. "I have a picture."

Erik slowly turned from a southwest heading toward the north, and in seconds, Karl announced, "Multiple targets at three hundred degrees."

Erik said, *"Abschalten!"*

Karl instantly confirmed, "Radar off."

Erik grinned. He heard no excitement or emotion from his new navigator—a good start. He watched the compass swing past three hundred degrees to three-twenty—he had added twenty degrees, his best guess at an intercept angle.

◇◇◇◇◇◇◇◇◇◇◇◇◇◇◇◇◇◇◇◇◇◇◇◇◇◇◇◇◇◇◇◇◇◇◇◇◇

Twenty minutes later, a yellow flare appeared in Erik's windscreen ahead and to port, and he turned slightly left to fly directly toward it. His instincts told him to maintain three thousand metres. Deelen was still silent, and Erik assumed they were on their own, as he preferred.

"Anschalten!"

"Radar on." There was no excitement in the boy's voice, although Erik knew that Karl had seen the flare.

Thirty seconds later, fuzzy bogeys dotted the entire screen. Karl shut off the set before they became sharp. "The sky ahead of us is full of airplanes flying over the yellow flare. A line of Radarechos is approaching from the west, but there are none more than fifteen hundred metres east of the flare." Karl added, "Radar is off."

"Roger on the Echos. Understand radar is off." Erik thought he knew what was going on. "It looks like the British are flying a circular holding pattern before they drop their bombs; God knows why, but perhaps a British general had a dream. Forget the radar; keep your eyes peeled for bombers, and I will set up the attack and fire the cannons. There must be a reason those bombers are stacking over that flare like a swarm of bees…until we figure it out, I need you to watch for traffic."

Karl said a short, *"Verstehe"* as he marked the flare's location on the chart.

Erik took the time it took to approach the yellow marker to figure out what was going on over that flare. He reasoned that a path of flares he could see leading south from the yellow marker was the road to the target. Only a desk officer with zero chance of flying the mission would contrive that brilliant idea!

Since Nürnberg, Erik had assumed there was no limit to Bomber Command's tactical stupidity—what he could see in front of him proved his point. He could not think of any explanation for this madness except that the Luftwaffe put the bright flares there to announce the bombers' location, but that wasn't reasonable. Had Bomber Command assumed that the Luftwaffe had run out of airplanes, gasoline, or both? Or did they think the Germans suddenly decided not to defend themselves?

Slowly descending, passing through two-thousand-four-hundred metres, Erik picked out a lancaster from the three he could see in the bright moonlight and began inching his way under it, trying to figure out the holding pattern it was flying. In his concentration on the victim, he missed a dark shape in front of him—Karl's young eyes saw it first, and he shouted, "Dive! Dive! lancaster dead ahead!" Before 'lancaster' was out of Karl's mouth, Erik pushed the stick ahead and yelled, *"Sheisse,"* as his canopy almost scraped the bottom of the lancaster's turret.

The moonlight shone full on the face of the young gunner, a few metres in front of Erik. The turret had no glass, and every detail of the young face etched itself forever in Erik's brain. They stared at one another briefly before what looked like a young boy swung and lowered his browning machine guns. He had stared at Erik just long enough to save Erik and Karl's lives. The diving messerschmitt gained speed and lost altitude quickly, but until Karl announced a stream of tracers passing behind him, Erik wasn't sure he was out of the lancaster's field of fire. He grunted, relieved when he felt no impact from bullets hitting the tail.

Erik squeezed the stick to control his shaking hands and forced the messerschmitt down five hundred metres before levelling off. He decided to survey the scene a little more before he tried again. Moonlight glinted off bombers all around him, and the magnitude of the British generals' stupidity made him shout, "The idiocy of this is embarrassing" into his intercom. "We are only losing this war because our idiots are bigger than theirs. Those bombers are actually flying in circles around that yellow flare!"

Karl's nervous voice cracked as he answered, "Yes, sir, if you say so, sir!"

Erik weaved his messerschmitt through the maze of circling aircraft until he was safely flying in a larger radius circle than the bombers were using. He soon realized the bombers were flying a standard rate two-minute turn, adding to the stupidity. Every aircraft on both sides of the war had a turn-and-bank indicator with only one turn marked on it, and it took two minutes to fly a circle at that bank angle with the ball centred—the slower the speed, the smaller the circle's diameter, and vice versa. Every bomber flew at the same airspeed, putting every British aircraft the same distance from the flare, telling German fighters where to find them and exponentially increasing the odds of a collision.

"Two more bombers down..." Karl announced the obvious, then said, "There must be a reason..."

Erik said, "No, this is war, run by politicians and generals, and by definition, there is no reason in anything. We've only begun to shoot bombers down. This clear sky and the bright moon should bring ten squadrons of night fighters to the party, but I'll bet a week's pay our generals won't let them use the fuel!" Erik doubted the Luftwaffe would ration fuel tonight if they knew what the British bombers were doing, but they would react too late.

"Karl, there are too many airplanes over this flare—watch out for our fighters—if the Luftwaffe wakes up, they'll be everywhere, and their eyes will be on bombers, not looking for our fighters."

Karl said, *"Verstehe"* again, and Erik was pleased to have a navigator who didn't need to say more than the essential confirmation.

Erik picked out a lancaster flying at two-thousand-five-hundred metres on the outside edge of the circling armada, descended fifty metres, set his aircraft in a two-minute turn that matched the bomber's path and kept the messerschmitt just outside it. Erik added power, steepened the bank angle, and watched the turret as the messerschmitt passed under the tail—and it didn't move.

When the lines in the reflector sight crossed the wing between the starboard engines, he closed his eyes and fired the vertical 30mm cannons for two seconds. The exploding shells severed the main wing spar, igniting thousands of pounds of fuel, and the ensuing explosion created an instant gap between the engines. The outer wing and engine flipped up, appeared to stop in the air, and then disappeared into the darkness behind Erik. The fuselage, lacking lift on its starboard side, fell to the right with the intact port wing pointing at the moon. Unsupported, the nose dropped until it aimed directly at the ground, the port side wing's lift slowly rotating the burning fuselage. Flames spread over the entire aircraft, splashing into a giant pool of bright light seconds later.

◇◇◇◇◇◇◇◇◇◇◇◇◇◇◇◇◇◇◇◇◇◇◇◇◇◇◇◇◇

Erik pulled his eyes back to the blackness and found that his night vision was gone. Even though the explosion occurred well below the Me110, the shock wave from the lancaster's exploding bombs threw it all over the sky, and Erik had to work to hold it upright. His vision destroyed, up and down unclear, Erik relaxed his grip on the stick and let the aircraft have its head while he sorted out what the instruments were telling him.

The wake of hundreds of heavy aircraft stirring up the air in the circular holding pattern tossed the little fighter around like a beachball tethered to a pole. But a messerschmitt 110 is a very stable aircraft, too stable to be even a mediocre one-on-one fighter against the modern agile Allied fighters, and when Erik recovered his night vision and sorted out what the instruments were saying, his aircraft was flying peacefully away from the melee surrounding the yellow flare.

Erik forced himself to concentrate. The proximity of the ground, shockwaves from exploding aircraft, and the wakes of hundreds of heavy airplanes milling around a yellow flare made flying the messerschmitt a full-time job. Erik decided to change his attack plans.

"Karl, I need you to fire the cannons, but tell me before you pull the trigger so I can close my eyes." He had nagged Karl ad nauseum about the dangers of hitting the fuselage. He said, "That's where the bombs are," until, on his ninth or tenth nag during a chess game, Karl had finally stopped him. "Enough, sir, I think I've got it." Erik didn't mention it again.

Until tonight. "If I set up on the inside of the bomber's wing, please don't hit the fuselage—it's full of really big bombs!" Erik smiled.

Karl said, "Understood. I will not fire if you set up under the fuselage." Erik whispered, "Touché."

The next bomber Erik picked out was a lancaster a hundred metres above him, and he carefully set up his attack on the inside of the circle, planning his escape toward the flare on his left, where logic said there would be no bombers or fighters. Consequently, he wasn't looking for aircraft on his left between him and the yellow flare when gun flashes appeared on the 110's port side.

◇◇◇◇◇◇◇◇◇◇◇◇◇◇◇◇◇◇◇◇◇◇◇◇◇◇◇◇◇◇

The tracers from the flashes marked a path over and behind the messerschmitt. Erik pushed the stick full ahead and to the right, slamming his foot on the right rudder, but he had reacted too late, and a stream of steel-jacketed .303 bullets tattooed the side of his messerschmitt. Following Erik's control input, the fighter lifted its port wing and dropped, sweeping the tracer stream away from the fuselage to the left engine. The deadly torrent of bullets stopped when Erik flew over another bomber, barely missing it. He used the left aileron and rudder to reverse the spiral, executed a ninety-degree turn, and straightened into a dive to the northeast, away from the bombers. Erik shut off the sick left engine, now spewing its oily guts over the wing, feathered the prop, and turned on the extinguisher to reduce the chance of fire while simultaneously cutting the throttle on the starboard engine. The airspeed was over six hundred kilometres per hour and increasing when he levelled the wings and eased the stick back, keeping the "G" load at what he hoped the likely damaged airframe would stand. The nose slowly rose, the airspeed decreased, and nothing broke.

"Scheisse!" Erik swore into his intercom, fighting a sudden panic as he asked, "Karl, are you alright?" There was no answer, and he couldn't see Karl in the mirror. He tried again, his heart in his black boots. "Karl, are you okay?" The intercom was silent. There was usually a bit of engine magneto noise in the intercom, but Erik's headset was utterly dead, and he guessed hopefully that this meant the intercom was the problem and Karl was alive—but where was he? Erik watched the airspeed back off the messerschmitt's structural limit as he levelled out at a thousand metres, unfastened his belts and turned around to check on Karl. His navigator waved at him from the floor, held up two ends of the white intercom wire that should have been together, and went back to patching. A few minutes later, Erik could hear the magnetos on the starboard engine firing.

"How are you receiving me, Oberleutnant?" asked his new mechanic.

"Five-by-five, Karl. It's good to hear your voice; how are things back there?"

"Drafty; otherwise, no problems. When we return, Fritz will have a few holes to patch, and I see we've lost the new engine. I suppose that means our night is over, and Fritz will be pissed."

Erik smiled, relieved they could fly home. Karl obviously didn't realize how close he had come to dying.

"Yes, it's over, but the plane is flyable. Fritz will be our biggest problem now—he won't be pleased we lost his engine!" Although Erik wished for rudder trim to help hold a steady course with one engine, the plane responded to the controls. His right leg was already beginning to tire. He shifted his left foot to rest on his right boot.

"I guess the RAF has more than one crafty gunner, or one of them has my number." He checked the fuel; the tanks weren't leaking. "Give me the course home and tune the radio to the field."

Karl tuned the wireless and, three minutes later, gave Erik the bearing and distance to the field. The starboard engine purred, Erik had the plane under control, and the moon was beautiful. The only thing left to worry about was whether the port landing gear would lower and lock—the landing gear legs were fastened to the engine mounts, and failure was a distinct possibility. Erik had no doubt they could survive a belly landing—and, at this point, Hitler's airplane was the least of Erik's concerns. He was more afraid of facing Fritz.

CHAPTER TWENTY-ONE

3 May 1944

Reprise

RONNIE CUMMINS WAS SO YOUNG when he learned to ride a horse that he had forgotten there was a first time—he was a part of the horse from the moment his butt touched the saddle or the horse's bare back—and the same was true of shooting.

When he was seven, Ronnie's father gave him a single-shot .22-caliber rifle for rodents and small game. He taught his son to safely handle the gun and shoot accurately, and Ronnie took to shooting like a newborn calf takes to walking.

The fine-tuning had come later from his uncle, one of the best competitive shooters in Rhodesia. When Ronnie was twelve, Uncle Josh gave him a British Lee Enfield 'three-aught-three' with a shortened barrel and stock, the 'cavalry carbine' version. Uncle Josh removed all extraneous paraphernalia and included lessons in shooting from all positions, including from a running horse.

Consequently, Ronnie learned to hit a fast-moving hyena from his galloping horse, and even a zigzagging gazelle had near-zero odds of escaping. He learned to fire accurately with both eyes open, instinctively leading his target.

When Ronnie sat in a canvas sling behind twin browning machine guns, he was at home, and it took only a few sessions before his accuracy with them was mythical. He saw, aimed and fired in one smooth motion and usually hit what he aimed at.

When Ronnie spotted a night fighter pulling up under an unsuspecting bomber, he swung his turret and swore into the intercom, "Jesus Christ, there's a one-ten on our starboard side!" while depressing the gun to the coaming. The twin brownings roared, cutting off the sentence at the second word, but the coaming stopped the browning's barrels from depressing far enough, and the line of tracers curved over and behind the German fighter. He almost broke the gun's mount in his effort to force the barrel down, but there was no joy there for him, and the night fighter didn't seem to notice.

"Did you hit him, Ronnie?" Willie had seen Ronnie's tracers, located the plane, and the chatter from his quartet of brownings drowned out Ronnie's answering curse. The German night fighter rolled away as Willie directed his stream of fire at the wing and one of the plane's engines but had to stop firing when the messerschmitt crossed over and behind another bomber.

"Sorry, I couldn't get my fucking guns down... " Ronnie's frustrated tone switched to a more optimistic one... "but I think you may have gotten him."

Willie wasn't as sure. "I didn't see him until you yelled, and all I had to fire at was a propeller. I'm pretty sure I at least took out an engine and ruined his night."

Willie's mind returned to the face he had seen in the close encounter with the earlier messerschmitt. The number painted on the nose came to him—it was 164, a number Willie knew he would never forget. His glimpse of the pilot was not of the cold-blooded killer he imagined would be flying a night fighter.

Willie reckoned that at least a dozen fighters were among the bombers—half of them Me110s. The first messerschmitt would probably have stayed with the bomber flow, and so there was a possibility he had killed the man he had seen in their close encounter. Willie was surprised when he found himself hoping the man had escaped.

Ronnie broke into Willie's reverie. "I doubt his port engine is still running, but I didn't see any fire, and he dove away from us so quickly I doubt he was damaged enough to be a kill." He slammed his palm against the breach of one of the brownings. "Jesus, I hate these popguns! The Germans use cannons against us, and we fire back with a rifle bullet! This fucking toy uses the same ammunition as my little Lee Enfield, and those bullets bounce off a rhino! God, I hate this stupid war and the idiots who are running it!"

Steve interrupted, "Agreed, but here we are; you've got brownings, and the stupid English are tearing Germany apart! Good shooting, Willie—you probably saved that crew's life! It's for sure that fighter won't shoot down any bombers for a few days, and that's the objective."

Steve added, "Okay, let's stop talking and concentrate on doing our job. I'm going to fly down that flare path, instructions or no instructions, and I will ask the rest of the squadron to follow me! Jeff, use the HF frequency."

Jeffrey Conway checked the master bomber's VHF frequency...it was still broadcasting American frivolity. He dialled the HF squadron frequency and informed the bombers of Steve's intentions.

It had been almost fifteen minutes since 'C for Charley' had begun the circling maneuver; mosquitos had refreshed the flare path, and the parachute flares over the target were visible. Bombs exploded at the tank base just as Steve turned out of the circle and followed the line of flares leading to the target—someone else had broken rank before him. As 'C for Charley' levelled out on the course, the American voice on the air stopped broadcasting, and the master bomber immediately instructed the bombers over the VHF frequency to fly to the targets, maintaining their assigned altitudes.

The flak was light but accurate, and the aircraft behind 'C for Charley' took a direct hit. Willie was looking at the plane when the shell hit the plane's bomb bay—twelve thousand pounds of high explosives disintegrated the aircraft before his eyes, temporarily blinding him.

Willie's eyes burned and itched as though full of sand as he strained to find the shapes, the spinning propellers, a glint of moonlight on a canopy, through the tears washing his eyes. However, as the flak increased, German night fighters didn't follow them into the cauldron of anti-aircraft explosions, and Willie's guns were no defence against the well-aimed shells. Every few minutes, a lancaster on the flare path to the target burst into flames and fell, a victim of the Germans' new radar-guided flak guns.

✧✧✧✧✧✧✧✧✧✧✧✧✧✧✧✧✧✧✧✧✧✧✧✧✧

Parachute flares lit up the details of the buildings in Jake Collier's bombsight—he had opened the bomb bay doors and taken over the lancaster's direction. Jake steered Steve exactly down the lighted line running fore and aft in his sight. Their assigned target buildings came into the front of the bombsight, rapidly approaching the lighted crossline. The target jerked in the lens as the lancaster thrashed through the shock waves of exploding bombs and flak. He lifted the covers on the bomb releases... the first building reached the approximate intersection of the bright lines, and Jake threw all four switches in sequence. The lancaster bucked violently upwards as twelve thousand pounds of bombs dropped into the night. The plane kicked sideways, intersecting the shock wave blasting upward from a 4,000-pound blockbuster.

Every lancaster carried sixteen 500-pound high-explosive bombs and one 4000-pound blockbuster. From this altitude, Willie could see the top of the overlapping blasts throwing the lancasters all over the sky. Dirt and debris from them blotted out the buildings. From Willie's perch, the destruction appeared to be total.

Steve held the southwesterly bombing course until the cameras flashed a picture of the devastation 'C for Charley' had inflicted, and Jake said, "Bombs gone—you've got it, Steve."

Steve turned right until the directional gyro settled on the heading for home. He said into his loose mask, "We survived a bad one, boys. Let's go..."

The blast from a flak shell exploding in front of the port wing interrupted Steve's sentence and the crew's cheers, shaking the lancaster and rattling shrapnel against the side of the fuselage. The outboard engine on the port wing burst into flame, and Phillip hit the fire extinguisher. An anti-aircraft battery had them in its radar site, and a second shell exploded on the starboard side, shaking the bomber like a rag doll in a bulldog's mouth. The inner starboard engine coughed up oil, vomiting a stream of it back across the wing, terminally ill. The engine spewed a cloud of black smoke and began to shake, and then, just before Steve thought it would depart the lancaster's wing, it died with a retching gasp.

Steve shouted into the intercom, "Shit, boys! It's time to find your parachutes!" Another explosion rocked the lancaster, and the intercom went dead.

◇◇◇◇◇◇◇◇◇◇◇◇◇◇◇◇◇◇◇◇◇◇◇◇◇◇◇◇◇◇◇◇

Black, oily smoke passed Willie's turret on both sides, eddying through the glassless windows into his face. He centred the turret, unfastened his belts, slid the door aside and fell back into the smoke-filled fuselage. Eyes watering, he turned and pulled himself to where his parachute should be. Working by feel, Willie got it on, choking on black smoke sucked back into the fuselage through the open turret. He cursed himself for not closing the door. Eyes burning, Willie blinked and squinted his way to the hatch, praying he would get there before the bomber exploded, or worse, the flames reached him.

Willie had just found the latch lever when Ronnie grabbed his hand. Coughing and cursing, Ronnie helped him get the hatch open, then pushed him into the night; Willie scraped the bottom of the plane as he exited, and the impact flipped him end over end into the blackness. He searched for the 'D' ring, found it and pulled, and the parachute yanked him to a stop, with his feet tangled in the shrouds. He rubbed his watering eyes with his overall sleeve and watched 'C for Charley' fly away with two engines belching smoke and flames.

The bomber disappeared behind the parachute canopy, and Willie turned his attention to freeing his legs. The tangled mess threatened to invert him; he wriggled around until he unwound the last shroud from his boot. Once oriented, Willie could see the edge of Ronnie's chute fifty feet above him and less than a hundred feet away. He saw no other parachutes and no explosion from the ground that would seal the lancaster's fate. If not for the fires and the distant rumble of flak and exploding bombs at Mailly le Camp, the world would have been at peace.

Willie shouted, "Ronnie, can you hear me?" Most of Ronnie's parachute was now visible, his small form hanging peacefully below it.

"No need to shout, pal; I can hear you just fine."

"Let's stay close so we can find one another when we land." Willie had no experience in this situation, and his training hadn't covered it. The instructions were to surrender if you must and find the friendlies if you can. As he hung peacefully under the white mushroom, Willie decided to avoid all contact with people—the French were not necessarily "friendlies."

"Right," said Ronnie, "staying close won't be a problem. On the other hand, I'll do my best not to land on you. I have no idea how we'll know where the ground is, so perhaps we should start being quiet soon—you never know who might be listening."

The quiet lasted for a few minutes, and Ronnie ended it. "I'm drifting over you, and I can't steer this damned thing. You got any idea how that works?"

Willie looked up at the motionless white canopy over his head, grabbed a handful of cords and pulled down carefully. Nothing happened. He pulled harder; still nothing. "Nope, no idea at all. I'm pulling the shrouds on one side, but I can't tell whether I'm moving in that direction or the opposite direction or not at all. Are you pulling yours?"

Willie held a steady strain on his right-hand shrouds, and he thought he might be moving toward Ronnie, but he wasn't sure.

"Yeah, I'm pulling on my left shrouds, but I can't tell if it's doing anything...." Ronnie sounded puzzled.

Which way are you facing?" asked Willie. "You might be going in the same direction I am, and that won't help." Ronnie had disappeared, except for a sliver of his parachute.

"I think I'm facing back towards where the plane went, but I'm not sure. Mailly is on my right. Where are you facing?"

"Hell. Right now, I'm not sure of anything, let alone direction. I'm having trouble with up and down. I can't see your parachute anymore, so you must be right over me. The fires are behind me, but I'm rotating to the left. Maybe we should pull the shrouds opposite the ones we are pulling now." Willie pulled the shrouds on his left side and held them, but nothing seemed to change.

"Okay, I've reversed, and now I'm pulling the right shrouds," Willie sensed from his voice that Ronnie was becoming irritated. "I was drifting away, but now I'm drifting over you again!"

"Where the Hell are you?" Willie searched for Ronnie's parachute, twisting, turning his body in the harness, grabbing a handful of cords, then a handful on the opposite side.

"Willie, stop whatever you are doing! I'm right on top of you and can't get away. Leave your fucking shrouds alone, and I'll pull mine—any direction will be away from you!"

The ground, and whatever was on the ground, relentlessly rose to meet them.

Willie still couldn't see Ronnie when the black ground suddenly appeared beneath him, rising at a surprising and frightening speed, giving him barely enough time to put his feet together and bend his knees. The parachute jerked him sideways, and he landed hard, grunting as the impact forced the air from his lungs. Despite his collapsed lungs, Willie managed to gasp, "Shit!" as he fell in a heap with his parachute dragging him through the mud. Ronnie struck the ground with his feet on top of Willie's parachute, collapsing it and stopping Willie's slide. Laughing, he rolled once and stood up, still on the white silk. He neatly tripped his chute with the bottom shrouds and pulled it into a pile in front of him.

Ronnie's relief poured out like a waterfall. "I must admit that was fun, but I don't want to do it again for a while—for sure not in the dark." He unfastened his harness and let it drop on the parachute, then helped Willie drag his chute into a similar pile.

Willie wiped a streak of mud from his face; Ronnie laughed and said, "Didn't your mother teach you not to play in the dirt, Willie?" Willie pushed Ronnie down on his back, and they both laughed like fools who had cheated death.

Still giddy, they gathered up the parachutes and picked a place to bury them. They had survived—the rest would be easy!

Digging in the soft soil was not a problem; the parachutes disappeared in fifteen minutes. Then, following enemy territory bail-out protocol, they tore off their rank insignias and stuffed them under the dirt fifty feet from the buried chutes.

<hr />

Willie opened his survival pack, dug out the compass, and levelled it in his hand. The luminous end of the needle pointed north, and Willie stuck his arm out 90 degrees to the left.

"That's West; let's walk in that direction until we find something to change our minds. We only have a few hours to find somewhere to hide before daylight." He started walking without waiting for Ronnie's reply.

"Righto, old chap!" Ronnie talked to Willie's back, imitating Steve's high-class London accent. Willie thought of Steve and hoped he and the rest of the crew had gotten out. If they had, he and Ronnie might find them when daylight came.

As they walked, the moon went into hiding behind clouds, leaving a narrow border of light around the edges. The ground became barely visible, but both men had grown up working and playing at night in a world without lights. The cloudy, moonless and starless nights Willie had spent on the ocean, where night vision was critical for survival, and Ronnie's nights camped out in the Rhodesian wilderness with nothing but firelight were paying dividends.

Both men were in their element, where a hundred-mile walk across fields and through forests wasn't even considered a challenge, and danger was the norm. Without discussing other options, Ronnie and Willie decided to walk to Dunholme Lodge.

Willie walked for less than two minutes before he stopped and checked the compass. "Shit, we're forty-five degrees to the left and headed southwest. I can't keep looking at the compass and the ground— there has to be a better way to walk in a straight line!"

Ronnie's teeth glinted in the dark. "You're right; there is a better way." He tried to see Willie's compass. "Which way's west?"

Willie stretched out his arm, and Ronnie sighted along it and pointed at the horizon.

"Okay, there's a small bunch of stars close to the horizon, a little south of our track... Do you see them?" Ronnie looked at Willie but kept his arm pointed at the stars.

Willie swore under his breath, "Yep, the seven sisters—keep them about ten degrees to my left, and that's all there is to it." He was embarrassed. "My grandfather taught me to use the stars to navigate on the water when I was knee-high...God, I feel stupid that I didn't think of it!" He started walking again.

"You should feel stupid, and, by the way, you owe me a beer because I just saved your life. If not for me, you'd be lost and alone, like the sheep that went astray. You'd go crazy; you'd walk into a nest of Krauts; they'd pull out your finger and toenails, shoot you two or three times, and you would never see Norma again!"

Willie didn't laugh as he was supposed to—he started walking...fast... too fast in the dark. Ronnie regretted using the 'N' word!

They walked in silence, and the night wore on. Willie's mind raced; he reckoned that the channel was at least a hundred-and-fifty miles from where they stood and that they could make three to four miles in an hour. If they only walked in the dark, they could safely walk twenty-five to thirty miles a night. The English Channel was a week's walking, and they had a week's rations.

When they reached the coast, they still had a slight problem with the English Channel, but he thought they might steal a boat—yes, he could steal a boat and sail it to England—that would work! With his navigation experience and knowledge of fishing boats, he could find something as big as England, even without a map. But a boat would probably have charts onboard.

Willie picked up the pace.

◇◇◇◇◇◇◇◇◇◇◇◇◇◇◇◇◇◇◇◇◇◇◇◇◇◇◇◇◇◇◇◇◇◇◇

They had been walking for an hour and had crossed four fields and

234

two narrow field roads when Willie finally stopped. He wanted to keep moving but decided to give Ronnie the option. "Do you want to rest and eat something?"

"Thanks for asking, but I'll tell you if I want to stop. I've been figuring out our schedule; we will need a week to get to the channel, and we have a week's rations. I suggest we eat and rest during the day and walk without taking breaks when it's dark."

Willie nodded without comment, and although Ronnie couldn't have seen the nod, they both began walking again, stopping in a few yards to climb a high wooden fence, the first they had seen.

Ronnie said, "There's always a reason for a fence like that, and it usually involves big animals."

On cue, shuffling hooves came toward them.

Willie said, "Cows. They're just curious," and didn't slacken his pace.

They walked across the field with the herd of cows trailing behind them. One inquisitive animal nuzzled Ronnie, almost knocking him down. He stopped to rub its ears, and the cow grunted softly. The others began to surround them, so they moved on.

"I see you know something about cows."

Ronnie said, "Yeah, we had all kinds of them on our farm—about a hundred milk cows and three thousand beef cattle. I've handled the meanest bulls and the sweetest mummy cows you've ever seen." Ronnie walked on with his female friend pushing him with her head, trying for another ear rub, until they came to a second fence and climbed over it. The herd watched their newfound playmates disappear in the darkness, and they mooed their displeasure.

Willie asked, "Will we be listed as 'killed in action' when they find our plane?" Ronnie knew where Willie was going with the question.

"I saw the plane fly away without any more parachutes. Maybe they made it home."

Willie pressed on, increasing his walking pace to a jog. "Yeah, we can hope. If they did make it—he breathed noisily a couple of times—wouldn't someone wonder what happened to us?" Willie found that talking and running were not compatible.

"Yeah, that's for damned sure!" Ronnie slowed to a walk, but Willie didn't, so Ronnie ran a few steps to catch him. "That's true whether they got home without us..." he puffed like a steam engine...

"or if there weren't enough bodies when they found the crashed plane…" He gasped a couple more times… "I guess that could mean we are missing in action." He wheezed a few big breaths to catch up on oxygen.

Willie asked, "Who would they tell if we were missing in action?"

He breathed deeply and tried to focus on the configuration of stars that had become dim as thin clouds threatened to cover them. He found a lump on the edge of the black horizon and shifted to it.

"They would tell our parents, and, of course, everyone at the base would know." Ronnie slowed, gasping for oxygen, and Willie slowed so he could hear him. "If our lancaster gets home without us…he wheezed…they will assume…he gasped…we won't return."

"How about girlfriends?" Willie began to walk faster, putting distance between himself and Ronnie.

Ronnie sped up a little and said to Willie's back, "I don't think they will notify Norma," He breathed twice and said, "Unless…did you ask them to?" Ronnie's tone was unsure. Willie was silent for a minute and then began to jog. "No, I didn't. If it takes us more than a week… He mixed a breath with a sob… Norma will find someone else… Two more breaths and another sob… I've got to get back sooner!"

Ronnie jogged hard to catch him, trying to see whatever they would run into before they hit it. "You know…we can't run all the way to Dunholme Lodge…don't you?" Ronnie used more effort to breathe, but he still ran smoothly.

Willie's voice broke; he began to realize the hopelessness of the task. "I've got to run… He sobbed, gasped, and slowed; his legs felt like lead… "Norma sings at the Blue Bell again on Saturday… I've got to be there… She'll find someone else!"

Ronnie pulled up beside Willie. "She loves you, even though you are an idiot." He breathed at the rhythm of his steps. "Everybody knows that…And everybody knows that you love her!"

Willie knew there was a good chance he would hurt himself running in the dark, but he couldn't stop. His voice broke as he gasped, "No, she doesn't love me… She lost the man she loves." He was staggering now. "She can't love a rear gunner…her husband was shot in his turret, and Norma still loves him, not me! I'm going to get killed, just like he did!" His body was wearing down from running, talking, and weeping.

Staggering more than running, tears blurring his vision, Willie's feet had trouble keeping up with his body.

Ronnie chuckled sympathetically between breaths. "She can't help loving you any more than your friends can. Willie—you're the most loveable guy I know."

Willie tried to keep running but had to stagger to a stop. He bent over with his hands on his knees, his breath coming more in sobs than gasps. Ronnie put his hand on his friend's shoulder and leaned over to speak into Willie's ear.

"Willie, I'm serious when I tell you she loves you. She will wait for you until someone shows her your dead body!"

Willie looked sideways at Ronnie, who put his hand on Willie's shoulder.

Ronnie slapped Willie's rounded back. "And what's this bullshit about getting killed? Do you know that a rear gunner has a better than one percent chance of surviving his tour? At least one, maybe even two in a hundred, pal! No need to get discouraged!"

Ronnie laughed and clapped his friend on the back again. "I'll even bet this trip will be upgraded to a full mission credit if they get us back. Hell, they may even give us another medal!"

Willie straightened up. "A full credit just because we were shot down? Now, that's too much to hope for!" His breathing approached normal. "I guess we need to slow down, but I don't believe you about Norma loving me. I'm not good-looking like you; I'm the son of a drunkard fisherman, and God knows I've learned that I'm not a good lover! She can replace me with a lap dog and a varnished broom handle!"

Ronnie pulled Willie's arm. "We're wasting time; let's walk while we talk. I'd like to hear more about you being a bad lover. Tell me every detail, and I'll try to help you with that."

Willie smiled at his friend and said, "Not a chance in hell!" He laughed as he found the group of stars disappearing under the horizon and resumed his fast walk using the bump.

◇◇◇◇◇◇◇◇◇◇◇◇◇◇◇◇◇◇◇◇◇◇◇◇◇◇◇◇◇◇◇◇

Steve fought to control the crippled lancaster as Phillip pulled the mixture on the inboard starboard engine, the second engine failure in less than a minute. He feathered the prop, shut off the switches and fuel supply, and pulled the fire extinguisher—the fire went out. The two remaining engines still ran perfectly; the smoke that had filled the fuselage flowed out the back, and Steve verified that the controls functioned by gently moving the plane around, just in case something was more fragile than it had been.

The intercom was out; Steve tapped Phil's shoulder, then leaned over to yell in his ear, "Go tell everyone that we're okay to get home." Phillip slid down from the jump seat and disappeared—he was back three minutes later, upset and barely able to make himself understood.

"Ronnie and Willie are gone—their parachutes too—they left the back door open!"

"Shit," Steve slammed his hand on the column. "They jumped when I said to get the chutes out. With all that smoke, they probably thought we were going for a damned Burton!"

"This is not good." Phillip wagged his head and said nervously, "If the Germans catch Ronnie, he'll have to dry out, which will probably kill him." He tried to force a laugh. "On the other hand, Willie will have new German friends in a week. They'll take him home, feed him, let him play with their children, and find a nice blonde Madel for him..." He slammed his fist on the metal panel above his head. "Fuck! Fuck! Fuck! Why in hell did they jump?"

Steve interrupted, "Well, they've got a better chance of surviving this war now than they had an hour ago!" Steve's face betrayed that his heart wasn't in the banter. "Jesus Christ, what are we going to tell Norma?"

◇◇◇◇◇◇◇◇◇◇◇◇◇◇◇◇◇◇◇◇◇◇◇◇◇◇◇◇◇◇◇◇

'C for Charley' made it home with six hundred pounds of fuel still in the tanks and a reparable airplane. They taxied to their parking spot and shut off as though nothing had happened, but the debriefing became an unpleasant affair when they notified Wing Commander Leech that both gunners had jumped out of the plane somewhere over France.

Leech waved his arms around his head with his fists clenched. "How in Hell did you lose the gunners? In the name of God, what did you say that made them jump out of a perfectly good airplane?"

Steve and Phillip looked at one another. Phillip said, "I wouldn't say it was a perfectly good airplane. One engine was puking like a kid full of green apples, and another was on fire!" He pointed across the grass at 'C for Charley,' and Steve took over. "Take a good look at that airplane, sir. There is considerable shrapnel damage on the tail and fuselage, and it took a heroic effort from the pilot and engineer to get that wreck back to base! In the dark, with all that smoke and fire, anyone could have made that mistake!"

Wing Commander Leech waved his arms again. "Oh, go to hell, both of you. I'm going to have to report them missing, but you had better fucking hope they show up, and soon." He grabbed a turning Steve by the shoulder and spun him back to face him.

"Do you know how hard it is to get a man to ride in the tail turret?" He put his finger on Steve's chest. "It's fucking dangerous back there, not to mention as cold as Santa Claus's attic!" He started to walk away, then stopped dead. He turned to face the two men.

He asked, "Who's going to tell Norma?" pointing at Phillip, then Steve.

Phillip grumbled, "Not me! I was only trying to help. I wasn't the one who told everyone to get their chutes!"

"Sorry about that." Steve winced. "Maybe they'll make it back soon, and we won't have to tell her."

Phillip sadly shook his head. "They won't be back anytime soon...not a fucking snowball's chance on a hot day in hell! And worse—without those two sharpshooters, we'll probably die on our next mission!"

⬦⬦⬦⬦⬦⬦⬦⬦⬦⬦⬦⬦⬦⬦⬦⬦⬦⬦⬦⬦⬦⬦⬦⬦

Filled with dread, Erik lined up his final approach to runway 25. The wheels had dropped with their usual thump as they locked, and two green gear lights were comforting, leaving only a flat tire to worry about. But it didn't help because Fritz was going to kill him anyway. As he added a bit of throttle to adjust the touchdown point in his windscreen, an idea formed—he would order Karl to talk to Fritz. Fritz liked Karl and would probably spare his life.

The starboard engine continued to run like the mercedes nameplate advertised it would. Erik cut the right engine, straightened the plane with the rudder, and the wheels touched gently in the first five hundred feet of runway. He let the aircraft roll without braking, coasting to a stop opposite the taxiway. At the parking spot, Erik pushed the rudder to the limit, added throttle, and spun the heavy fighter into its place. He shut off the mixture on the healthy engine, robbing it of fuel, and it slowed to a stop. Four ground personnel pulled the messerschmitt's tail back and tied it down.

Fritz didn't wait for Erik to put his foot on the ground.

"What have you done to my beautiful new airplane?" Karl waited in the plane, fiddling with the logbook, charts, and his headset. Erik gave him his most evil stare—this wasn't following the plan.

Erik decided to let Fritz vent a little before he tried pulling rank—his last hope. He waited with his head down, examining his immaculate boots.

"I left this aircraft in your care, and now look at it—holes in the wing, holes in the fuselage, holes everywhere!" Erik sneaked a peek at Fritz's flailing arm. "Erik, you've just got to be more careful!" Erik realized Fritz was upset about more than his airplane. He kept his eyes down as he spoke with a hint of sarcasm.

"I'm sorry, Fritz, but unless you can find a way to shoot at bombers without them shooting back, they will occasionally mess up your airplane. Look at those holes in the fuselage and try to figure out why Karl isn't dead! The armour plating saved me, but he hasn't got anything but an aluminum skin to protect him!" He swept one hand across the sky for emphasis and put the other on Fritz's shoulder.

"Try imagining yourself in a pack of bombers in the dark—imagine you have to shoot one down without the gunners seeing you! I just thank God that the British gave the lancasters guns that can't kill a tough goose beyond a hundred metres—that's all that saved Karl!"

Erik figured he had Fritz in the palm of his hand. He smiled wickedly and added a carrot. "I admit that I made a mistake, and to make it up to you, I will help you fix this plane, even if we have to work all night!"

Fritz's face turned red, and he turned to walk away but took only a few steps before returning to face Erik. He wagged his finger, increasing the volume with every word. "If you help us, it will take twice as long, and the plane might not fly again!"

He started to turn away, turned back and pushed his face up to Erik's.

"Now, you tell me why we're doing this nonsense! I get you a brand new airplane with all the doodads and gizmos, and I fit it to suit you. Then you take it up, and on the first flight, you return with this pile of junk! Karl and I worked all day and night to make this airplane perfect for you, and now we have to do it all over again. I was looking forward to an oil change and a wash job, maybe even a little wax, before your next mission—now it looks like we'll be working day and night for a week!" His voice broke. "And if I do that, you will just take the plane and get both of you killed!" He wiped tears from his face. "Why in hell can't we just go home?"

Erik waited for Fritz to go on, but he stayed silent, facing him, fighting tears with his sleeve.

Erik said quietly, "I understand why you are frustrated, but the British are getting smarter at finding ways to get around our equipment. The men flying those damned mosquitos are very good at finding our night fighters, and when they find us, we don't often see them coming. The bombers' gunners seem to know where we are, and their formations are becoming more effective. I will tell you the truth—they scare the shit out of me!" His voice rose, "My ambition is to survive this war, not to save the fucking Third Reich's airplane!"

Fritz stepped back, looked at his feet, then turned to look at the damaged engine. He had never before heard Erik say anything worse than "Scheisse."

Fritz's tears kept coming; he wiped them with his sleeve. "I have another engine in the repair shed, and Karl is a big help. I will replace your damaged armour, and I suppose we can find an extra piece or two for Karl's seat. If we begin right now, we could have you ready to go tomorrow night—will that be okay?"

That was as close to an apology as Erik had ever heard from Fritz. He said, relieved, "Yes, Fritz, that will be just fine, and I wasn't kidding; I will help if you need me."

Fritz laughed and wiped his eyes, back in control. "Some people shouldn't be allowed to own a fingernail file or a pair of scissors, and I'm afraid you fall into that category—if you help us, we will need an extra day."

Erik tried to look hurt, but Marita had already destroyed the mechanical abilities part of his ego. She wouldn't let him change a light bulb.

Karl came down the ladder and exchanged back-slaps with Fritz, who clapped Erik on the back and said, "Erik, you're the only person I know who can cross-thread a light bulb! I know you are a good pilot, but I have no idea why. It's amazing to me that you figured out how to get your wife pregnant!" Fritz and Karl laughed harder, and Erik reluctantly joined them.

Fritz took his hand from Erik's back. "Now you two go and get some sleep, and we'll remove this engine. Karl, you can come back after sleep and breakfast." He turned to Erik. "I don't want you to touch anything, and stay away from here until we've got your toy repaired." Fritz walked back to the shop, a hundred metres from where Erik had parked the plane, with his head down.

Erik and Karl headed in the opposite direction for their debriefing.

Karl looked straight ahead as he said, "You know, if you die, Fritz will too."

"I know that. But we won't talk about it again, will we?"

"No, sir." Karl smiled at Erik, but Erik didn't look at him.

It wasn't yet one-thirty; there was plenty of time to sleep before a late breakfast.

CHAPTER TWENTY-TWO

4 May 1944

The wind of absence either blows out the candle or fans the flames.

THE PRE-DAWN SKY WAS BRIGHTENING FAST when Willie and Ronnie approached a narrow strip of trees growing along both sides of a small brook. They could see almost all the way through the narrow strip of forest; it was barely thick enough to hide them during the daylight hours, but their choices were limited to one.

They walked a hundred feet into the trees, crossed the brook by stepping from stone to stone, and found a small thicket beside it where they had cover on both sides. They broke short ends off spruce branches to build a dry bed and broke off a few larger boughs for cover over their bodies. When they finished, the sun had evaporated the damp morning mist, lifting their spirits.

Ronnie pointed up a slight hill on the west side of the woods. "I can see a road at the top of the hill. I'm going to walk in the woods parallel to it and see if there are any signs we can use to get our bearings."

"Good idea. I'll go with you to keep you out of the bars." Willie walked behind Ronnie, weaving his way through the trees, instinctively trying to avoid stepping on dry twigs or leaves. Most of the spruce trees, roughly uniform in size, were without branches as high as a man could reach, making walking easy but limiting the cover.

As the morning sun lifted their spirits, Ronnie began to whistle a tune but stopped when Willie poked him in the ribs. Nothing could spoil their solar-driven positive mood, and they grinned like children, happy to be alive.

Working their way along the edge of the trees, keeping under cover, they arrived at an intersection where the narrow dirt road they had been paralleling crossed a wide two-lane paved road running north and south. There were signs at the intersection with place names and distances, but they were unreadable without leaving the trees.

Ronnie said, "You can read French…check it out…I'll wait here."

Willie had grown up with a French-Acadian grandmother, born and raised on the "French coast" southwest of Digby, and because he and his sister had spent half their lives with her, had learned more than enough French to read a road sign.

Willie returned to the trees' cover in under a minute.

"It's fifteen kilometres north to Vertus, and we are near Fère-Champenoise in the other direction. That's enough to plan our trip using our maps."

Ten minutes later, they were sitting on their dry boughs, the sun streaming through the trees from a clear morning sky. Willie unfolded the silk map that was part of his survival kit and located Vertus. He found the intersection fifteen kilometres south of Vertus, just outside the village of Fère-Champenoise. He calculated the distance to the coast using the scale and a straight twig.

"It's about two hundred miles to Calais but only about a hundred-and-fifty to the nearest point on the coast. What do you think we should do?" Ronnie had spread out his map and was studying it intently. He slid his finger from right to left. Willie leaned over to see where Ronnie was pointing.

"If we go directly to the coast, we will pass close to Paris, and, with these uniforms, there's a good chance the Germans will catch us. If we go here, northwest, between Reims and Paris, we should be able to find shelter every day before daylight—another fifty miles walking is better than getting caught."

Willie silently agreed with a nod, then curled up on the bed of boughs and pulled branches over his body until nothing was visible. "So, we cross the road tonight and go northwest when it gets dark—let's get some sleep."

Ronnie lay beside Willie, pulled a few tree limbs over his body, and began to shake despite his insulated coveralls and the warm sun gradually finding its way through the trees' lower branches. Willie had seen the signs in his father—the increasing restlessness from a shortage of nicotine and alcohol in his blood, then the shaking that worsened until he found some liquor. Willie lay still as Ronnie twisted and turned, trying to control his shaking body with all the will he had. Ronnie's body needed a drink of anything with alcohol in it.

Willie knew nothing he could do would help, so he closed his eyes.

During the short periods when Willie was awake, he was aware of lorries and smaller vehicles travelling along the main road, but didn't hear anything on the narrow dirt road parallel to the woods. He awoke for good in the middle of the afternoon to find that Ronnie was gone. He got up, splashed water on his face, drank from the brook, and then walked toward the road where he found Ronnie sitting on a patch of dry moss, hidden behind thick bushes, intensely watching the main road.

Willie said, with a deliberately sharp edge, "When did you get up?" He knew that Ronnie hadn't heard him approach and laughed when he jumped. Ronnie turned quickly to find Willie five yards from him. Willie grinned, Ronnie cursed, and Willie sat beside him, chuckling. He asked, "How long have you been watching the road?"

"Two hours—and the only vehicle I've seen on the side road was a bicycle with two kids on it. There's been a steady flow of Bundeswehr lorries and those noisy, topless German military cars on the main road, but no civilian traffic. There were canvas tops on the lorries, and the one half-track I saw had four soldiers hitching a ride on it.

"What's the verdict?" Willie watched two lorries drive north.

Ronnie gestured in the direction of the traffic. "We will need to stay off the main roads, but this side road doesn't seem to have any traffic. We might be able to walk on those roads if we are careful."

Willie shook his head. "Not in these uniforms! I want to keep to the fields and woods—speed isn't as important anymore. Norma will find another lover this weekend, and I'll be out."

Ronnie kicked the dirt with his boot and said, "That isn't what's going to happen—I will bet a month's pay on Norma waiting for you."

Night came late in May and lasted little more than eight hours. Willie impatiently watched the daylight slip behind a beautiful sunset as the world continued to turn despite the turmoil on its surface. The day had been warm, but the clear sky allowed the warmth to escape, and Willie and Ronnie pulled on their overalls before the darkness was complete. They distributed the bed branches through the small line of trees and gathered leaves to cover the spots they had trampled. They worked without saying a word, each doing his job in the order that was obvious to both of them.

Willie and Ronnie crossed the main road and headed northwest with only the dim light supplied by the stars. Using the compass, they agreed on a group of stars to hold them on course. Smooth, freshly planted fields made the walking easy, and an early-rising moon gave them enough light to see any significant obstacles.

As the night wore on, the stars they had picked disappeared, the seven sisters constellation appeared, and they began to climb low hills. Small patches of woods became more frequent, as did narrow dirt service roads. They checked for vehicle tracks on a service road that was barely a path going in their direction and, finding none, chanced walking on it for a full hour.

When they guessed the short night was about half over, they stopped by a fast-flowing brook to eat part of a ration stick and drink cold water.

"Have you ever been afraid of the dark?" Ronnie asked Willie, leaning back, his fingers interlaced behind his head. "The way you sneak through the woods and shoot those brownings, I can't imagine you've ever been afraid of anything!"

Mice scurried noisily in the leaves, but Willie didn't look in their direction except out of curiosity. Nothing about the night startled him.

"No, I can't remember being afraid of anything except my father." Ronnie said nothing, so Willie added, matter-of-factly, "Man and beast give my father a wide berth when he's drunk!"

Ronnie looked far away. "I wasn't afraid of my father. He never touched me when I was little except in affection, and he taught me not to be afraid of the dark or anything else. Dad trained me to value the night and to use it to my advantage. He took me hunting hyenas at night. When you hunt those bastards, you learn to wait for opportunity; when you get it, you had better not miss!" He turned back to Willie.

"Why were you afraid of your father?"

Willie poked the ground with a dry stick. "My Dad beat me and my sister, and he beat my mom...the bastard almost killed my mother twice, and no one did anything about it!"

Willie tossed the stick away. "I remember when my mother was in the hospital with a concussion and a broken back. Dad told everyone she had fallen down the stairs, the ones to the second floor, but Mom told the doctors she had fallen down the cellar stairs. Almost everyone in Digby, including my uncle Rowley, Mom's brother, knew we didn't have a cellar. Uncle Rowley faced Dad down about it, and my dad threatened to kill him with an axe!"

"Jesus, Willie, why didn't you kill the bastard?..." Ronnie said it so naturally that Willie cringed... "I sure as hell would have!"

Willie waited, trying to remember why. "I suppose I didn't because when I got old enough to do something like that, my mother wouldn't let me. She said she still loved my father—Mom said she only hated the liquor that made him do those things, not the man."

It was Ronnie's turn to be silent and poke the ground with the stick Willie had discarded. Willie picked up another stick.

"I guess that's why I hate booze so much. I've tried a few sips of wine and beer, but I can't stand the taste—I don't see the need for it."

Ronnie leaned ahead and locked his fingers together in front of his knees.

"Unfortunately, I love the taste, and I need it."

"What does it do to you that you need it?"

"It makes me forget my fear of flying. I'm terrified of dying in a flaming coffin—I'm scared shitless all the time!" Ronnie looked at Willie, his expression crying for help. "Other than that, I'm not scared of man, the devil, or the dark, but I suppose that still makes me a coward, doesn't it?"

"No..." Willie hesitated, looked sideways at Ronnie... "I guess that makes you the same as everyone who climbs in a lancaster, and I don't think anyone who does that can be a coward. I'm euphoric the morning after a mission because I survived another one, but by nighttime I'm depressed and starting to get scared again. Every day, it gets worse; I have nightmares about burning, and if we get a few extra days off because of the weather, I get sick to my stomach and can't eat. Even though I want to piss on the tire for good luck like you do, most of the time, I can't. I'm like that until we take off, climb to altitude, and I get busy looking for fighters."

Ronnie leaned his head back against his locked fingers and stared at the stars. "Yeah, me too. I'm okay once we enter enemy territory, where I have to concentrate on finding those damned night fighters. I guess the fear makes me good at my job."

"Yeah, I think that's true for everyone." Willie stared at a familiar dense group of stars and realized with a start that they were the ones he had been following, already burying themselves under the horizon. "I concentrate so hard I don't blink, and my eyes feel like someone rubbed sand in them. I'm terrified when I can't see through the tears. Every ten minutes, I try to look into the distance at another bomber, and I blink fast to wet my eyes, but when I forget..."

"Yeah, the dryness makes my eyes water, but it disappears after a few minutes. I worry about a fighter coming when my eyes are watering, so I rub them to get it over quicker."

Ronnie spoke a little louder. "You know, after this, I'm going to quit drinking!"

Willie quickly reminded him, "You quit drinking yesterday; that proves you can do it if you want to, but I won't hold you to it. My dad is one tough son-of-a-bitch, but he can't lick that problem even though it will eventually kill him, my mother, or both of them."

Ronnie rose to his feet. "Let's get going—time's a-wasting."

Willie followed, dodging tree trunks in the dark as they walked towards their group of stars twinkling in the northwest sky.

CHAPTER TWENTY-THREE

6 May 1944

Birds fly because they have faith—they sing because they have hope.

Every man on the Dunholme Lodge base knew that Norma sang at the Blue Bell every Friday night, and, in a matter of hours, while 'C for Charley's' crew slept, the rumour spread over the base that her rear-gunner boyfriend was missing and half the base wanted to be there when she found out.

Their reasons varied from ghoulish to innocent curiosity. Would Norma shrug it off and take someone else home with her? Would she break down in front of everyone? For the men on the base, it was like plucking petals off a daisy... She loves him... she loves him not... Bored soldiers grasp at anything with the potential to become a betting pool—which of two crows sitting on the fence will fly first? Will Willie make it back? How many men will die this month? Hundreds of pounds found their way into the hands of the base bookie.

Late in the afternoon, it became apparent that there wasn't transportation for everyone, although Commander Leech had confiscated everything on the base with wheels and seats. He reserved the bus for himself and Steve's crew then filled it with every man they could squeeze in.

The lorry left the base early, but when it arrived at the Blue Bell, men were already lined up at the door to get in. Somehow, the rumour of Willie's possible demise had reached other squadrons.

Norma's reputation had spread throughout Lincolnshire; she was the darling of RAF Bomber Command, and tonight, the place would be filled with her worshipers, many of them hoping to replace Willie!

When the door opened, Leech, Steve, and what remained of his crew headed straight for their usual table. Commander Leech took Ronnie's seat, and Willie's was conspicuously vacant. They ordered drinks all around, and Steve noted that the barmaid hurried through the door behind the bar before she went for the drinks.

Twenty seconds later, Norma stood beside the table, buttoning the last button on her blouse. The fear in her eyes shook Steve, but he faced her, knowing the answer to the question on her lips would not be something she wanted to hear. The chatter and swearing suddenly stopped.

"Is he dead?" Norma's eyes brimmed with tears, her resonant voice carried throughout the room, and someone choked a sob.

No one made a sound except Steve. He said, "Willie and Ronnie jumped by mistake, and it was all my fault!" The room sucked in its collective breath, and Steve reacted quickly. "Hell, no, he's not dead!" He looked into her eyes, lowered his head, and the truth poured out.

"I don't really know. We haven't received any word that the Germans got him, but it's too early for that." He looked at her pathetically, helplessly. "I just don't know whether he made it or not." Most of the men in the room lowered their heads and shared her pain, lamenting her loss, but more than a few cynics had bet on Willie's demise, hoping he wouldn't return, secretly wishing Norma would become available again.

Commander Leech stood and took Norma's hand. She turned to him, tears magnifying the hope in her eyes. She wiped her white sleeve across her face, streaking her makeup and painting the fabric pink.

Leech said earnestly, "Norma, he's the toughest, most capable man I've ever met, and he's got the second toughest man I know with him. Ronald and Willie bailed out together, and I'm assuming our excellent parachutes got them safely to the ground. France is full of people who will try to get them back here. Every day, the Résistance smuggles shot-down airmen out of Belgium and France, even Germany, through Switzerland and Spain."

Norma hugged Commander Leech, her eyes filled with tears. "I've been here before, Commander, and I don't know if I can bear it again!" She hurried away and disappeared through the door behind the bar. Gradually, men began to speak, first in whispers, then in soft murmurs. A few paid for their drink and wandered out the door, assuming Norma wouldn't sing tonight. Their replacements were inside before the door swung closed.

◇◇◇◇◇◇◇◇◇◇◇◇◇◇◇◇◇◇◇◇◇◇◇◇◇◇◇◇◇◇

Scarcely fifteen minutes had passed since Norma had disappeared when the piano began the introduction to "The White Cliffs of Dover," and every man in the room stared at the door behind the bar. It opened on cue, as it always did, and Norma stepped into the room, then stopped and let her eyes wander from one man to another, like she always did. Gradually, the men stood up, clapping softly at first, then louder as Norma scanned the room. The men who had bet against Willie looked down to avoid her gaze because, at that moment, everyone in the room wanted Norma's Willie to return.

Norma started to sing as she reached the center of the room, and the applause stopped as though someone had thrown a switch, prompting the men to sit down as quietly as they could. Her voice was as beautiful as it had ever been…she radiated the hope that every man in the room felt. She sang of war and home, returning to girlfriends, wives, and a world without killing. Men who faced a horrible demise three times a week, themselves instruments of death, wept like broken-hearted children. She sang with a broken heart, and every man loved her for it.

Norma made the rounds of the tables, avoiding 'C for Charley.' Steve drank his beer in silence, nursing it while fiddling with his food. John Leech tried to cheer him up by rescinding his threat to make him a tail gunner, but Steve was still depressed when they rose to leave early and let others in to hear Norma. She intercepted them at the door.

"I want you to know that I won't give up hope if you don't. If you tell me there's no chance, I'll cry my eyes out and eventually get over it, but for now, I will assume he's walking back to me."

Norma hugged Steve, planted a kiss on his cheek, and said, "I don't know what happened in that plane, but it wasn't your fault. There's a war going on, and bad things happen when men try to kill one another." She showed them a piece of paper she had in her hand. "I want you to immediately tell me everything you learn. The phone numbers for the Blue Bell, the Petwood Hotel, my home, and my parents' home are all on this paper. And please, don't be afraid to tell me the truth!" She held it in front of Steve. He hesitated, Norma waited, and he took the paper. Norma reached up and again hugged him, adding another affectionate kiss.

When she let Steve go, he said, "I'll let you know what we find out," while thinking what a lucky bastard his rear gunner was. And then he forced an evil gremlin out of his mind.

✦✦✦✦✦✦✦✦✦✦✦✦✦✦✦✦✦✦✦✦✦✦✦✦✦✦✦✦✦✦

Walking through the forest at night tested Willie and Ronnie's patience;

the thick woods allowed only a tiny amount of light from the waning moon to filter through. Despite falling often, whip-like branches raising red welts on their faces, and crawling through thickets that didn't seem to end, the fugitives did not dare leave the woods' safety. They had agreed that walking in the daylight would be suicide, but when the stars disappeared into the new morning, Willie navigated by keeping the lightening sky on his right rear quarter.

Daybreak came, and neither suggested they stop working their way through the trees. They could see the ground and duck the swatting branches in the half-light before dawn, so they continued to walk until the sun had risen in the trees. In thirty minutes, they doubled the progress they had made in the previous hour. The daylight was full when Willie and Ronnie stopped on a dry knoll, and Willie said, "This looks like a good place to spend the day."

Ronnie picked out a dry bed of pine needles and swept the sticks and cones aside. "It's already warm, and the ground is dry; we won't need to cover ourselves." He and Willie spread their coveralls on the bed.

Willie rolled his flight jacket under his head and fell asleep watching Ronnie search his pockets for non-existent cigarettes.

◇◇◇◇◇◇◇◇◇◇◇◇◇◇◇◇◇◇◇◇◇◇◇◇◇◇◇◇◇◇◇◇◇◇

Ronnie had always spent all his money on beer in the pub, bumming cigarettes where he could. When he bailed out, he had none in his pockets, and now, lying on his coveralls and laying his head on a pile of his flight jacket, he fought the combination of nicotine fit and alcoholic tremors that threatened to overwhelm him. Ronnie tried to sleep, but Willie's quiet snoring infuriated him, so he got up and walked away.

He stopped for a few minutes to watch Willie through the trees, marking the spot by taking a detailed picture with his mind. He walked downhill, carefully noting the direction of the sun and the lay of the land with every step. Five hundred yards farther, Ronnie reached a narrow road. He watched the dirt track from the shelter of the trees, then moved closer and sat behind a small thicket. A few minutes later, he lay back on the soft moss and fell asleep in the warm sun.

A sharp escalation of his senses shocked Ronnie awake. A woman's voice spoke to someone in the trees on the opposite side of the road and Ronnie sat up, looking between the thicket's branches. Minutes later, a woman walked up the road toward him, stopping to stare at the thicket where he was hiding. She looked directly at him and spoke in English, spiced with a sexy French accent.

"Come out, English flyer—we won't hurt you." She beckoned to him, and he cautiously stood up. "Don't be afraid…come here," she said, waving him to her.

Ronnie heard a noise behind him and turned to see three men standing twenty feet up the hill, British 'Sten' guns in their hands. He had already decided to do as the woman asked, but the men carrying machine guns removed any other thoughts as he circled the thicket. She beckoned for him to follow, and Ronnie crossed the road. She walked slowly until he caught up, then walked faster as she left the road and went into the trees. He noted that the three men behind him walked spread out, and a hundred yards down the hill, they met three men carrying rifles, who joined them.

"Who are you, and where are you trying to go?" The woman had a musical rhythm to her speech, but she spoke clearly. Ronnie decided to trust her.

"I was the mid-gunner in a lancaster that attacked Mailly le Camp the night before last, and I'm walking to the coast."

She nodded. "Are you alone?" When he hesitated, she smiled and waited.

Ronnie said, "Tell me who you are and why I should trust you." He was pretty sure he knew who they were.

She said, "We're French Résistance, the Maquisard," and continued to smile at him as his apprehension vanished. "We can help you, but you must do as we say." Her accent was as beautiful as she was.

She looked at his hands, said something to one of the men in French, and the man pulled a nearly full package of cigarettes from his shirt pocket. She said something more forceful to him, and he reluctantly handed them to Ronnie. The man had a match ready when he shook a cigarette out of the pack and put it in his mouth, and he lit it for Ronnie, who inhaled deeply and nodded his heartfelt thanks. He held up his hand and watched the shaking subside.

Ronnie told the woman, "I bailed out with the rear gunner; he's asleep a few hundred yards up the hill. I should take you to him so he won't panic when he hears you coming."

She said, "Okay, I'll go with you." Ronnie was surprised; she was unarmed and didn't ask any of the men to go with her. Dressed as a peasant in a checkered shirt and dark red skirt held up by a narrow black belt, she looked like the most harmless person in the world. Brown leather boots covered her legs to the top of her calves, and long black stockings hid the rest of her shapely legs. She had a generous heap of black hair bunched on her head, held firmly in place with a three-fingered wooden comb. She walked fast up the hill, and Ronnie didn't catch up until she stopped at the road.

"Wait here until I check the road." She put her hand out to indicate he should stay at the edge of the woods, then casually crossed the road. She looked up and down the road, climbed the other side to the thicket, and beckoned to him from behind it.

Ronnie led her up the hill, following the trees and ground depressions, reversing the sun's position and remembering details of the vegetation growing on the slope that he had noted on his way down the hill to the road.

He stopped the French woman fifty metres before they reached Willie, who was sleeping like a child and didn't stir as Ronnie approached him and touched his friend's side with his foot.

<hr>

Willie slowly opened his eyes. "What's up, Ronnie? It can't be time to get up yet!" Willie squinted at the sun still rising in the trees.

Ronnie grinned at him. "If I had been a German, you'd be dead!"

Willie grinned back. "Yeah, and pigs could fly if they had wings. Now, what's the big problem you had to wake me to solve?" Willie sat up, noticed Ronnie's cigarette and pointed at it. "Where did you get that?"

Ronnie cocked his head toward the woman. "From a friend of hers."

Willie stared, then pointed. "Who's she?"

"She didn't tell me her name, but she's French Résistance…she knows a lot of people who have guns." Ronnie waited for Willie to adjust to the new situation.

"Are you sure they're friendly?" Willie looked at the cigarette. "I guess that's a stupid question, isn't it?"

Ronnie pulled out the package of cigarettes. "Yes, it's a stupid question. And I'm pretty sure she's unarmed, but I didn't frisk her." Ronnie chuckled. "They let her come with me to get you, so I guess we should trust her."

Willie nodded and said, "This could be good, Ronnie..." He stood up. "Let's go see how soon they can send us home."

Willie and Ronnie gathered their clothing, then scattered cones and sticks over their bed, leaving the forest floor as they had found it. Obviously impressed with their handiwork, the French woman didn't try to hurry them and, when they had finished the housework, led them down the hill to the road, leaving them in the shelter of the bushes. She crossed the road and waved them over when she was satisfied. The men with machine guns were gone.

She led them, seemingly aimlessly, through the pathless forest, and a half-hour later, everyone scampered across a narrow field to a small farmhouse and entered through the back door. Inside, Ronnie recognized two of the gunmen, now without their Sten guns. They sat at a rough wooden table, each with a plate of stew before him. A board with bread, butter, and a long knife sat in the center of the table. Ronnie and Willie noted three empty plates with spoons and forks beside them.

The woman motioned for her charges to sit, took a big iron pot from the wood-fired stove, and put it on the table with a thump. "The pot's too heavy for me to hold. You can take what you want."

Willie and Ronnie ladled a generous portion onto their plates and sat down. The woman cut a substantial chunk of bread from the long loaf in the centre of the table, handed it to Ronnie, and then did the same for Willie before cutting a small piece for herself. One of the men on the other side of the table muttered a short prayer, and everyone but Willie and Ronnie expertly crossed themselves. The only Protestants in the room, they made clumsy attempts to emulate the motion, but the Catholic God probably guessed that they were not from His flock.

The stew was spicy and hot. The vagabonds held their heads down and shovelled without pause until, with their plates half-empty, they came up for air. Ronnie burped unexpectedly, and everyone at the table laughed. Coffee appeared in front of the young aviators—Willie took his black—Ronnie added three teaspoons of sugar, then poured enough milk into his cup that some of the coffee spilled on the table.

∞∞∞∞∞∞∞∞∞∞∞∞∞∞∞∞∞∞∞∞∞∞∞∞∞∞∞

The beautiful French woman smiled at Ronnie and said, "My name is Simone, and these gentlemen are René and Camille. Now, if each of you will tell us your name and squadron, we will get the word out that you are safe and on your way home."

Willie restrained the impulse to hug her and immediately answered, "I'm Pilot Officer Willie McLaughlin, and this is Pilot Officer Ronald Cummins. We're from RAF No 44 squadron, and 'C for Charley' was our aircraft." Simone relayed the information in French to Camille. He wrote it down, then left the room.

The stew in Willie and Ronnie's bowls disappeared in ten minutes, and both men waved her away when Simone jumped up to refill them. Simone took their plates to the sink and returned with small bowls filled with sweet bread and raisin pudding covered with milk. Willie and Ronnie made quick work of it.

When Camille returned and said something to Simone, Willie and Ronnie were scraping the bottoms of their bowls. She turned to them with a broad smile that showed her perfect teeth and said, "Your plane made it back on two engines. Eyes shining, she looked at Willie. They said to tell Willie that Norma is waiting for him."

"Oh, thank God!" Willie stood up, so excited that Simone laughed, filling the room with music. "How did you do all that? How can you talk to England without the Germans catching you? Don't they have something that can find a radio signal?"

She said, "Yes, it's no secret to the Germans that we can communicate easily with our Allies, and they can find us if we're not careful. We change frequencies and use codes that sometimes change by the hour, patrolling British aircraft relay messages, and we don't transmit long enough for them to find us."

She smiled, "We are already arranging your transport, and by morning, you'll be on your way."

Willie tried to remain calm, thinking it couldn't be this easy. He asked, "How long will it take, and what are our chances of getting there?"

"You will get home safely; we will protect you until you are in Spain. As for the time it takes…" Her voice softened, "It can take several weeks, but with the invasion close, I doubt it will be more than a few days before you're in Spain. We have no control from there, but you will likely take a commercial flight to England." She turned away from Willie and looked at the wall where it met the floor. "It is our job to take the risks required to get you home." Tears overflowed her beautiful eyes and ran down her cheeks.

Ronnie, proving that he possessed no tact, asked, "What happened? Did someone get killed?"

She hesitated, then said, "Yes, I lost my husband."

Ronnie asked, "What happened?" Willie squirmed at Ronnie's lack of judgment.

"He was tortured, then shot by the Gestapo." She lifted her head and looked into his eyes. "He refused to reveal the hiding place of an American fighter pilot we were protecting, so they killed him." She didn't drop her gaze, and Ronnie wilted.

"Oh, God... Simone, I'm sorry." It was obvious that Ronnie wanted to fix it, but she left the room, and René shook his head, saying something that was probably better not translated.

<hr>

Camille showed the British gunners to a room with two cots and children's drawings pinned to one of the rough plaster walls. Children's clothes piled in the corner, and unmade beds indicated the young ones weren't far away. Willie straightened the blankets on one of the beds and lay down on top of them. Ronnie sat on the edge of his bed with his head in his hands.

"What was I thinking?" He pushed his fingers through his hair. "How could I have been that stupid?"

Willie couldn't think of anything to say except, "Good questions... both of them!"

Simone came into the room with two blankets and pillows in her arms. She laid them on the bed behind Ronnie and sat beside him, taking his hand in hers.

"I loved my husband very much, and the sacrifice he made for all of us breaks my heart every day, but you, flying so high above us, can't know about these things. The war for you is between machines and an enemy on the ground that you will never see—but our war is personal. If one of us dies or kills the enemy, we sometimes have to watch it happen. Too often, when we shoot a German soldier, we are close enough to see the light in his young eyes go out. When they wound or capture one of us, the rest must run away and leave their friend to die, or worse.

This war is evil for all of us, but from different points of view, and you can't accept responsibility for the people who might die getting you home." She rubbed his hand and leaned over to kiss his cheek. "Unfortunately, we need you to keep killing Germans."

She went to a cupboard and came back with an unopened pack of French cigarettes. "Camille said he recognized you as a fellow nicotine addict, and he said you will need these to get you home."

He opened his mouth to remind her he still had half a pack, but she said, "You will need two packs, and we have lots of cigarettes." He put the cigarettes in his pocket, took one from the open pack and lit it. His nervous hands became quiet, and he asked, "When did your husband die?"

"Ten days ago—you will be the first flyers we've rescued since then."

Ronnie dared not lift his head. "Jesus Christ, I'm sorry for being such a jerk!"

He said it so softly that Willie wasn't sure of what he'd heard.

Simone quietly left the room.

CHAPTER TWENTY-FOUR

5 May 1944

Oppression, Struggle, Sacrifice, Liberation, Freedom—Repeat.
The People's Political Circle.

KARL ATTENDED HIS FIRST LUFTWAFFE DEBRIEFING and listened to Erik dictate his report accurately. But, when the interview was over, the rookie navigator understood that any resemblance to the truth in the final document was purely coincidental and probably not what the report was intended to reflect.

Karl's boss explained to the interviewer how they had found the bombers, noting the usual jammed Deelen frequency, and the intelligence officer said, "I understand that you experienced some radio interference, but it didn't affect the mission." Erik then described his victory as a standard "Schrägemusik" kill and the officer wrote for a minute, filling half a page. Erik then told him about how they had been ambushed by a lancaster rear gunner and estimated the damage to his messerschmitt as "substantial." The briefing officer corrected the ambush to 'random enemy fire,' and the damage to his aircraft from "substantial" to "light." The officer described the mission as "successful" with a downed British bomber at a cost of light damage to the night fighter. Technically, that was true, aside from the word, 'light.'

The briefing lasted ten minutes, with the last three standard senseless questions framed to elicit prescribed answers. When they were done, the intelligence officer asked Erik to press hard when he signed the report—there were two carbon copies. Erik signed it without reading a word, and they left the briefing with Karl wondering why.

On the walk to the barracks, Erik was surprised at Karl's unusual silence, but he could sense the young man's mind whirling. Karl was not an impulsive talker, but Erik knew he would hear from him as soon as the boy figured out how to say what was on his mind.

Breakfast was the usual spread of boiled eggs, cheeses, three kinds of wurst, jams, and several types of bread—the only flaw was the zero-caffeine ersatz coffee. Karl had a teenager's appetite and was still eating long after Erik had finished. When he finally stopped, Erik braced himself for a conversation about the briefing, but Karl announced he would help the maintenance crew and invited Erik to come along. Erik declined, heading instead for the command center to get an update from Major Fischer on the Mailly operation.

<hr>

When Erik walked in, Major Fischer sat by himself in his outside waiting area. Erik saluted as his boss rose, noting that the adjutant who usually separated the commanding officer from unwanted visitors was absent. He got a sloppy effort in return.

"I'm glad you're here, Erik. Sit down...I want to talk to you about something." Major Fischer waited until Erik sat in the leather chair next to him. "I would like to offer you a drink, but unfortunately, we're short of such pleasures these days."

"It's a little early for that anyway, Georg. I came here to try and understand what we should expect in the next few days. Last night, I lost an engine to an English gunner, and Fritz was upset—he had just finished replacing that engine. Karl is helping with the repairs, but parts may be a problem, and Fritz tells me the fuel and ammunition issues aren't getting resolved either. On top of all that, I see those damned mosquitos on almost every mission." He looked into his friend's eyes. "Can you tell me what the hell is going on?"

The major kept his attention on Erik momentarily, then dropped his gaze to the floor. Erik waited. When Major Fischer lifted his head, he spoke carefully and a little quieter than usual.

"The spare parts problem is not going to improve. The parts are in the factories, but distribution is a problem that will probably worsen. We have no fighters to protect the trains during the day, and the Résistance sabotages them at night. I don't know what percent of them get through, but it would probably disappoint us if we knew."

Major Fischer poured two cups of ersatz coffee from a silver coffee pot with a long, graceful neck and a magnificent buck deer etched around its waist. Erik knew that the urn was a loan/gift from Georg's wife, who stipulated that he bring it back. The major talked as he poured.

"On the matter of fuel, there is worse news. The British bombers have turned their attention to the synthetic fuel plants in Germany, and no oil is coming from the east since we've retreated from Russia and Romania. Until a few months ago, the Judas capitalist Americans—bless their greedy souls—had defied their government and shipped oil to us at a tremendous profit to themselves. However, with the losses in our Russia campaign and an imminent invasion of France, it is assumed they have become convinced that we will not survive. It would be bad for business to get caught supporting the losers!"

Erik sipped the hot but unsatisfactory substitute for coffee while waiting for the major to return the pot to the center of the low table. Georg took a sip before he put his cup down and leaned back. His tone gloomy, Fischer said, "Because the already bad fuel and ammunition situations are worsening, my orders are to send you up with only enough fuel and ammunition to complete the mission. Of course, the tone of that order is wishful thinking because every mission requires full fuel and ammunition..." Erik nodded... "and, of course, you must decide what is enough. If you don't have fuel in the tanks or ammunition in the guns, you have the answer to whether to fly the mission before you start the engines!"

Erik expected Major Fischer to smile, but he didn't, and Erik waited for him to go on. Fischer unhappily said, "My orders are to cancel all leave for the immediate future—there will be an invasion of France any day now. The bomber attacks over the last month, both day and night, have been exclusively on military targets, mostly in France and Belgium. We both play chess, and we should see this as the end game in this war. We're black, we've lost our queen, and white has cornered our king. If this were chess, black would tip his king now. Unfortunately, that option isn't available to pawns."

Major Fischer was the commanding officer of a critical Luftwaffe base, and he had just told Erik that Germany would lose the war, that they had no chance... It was a statement that carried a death sentence.

Erik sat silently, thinking, his cup of hot liquid perched precariously on his knee. He went back to his conversation with Kriminaldirektor Richter...The message Erik had carried to him was playing itself out as he had predicted.

The major continued, "Of course, I want you to do your best with what we can provide you, but a dead hero on our side will get no glory." The major motioned Erik to remain seated as he stood up and began pacing.

"The raid last night was on a Wehrmacht training and supply camp in Mailly le Camp, and the British bombers wiped out the base, killing hundreds of men and destroying all the buildings and machinery, including forty panzers. Other bombing raids have been devastating; hundreds of bombers destroy our shore defences and submarine bases, and they operate with impunity because we have no fuel and ammunition. The attacks involve hundreds of heavy bombers dropping hundreds and sometimes thousands of tons of bombs." He waved his arms in frustration.

"What were our skies a year ago are now theirs, and nothing we own, from fighters to tanks to trains, moves in the daylight. If we move something on the ground, their attack aircraft are there in minutes, and the vehicle is no more.

The Résistance used to be a disorganized bunch of ragtag revolutionaries; now, it is everywhere, carrying machine guns and explosives, attacking our roads, canals and trains. That little episode we had with the mosquitos strafing and bombing our base is happening regularly at all our military installations in France and Belgium, instigated by information the British get from the Résistance."

Major Fischer stopped pacing, stood behind his chair, and leaned on its back with a black mood plastered on his face. "Someone at a desk in Berlin will now give the orders for where and when we are to intercept bombers, and we will only protect essential factories and supplies in Germany. Except for flak, the British and Americans will raid our rocket sites and other military targets unchallenged. During the day, Allied ground-attack fighters will destroy whatever they choose to, essentially without opposition."

Major Fischer straightened up and indicated he was done with Erik, so he stood and faced him. "I understand, sir. We will do our best with what we have, and I want to thank you for your honesty. The talk on the base paints an even bleaker picture than you do, but that kind of talk doesn't interest me. Thank you again." He saluted, but Major Fischer took his hand and shook it, in no hurry to let it go.

Erik said, "Yes, sir, I understand." but Georg held onto his hand, grabbed Erik's shoulder with his left hand and said, "Do you really understand what I am saying?"

Erik said, "Yes, sir, I understand, and I promise I will do my duty..."

Major Fischer let him go and said emphatically, "Erik, I am telling you that your duty is to survive…you must forget about winning the war!"

◇◇◇◇◇◇◇◇◇◇◇◇◇◇◇◇◇◇◇◇◇◇◇◇◇◇◇◇

Erik's depression deepened as he walked to the maintenance shed where Fritz and his crew worked on his messerschmitt. He walked through the open door into the sunlit hangar—it faced south, allowing the sun streaming through the wide opening to warm and light the interior. Karl, a pair of safety-wire pliers in his hand, sat on a scaffold beside the new port engine.

Erik stood under Karl's plank seat, looked up at his navigator and asked, "How's it going, Karl?"

"Great, Sir," he managed to sound cheerful. "I will have the engine safety-wired in another half-hour, and we could be ready tonight if nothing unforeseen comes along to bite us."

Erik asked, "Has anyone said anything about getting us fuel and ammunition?"

Fritz came out of the back of the hangar with the repaired cowling in his arms. "No fuel until the aircraft is airworthy, but no fuel for a test flight to find out if it is airworthy." He shrugged and grinned, "If your luck holds and we obey our orders, you may never fly again!"

Erik touched a fuel line on the new engine and put his hand on something he thought might be a carburetor. Fritz had told him several times that the engine was fuel-injected, but Erik hadn't grasped the connection…that fuel injection replaced a carburetor. He said, "I trust your work—the test flight isn't necessary if we can test-run the engine for a few minutes." Fritz scowled, and Erik stopped smiling.

"Have you slept, Fritz?" Fritz looked at him through bloodshot eyes and moved like a drunk.

"No, your majesty…and take your hands off that magneto…sir." He made a motion that, with enough imagination, could have been a salute. "I have orders to get your steed ready as soon as possible, and I don't have time for sleep or unnecessary food until I've done that." He set the piece of cowling down on its end and leaned on it.

Erik motioned toward the barracks with his head. "Come with me, Fritz. It's time for a break and some food and rest." He looked up at his navigator, "Karl, come down from there." Erik put a hand on Fritz's shoulder and tried to steer him away from the plane, but Fritz pulled away and headed for the back of the hangar. "I've got to take these coveralls off, and I'll be right with you. He changed gears, washed in four minutes and joined Erik and Karl.

◇◇◇◇◇◇◇◇◇◇◇◇◇◇◇◇◇◇◇◇◇◇◇◇◇◇◇◇

As they walked, Karl asked, "Sir, do you know how to tell a pilot from a mechanic?" Erik shook his head, although he knew the punch line, and Karl continued. "A pilot washes his hands after he pisses; a mechanic washes them before." Fritz and Erik had heard the joke before, told by every new mechanic, but they laughed heartily.

The next afternoon, Erik and Karl took possession of the healthy messerschmitt Bf 110, but there were no missions for another three days.

They flew eight intercepts and shot down two British bombers by the end of May, increasing Erik's total to twenty-six confirmed kills. As expected, Karl proved to be an excellent navigator and a magician with the radar, picking out targets in an unbelievably short time. No mosquitos found them, and Erik brought the messerschmitt back unscathed. Fritz was as happy as he ever allowed himself to be, and Karl continued to beat Erik at chess. Life became monotonous, as it often is in war, broken sporadically by short periods of sheer terror.

On June 6, despite the inevitability, the news of the Allied landing in Normandy shocked the base.

CHAPTER TWENTY-FIVE

6 May 1944

No one can solve the Problems of Life because the only constant is change.

Commander Leech double-timed out of the communications building and across the field to the Quonset hut that housed 'C for Charley's' crew. He charged through the open door, stopped in front of Steve, grabbed his shoulders, and said, "They're on their way home! They're alright!"

Steve yelled, "Good God, man…Willie and Ronnie?" He added in a more civilized voice, "Sir?"

Commander Leech laughed like a kid. "Yes, they're in the hands of the Résistance and on their way home. Let's go to the Blue Bell tonight and tell Norma personally. I'll go and find a bus." He turned to leave, then stopped, turned his head, and said, "I can't wait to see Norma's face!"

It was almost five; they hadn't had supper and would be there early, but Steve and Leech left the hut with 'C for Charley's' excited crew behind them. Leech found a bus with the keys in it, and minutes later, they took off for the Blue Bell Inn, forty minutes away. It was Saturday night, always a reason to celebrate, but more momentous; tonight, they would celebrate finding their lost sheep.

The usual course of the war was a string of disasters and lost friends—on the rare occasion when lost friends reappeared, a celebration became the order of the day. Their return to the flock proved the possibility of survival.

The bus ride was bumpy, especially with an excited Leech driving like a maniac. The euphoric crew laughed, joked, and bounced around in their seats all the way to Tattershall Thorpe. They recounted feats attributed to their returning pals, exaggerated everything, and repeatedly recited the story of the night Norma had kidnapped Willie from their table.

Phillip hee-hawed, "Hey, remember the look on his face when she grabbed his arm and pushed him out the door?"

Steve said, "Yeah, but what about the look on his face when he got back on the bus?" And then his tone became serious. "I've never seen two people so much in love. You know...I didn't believe in love until I saw Willie and Norma together." He paused, but no one broke the silence. A moment later, he said, "I'd give anything to feel like that."

<hr>

The conversation turned to the next mission without their gunners, and Commander Leech reassured them. "I don't think you need to worry about that. Your targets will be in France and Belgium for the next few months, where the flak should be light, no night fighters, and a short flight time." He added, "Military Intelligence says that the Luftwaffe is running out of gas, ammunition, and dedication to the cause."

Every man hooted, each making a case for the oxymoron 'Military Intelligence.'

Leech went on, "Remember, Mailly was an exception. Otherwise, the last two months have been a lark, with no fatalities in the squadron. For some reason, the German night fighters let us bomb civilians and some military installations with impunity—just stay away from their synthetic fuel plants. mosquitos attack the German bases at night; mustangs, thunderbolts, Tornadoes and spitfires by day, and the proximity of Allied bases means there are constantly Allied aircraft over the German's heads. That makes it tough for German fighters to take off without horrendous casualties. Our bombers mark a flak battery, and, in a few hours, thunderbolts and Typhoons arrive with bombs and rockets."

He shifted down and revved the engine for a hill. "It won't be long before Hitler eats his own shit!"

The men mumbled their agreement—every man there knew that armour, lorries, and tents filled all the fields in southern England. The invasion of France had to happen soon, or England would have nowhere to farm or fish. There was no room to park a rowboat in the harbours, and airmen, seamen and soldiers took shifts at the overflowing taverns and pubs. The patient English population soon learned that the Americans had money, the Colonials had courage and loved to fight, and never to trust a Canadian with their daughter.

Leech said, "I have the report on the Mailly raid." He spoke as though he were reading the report. "Three-hundred-and-forty-two heavy bombers dropped fifteen-hundred tons of bombs, destroyed one hundred and fifteen buildings, one hundred and seven armoured vehicles, and killed four hundred Germans. Our reconnaissance shows that the destruction of the base was total. We lost forty-two bombers and two-hundred-and-eighty men, but General Harris calls the mission a victory and guarantees that Bomber Command has corrected the problem with the radio."

Leech waited; the men looked at one another as though they knew a secret—a few laughed. He said, "All right, I'm not so sure either… So, just in case, I'm designating an alternate VHF frequency for the forty-fourth squadron, and the master bomber will have it. You never know—we might have another 'easy as pie' mission."

∞∞∞∞∞∞∞∞∞∞∞∞∞∞∞∞∞∞∞∞∞∞∞∞∞∞∞∞

The 'C for Charley' aircrew waited over an hour for the Blue Bell doors to open, then followed a bomber crew from Spilsby Aerodrome through the door. Unfortunately, no one had briefed the new lads on 'C for Charley's' table rights, and they slid behind it just as Steve and his men stopped beside them, with Charley in the lead.

"Fin' anither table chaps. Thes a body belongs tae 'C fur Charley,' an' that's us." He pointed at his chest. The new arrivals looked at one another but didn't move to get up.

Charley leaned over the sergeant sitting on the corner. "Noo, I'm gonnae ask nicely a body mair time, friendly force tae friendly force. We jist foond it uir lads ur alife an' walkin' back haem frae France—we've come tae celebrate, an' ye ur in uir seats!" Charley had spoken in the sergeant's ear. The sergeant smiled sweetly, stood up and pointed at his derriere.

"Kiss me bloomin' arse, ya Scottish sheepfucker!"

Charley kept the smile fixed on his face as he balled his fists into clubs.

Commander Leech stepped around Charley and pushed him away from the sergeant before he could hit him, which Charley's clenched fists and cocked arm made clear he was about to do.

Leech leaned over until his face was an inch from the sergeant's. "You cockney prick, I'm going to give you an order, just once, and then I'm going for the MPs, and you will miss the show. My name is Wing Commander Leech, and these are my boys—now, get out of those damned seats!"

The cockney prick stayed where he was, pleased with the fixed smile plastered on his face.

"Nah shit, ya canuck bastard. Ya've got nah rank in 'ere, and ya'll be in 'ell before I give ya me seat!" Commander Leech turned beet red and shifted his weight to throw the first punch, but one of the sergeant's mates spoke up before he did.

"Christ Jerry, that's John Leech; 'e won the Victoria Cross, 'e did, and we'll be drawn and quartered if we was ta pick a fight wi' 'im! Count me out." He pushed on the big man, who had the speaker blocked. Staggering to his feet, the sergeant took off his cap and reached for Leech's hand. John took it and pulled the sergeant away from the table before releasing him. The man, appropriately humbled, stood to one side to clear a path for his friends, and John tipped his hat to him before he sat down.

◇◇◇◇◇◇◇◇◇◇◇◇◇◇◇◇◇◇◇◇◇◇◇◇◇◇◇◇◇◇◇

Norma began her show as usual with "The White Cliffs of Dover," drifting over to Steve's table as she had when Willie was there. Steve squirmed in his seat like a little boy who desperately needed to go to the toilet and, as she brushed by the table, still singing, grabbed her and spun her around. She stopped in the middle of a phrase, and he yelled, loud enough for everyone in the building down the road to hear, "Willie's alive! We just heard that he and Ronnie are on their way home without a friggin' scratch!" He laughed and danced Norma onto the open floor.

The entire room cheered—even the ones who had lost money in the pool. The clever pianist broke into "For He's a Jolly Good Fellow," and men came from every cranny in the building to hug Norma and congratulate her. She had to break a few robust grips, but she survived, and when she raised her hand, the Blue Bell became silent. She let her eyes drift around the room, waiting for the perfect time. She was an entertainer, and her gift of timing showed.

"I can't put into words how happy I am right now. Willie is the best thing that's ever happened to me, and you all know how I love him." A hearty "Yeah!" resounded through the room. "Not that I don't love all of you..." She laughed, and everyone except those who had lost a lot of money erupted with cheers.

"Now, I'm going to sing to you—let's celebrate something good in this damned war!"

The cheers started, and the pianist, a brilliant chap, rescued her with the introduction to "We'll Meet Again." The men in the room laughed, cried, and cheered. Because of the din, she had to guess the pitch and the timing, but the room became silent when her beautiful voice resonated on the first note. It was as though someone had thrown a switch, and every man in the room stopped breathing.

A month later, just before dawn on June 6, 1944, an RAF Air Transport DC-3 left Gibraltar for Lyneham airbase, eighty miles west of London. The American DC-3 was one of several the British government had converted to an airliner to shuttle diplomats, spies, and rescued airmen in and out of neutral Spain. Willie and Ronnie sat in comfortable airline-style seats, each with a window to watch the miles and miles of tiny white specks dancing on the gray Atlantic Ocean. The flight was a day late due to bad weather in England, but it finally left Spain in the pre-dawn light. Willie rested his elbow on the seat rest and his chin on his hand, watching the coast slowly creep past. His thoughts centred on Norma, anticipating their reunion—the day's delay hadn't diminished his elation.

Ronnie's excited voice broke Willie's trance, "Holy shit, Willie... Look ahead!"

Willie looked over the wing at the sea gap connecting the British and French coasts just coming over the horizon.

"Jesus, Ronnie, I didn't know there were that many ships in the world!" Willie pressed his face against the window to see the edge of the land at the southern tip of England. He started counting ships, lost count in the fifties and began again.

More ships appeared as the rolling horizon exposed them like pencils dropped on a gray mat, all pointing east. Willie whistled, "There are hundreds of them!"

As the aircraft progressed toward the southeast tip of England, the sea floated a mosaic of ships, large and small, some trailing long tails of black smoke as they crept to a point on the French coast almost at the horizon. As the plane ate up the distance, Willie saw dozens of ships waiting off the French coast and small boats fanning out toward the beaches. Clusters of black dots moved back and forth under the clouds like blowflies buzzing around a dead carcass.

"Those dots are fighters and bombers heading for France." Ronnie tapped on his window.

Willie noted that the dots moved both ways. He said, "Some are coming back." He lifted the little yellow curtain back from the upper corner of the rectangular window. "They're flying higher than we are, and some are going home to refuel and rearm. They've been at this for a while already."

Ronnie noted a slight change in the DC-3's course. "We're turning west to go around them."

People on the port side stepped into the aisle to look out the starboard windows, but the flight attendant chased them back to their seats. No one on the starboard side offered to trade seats—everyone knew they were watching history—this was the beginning of the end for Hitler's Germany and the Third Reich!

The DC-3 flew inland to approach Lyneham from the west. When they landed and walked down the steps, a bus awaited the London-bound passengers, and a WAAF waved from a car waiting for Willie and Ronnie. The invasion had closed all the essential combat airfields to non-combat aircraft, and Lyneham was one of few destinations in England for civilian flights from Spain.

It took the WAAF driver four hours to get Willie and Ronnie to Dunholme Lodge airbase, and they stepped out to a small group of celebrating comrades. The airfield was a buzz of activity; fuel trucks and lorries pulling trailers loaded with bombs and rockets crisscrossed the field.

◇◇◇◇◇◇◇◇◇◇◇◇◇◇◇◇◇◇◇◇◇◇◇◇◇◇◇◇◇◇◇◇

Commander Leech welcomed Willie and Ronnie, then led a parade to the officers' mess for an alcoholic celebration. The cook had made a special dinner of roast beef, Yorkshire pudding and mashed potatoes, and the prodigal sons made speeches and answered endless questions about their adventures.

Ronnie described the armada in the channel—hundreds of Allied ships and aircraft on their way to France, and the room cheered. The field at Dunholme Lodge was a jumping-off and refuelling point for RAF spitfires, Typhoons, and American 8th Air Force thunderbolts and mustangs stationed further west. Even without official confirmation, the sudden increase in traffic confirmed that the invasion was underway. Ronnie, well off the wagon and into anything that contained alcohol, increased his estimate to "thousands of ships, so close together, you could jump from one to another." And then, "The war will be over in a year...no, a month," and finally, "...they are negotiating with Hitler's generals as we speak; they know that nothing can stop us now!"

The gig continued until the already inebriated crowd broke up for evening celebrations in the Blue Bell Inn. Willie temporarily shut down his disgust with alcohol and joined in the festivities, matching his frivolity level with those who were happily inebriated but still rational.

John Leech, one of the few still relatively sober, talked some fool into loaning him their Austin sedan so he could chauffeur the homecoming heroes to the party. Willie steered Ronnie into the back seat, where he collapsed and threw up on the floor. Willie rolled down the back-seat windows, and Commander Leech fitted the Austin between a lorry and a bus for the drunken parade to the Blue Bell.

<hr>

At the tavern, a swarm of airmen pushed Willie in front of them to the main door, but Steve stopped Willie before he opened it. Commander Leech reached around him and knocked. The door flew open, and Norma grabbed Willie before he could step over the threshold. Commander Leech and Steve caught the locked lovers as Willie tumbled backwards with Norma on top of him, her mouth pressed on Willie's so hard it hurt him. She pulled him into the barroom.

Four men towed the heroes to the dining room, where they picked Willie and Ronnie up and put them on a table so they could sign the ceiling, the custom for local RAF heroes. The noisy crowd gathered in a circle as Willie and Ronnie signed their names over the spot where some joker had written "Victims of Premature Ejection" next to Leech's signature from when he had won the Victoria Cross.

Finally, everyone retired to the main room, where Norma sang a verse of "We'll Meet Again." There had been no plan for her to sing, so she sang it unaccompanied. No one breathed; when she finished, the crowd remained silent for a long ten seconds before a smattering of applause became a roar.

Before the applause died, a British flyer from the nearby aerodrome at Woodhall Thorpe burst into the room, interrupting the celebrations. He attempted, without success, to shout above the applause of Norma's fans. When the room finally noticed him and became quiet, he repeated his announcement. "They've landed in Normandy! We've done it! Our boys are fighting their way off the beach and headed for Berlin—it's Hitler's turn to go for a Burton!"

Their high expectations confirmed, the men's excitement for Norma and Willie changed focus, and everyone gathered around the new arrival. Someone lifted him so he could speak from the top of a table, and the gunner said that rumours were already flying around that the Canadians had taken their beach and driven inland past the German defences, bringing a roar from the Canucks in the crowd. He said the Americans had established a beachhead and dug in at the bottom of a cliff, waiting for reinforcements, and someone said, "Give 'em 'ell, Yanks!" The place erupted when he announced that the British were over the seawall and working on the big guns above the beach.

The crowd lifted the messenger from the table and took him to the bar, now open and ready to do their part for the war by circulating British currency.

Norma and Willie lost interest in the war news—they had eyes only for one another. Willie jerked his head toward the door, and Norma took his hand. They ran out on the road and kept running until they reached the Petwood Hotel.

The evening sky was ablaze as they stopped, panting for breath on the small hill above the familiar maze of chimneys perched on the roof of the complicated building. They spontaneously kissed—a long, passionate kiss that, combined with breathlessness, left them both dizzy. They separated and staggered arm-in-arm down the driveway.

It was Tuesday, June 6, 1944, the day Willie established for sure that Norma loved him, and he knew he would remember it for as long as he could stay alive.

✦✦✦✦✦✦✦✦✦✦✦✦✦✦✦✦✦✦✦✦✦✦✦✦✦

The week flew past. No 44 squadron flew four missions to support the invading Allied forces as they moved inland, but Willie stayed on the ground. Norma sang again on Friday night, and when she finished her last set, Willie went to the Petwood Inn with her. On their way, they scampered back and forth on the road, playing like children. But Norma's mood changed as they approached the inn—she walked slower, with her arm entwined around his.

They made slow, tender love, and again, in the morning, with the thick blackout drapes pulled to the sides and sunlight streaming in on them. She lay down next to him so that he could stroke her. He had learned where to touch her, what to avoid, and had become very good at reading her shifting moods. She sent subtle signals she couldn't explain, and he was learning to interpret them. Most of the time, she preferred a more gentle approach than she had used on the night she had taken his virginity, but sometimes...

As they cuddled together, Norma's head on Willie's shoulder, legs wound together, she whispered in his ear. "Willie, I've got to tell you something, and you may want to leave me when you find out."

He laughed, "Don't tell me you've got gonorrhea!" She didn't laugh. He said thoughtfully, "In that case, it's too late, and nothing else matters a whit."

She sat on the bed with her legs bent and arms locked below her knees.

"No, I've got something much more serious than that." She looked at him. "I have a little boy, and Brian is his father."

Willie said nothing for a few seconds, then leaned over and lifted her face so he could kiss her.

"I'll only forgive you if you teach him to call me daddy."

"You want to marry me and take another man's child to be your own?" She began to tear up but quickly wiped them away.

"You're telling me that I get a little boy, and I don't have to put up with a pregnant wife for nine months? And no after-birth blues? No babies crying all night?... I've always wanted children but never expected to get one for free! Now, what's the catch?"

She sat on the edge of the bed. "Nathan will be two years old at the end of this month. His official last name is Jones, but that can be changed when I change my name."

Willie sat up and swung his legs over the side of the bed to sit beside her. He put his hands on his knees and looked thoughtfully at the opposite wall.

"So—am I reading this right? You're telling me I have to marry you to get the boy?"

Norma looked at the wall; she grasped what he was doing.

"Yep, that's the deal." She looked at him, sliced her hand horizontally in a quick motion. "Take it or leave it!"

"Thank you, Norma, but...." Norma stopped breathing, and her jaw dropped. Willie put his hand on hers and looked into her beautiful eyes. "Neither you nor Nathan will need to change your names when we get married. You will always be Norma Collette Stanfield to me, and besides, another name would be confusing."

Norma stood up and pushed Willie down on the bed. "You joker! Of course, I will marry you! We will talk about names later." She kissed him, rolled off him and said, "You'd better listen to me. If anyone asks, you pleaded for me to marry you, down on one knee, cowering like a whipped dog. If you tell anyone anything else, I won't marry you!" She pushed on his chest with the end of her finger.

"Okay, okay, I get it...I grovelled!" Willie took her hand and changed the mood. He said earnestly, "When Nathan is old enough, I want him to know about his father, what he sacrificed and how he died. Brian deserves better than to die without his son honouring him as a hero and proudly carrying his name." Willie kissed Norma's hand.

"Norma, the world has changed; this time will live forever in history. Now that the Allies are in France, the Germans won't last long. They're out of gas—the lads say they haven't seen a fighter in weeks, not since Mailly. The Russians are coming from the East—a month, maybe two, and the war will be over. Even if it isn't, I only have another five or six missions and probably won't have time to do them. My survival chances are better than good, so I want to ask you to marry me, seriously, because I love you."

Norma glowed. "Yes, Willie, I will marry you. I don't know when—I will let Mother decide that—but in my heart, I've been married to you since I met you. I love you more than anyone, except my sweet Nathan, of course. I hope you don't mind sharing."

"Well, I don't mind, but I warn you; when that boy gets to know me, he will forget about mummy!" Willie grinned and hugged her—she turned the hug into something more.

"Now, Norma, don't you start anything! You surely don't expect..."

They kissed tenderly; she threw his clothes at him. "Well, if that's all you've got..." She laughed at him when he missed, and the pants hit him in the face. "We don't have time anyway; Mother will be here in an hour, and I must eat. I'm famished."

<hr>

Willie asked, astonished, "Your mother is driving here? Are we going somewhere?" He pulled on his underwear and shoved an arm into his shirt.

Norma spoke as though she had everything arranged. "Yes, I spoke with Commander Leech, and we'll live in my apartment for the next few days. You will meet Nathan this morning." Full of joy, Norma laughed at Willie as he fought with his shirt. She lifted it over his arm. "I just don't see how you can live without me!" She whacked his bum.

Willie caught her and kissed her again. "You're right; I can't live without you," he patted her backside, "but it's got nothing to do with my shirt."

A few minutes later, when they were in the dining room, Willie caught the saucy Lincolnshire girl waiting on them winking at Norma as she added a bowl of flowers to the table. Willie gestured at the retreating waitress with his head.

"How long have you known her? Tell me about her."

Norma looked at the swinging door where her friend had disappeared.

"We've been friends since I began singing at the Blue Bell. She's the one who made me find someone after Brian died, so I guess we should thank her."

"Yes, we should do that, but first, tell me her story." Willie poured tea from the pot the waitress had left on the table.

"If she hasn't got a steady, she's at the Blue Bell almost every night, more to flirt with the RAF crews than to hear me. Most nights, she doesn't return home empty-handed, and presently, she's madly in love with an Australian mosquito pilot stationed at Woodhall Spa. The Petwood Hotel is the Spa's official officers' mess, and instead of drinking with his mates, he visits her room. Most nights, her pilot sneaks back to the base just before daylight. mosquito pilots live longer than lancaster crews, and the war is almost over, so perhaps this one will be her last."

"Has she lost someone too?" Willie regretted the question.

"Yes, most girls around here have lost at least one RAF lover. Carol has lost two men to the RAF casualty list, but she's found a way to get on with her life. She took a few weeks to mourn after receiving the "killed in action" report and then was back at the Blue Bell with her red dress on." Norma answered Willie's unasked question, "I suppose grief is like everything else—it gets easier with practice. She loved those men with all her heart, but life goes on, and loss has made her a strong woman."

Willie wondered how long it would take Norma to find someone else if he went for a Burton. For the first time, he dared to believe that it wouldn't happen.

Norma turned the conversation to her mother and Nathan's affection for his grandmother. The crumpets and boiled eggs arrived, and they ate, happier with every bite.

<hr />

They were back in the room for only a few minutes when a soft knock interrupted Willie's packing, and he opened the door. A woman who could only be Norma's mother swept into the room, passed him, and headed straight for her daughter. In her late forties, she was a stunning woman, definitely not what Willie thought of as an average grandmother. Wearing a printed skirt that cheekily covered half her knees and a white cotton blouse unbuttoned dangerously low, she showed a generous amount of leg and cleavage. A silver clasp held her black hair together at neck level, forcing it to cascade down her back to just above her belt. She had the same dark complexion and eyes as Norma, and it was plain to Willie where Norma got her beauty.

She looked at Willie, top to bottom—bottom to top. "Well, you're a little small, but you'll do!" She laughed at what he expected was a look of surprise that had swept over his face, then turned away from him to face her daughter with a questioning look. Norma very slightly nodded.

"How long have I got to prepare?" she asked. "I have to get invitations printed, and the reception absolutely must be in the… "

"Blue Bell," interrupted Norma. "The party will be at the Blue Bell."

"All right, dear, it will be in the Blue Bell. But will you please, please, please get married in the cathedral this time... No scurrying away to a justice of the peace? Your father and I will not miss your wedding again! You are our only child, and I want to see you married in a beautiful white dress in that beautiful cathedral, and I want your father to walk you down the aisle. Please, darling, do this for us!"

Norma put her arm around Willie's waist. "I will be proud to walk down the aisle on Dad's arm as long as Willie is at the altar waiting for me. The only condition is that 'and obey' be struck from my oath."

"Your father and I will take care of that, even if we have to speak with the bishop." Her mother spoke as though Norma's father could change church doctrine at will. "Now, when do you two want to tie the knot?" She looked straight at her daughter and asked, "Are you pregnant?" Before Norma could answer, she turned to Willie, then back to her daughter. "Norma, you must stop using that silly name. His name is William, not Willie." She took Willie's hand. "William, I am Gianna Collette, Norma's mother."

Willie swallowed hard and was about to say how pleased he was to meet her when Norma said, "No, I'm not pregnant yet, but I'm taking no precautions whatsoever—I want Willie's baby."

Willie, overwhelmed, said stupidly, "You didn't tell me that! You wanted my baby right from the beginning?"

Norma laughed and said coquettishly, "Yes, almost from the day I met you and started teaching you how to make love."

Willie's face turned red—his neck burned in his collar. He thought he should probably be insulted but found that he was pleased.

Gianna laughed at his embarrassment. "You want more babies, and I want more grandchildren, so that's okay with me. As usual, your father does not need to know your plans; he has far too much on his mind." Gianna checked her fingernails. She had the same twinkle in her eyes that Willie had grown to love in Norma's.

Norma pushed Gianna out the door and followed with her small bag. She left her heavy suitcase for Willie; he picked it up, slung the strap of his duffle bag over his shoulder, and followed her.

The car Gianna headed for was a long silver Bentley, complete with a capped chauffeur in the driver's seat. The chauffeur jumped out and hurried around the car to open the door for Gianna and Norma. He held it while they climbed into the back seat, then took the bags from Willie and put them in the boot while Willie opened the left front door and slid into the soft leather seat. Before he could shut the door, the chauffeur gently closed it behind him. The latch clicked with the slightest pressure. Gianna leaned ahead and whispered in Willie's ear, "William, the only rule is no smoking in the Bentley—James will kill you if he smells smoke in his Rolls!" Willie assumed James was Norma's father.

"No, ma'am, I won't." Willie added, "I don't smoke."

Gianna pursed her lips and looked approvingly at her daughter. The chauffeur started the Bentley and smoothly drove away while Norma and Gianna chattered in the rear seat like long-lost friends. Willie smiled as he thought of being a part of this family—the rolls royce didn't hurt.

<hr>

At one o'clock, George—Willie had learned the chauffeur's name—stopped the car in front of the most beautiful church Willie had ever seen! Three massive ornate towers rose out of an enormous Gothic building that dwarfed the red roofs of the two-storey townhouses surrounding it. Immaculate lawns surrounded the church at ground level. Thousands of ornate details that would have taken thousands, probably millions of hours to create decorated every nook, cranny, and corner of the building. Willie was awe-struck. There was nothing like this in Digby, Nova Scotia.

Norma leaned over the seat, kissed him on the neck and said, "I'll see you later, darling," then slipped out the back door the chauffeur held open. She ran up the stone steps and through the imposing main door.

Gianna answered his question before he asked it. "I'm taking you to Norma's apartment to meet Nathan. And then you and I will spend the afternoon chatting and drinking tea while Norma rehearses. George will pick her up at four when the rehearsal is over."

"Yes, ma'am," Willie replied. He was pretty sure the afternoon would be his job interview.

"My name is Gianna, and if you call me 'ma'am' again, I shall forbid my daughter to marry you—not that she listens to anything I say..."

"Yes, m..." he caught himself... "Mrs. Stanfield."

She sat back in the seat and looked out the window as if talking to some unseen person far away. "That's the only name you could call me that I hate worse than 'ma'am.'" She turned back to Willie. "Call me Gianna, and I shall call you William. William is a fine English name; you should train your headstrong future wife to use it. Willie, on the other hand, tempts one to add wee, as in wee Willie, not at all appropriate for a man."

"Yes, Gianna," he said, grinning to himself; "I will change my name to William, just for you."

The big car slowed in front of a long stone building, a row of townhouses with thick masonry walls separating the units, their tops extending above the roofs. Each house had identical bay windows beside identical ornate oak doors with identical round black knockers in the centre. The second story of every unit had two identical dormers growing out of a red clay-tiled roof. The Gothic number on the door was the only way to differentiate the units.

As they climbed the stone steps, the door opened, and a small boy peeked out from behind a large woman who restrained him from running out to greet them.

"Granny!" He shrieked and tried to push past the large woman.

Gianna pointed her finger at Willie. "Don't you say a word! That child is as stubborn as his mother!"

Gianna ran up the steps, and the woman stepped aside, letting the little boy go so his granny could scoop him up and kiss him.

"Granny was the second word he learned," she told William. "I hold Norma responsible for that."

"I'll bet the first was mummy," he said, pleased with himself.

Gianna hooted, "You don't know much about children, do you? The first word is always 'no;' he said it for a month before finally saying, 'Granny.' I've been trying to teach him 'Gianna,' but he won't even try." She laughed and pointed at William. "Nathan, his name is William, and he's going to be your new daddy. Can you say, William?"

He said, "Daddy," and stretched his right hand out to Willie, working his fingers back and forth. Willie touched the tiny fingers and said, "I'm very pleased to meet you, Nathan." He kissed the wiggling fingers, and Nathan smiled.

Gianna put Nathan down. "You two will be fine." Nathan ran into the house, and everyone followed him.

Gianna introduced Nathan's caretaker as Cynthia Caldwell. She politely shook Willie's hand, then disappeared to prepare lunch.

Willie sat on the floor beside Nathan, who immediately knocked down a pile of blocks he had built, laughing at the destruction he had wrought. Willie picked up the blocks and began building while Nathan watched. It quickly became a reasonable facsimile of a house.

Half an hour later, Cynthia interrupted them. "Time for lunch, you two." She tried to pick up Nathan, but he was having none of that. He took Willie's hand and walked to the table with him, steering Willie to the chair next to his highchair.

Gianna tousled her grandson's hair and winked at Willie. "It looks like he's adopted you as his father—Norma can't change her mind now!"

Willie laughed. "He'll be fine until I change his diaper and put him to bed."

Gianna and Cynthia exchanged looks and knowing smiles.

<hr>

Norma came through the door at a quarter after four. Willie pointed to her and said, "Mummy's home!" Nathan smiled, pulled Willie to the pile of blocks, and returned to his building. Willie picked up Nathan, carried him to meet Norma, and handed the boy to her. Nathan twisted, but she held him tight, sniffing his diaper.

"Who changed your diaper?"

He pointed at Willie.

Norma looked at Willie and her mother. Gianna nodded, and Norma said, "Thank you, Willie. Is there any chance this behaviour could become permanent?"

"Willie!" said Nathan.

"William!" corrected Gianna, pointing at Willie. Everyone but Nathan laughed. Norma put her little boy on his feet, and he grabbed Willie's hand.

Norma said, "What have you done to my son?"

Willie, pleased with himself, said, "Right now, we're working on the toilet thing. I'm going to take him there now before I have to change his diaper again. We'll be right back."

"I've got to see this!" Gianna started up the stairs behind him.

"Me too!" said Norma, catching up to her mother.

Willie held up his hand. "No, we men will do this—no women allowed. The ladies will have to wait here!" Nathan smiled at them and hurried to keep up with Willie. Even though the steps were too high, forcing him to use his hands and feet to climb them, Willie waited for Nathan without offering help. They eventually reached the top; Nathan turned to smile at his mother and grandmother, then took Willie's hand and disappeared.

As Cynthia pulled on a sweater and followed Gianna to the door, she asked, "Does Willie have a brother?"

Gianna opened the door and told Norma, "Cynthia and I are going now to take care of your father, but I could stay if you need me..."

Norma pushed her mother out the door. "Go, please, Mother, and thank you for everything. As for the wedding planning, I will marry him whenever and wherever you want. But I want the reception to be a party at the Blue Bell, and I will arrange that. We'll get the whole place for the afternoon." She added, "Don't bother to speak to the bishop about the 'obey' word—I'll cross my fingers."

Norma watched Gianna and Cynthia go down the steps, then closed and locked the door. Willie returned to the living room with Nathan in tow.

"Did he do it?" she asked. Willie nodded, and Nathan left him for his blocks.

<hr>

Norma and Willie ate late in the evening after Willie had tucked Nathan in bed. He insisted on a kiss from Daddy and Mummy, then put his head down and fell asleep before they were out of the room.

Norma pulled out a novel she had been reading and showed Willie her collection of books. He picked out 'Moby Dick,' Herman Melville's tale of men and the sea, flipped a few pages and said, "I always intended to read this but never got around to it."

Norma pointed to a soft chair with broad arms, a footstool, and a floor lamp beside it. In minutes, he was engrossed in the book.

Norma closed her book at ten o'clock and pulled Willie from his chair,. playfully shaking her finger at him. "Rule number one, William. No sex when I have serious music to sing the next day!"

He smiled. "Hmmm... Because it makes you happy, and then you can't be serious?"

"No, serious music can be happy too." Norma pushed his chest with her hand. "I sing better when I feel desire."

"Then I'll have to sleep on the sofa." He went to the bedroom, picked up his duffle bag, and untied the cord.

She closed the door and began to unbutton her blouse.

Willie straightened up, watched her unfasten her bra, and shook his head. "Nope, we can't." He pulled his pyjamas out of the bag and headed toward the door.

Norma intercepted him. "We have to practice this," she said earnestly, "I'll be singing a lot, and you need to learn to control yourself." She motioned for him to undress. He spread his hands in a gesture of defeat and took off his clothes. He pulled on the bottom of his pyjamas and put his left arm in the top pyjama sleeve.

"I didn't know you had those." She pointed at the blue-striped pyjamas. "You look sexy in them."

Willie laughed. "You've never let me get that far."

Norma watched Willie climb into bed, threw the nightie in the corner and said, "Oh, what the hell... So, I'll sing shitty!"

Before he figured out what she was up to, she pulled the sheets down and grabbed the waistband of his pyjamas.

Twenty minutes later, she lay on him, exhausted and satisfied, and they slept like the dead until daylight when Nathan began yelling for Daddy.

◇◇◇◇◇◇◇◇◇◇◇◇◇◇◇◇◇◇◇◇◇◇◇◇◇◇◇◇◇

Willie got up, tiptoed into Nathan's room, changed his diaper and took him downstairs. He found oatmeal in the pantry, enough for all of them, cooked it, filled a small bowl for Nathan and covered it with a layer of brown sugar. He found milk in the icebox and drowned the boy's porridge. Then, when Nathan began eating the sweet concoction, Willie checked on Norma. She was sound asleep—he watched her for a few minutes, worried that their busy night had ruined her voice.

CHAPTER TWENTY-SIX

11 June 1944

La musique exprime ce qui ne peut pas s'exprimer avec des mots et sur quoi il est impossible de se taire.
(Music expresses that which cannot be put into words, and that which cannot remain silent.)
Victor Hugo

NORMA WAS STILL IN HER NIGHTDRESS when she came down the stairs for a late breakfast. She kissed Nathan and Willie, interrupting their play in the living room, and went to the kitchen. Time had ruined the porridge, so she found a biscuit, sliced it in two, spread a thick layer of jam on each half, and poured hot water into a cup through a strainer full of Earl Gray tea. She watched Nathan and Willie for a few minutes while she ate the biscuit. When it was gone, she interrupted.

"The music we're doing today is called a Requiem Mass. It's a religious piece for those who've died, written by Wolfgang Amadeus Mozart in the late eighteenth century, and ironically, Mozart died before he finished it. One of his students finished it from his notes."

Willie asked, without looking up, "All right, tell me, what is a Requiem Mass for dead people? I know a mass is a church service, but what's a requiem?" Willie whittled a door frame for the house he and Nathan were building.

Norma swallowed a sip of tea while she decided how to put this in layman's terms. "I guess you could say it's a funeral service for all the dead—a prayer, or I suppose one should say a sequence of prayers for their souls' salvation and eternal peace. It's sung in Latin, the universal language of the Roman Catholic Church."

Willie looked puzzled, so Norma reassured him, "You will be given a translation at the door."

As he continued helping Nathan install the frame, she touched his arm.

"I want you to sit with my Mother and Father. I guarantee my Father will cry, so don't feel embarrassed if you do too."

Willie half-laughed. "Why would I cry? I never cry when I listen to music." He smiled at her... "Except maybe when you sing Lili Marlene."

Norma shook her head. "This isn't Lili Marlene—it's much, much more powerful. I can't help crying inside when I sing it. I weep for my Brian and all the other boys I don't see in the Blue Bell anymore." She patted his knee. "You'll understand when you hear the music."

Willie waved her off, smiling, "Don't worry about me. I just hope we didn't ruin your voice last night. Next time, you won't talk me out of sleeping on the sofa!" He turned to Nathan, who had torn the house down and was building a complicated, undefinable structure. Willie tried to see Brian in his little face but could only find Norma's beautiful southern European features.

Norma finished the last bite of her biscuit, chuckled, and drained her teacup. "My voice feels fine now, but I won't try it in earnest until after lunch. The performance isn't until three."

Norma kissed Nathan on the cheek, and the boy pretended not to notice. "We've already missed the church service, but I told Mother yesterday not to expect us. She only said, 'Of course not, dear,'" Norma mimicked her Mother perfectly. "It frightens me how she reads my mind."

Willie helped Nathan fit a problematic block in place. "I like your Mother... I wish mine had some of her guts!"

Norma said, "She got those 'guts' the hard way." She gathered the dishes from the table and spoke from the kitchen, "Someday, I'll tell you her story, but not today." She laid the dishes on the kitchen counter, then looked meaningfully at Willie before she went up the stairs.

Willie took Nathan to the kitchen and pulled a chair over to the counter so the little boy could help him wash the dishes. Nathan laid the clean dishes on a rack beside the sink. He dropped one, but it didn't break on the soft pine floor, and when Willie picked it up and said, "Oops," Nathan repeated it.

Norma dressed and went to the living room to read her book while Willie made peanut butter and jelly sandwiches for lunch. She had made it clear to Willie that she found the sandwiches disgusting, but Nathan loved them, which sealed the deal for Willie.

◇◇◇◇◇◇◇◇◇◇◇◇◇◇◇◇◇◇◇◇◇◇◇◇◇◇

Lunch was over at one, and Willie listened to Norma warm her voice

284

with a few arpeggios and phrases from the Requiem—the voice he heard was not the one she used at the Blue Bell. Nathan stopped playing to watch his Mother, and Willie watched both of them. With a gloating smile at Willie, Norma pronounced her voice healthy and ready to sing.

Willie obediently followed Norma to the bedroom and didn't complain when she helped him dress in clothes he assumed had been Brian's. When she finished, she stood back, delighted with her work. Willie detected a fleeting sadness in her eyes, and then it was gone.

"You clean up real nice," she said, imitating the airmen in the bar. "In fact, you are smashing!" She kissed him on the cheek, then kicked him out of the bedroom. "Get out of here before I really ruin my voice!"

Ten minutes later, Norma walked into the living room—Willie moved his mouth, but no sound came out. She twirled once and stopped.

"Well, what do you think?" The fabric made an extra quarter turn, swung back, and came to rest. The exquisite black gown covered her ankles but left her black leather high-heeled shoes still visible. Willie swallowed and opened his mouth to try again, but the doorknocker interrupted him.

The knocker was louder when it banged for the second time just as Willie opened the door. Cynthia's smile contained a bit of finger-wagging, but she said nothing and went to Nathan, who was staring at his Mother. Cynthia picked him up as Willie took Norma's arm and led her to the door, so proud he looked foolish. Cynthia's grin, aimed at Norma, told Willie she was more than a maid in this house.

The Bentley waited at the curb; Norma's parents sat in the back seat. George, the chauffeur, held the rear door open for Norma while she gracefully backed through it. He deftly lifted her dress as she rotated and lifted her legs into the floor well. Before George could get to Willie's door, he opened it and slid in, closing it gently.

A hand landed on his shoulder; Willie turned and found himself facing an average-looking man with ordinary brown eyes and gray-streaked brown hair beginning to recede from his forehead. The man was six inches taller and fifty pounds heavier than Willie, and he squeezed his future son-in-law's hand with an uncomfortably firm grip.

"I'm Norma's Father, and you shall call me James, but not Jim any-where Gianna can hear you. I'll call you William if that suits you. And

William, I want to thank you for saving my daughter—at least that's what my wife tells me you've done." He finally released Willie's hand, and Willie resisted the urge to shake it to restore blood flow. James added, "There is only one thing I want you to do for me. Please stop changing diapers—you make me look bad!" He laughed good-heartedly and slapped the back of Willie's seat. "I've never changed a diaper in my life!"

Willie said, "Thank you, sir; William will do... But about the diaper thing—I'm afraid I'll have to ask Norma what she wants to do about that."

James scoffed and chuckled as he said, "William, don't you dare let that girl push you around. I can tell you from experience that you must keep a tight rein on that filly!"

Willie looked at Gianna, and she sniggered. He turned and looked ahead. "Yes, sir, but you'll have to show me how to do that—I haven't had any luck so far."

James leaned back, laughing, clearly amused. "Good heavens, William, I didn't say I knew how to do it, nor does her Mother. Let us know if you figure it out!"

<hr>

With the cross as its footprint, the massive Lincoln Cathedral impressed Willie more the second time he saw it. Rows and columns of windows lined the walls in perfect geometric order, with pointed arches separating buttresses, dozens of them rooted deep in the ground, pushing against the outside walls to keep the building's walls from squeezing outward and falling. Spires eliminated every sharp corner of the building, and Willie's eyes shifted from one marvel to another as he tried to digest it all.

George stopped the car, and Norma got out, waved, then hurried up a stone sidewalk leading to a door into one of the building's half-dozen protrusions. George drove to the nave entrance, where everyone got out, and Willie followed Norma's parents through the open doors. Inside, the Priest greeted every parishioner by name as they passed him but shook and held Gianna's hand when she reached him. He raised his eyebrows when she introduced Willie as her future son-in-law.

"The Priest is always the last to know." He laughed in a way that told Willie there was a unique affection between them. "I hope you'll allow me to do the dirty deed this time!"

Gianna winked at the Priest, and he released her hand. "This time,

I have complete control, but you must do it quickly—I don't want this one to get away!" She leaned toward him and spoke into the Priest's ear. Willie heard her whisper, "He changes diapers...among other qualities that seem to appeal to my daughter."

The Priest chuckled, and Gianna took her husband's arm and steered him into the sanctuary. Willie followed them to seats in the second row, and Gianna motioned him to sit in the third seat from the aisle. She sat beside Willie, and he noted she had trapped him. James sat next to the aisle, blocking all chance of escape.

While they waited for the performance to begin, Willie looked around, fascinated. Ribbed columns separated triple windows high above him; pointed arches sat on the top of the columns, forming a structure that supported the roof. The remarkable stone ribs that formed the arches curved upward and inward to meet at a single backbone running along the centre of the ceiling—joined in a pattern that made no sense to an amateur engineer. An exquisite carving at every stone boss and joint each deserved an hour of scrutiny.

Willie was only beginning his study when the orchestra filed in, interrupting his education. They waited with their instruments in hand until a man carrying a violin entered and acknowledged a ripple of applause from the audience. Norma had told Willie about this man—he was the Concert Master, the first violin, and would tune the orchestra. Except for the violinist, the orchestra sat down. The Concert Master turned his back to the audience and nodded to a wind instrument—Norma had said it was an oboe. The First Oboe played an 'A,' and the other players picked it up. The oboe repeated the note, and every player duplicated it until the violinist nodded his satisfaction and sat down. Although he could not hear a difference, Willie assumed the orchestra was tuned.

The choir entered from both sides, dressed in purple and dark red gowns. The men filed into the back row; two rows of women formed an arc in front of them, curving behind the brass and percussion instruments. Willie looked for Norma, and, when he couldn't find her, assumed she would occupy one of the four empty chairs in front of the orchestra. After a brief silence, Norma led a woman and two men to the empty chairs, turned to the audience, and waited.

Willie couldn't take his eyes off her. The scene was surreal—Norma standing on the stage in front of a hundred musicians was not the Norma he knew!

The orchestra stood as the conductor entered, nodding as he walked briskly in front of the ensemble and stepped onto the podium. He waved to the soloists, instrumentalists, and choir, and they sat down. He bowed to the now applauding crowd, turned to the musicians and raised his baton, silencing the room. The baton dropped twice before the music began, softly and beautifully. Willie's emotions churned as he stared at Norma. He felt a strange excitement, a fear of something without knowing what it was.

The first sweet phrases filled the church with melodies intertwined like vines climbing a trellis, and the beauty of the sound banished his fear and brought a sense of tranquillity Willie hadn't expected. He had read the English translation of the first movement, a prayer for peace and eternal rest, but couldn't have described what he felt if someone had asked. Beauty mingled with peace, creating something he could find no words to describe.

His mind drifted to a nightmare that frequently tormented him: his Mother lying on the floor, bruised, bleeding, reaching out to his Father, begging him to spare her children. And then profound regret that he couldn't defend his Mother because he couldn't fight his Father. He always woke up crying, overwhelmed by a feeling of helplessness.

The brass instruments interrupted his Mother's plea for mercy, a crescendo of emotion that moved Willie beyond anything he had experienced in battle.

The choir sang a prayer for mercy that became a shout to heaven, and Willie's Mother faded, then disappeared, replaced by a feeling of exhilaration, fear, and impending doom he experienced every time the ground fell away from his turret as 'C for Charley' lifted off the Dunholme Lodge Lodge runway.

When the choir retreated with a soft plea for lost souls, a prayer for peace and eternal rest, Willie saw crews trapped inside burning airplanes.

◇◇◇◇◇◇◇◇◇◇◇◇◇◇◇◇◇◇◇◇◇◇◇◇◇◇◇◇◇◇◇◇

And then, Norma's clear voice drove the images away. She repeated the choir's prayer—sweet tones floating on a cloud of beautiful sound, and Willie thought, "Surely, a merciful God would grant this woman's prayer!"

The choir interrupted her, begging God for an answer, returning

Willie to his cold turret, suspended in blackness, held up by the sound, surrounded by silver stars painted on black velvet. His hands instinctively checked that his brownings were loaded and racked.

Willie closed his eyes; the choir's driving rhythm became the pulsing of four synchronized Merlin engines, six thousand horsepower pulling the lancaster bomber through the void. Adrenalin heightened his senses—he must find the night fighters before they killed him. Flexing his hands on the cold handles of the familiar browning machine guns, his head traced the scan he used to find a night fighter before it sent 'C-for-Charley' to earth in a ball of fire. His heart raced, his breath shortened—he scanned the darkness, picked out shadows of bombers surrounding him, and moonlight, glinting off whirling propellers, reflecting from the perspex of dozens of canopies.

The music rose; Willie desperately searched for the night fighter before it fired. He could hear the fighter pilot laughing, and then, out of the darkness, the messerschmitt pilot's face, smiling at him. The fighter's cannons flashed—explosions all around him—he had to get out!

The music stopped—sound reverberated from stone arches—then silence.

✦✦✦✦✦✦✦✦✦✦✦✦✦✦✦✦✦✦✦✦✦✦✦✦✦

Willie watched the conductor, anticipation building. He couldn't shake the feeling of doom.

The conductor raised his baton; Willie dared to glance at the third movement's name. Dies Irae, 'day of wrath.' The words, the musicians poised like horses in a starting gate, a fighter pilot with his thumb on the cannon's firing button, the lancaster's fuel tanks in his gunsight, waiting to explode when he moved his thumb.

The conductor's baton swept violently downward—the sound stopped William's heart, then restarted it, the music's ferocity ripping Willie back to the thrashing lancaster, pummeled by bursting flak shells. The night fighter disappeared, replaced by a new terror gripping Willie—the flak—orange explosions drenched in black smoke, shaking the sixty-five-thousand-pound bomber. Flak exploded where stars had been; black smoke and orange fire filled the space between hundreds of bombers. Willie tightened his belts and braced himself in the flailing turret, expecting each breath to be his last. The music intensified; he saw death's face.

The lancaster jumped as it spewed eight tons of bombs out of its belly into the fires below.

And then the music stopped. The bomber left the explosions behind, leaving only the fading hypnotic drone of engines, and finally, peace.

◇◇◇◇◇◇◇◇◇◇◇◇◇◇◇◇◇◇◇◇◇◇◇◇

Gianna patted his hand; he pulled away. Willie glanced at the translation, hoping for a respite, but the fourth movement began with a trombone solo and then the bass soloist calling the dead to judgment. Willie read: "The dead will rise from their sleep to face their day of judgment..."

The soloists began to sing, one after another. Norma's sweet soprano voice, resounding from the stone walls and arches, liberated Willie from the lancaster, washing him in its beauty and soaking it into his soul.

The soloists, singing as a quartet, asked the question that ended the movement: "What will I reply when the Lord asks me, 'Why should I spare you from Hell's fire?'" Willie lowered his head and closed his eyes. The target, an ocean of fire, flowed under his turret. A city burned, an inferno miles behind his turret, miles wide. Women, children, trapped in the flames—horrible death. He blinked to rid himself of tears that pushed out of his eyes, and they flowed down his cheeks.

The movement ended, Willie wiped his wet nose on his coat sleeve, and Gianna's hand appeared under his face, holding a white handkerchief. He took the beautifully embroidered bit of cloth, reluctantly blew his nose and tried to return it, but she refused to take it.

◇◇◇◇◇◇◇◇◇◇◇◇◇◇◇◇◇◇◇◇◇◇◇◇

The fifth movement began with the choir begging a merciful Jesus for salvation and forgiveness, forcing Willie's unbearable guilt to the surface. When Jesus didn't answer, their loud, sorrowful pleas for help suddenly became a whimpering "Salva me! Salva me!" that took Willie to his Mother, sitting on the floor with blood in her tear-filled eyes. In his dream, he begged her for forgiveness, and she reached for him, then faded, replaced by children's faces in walls of flames. Where was God's mercy? His Mother stretched out her arms; Willie closed his eyes; the darkness made her desperate plea more poignant. Willie whispered, "But Mother, I'm too small!" Gianna squeezed his hand.

290

The movement ended; the conductor paused for over a minute, and Willie's guilt retreated to its hiding place.

The soloists silently stood; the conductor's baton fell in a graceful swoop, curved upward and turned. The orchestra began as one instrument, playing the sweetest music Willie had ever heard. They played so softly and with such resonance that the sound penetrated the stone in the church walls. The soloists begged Christ to remember that the humiliation and pain He had endured was for them, imploring Him to fulfill his promise of forgiveness. They ended their supplication with a frail, hopeful, "Jesus, pity us." Willie slowly relaxed, his nightmare gone to its dark corner.

Norma began to sing, her pure, resonant voice stiffening the hairs on the back of Willie's neck. The other soloists joined her in begging Jesus to save them, and the sheer beauty of Norma's voice carried above the others—an angel singing from heaven. Willie's guilt and apprehension steadily subsided bar by musical bar. When the movement ended, his heart held a glimmer of hope. The beautiful woman who had become part of him was praying for his salvation. Jesus, suffering on the cross, must have heard such angels sing, and the exquisite sound would have dulled the pain.

When the movement ended, the conductor paused only long enough for a single breath, then flung his baton into the next movement, damning the wicked to burn in Hell!

The choir shouted: "Confutatis Maledictis, flammis acribus addictis!... 'Doomed are the guilty to burn in misery's flames!'" Willie revisited the firestorms, his victims—women and children dying under his bomber without understanding why.

But, just as suddenly, the choir pleaded, "Salva me; voca me cum Benedictus... 'Save me; count me among the blessed,'" but Willie could think of no argument for his salvation...no possibility of atonement, and his grief became unbearable. He wanted to escape the church and its righteousness, but Gianna and James had him trapped. He hung his head and wept, not caring who saw or heard him. Gianna took his hand between hers—Willie left his hand there.

The conductor paused at the end of the movement, freezing time. While he waited, Willie resolved never to fly in a bomber again, no matter the consequences!

The choir and orchestra began the most beautiful music Willie had ever heard. "Lacrimosa dies illa... 'The day of tears,'" and the beauty of the lilting melody returned Willie, phrase after beautiful phrase, to a place where hope dried his tears.When the movement ended, the conductor turned to the audience and paid homage to the end of Mozart's writing and his life. As he spoke, Willie relaxed. But when he finished, and the music began, joyously praising Jesus, Willie remembered friends who had fallen to their deaths in burning planes. When they stood before God and the people they had killed, would God grant them forgiveness? Would Jesus witness for them? Would Freedom's name be enough? Was it enough that they gave their lives to save others who might have died had they not dropped the bombs?

The soloists picked up the choir's theme, and Norma's voice calmed Willie, carrying him through the pain. But his sense of logic intervened—the message of hope and assurance in Jesus's absolution was not for him—for something so hideous, there could be no forgiveness.

The last movements blurred together in Willie's grief. Beautiful music, promises of redemption and eternal life—nothing helped—he couldn't accept forgiveness. Even Norma's soaring tones, touching his heart and soul, couldn't save him. Burning cities and fallen friends— friends he would yet lose. A frigid cold gripped his heart. He would never forgive himself, and the concept of a God who would forgive him slipped away. There was no merciful God, only grief and guilt.

The Requiem ended with a soft, moving prayer for the salvation of the dead. It left Willie exhausted, and he stayed in his seat when Gianna and James stood to applaud.

With applause that violated the church's rules of decorum, the audience enthusiastically praised Mozart's work and the performers who had brought it to life.

The Priest walked to the front and raised his hands to signal his intention to speak. The audience, assuming a sermon, sat down.

"Ladies and gentlemen..." Willie felt the reverend looking straight at him... "Mozart was dying and broke when he wrote this work almost two hundred years ago, and he died before finishing it. He couldn't have imagined the carnage this world would experience two hundred years later, during our lifetime, all because one man decided to replace God.

"Despite that, this music overflows with hope. Millions of good people have died, and I fear many more will perish before the world finishes with this hideous war! We all know that we are nearing the end; if not in weeks, then indeed in months. This music teaches us to forgive as we are forgiven." He swept his eyes through the silent room, waiting—almost everyone in the room had lost someone, most had lost many. He said, "When this horror is over, that is what we must all remember, and that hope is enshrined in Mozart's Requiem Mass." The walls and ceiling reverberated his voice back into the room until the stone was as quiet as death.

Willie wanted to get out of the church, away from people. He wanted more than anything to be alone with Norma and Nathan. They were already a part of him, one that would live there until he died, and he could no longer bear the thought of killing or dying.

The Priest broke the silence. "We must all remember that the men who must kill other men do it so you can live without fear. They bear the most unbearable burdens of war—death, loss of friends and comrades, mutilating injuries, and, in the end, the most unbearable and permanent cost...They bear the guilt of those who command them."

The Priest held his hands high and bowed his head.

"God, bless us in our hour of need and help us accept the task you've assigned us. Amen!"

The congregation began to applaud again, and the Priest nodded his encouragement. They stood, clapped harder, and didn't quit until he left through the south transept.

Willie hung his head, but his load had lightened. Hitler was on his knees, and if they didn't finish him off, he would rise, and Norma and Nathan could become the faces in the fires. He must join his crew on their next mission—he would find absolution in his new family and leave atonement for later. He desperately wanted peace, but paradoxically, he knew he would have to fight for it.

Gianna sat beside him and James looked down at Willie. Their warm smiles, more than words, comforted him. William knew he would be a part of this family until he died—his fight would now be for them.

CHAPTER TWENTY-SEVEN

28 June 1944

"I do not believe in miracles. I've seen too many of them."
Oscar Wilde

Ten days after the Mozart Requiem concert, 'C for Charley' lifted free of earth's powerful grip with fourteen thousand pounds of high explosives in its bomb bay, cleared the boundary fence by a few feet, and left the runway at Dunholme Lodge Lodge behind.

The mission would be the third for Willie and Ronnie since they had returned from leave. The first two had been attacks on German troops, tanks and artillery; tonight's objective was a synthetic fuel plant near Wesseling. Once again, civilians were not the objective, and 'C for Charlie's' crew flew into battle eager to strike another blow for humanity against an inhuman tyrant.

The briefing forecast was for clear skies with a low probability of night-fighter activity. The briefer predicted light to medium flak over the objective. The mood in the briefing room was almost jovial, given recent successes. But No 44 squadron's experience with briefing predictions was not good, and 'C for Charley's' crew made contingency plans for clouds, heavy flak, and flocks of night fighters.

Following the briefing, Jeffrey Conway, the crew's resident and eternal pessimist, commented on the "low probability" of night fighters as "Rubbish mates, pure rubbish. Those Nazi bastards will not like us going after their bloody fuel, and they will throw the goddamned kitchen sink at us. It will be a bad one, mates—I can feel it in my bones!" Jeffrey's intuition had consistently been uncannily accurate at predicting disaster, mainly because he consistently predicted a calamity of some sort, and calamities were 'C for Charley's' business; it was only a matter of degree. But tonight, the crew took his prediction more seriously than the briefing. Logic told them that the Germans would protect their life-blood—fuel, with everything they had. Every man in the aircraft prepared themselves for the worst.

They checked, then re-checked their guns, safety harnesses, and parachutes with diligence that had been missing in the last few missions.

Mailly had taught Willie that fighting his way out of the turret, then forward through smoke and flames to get his parachute, was not a good idea. He had experimented with wearing the chute in the turret and was now sure he could roll out the door with the chute on. He had rehearsed it on the ground and decided he could do it in under three seconds.

Every man in the crew felt an extra sense of urgency; if the Luftwaffe were going to defend anything, it would be their fuel supply.

On this mission, Jeff Conway had a new toy. While Willie and Ronnie were finding their way back to England through French fields and forests, the RAF had installed 'H2S' ground radar on their lancaster. The technology made it possible to hit bombing targets accurately, lessening friendly citizens' losses from "friendly fire." The second benefit of H2S, equally critical to the crew, was an add-on installed before this mission—rearward-looking radar that was somewhat effective in spotting night fighters. The add-on system necessitated installing a second, smaller-scale radar screen beside the standard H2S screen, dubbed "the fish pond."

The operator's challenge was figuring out which aircraft on the tiny screen was 'theirs' and which was 'ours.' He must memorize geometric shapes that perpetually changed as aircraft moved around in the formation, always cognizant that a British mosquito and a German night fighter returned the same blip on his screen. Luckily, Jeffrey had a quick, pattern-conscious mind and could organize the bomber stream's shifting blips, constantly comparing what had been with what he could see on the screen now. He played chess at a high level and considered the 'fish pond' nothing more than simplified chess.

The 'clear skies' forecast and the nineteen thousand foot flight level assigned to Steve White's lancaster were eerily reminiscent of the Nürnberg raid. No 44 squadron was the second squadron from the rear, ahead of No 619 squadron and at the same altitude. Before boarding, the crew gathered to hear familiar words of encouragement from their captain, but this time, Steve had more than reassuring words…he had a plan.

"I've been thinking about the new "fish-pond" radar and Jeffrey's prediction of fighters, and I have something I'd like to try. Jeff is confident that no night fighter can approach us without him seeing it on his screen, but the gunners still have to find the plane to shoot it down. Both Ronnie and Willie have blind spots, and I think we can eliminate them while at the same time confusing the fighter." The gunners exchanged looks—this had to involve something more than flying in a straight line.

"My idea is this: if Jeff announces a strange bogey behind us, I will begin a series of random turns, staying on the same average course and station, increasing the throttle so we keep our position. This should expose the approaching night fighter to Willie and Ronnie, no matter where it comes from. It will be more difficult, possibly impossible, for him to line up under us. The fighter will try to synchronize his moves with ours, but I will turn often and as randomly as possible, making the bastard easier to find as he bobs and weaves behind us. Instead of coming from a stationary point, the fighter will move back and forth across Ronnie and Willie's field of vision." He examined the faces around him. "Is everyone clear on the tactic? Does anyone have any questions?" The men muttered their agreement and lined up to piss on the tire.

While they waited their turn to wet the tire, Willie said to Ronnie, "I wish I'd thought of that! I think Steve just made our job a whole lot easier!"

Ronnie, ahead of Willie in the line, turned around. "We'll have a lot better chance of seeing the bastards, but hitting them will be harder." He grinned, "But still easier than hitting a running hyena from a horse!" Ronnie drenched the tire, and Willie tried but had nothing to add.

The English coast passed under Willie's turret five minutes after lift-off. He checked, racked and test-fired his guns, ready for battle, and while he waited for the inevitable fighters, let his mind drift back to Norma and Nathan.

He was growing closer to the boy every day. Nathan's toilet training had reached the point where accidents were rare, and he refused to wear a diaper. The boy could put words together in sentences and had developed an impressive vocabulary. Willie constructed their fun around education; he never played with him without teaching new words and motor skills. Willie taught him how to hit a nail with a small hammer, and his little hands had learned to twist a screwdriver in the appropriate direction to loosen or tighten a screw.

One afternoon, when Willie and Norma sneaked into the bedroom for a "quickie," presuming Nathan was asleep, they returned to the kitchen to find his booster seat completely disassembled; every screw had been removed and the parts neatly stacked. When Norma began to chastise her son, Willie intervened, praising him for his ingenuity and neatness, then spent the rest of the afternoon teaching him how to put the seat back together.

Gianna had scheduled her daughter's wedding for July 22, and Willie refused to consider the likelihood that he might not live that long. Since Norma and Nathan had entered his life, he had suspended his faith in statistics. He lived his life one mission at a time, allowing his emotions to reject the possibility of death.

◇◇◇◇◇◇◇◇◇◇◇◇◇◇◇◇◇◇◇◇◇◇◇◇◇◇◇◇◇◇◇

A young Luftwaffe sergeant stuck his head in the open door of Erik and Karl's room, said, "Bombers up... Time to fly," received a wave from Erik, and disappeared. Karl moved his rook, Erik tipped a black pawn, indicating it was his move, and they abandoned their chess game. Neither Erik nor Karl was superstitious and often left their room in the middle of something they would finish later, unlike most crews who cleaned their rooms, made the bed, and stowed everything carefully away as though they would not be returning. They left a last will and a letter to their wife or girlfriend. Erik's will was in a drawer at home, and Marita knew how he felt about her and the children.

A Kubelwagen drove them to their Me110, parked a thousand metres from the barracks. Their night fighter group, NJG-4, had relocated to Gütersloh when the Allies advanced through France and the number of Allied strafing and bomb attacks had become intolerable.

Since the move, marauding Allied fighters hit the Gütersloh airfield twice weekly, but repair crews were able to fix the damage before the next attack, which led Erik to wonder if the attacks would stop if the repair crews stopped fixing the damage. But the repairs were made, mosquitos attacked at night, thunderbolts by day, and life for the pilots and crews was as hectic as the Allied air forces could make it.

It was already dark, and Erik and Karl wanted to be out of there before the mosquitoes made their pre-raid attacks. Fritz had the engines running, and everything was green by the time Erik and Karl had run through the checklists. With the engines turning a thousand revolutions a minute, the bite of the big propellers gently rocked the plane. Erik slowed the engines to seven hundred before releasing the brakes—the runway was less than two hundred metres from the parking area, leaving Erik and Karl little time to do moving checks. Using a combination of rudder and brakes, Erik weaved the plane back and forth while moving the aileron, elevator, and rudder controls to maximum deflection and announced, "Controls—check." Karl noted that on his mission sheet.

Erik stopped short of the runway, locked the brakes, ran each engine up to two thousand RPM, switched each magneto off, then on, noting the drop in revs. The dual Bosch magnetos spark system bolted to each of the new daimler benz 605B engines checked out with less than the maximum permitted rpm drop.

"Mag drop—check." Erik pulled the throttles back. "All set back there?" He glanced in the small circular mirror that Karl had installed so they could see one another.

"Roger—all set—reading you five by five."

Erik lined up on the airstrip's centre line and held the brakes until the runway lights flashed on, then eased both throttles forward to their stops. The tail came up, and the moon rose in the messerschmitt's windscreen; it was a beautiful night to fly, and despite the mission, Erik felt a sense of exhilaration as he released the brakes.

The first fighter to take off, Erik held the Bf 110G on the runway until the airspeed was twenty kilometres per hour above acceptable rotation speed, gently eased the stick back and climbed to a thousand metres as quickly as he could. He lowered the nose and set the trim for a shallow climb on the southwest bearing Karl had gotten from ground control. Deelen had no accurate idea of the bomber stream's destination this early in the attack, so Karl turned on the radar as they passed through two thousand meters. Erik's new messerschmitt had the latest SN2 set, and other pilots assured him that the British mosquitos had not yet figured out its frequency. The tubes warmed, and Karl began his search for the bomber stream.

He reported, "The bombers are not dropping 'window' to jam our radar, and Deelen ground control is loud and clear."

"The British aren't afraid of German night fighters; they've become as arrogant as we used to be, and that will work to our advantage." Erik wasted no time wondering why the British would be so foolish.

He climbed at full power, something Fritz had verboten. With the Me110 drinking nine litres of avgas every minute, the modern fluid-coupled altitude-compensating superchargers maintained almost fifteen hundred horsepower on each engine until the fighter reached six thousand metres, well ahead of the bomber stream.

His usual plan of attack, getting in front of his victim, waiting above and to one side, then sweeping down in a shallow diving turn to intercept the bombers, had worked faultlessly many times, and he saw no reason to change it. The messerschmitt could use the extra altitude to gain the speed it would need to catch its intended victim. It was dangerous to turn too early and end up too close to the target, but too late would extend the time it took to catch the bomber, exposing the slow messerschmitt 110 to marauding mosquitos.

Karl announced radar contact at the same moment he received a new bearing to the target from Deelen—he acknowledged the bearing and repeated it into the intercom. Erik turned ten degrees left to the intercept heading.

Karl looked at Erik in the little convex mirror. "The blips are all over the screen. There are two groups of bombers; at the moment, the smaller group is heading north, and the larger force is turning more easterly. Which group do you want to follow?"

"The small group is a diversion; the larger group is going to the main objective, and they will be our target."

Erik had played this deadly game for three years but still marvelled that the British would consider their silly diversions worthwhile. The implied British assumption that Germans were stupid irritated him.

Half an hour later, Karl instructed Erik, "Turn to two-eighty degrees," and Erik banked to the right. Ahead of him, moonlight glinted off painted aluminum.

"No more courses, Karl, I can see them. Leave the radar on, watch for targets, and don't forget the mosquitos."

"Yes, sir."

It was too late to get in front of the bombers, and as they flew parallel, above and behind the bomber stream, Karl picked up several blips trailing behind the flotilla. "It looks like we've scrambled the entire night-fighter force. I can see fighters all over the sky!" He hurried to clarify his remark., "They're too slow to be mosquitos, and there are too many of them."

"All right, Karl, I'm turning to get under the rear bomber on this side. Make sure everything is ready, and I want you to fire the gun. I will slip sideways after the kill and take the adjacent bomber before we leave." The second bomber was too close to his friend, oblivious to the danger of close proximity.

"Understood. I will shoot," Karl verified.

Erik took the messerschmitt down to five-thousand five-hundred metres in a shallow dive, catching his victim quickly, then climbed to 75 metres below the lancaster's right wing. He occasionally glanced at the gunsight as he approached, and as the lines lined up with the main spar between the starboard engines, he closed his eyes. Following the loud explosion, ear-splitting even above the smooth Daimler engines, Erik opened his eyes in time to see the fading flare from the exploding fuel tank, and half the lancaster's wing and outer engine tumbling down behind his fighter. He turned away from the falling debris, opened the throttles, and lowered the nose.

The turn caused the fighter to lose ground to the adjacent bomber, but the additional throttle and momentum from the descent brought the messerschmitt 110 to where Erik wanted to be—below and behind the port wing of the next victim. He left the throttles open and waited until he was under the bomber to inch upward to a shooting position. The unsuspecting aircraft continued to fly straight ahead—Erik closed his eyes, Karl fired a short burst, and Erik saw that the wing had stayed on. Seconds later, the aircraft was burning from the port wing to its tail. Erik dove and turned left, away from the bomber stream.

He said calmly into the intercom, "I will set up again, but they are more vigilant now. We will move away for a few minutes."

"Yes, sir," Karl replied, not as calm as his boss.

CHAPTER TWENTY-EIGHT

28 June 1944

"It always seems impossible until it's done."
Nelson Mandela

THE FIRST INDICATION OF IMMINENT CATASTROPHE was Jeffrey's announcement of "Multiple bogeys behind us," followed a few minutes later by an explosion that destroyed a lancaster to Willie's right. Four minutes later, another bomber in the same space burst into flames. Ten minutes passed, two more aircraft fell, and it was still over thirty minutes to the target! The strain to find the enemy in the dark filled Willie's eyes with tears that fell and froze on his uniform. His vision blurred—he rubbed his eyes to clear it and cursed the night.

Jeffrey announced, "There's a bad bogey at our six o'clock and a thousand yards!" His voice rose. "He's below us and closing fast!"

Steve began oscillating the aircraft in three to four-second intervals, banking from side to side in an unpredictable, irregular pattern.

"He's still coming!" Jeffrey confirmed a minute later, "He's under five hundred yards and closing!" The pitch of the engines changed as Steve added power to compensate for the maneuver.

Willie and Ronnie adjusted their scan to sync with the rolling motion of the lancaster. At the apex of the turns, they had a clear view of where the fighter should be, and on the third swing, both gunners saw moonlight glint on the fighter's canopy and opened fire simultaneously. The coaming below Ronnie's gun prevented him from depressing it far enough to hit the fighter; his tracers missed high, but Willie's four streams converged on the fighter's nose and swept smoothly back along the fuselage. He held down the firing button and directed the curving tracer string forward to where he knew the port engine and wing should be. His reward was a small explosion, then fire sprouting from the engine and spreading along the fuselage. The fighter dropped its nose, two parachutes blossomed in the faint light, and the junkers 88 dropped in a terminal, fiery dive.

Steve levelled the aircraft and adjusted the power to hold position in the squadron; Jeffrey's excited voice said on the intercom, "It worked! Those fucking fighters haven't got a chance! Come and get it, you bastards!"

The words still echoed in Willie's ears when a No 44 squadron aircraft ahead of them was hit in the bomb bay and exploded in a burst of white light. Small pieces of burning aluminum fluttered out of the ball, and then there was nothing. Another lancaster ahead of them began a shallow dive without a sign of fire, but seconds later, the right wing separated between the engines. Two parachutes appeared behind the plane. Without any support on the starboard side, the lancaster flipped onto its edge, pointed its nose straight at the ground and dropped so fast it was impossible to tell if others had escaped. The explosion on impact was enormous, a ball of white light leaving a dull red glow that faded into darkness as it receded behind them. Willie's stomach heaved—he forced the bile back where it belonged and picked up his scan.

<hr>

Karl reported, "There are no night fighters on the left side of the bombers ahead of us. We are on the edge of the flotilla."

Erik decided on a lancaster, added full power, and slid sideways toward it, happy not to worry about a collision with his comrades. He lined up with the bomber's fuselage on his right and seventy-five metres above him. Throttles fully open, superchargers automatically at full boost, he steadily gained on his victim. The rear turret remained stationary as they passed. The bomber's wing entered the sight, and Erik closed his eyes. Karl fired; the flash of the lancaster's exploding fuel tank registered through Erik's eyelids, and when he opened them, the bomber's wing fluttered out of his peripheral vision while the rest of the plane fell to earth behind him. He banked hard left, away from the formation, spiralled a complete three-hundred-sixty-degree turn in a 'red line' descent to four-thousand-five-hundred metres.

Erik said into the intercom, "Search for mosquitos; we'll stay out of the battle until we assess the situation." The spiral had put them well behind the bombers, but they had plenty of fuel, and the new thirty-six-litre DB 605 engines added fifty kilometres per hour at this altitude. The messerschmitt could easily catch the bombers, and the mosquitos would be there shortly, so Erik decided to wait for them well below and behind the stream, where Karl's radar would pick up the escorts. They were approaching Stuttgart, nearing the limit of the bombers' range, and their target couldn't be far away. The stream would soon face flak, as deadly to Erik's ME 110 as it was to the enemy, and Erik planned to save the last of his ammunition until after the bombers had released their loads and turned for home. He would cut across the loop they must make after the target and intercept them after the turn. Gunners were often less attentive after the bomber finished its job.

Cruising ten kilometres behind the lancasters, Karl and Erik watched the tragedy unfold. Bombers fell like burning leaves—Erik counted twenty in the twenty minutes before they reached their objective. The city of Wesseling was nearby, but the track was west of it. The bombers dropped their loads near the Rhine on a target not marked with the usual flares. Thin clouds obscured everything below, and Erik guessed they were using ground radar to find their aim point.

Flames reached skyward, and Erik announced, "They hit the fuel plant."

Karl said, "Yes, sir, and they are turning right immediately after they release their load."

"All right, Karl, we'll cut across and join the returning stream. I'll fly a bit to the east and out of sight below them. You should figure out a course to intercept them, but remember, mosquitos are hunting for us in that stream, so keep an eye on the radar."

One of the flaming wrecks he had seen looked a lot like a night fighter, too small for a lancaster, and he doubted that a German night fighter had nailed a mosquito. Erik had expected mosquitos sooner, but there was no predicting the British.

Five minutes later, the first bombers passed Erik's position on their way home, a thousand metres above his messerschmitt, and Karl gave him the timing and the intercept course to the middle of the stream. Erik edged under the flotilla, set up a shallow climb, slowed his plane, and deliberately let a lancaster pass over him. Intelligence had reported that the RAF had a new type of rear-looking radar, and, if that were true, he wanted them to see his aircraft falling back—and mistake it for a troubled lancaster.

✧✧✧✧✧✧✧✧✧✧✧✧✧✧✧✧✧✧✧✧✧✧✧✧✧✧✧✧✧✧✧✧✧✧✧✧

"Course correction, ten degrees right." Jeffrey watched the course line on his H2S radar swing left over the Rhine loop where the fuel plant was supposed to be. According to his radar, the area marked by the pathfinders was a large field. Steve banked the lancaster slightly and levelled the wings.

Jeffrey said, "Okay, Jake, we're on course to the target. Can you see the ground, or should I tell you when to release?"

Jake Collier watched the sight—buildings at the target appeared intermittently through the clouds. "I've got it, Jeff." He lifted the switch guards and, directly over the fuel plant, flipped the switches and announced, "Bombs gone." His bombs fell well to the right of the previously marked area, but flames reaching skyward into his sight indicated a direct hit on the target. Steve maintained his course until the camera flashed.

Jake said, "Okay, Steve, we hit the target, and we can prove it—let's go home!"

Steve held his course for another thirty seconds to clear the aircraft behind 'C for Charley,' then pushed the right rudder, turned the wheel to add aileron, and, relieved of a third of its weight, the aircraft turned smoothly in a two-minute turn to the right. Steve levelled the wings as the directional gyro approached the westerly heading on the navigation instructions and settled the plane on the course for home. He checked the gyro against the compass, pulled the adjustment screw and added three degrees to the gyro heading.

Clear of the sporadic black and orange puffs of flak, Willie watched four more lancasters become funeral pyres for their crews. He had already seen over twenty bombers fall, most of them leaving no hope for the crews' survival. Willie's confidence in his survival was gone; something sinister had taken its place.

"Captain, we are passing over a slow bogey; I assume it's a crippled bomber." Jeffrey marked the blip's progress on the glass with a wax pencil.

Steve shouted into the intercom. "Don't assume anything! Watch him, and if he speeds up, let me know."

Less than a minute later, Jeffrey's surprised voice returned. "Sir... His speed is increasing—he's staying on station about three hundred yards behind us."

Steve banked left and began the swinging motion that had gotten them a kill an hour ago.

On the second swing, Ronnie spotted the Me110, pressed the firing button on his brownings and shouted into the intercom at the same instant Willie fired. The lancaster was in a fifteen-degree bank, and, with his mid-turret gun fully depressed, Ronnie saw his tracers pass just above the glinting canopy and strike the port wing. Willie's necklace of fire streaked into the messerschmitt's left engine. The wounded fighter pitched up and turned toward 'C for Charley,' its cannons spitting fire in a desperate attempt to save itself by killing its tormentor.

Willie recognized the flashes coming out of the 110 as cannon fire and knew his life would end in seconds if he didn't kill that messerschmitt! His tracers arced to the 110's left engine. He had to hit a fuel tank—the centre of the ME 110 was armoured, and the browning's .303 shells wouldn't penetrate it.

Something slammed into Willie's feet, and suddenly, he was spinning through the darkness.

◇◇◇◇◇◇◇◇◇◇◇◇◇◇◇◇◇◇◇◇◇◇◇◇◇◇◇◇◇◇◇◇◇◇◇◇

When the lancaster banked left, Erik's senses sounded an alarm. The move startled him, and when a stream of tracers from the mid-gunner passed inches from his head, striking the top of the left wing, he moved his hands and feet. Another stream of tracers from the rear turret flowed into the left engine and threatened to rake the fuselage. Erik turned into the line of tracers, seeking the protection of the forward armour plating while pushing the firing button on his forward cannons. Without tracers, he could only guess where they were going until flashes of exploding cannon shells lit up the bottom of the lancaster's turret. It flipped off the aircraft's tail, falling end-over-end into the night.

There was no time for rejoicing. The left propeller separated from the messerschmitt's sick engine, and the plane pulled sharply left. Without the load of the propeller, the DB 605 engine screamed, over-revved, and shed essential parts in all directions. It belched a final flood of oil through the cowling as it died.

Before he could catch it, the wide-open starboard engine had whipped his messerschmitt into a steep left-hand turn, and Erik glimpsed moonlight reflecting off the flipping turret falling ahead of him. He cut the throttle to the healthy engine, pushed the column forward, added right aileron and rudder, and dove to get out of the bomber stream.

As Erik snapped the fighter out of the turn, his training told him to feather the sick engine's propeller, but it was missing, so he automatically fired the fire extinguisher before slowly adding power to the healthy right engine. He added starboard rudder trim to keep the fighter flying in a straight line and levelled out at three thousand metres, well below and behind the bombers.

"Oh, *Sheisse*, Karl, we lost the port engine again—Fritz will not be happy!" Erik sounded as worried as he was—Fritz was at the end of his rope.

Karl laughed nervously. "I'm not taking any blame for this one; it was your idea to fly under the bombers..." Karl hesitated. He had overstepped, and he knew it.

At that moment, Erik didn't care. He said, "Right now, I want you to plot a course for home," and a minute later, Karl said, "Steer two hundred and ninety-two degrees for the field."

Erik immediately swung to it, smiling in the red glow of the instrument lights. Karl owed him one.

He warned the young man to "Keep an eye out for mosquitos."

Karl laughed, "What will we do if I see one?"

Erik detected a hint of sarcasm, but he had the answer ready. "We're going to jump out before he kills us—I can tell you from experience that parachuting is fun—and someday, people will jump out of airplanes just for the fantastic ride to the ground under a parachute!"

Erik noted the absence of 'sir' in Karl's conversation and started to say something to him about growing up but decided to hold his tongue.

An hour and a half later, Erik landed his wreck in Gütersloh. The gear worked, and, as usual, Fritz was waiting for them. Erik parked the messerschmitt and shut down the healthy starboard engine. The ground crew pulled the fighter back into its place, and Erik climbed down with a silly grin, ready to begin the fencing match with Fritz.

Fritz didn't disappoint him. He asked, "What is that dirty black shit all over the port engine cowling? That crap belongs inside the engine." Fritz pointed to the streaks and then to the front of the cowling. "And where's my propeller? And please tell me, why are all those holes in the cowling and the wing?" He stood for a moment with his hands on his hips, looking at the mess, then turned to face Erik while Karl fiddled with his paperwork in the back seat.

Erik looked toward the major's office, hoping Fritz would take the hint. "We had a little encounter with a clever lancaster, but we did shoot down two before that." He looked at his mechanic, grinning sheepishly.

"Either they have a tail gunner who can see in the dark and shoot the whiskers off a cat, or they have some kind of secret weapon that tells them exactly where we are—maybe both!"

Fritz couldn't keep it up. His face and his voice softened. *"Verdammt Sheisse,* Erik, you are scaring the hell out of me!" He took Erik's hand, shook it, then pulled him into his arms in a bear hug. When he pushed back from him, tears glistened in his eyes. "We lost three to the mosquitos and gunners tonight, and I was afraid one of them was you." He waved his arms helplessly in the air. "I'm getting very tired of this."

Erik put his arm around Fritz's shoulders as Karl stepped off the ladder and approached them. "Fritz, it will all end soon…very soon."

Fritz had brought a Kubelwagen to the plane and drove Erik and Karl to the debriefing in Major Fischer's office. As they removed their parachutes and kits from the back of the vehicle and turned toward the building that housed Major Fischer's office, Erik wondered why the major was shorting the process. He was considering the possibilities when Fritz said, "Erik, I'm going to take my time fixing her."

Erik replied without turning around, "That's okay, Fritz. It's for sure I won't need it before tomorrow night."

◇◇

Willie and his turret fell at 200 miles per hour…giving him seventy seconds to get out through the door that, until a few seconds ago, had led to the fuselage. He had rehearsed getting out, but in his wildest imagined scenarios, the turret and the lancaster were one entity, and the turret wasn't flipping end over end.

The force of the exploding cannon shells had flipped the bottom of the turret outward and started it's gyrations. With the vessel containing Willie falling, gravity was neutralized, but centrifugal forces inside the spinning turret still pulled and pushed his weightless body in unpredictable directions. The openings where he had removed the perspex were too small to offer a way out, so he had to find the door…if he could unfasten his belts.

With dizziness threatening to overwhelm him, Willie found the belt release and pulled it, and as his body floated out of the seat, his head hit the edge of a window. The door latch swam past; Willie grabbed for it, missed, braced his foot to steady himself and found it again. The door slid sideways—he let go—the door latched itself again. He yanked the handle, forced his hand through the opening, and held the door open. Gripping the doorjamb with both hands, Willie heaved himself outside. The wind ripped at his upper body and dragged his legs out of the turret as he tore the 'D' handle out of the pack. The parachute opened, the shrouds jerked him to a stop, and the turret disappeared, almost immediately slamming into the ground with a loud thump.

Seconds later, Willie swung in an arc that ended with his back slamming against soft grass and dirt.

Willie tried desperately to get air into his empty lungs. He vomited, the world spun—he gasped, gaining a little air—he prayed he wouldn't die. The parachute pulled him through the damp earth. He rolled to his stomach, lifted his head, grabbed the shrouds, and tried to pull them in. They slackened, and he fumbled for the harness release but couldn't find it. He gasped, gained more air and vomited—he knew he had cheated death again.

Short, frantic gasps became short breaths; the ground stopped trying to throw him back into the sky, and slowly, his lungs inflated. He found the parachute release, twisted it, and the harness fell away. Willie rolled onto his back and looked at a rotating blanket of stars swimming in a black sea. He breathed, each breath bringing more relief than the last.

The world revolving around Willie slowed, and he found the strength to prop himself up on his elbow. His head hurt, and though the spinning had almost stopped, his stomach tried one more time to empty what wasn't there.

He looked around.

A bright moon shone through scattered breaks in the low clouds, and the sounds of animals shuffling around him brought Willie to his feet. But the ground slid away, and he fell. Willie decided to wait on his hands and knees, then tried a sitting position. He jumped when a soft nose nuzzled his back, and another wet nose touched his right hand. They were cows' noses, Holstein cows, the same German/Dutch breed his grandfather raised.

He looked around in the moonlight and saw the parachute move.

Willie stood, staggered, then walked a circuitous route to the moving silk, noting that he had lost a boot. His bootless foot was muddy and wet.

A cow's horn protruded through the parachute; the rest of the cow was covered by the eighty yards of thin silk cloth that had saved Willie's life a few minutes ago. Willie talked to the cow quietly, saying, "Now, didn't I get you into a nice pickle?" as he patted its back.

The cow patiently waited while Willie rolled up the parachute. When he reached the cow's horns, it stood still while he pulled the canopy away, but its front hoofs were still on a corner of the cloth. Willie stood on the parachute, pushed the cow's shoulder and asked her to step back—which she obediently did. He looked around for his boot but soon realized that, for now, it was too dark to find a brown boot in brown mud.

Next, Willie searched for and found the turret a hundred feet away. Dragging the parachute behind him, he stuffed it inside the turret and discovered his missing boot wedged in the doorway. Sitting down on a patch of grass to put it on, Willie smiled as the cows gathered in a circle with him at the center.

"Can you girls direct me to the nearest patch of woods?" He laughed at himself and got to his feet—he needed to get as far away from the turret as possible before daylight. Using the logic that searchers would expect him to go west toward the coast, he decided to walk northeast toward the Rhine, thinking that Switzerland might be the best bet to get home. He was south of the Rhine River, probably in Belgium, and thought there would likely be forests nearby.

Willie dug his compass from the survival kit, opened it, and walked without looking at his feet—there was barely enough light to see where to put them anyway. He stepped in cow dung several times before arriving at a wooden perimeter fence and, climbing over it, left his cow girlfriends behind.

He walked northeast, stopping twice in a hundred yards to look at the compass. At the second stop, he heard a snort, and it was close. A heavy foot stamped the ground once, twice, and then a big animal's heavy breathing rang a bell in Willie's brain.

"Oh, shit!" Willie began running away from the sound; powerful hooves hammered the ground close behind him. He looked for a fence, couldn't see one, but spotted a big tree standing alone against the moonlit clouds.

The animal gained fast; Willie could hear its heavy breathing getting closer. He found the fear gear, received a charge of adrenalin, and reached the tree before the bull but knew he wasn't far enough ahead to climb it before the horns got him. Using his superior maneuverability, Willie grabbed the tree's trunk and swung himself around it; the bull's momentum carried him past Willie—it tried to stop, slid sideways and fell in a tangle of feet.

The tree was about a foot and a half in diameter, with low branches, and while the bull struggled to his feet, Willie caught a low-hanging limb with his arms, swung himself up, and found a second one with his feet. He wriggled over the branches and struggled to stand up as the bull snorted and pawed the ground under him.

Willie was safe and couldn't help himself—he laughed and couldn't stop laughing for a full minute. Even with the stalemate with a bull, he was in a better place than he had been an hour ago.

The bull snorted, backed up a few feet, and dropped to the ground with a thump. He looked at Willie, moaned, and laid his head between his front legs. Willie took that to mean he was a patient bull and would not be leaving anytime soon.

Looking around at the lower branches, Willie found a split in the trunk ten feet above the ground, with a large limb growing out of each side. He lay down in the natural cradle and closed his eyes—but found he couldn't sleep and safely balance himself, especially with branches digging into his back. Willie began to talk to the bull; he told him all about Norma and Nathan and the wedding.

"I suppose a wedding is not in your future, Mr. Bull, but me…I'm a one-woman man." He spoke as though to a friend and laughed when the bull looked up at him, blinked, and licked his lips with a big, thick tongue.

"Yeah, I bet a handsome bull like you gets all the girls!"

The bull grunted.

"I've got to be on my way in the morning, and you've got to let me; otherwise, it's hamburger for you!" He fished in his pocket and pulled out the pocketknife he always carried. He opened it, showed it to the bull, then cut off a small branch digging into his back. The bull grunted, unimpressed with Willie's knife.

Eventually, Willie braced himself as well as he could and fell asleep almost instantly but woke with a start when he nearly fell from his perch. He fell asleep a half-dozen more times before the morning sun shone blood-red, paling to pink on the underside of the few clouds remaining in the sky. He looked down; twenty feet from the tree, the bull munched his breakfast of green grass.

"Good morning, Mr. Bull; you certainly are a big brute!"

The bull trotted over to the tree, looked up, cocked his head to one side, and groaned. Willie decided not to try the bull's temper just yet.

He looked around the horizon and found the turret about two hundred yards away on the other side of the fence he had climbed. He immediately regretted not burying the parachute. If someone found it, they would know the man had survived and left the chute there. Without it, they might have believed he had fallen out and died; his smashed body could be miles from here! It would even have been conceivable that he had escaped into the tail of the plane. He decided he had to bury the parachute, but first, he had to outwit the bull.

The western end of the fields looked like the edge of a forest and was closer than the fence he had climbed last night. He decided to run for it if he could get the bull to wander to the opposite side of the tree so he could get a head start. Once in the trees, he could get to the cow pasture and the chute. He would bury it in the woods, then walk to Switzerland.

<hr>

Major Fischer was waiting for Erik and Karl when they entered his new office and waved them to two soft leather chairs. He poured three steaming cups of ersatz filter coffee he had made on a small electric hotplate. A tray of pastries, mostly French, baked by a German, occupied the center of a small table. Major Fischer began speaking while he returned the silver coffee pot to its place.

"The bad news is that we lost six good men tonight, and judging from what I hear, we almost lost you. The good news is that we have an engine for your plane"—he spread his hands in a gesture of futility—"but I have no fuel for it!" Shaking his head, he sat in a leather chair opposite Erik. "I want the story of the mission as you saw it happen, not as a political lackey interprets it. There is a gap between the reports I'm getting and what my eyes and ears tell me."

Erik sipped from the cup Major Fischer had handed him, then put it on the table. "Well, sir, I suppose I can say we had a good night. We shot down two lancasters and killed their crews—they had no chance at all." He paused, watching the major's reaction—there was none. "The new 30mm cannons are devastating—we get a sure kill every time."

Erik waited again, but still, Major Fischer said nothing. "We also shot the turret off the lancaster that ruined our engine, complete with rear gunner...I don't see how he could have survived. However, the plane might have made it back to England—that big double tail could probably handle the change in the centre of gravity."

"That sounds like good news for the fatherland and great news for your career. Tell me how you feel about the war—you can be candid— we are 'under four eyes.'" Major Fischer passed the plate of pastries to Erik, who took one and offered them to Karl, but Erik's young navigator declined.

Erik gave the plate to the major. "I lost interest in my career two years ago. I'm fighting now to survive and to save as many people from the bombs as I can. In doing that, I have a long list of deeds to account for when I meet St Peter. But at least I will have lots of good men to drink with me in hell!"

The major smiled. "I wouldn't lose too much sleep over that; we all have to deal with our monsters the best way we can." He leaned forward, "It's time for some war news—you have a right to the truth, and that's the second reason you're here."

Erik returned his smile. "Yes, I suppose the truth is important; I haven't listened to Hitler's lies for a long time. I know the Allies are off the beaches and on their way to the German border. I have heard from the recon boys that British and American equipment is cluttering the French roads, unmolested by our Luftwaffe. At the same time, our tanks are practically useless because the American and British aircraft destroy everything with an iron cross on it that moves. Is there more?"

Major Fischer leaned back. "I think you've got the picture in the West, but the Russians coming from the east are more worrying than the advancing Western Allies. They are at the gates of Warsaw and, without a miracle, will advance to our eastern border before winter. It took them only seventeen months to get there from Stalingrad, and they become stronger every day. The Führer still speaks of a wonder weapon, a super bomb, and I've heard of a new jet-engine fighter, even a jet-powered bomber, but it's too late—we can't build enough of them to make a difference in the time we have. As for the miracle weapon, what could it be? There is a limit to physics and no limit to the power aligned against us!"

"I will do my best to keep you in a safe airplane, but I don't know how much longer I can do that. Our Führer seems to have lost what little connection he may have had to reality, and the people around him are in too deep to quit."

He stood up and extended his hand to Erik. "I'm sorry for all this; I hate to send good men to their deaths in a lost cause, but, unfortunately, none of us can turn the tide or roll back time. I pray we live to see a better world."

Erik stood and took his outstretched hand. "I haven't entirely given up on that better world, Major, but I am afraid that the bad guys always win in the end." Erik turned to leave; Karl waited.

Major Fischer asked, "Who are the bad guys?"

Erik opened the door, turned, and answered, "The bad guys are the ones who send us out to kill one another."

He walked out into the cool night air.

∞∞∞∞∞∞∞∞∞∞∞∞∞∞∞∞∞∞∞∞∞∞∞∞∞∞∞∞

"Jesus Christ, we lost Willie!" Ronnie screamed into his mask as the lancaster's nose dropped. The autopilot tried unsuccessfully to return the bomber to level flight; the dramatic forward change in the center of gravity was more than trim tabs—the primary control the autopilot used—could correct.

"What the hell just happened?" Steve yelled. He adjusted the elevator trim full nose-up... It wasn't enough. He held back pressure on the column, and the plane levelled itself.

Ronnie spoke through the intercom so fast his words were barely understandable, "A fighter blew Willie's turret off! It just flipped off the back and fell like a stone. And the bastard followed him down to make sure he killed him!" His voice broke.

"Jesus, almighty Christ!" Steve slammed his hand on the control column.

There was a moment of silence on the intercom, broken by Charley. "Och mah God. Whit ur we gonnae teel Norma?"

Ronnie, a little calmer, said hopefully, "He was wearing his parachute... He may have gotten out." Ronnie didn't sound confident. "That Goddamned German fired at him for a good five seconds, and Willie held down his firing button until...." He couldn't finish, and, in any case, Steve interrupted him.

315

"Shit! Shit! Shit! They were going to be married in a couple of weeks!" Steve banged his fist on the control column so hard he hurt his hand. He yelled, "I need everyone except Jake and Charley to go to the rear of the plane and sit on the floor. Take anything you can carry; the heavier, the better." As they moved back, Steve let the pressure off the column and adjusted the trim. The lancaster was again flyable. He switched on the autopilot.

The crew was silent as the aircraft made its way back to Dunholme Lodge. Steve came in hot and landed with the tail high but stopped well before running out of runway. He taxied to 'C for Charley's' parking spot, and the dejected crew climbed out. They examined the broken shaft that had held the turret on the plane, then gathered at the wheel to wait for the lorry that would take them to the debriefing.

Ronnie queried the worried faces around him. "We've got to tell Norma today...do we draw straws, or what?" They were used to death— but telling Norma that Willie had gone for a Burton...?

"Let's talk to Commander Leech; maybe he'll do it." Steve failed at his attempt to sound optimistic.

When Wing Commander Leech attended the debriefing, he had already heard of the missing turret and its rear gunner. Theirs wasn't the first RAF lancaster ever to come home with a missing rear turret, but unfortunately, none of the gunners had survived.

When the debriefing ordeal was over and the target-marking problems hashed through, 'C for Charley's' crew stayed behind. Steve went straight to the Wing Commander. "Sir, we've got a problem we need to discuss with you." His crew bunched up behind Steve, all knowing that Leech knew what the problem was.

Leech waved his hand in frustration. "Alright, yes, I will go with you to tell Norma and her parents. As aircraft captain, you have to come, and you will bring the witness, Pilot Officer Cummins."

Steve had hoped to avoid the meeting entirely, but John Leech's offer was better than nothing.

"Thank you, sir. Norma gave me her parents' number, and we should call them before we go." He handed Leech the piece of paper Norma had given him.

Leech took the paper, gave Steve a sour look and said, "Yes, we will do that..." He made a face as though stomach bile had reached his vocal cords..., "but not yet. We may hear that he's with the Résistance, or maybe the Germans have him as a prisoner. I suggest you go and get some sleep. I'll call them late this afternoon."

Steve, relieved to put the deed off, even for a few hours, led his men out of the building and headed for the Quonset hut barracks.

At the evening meal of roast beef and potato, Leech reported that he had chickened out and postponed the call until the following day after breakfast.

The crew ate their breakfast with Leech, and when they were seated with their food in front of them, Leech began discussing Willie's misfortune.

"We owe it to Norma to tell her the truth, and the truth is that there isn't a snowball's chance in hell that Willie got out of the turret with his parachute on before it hit the ground. I made a phone call before I came to breakfast, and in eleven turret losses, the gunner has never survived—not even close. Some genius figured out, assuming 'C for Charley' was at 20,000 ft, that Willie had sixty-eight seconds to get out of the turret and open his parachute—seventy-five seconds max!"

"Shit, I was afraid of that!" Steve played with his scrambled eggs. "That little bugger is damned good at getting out of a scrape, though... Remember, he made it back once already when someone said, 'Not a snowball's chance in hell!'" He looked at Phillip, and the big man grinned stupidly.

Ronnie shook his head. "Yeah, but I saw that turret blown off—it flipped end over end, and even Willie couldn't have gotten out of that! Anyway, the cannon shell that tore the mount apart probably killed him, or at least injured his feet so that he could never have gotten out." Ronnie hardly touched his food. He kept his eyes down, looking at the table.

John Leech looked around the table at the sad group of men. "Okay, are we all agreed that we tell Norma there isn't any hope?"

Charley spoke up, clearly upset. "When Ah was sixteen years auld, Ah feel aff a cliff ontae rocks awash in a ten-fit surf. If ye looked at th' cliff, ye woods say 'at nae a body coods survife 'at faa, but Ah did, an' withit a body broken bone!" The crew looked at one another, not positive they had understood all of Charley's ramble. He clarified. "I'm nae givin' up oan th' wee bloke until Ah see his deid body!"

Everyone at the table mumbled their half-hearted agreement. Faint hope is the hardest to kill; the fainter it is, the more determined it is to live. Willie's friends ignored physics and conjured up a miraculous survival scenario for Willie.

Phillip ended a thirty-second gap in the conversation by addressing Wing Commander Leech and his captain. "Why don't you call her parents and make an appointment to see them? Tell them something has happened to Willie, and we need to talk to them before talking to Norma. They'll make sure she isn't around, and you can let them decide what to tell her."

"Excellent idea, Phil." Leech grabbed the lifeline. "If we all agree, I'll call her parents now, and they can take it from there." His relief at the opportunity to pass on the decision was painfully obvious.

Everyone nodded, eager to pass the dirty buck. Wing Commander Leech left to make the call and returned in ten minutes, happier than when he'd left.

"I explained the situation to her father, and he thinks we should wait until at least tomorrow afternoon before we meet, and he wants Norma to be there—I got the feeling he doesn't want to tell her any more than we do."

There was relief all around the table—another day—maybe they would hear something. And, who knew, perhaps the world would end before tomorrow afternoon, letting them all off the hook.

The crew returned to the barracks hut, talking about Willie and his now-legendary abilities with his browning machine guns. By the time they had walked the half-mile to the Quonset, Willie had joined the ranks of heroes as great as John Wayne and Errol Flynn.

The cards came out; five-card stud poker was the game. The conversation continued, occasionally diverted to other matters but always returning to Willie and his chances. They dissected how Willie could have gotten out of the flipping, spinning turret and how much protection the turret floor offered against a cannon shell. Before they went to bed, they had talked themselves into believing there was a slim chance Willie might have survived.

CHAPTER TWENTY-NINE

29 June–20 August

Einmal ist wie nichts, zweimal wie zehn.
(To do it once is nothing; do it twice and you can do it ten times.)

THE DAYLIGHT STRENGTHENED, the morning mist lifted, and Willie could make out the outline of a house with an attached barn on the west end of the field. He could hear the farmer's cows mooing as they waited at the gate that barred their way to the barn, food, and relief from the discomfort in their full udders. The farmer came to the gate, opened it, and the anxious cows trotted to the barn. He stood for a few minutes, looking up the field, his hand shielding his eyes from the brightening rays of the rising sun. Willie assumed the man was looking for wayward cows until he started walking down the field and stopped partway to the half-buried turret—close enough to identify it. The farmer broke into a run, and when he reached the turret, he looked around for the missing gunner. Stopping his scan at the tree, the man stared at Willie and the bull standing guard. He gathered up the parachute, carried it to the house, and seconds later, Willie heard an engine start. A small 'camion' left the yard in a cloud of dust.

Willie said, "Mister bull, I've got to go," as he stepped down to the bottom row of limbs. On cue, the bull got to his feet, looked up at Willie with big black eyes, snorted, and pawed the ground with his right front foot. Willie sat on the bottom limbs, legs dangling just beyond the bull's reach.

"Your master has gone to get someone, probably not anyone I would like. I can't wait here, so, mister bull, it's you or me!"

Willie unfolded his pocketknife, edged down until his feet were just above the bull's head, leaned over and looked into the animal's eyes, his face inches from its upstretched wet nose. The bull opened its mouth and pushed out a blat that almost caused Willie to lose his tenuous grip on the tree. Willie looked at the knife, the bull's massive head, and pulled himself back up on the branch. "All right, you win. I only ask that you don't tell anyone I'm here." Willie searched for more cover higher up, where the branches became dense and small. He tried to make a hole to climb higher by breaking them off but soon realized his plan was hopeless—his only hope was that the farmer was friendly and had gone for help.

But what if he had gone to get German soldiers? They probably paid well for such information.

Willie considered his chances of making it to the fence next to the woods, but it was close to a hundred yards, and a mean bull stood between him and freedom. After surviving this long, it would be stupid to die on a bull's horns!

The farmer had taken the parachute into the house, so there was a real possibility that the man was on his side... If he were going to tell the Germans, he would have taken the parachute with him to prove his story...wouldn't he?

Willie looked at the bull, weighed the odds, and decided to wait.

◇◇◇◇◇◇◇◇◇◇◇◇◇◇◇◇◇◇◇◇◇◇◇◇◇◇◇◇◇◇◇◇

Twenty minutes later, the farmer returned in another cloud of dust, with a small Renault camion close behind. The farmer's vehicle stopped at the house while the Renault continued to the edge of the bull's field. Two men exited the car, climbed over the fence, and walked straight toward the tree. The bull greeted them with grunts but stepped aside when one of them pushed him. He said something to the animal, and the other man patted the bull's forehead.

The taller man looked up and smiled. "Come down, British flyer; the cow won't hurt you." Willie swung down, landed beside him, and said, "You have a French Canadian accent."

"Yes," said the man, "I'm Acadian, from Cap Pele, New Brunswick—that's in Canada."

Willie laughed, saying, "I'm from Digby, Nova Scotia, and my grandmother lives on the French Shore of Saint Mary's Bay." Willie reached out to pet the big animal. "And it's a bull, not a cow." The bull groaned with pleasure.

"Small world... He seems to like you." The man chuckled, then motioned to the Renault. "We have to leave now." He was built like an athlete, was almost a foot taller than Willie, and needed a haircut.

Willie's saviours led the way, with the bull walking peacefully behind. They seemed in a hurry, so Willie felt it better to ask no more questions.

The smaller man motioned to the back of the little camion—a canvas tarp covered the bed, fastened at the corners.

"You must get in here until we can get you to where you can change those clothes."

Willie looked at the confined dark space and said, "I can't."—He felt better getting into his drafty turret than into that box, despite the cold and the fighters—"I'm claustrophobic!"

"Get in, or you'll be dead, and so will we." The man pushed Willie, who wanted to fight back but was reasonably confident he knew who these people were—they were his only hope to get back to Norma. He closed his eyes, crawled under the canvas, and lay down on the floor with his knees bent; they closed the tailgate, and Willie stifled a cry. Ten seconds later, the engine started; the little Renault drove down a rough road for a few minutes, and then the ride smoothed out.

∞∞∞∞∞∞∞∞∞∞∞∞∞∞∞∞∞∞∞∞∞∞∞∞∞∞∞∞∞∞∞∞∞

What to Willie seemed like an eternity later, the vehicle slowed, bounced over what felt like a ploughed field, then stopped. The tailgate opened, the smaller man helped him out and led him to a brick farmhouse surrounded by trees. The taller man walked behind Willie.

Inside, the man who spoke Canadian English spiced with Acadian French introduced himself as René and his companion as Camille. Two young women came through a doorway; he presented them as Simone and Michelle. A teenage boy sat silently at the table.

"I met another Simone and, come to think of it, a René and a Camille in France!" Willie smiled at the coincidence, knowing it was not.

"You've been shot down before?" René seemed interested.

"Yes, early in May...the French Résistance got me home. They walked me through the mountains across the Spanish border."

René nodded and said, "We have better choices now that the Allies have landed. You are in Belgium, near Florennes, and we will get you through the Allied lines tomorrow afternoon. It will be a difficult trip, some of it in the trunk of a car and some hidden in a 'petite camion,' but we will get you safely through. First, you must change your clothes and eat, and then we'll go. It may be your last meal for a while, so eat well."

Everyone ate quietly. Willie tried to start a conversation, speaking slowly and a bit too loud. "I'm getting married when I get home. My future wife, Norma, is a singer."

321

René asked, "What kind of music does she sing?" and then translated the conversation for the others.

"I heard her sing the Mozart Requiem Mass in the Lincoln Cathedral a few days ago." No one said anything—Willie added, "It was the most beautiful music I've ever heard."

Simone said in heavily accented English, "The Mozart Requiem always makes me cry, especially the Lacrimosa." She was slightly smaller than Willie and resembled Norma in so many ways that he felt an affinity with her. Her English lacked polish, but her accent was charming. "The Gestapo murdered my husband a few months ago. We sang together in German opera houses before the war, and I have sung the Mozart Requiem with him… but it would break my heart to sing it now."

René said, "The Gestapo caught Simone, and if not for your British mosquitos blowing up the walls of the Amiens prison, she would have died as her husband had."

Willie sensed that René was in love with Simone. He asked, "…And you and your Résistance friends rescued her?" René nodded.

"Everyone in the RAF has heard a rumour about such a mission, but officially the operation never happened." Willie looked at his hands. "I know what you risk getting me home, and I also know that my thanks are pitiful compensation for your sacrifice."

The young singer woman struggled with her English again, but the meaning was clear. "I do this because I hate the Nazis, not because I love the British—and we do much more than rescue airmen."

Willie imagined Norma in the same situation and had to pull himself away so he wouldn't break down.

"I take it Michelle isn't your real name? Nor yours, René? Do you mind telling me your real names?" He didn't expect an answer.

"Juliette Durand and he is Marcel Guignard, my guardian angel."

"Damn, Juliette, you know the rules." Marcel tried to sound angry, but Willie could hear he didn't have his heart in it. It was evident to Willie where Marcel's heart was.

"And the boy?" Willie looked at the smooth German face opposite him.

"I found him in the woods. He's a *Kindersoldat…*" Juliette didn't offer a name… "and he belongs to me."

<hr>

A half-hour later, Willie was in the back of the Renault, dressed in one of their fallen comrades' clothes. For an hour, he bounced on the steel lorry bed, wedged against the sides. He wondered whether Norma thought he was dead, thought of Nathan and his blocks, and still, the ride was long and painful.

The little camion stopped at the edge of a village, and two men whisked Willie down a narrow street to a forest. They spent an hour fighting branches and tripping over stumps, finally emerging in a freshly planted field torn apart by tank tracks. Four American infantrymen appeared, checked their identities and led them across the open area to a group of tents that turned out to be an American Army command post. Two idling tanks sat on a narrow road a hundred yards to each side of the station, their cannons pointing down the road away from the tents.

The busy lieutenant who was in charge turned the crank on a field telephone, said a few words, mentioned Willie's name, nodded, listened for a few minutes and hung up. "You seem to be important to someone. I would love to hear how you got out of that turret, but we don't have time." He pointed to a jeep sitting outside and yelled at the corporal sitting in it. "Take this guy and put him on the C-47 that's going to London. They're holding it for him!"

Willie was on the plane before two in the afternoon. It landed in London, unloaded twenty wounded soldiers, and, an hour later, its wheels touched the Dunholme Lodge runway. Willie climbed down the short steps to the tarmac, and a lorry took him to the command post where half the base waited for him.

After an intelligence officer debriefed him for fifteen minutes, a grinning Charley steered him to the Sergeants' Mess. Laughing and jostling one another to get to Willie, everyone in the Mess slapped him on the back, shook his hand, and generally confirmed that he was indeed alive. Someone put a beer in his hand, and he lifted it to his lips, took a sip, then put it on the bar. Charley confiscated it, saying, "Noo laddie, we wooldn't want ye tae learn onie bad habits, nae woold we?" Charley tipped it up and poured its contents down his throat.

Willie said, "If you don't mind, I want to see Norma as soon as possible." He looked around at the laughing faces. "If someone doesn't find me a car, I will steal one."

Charley put down the empty beer glass and picked his hat off the bar. "Ah've awready got yer car, but yoo've got tae direct me tae yer in-law's hoose. Yer bride's thaur reit noo, bein' tauld by yer crew 'at yoo're deid!" He pulled Willie outside and pushed him into the passenger seat of an old Austin. He ran around the car, started the engine, and, at precisely 4:30, they drove away from the base amidst cheers and shouts of "good luck."

Charley drove much too fast, but Willie balanced the chances of being splattered against a stone wall against getting to Norma sooner and decided to keep his mouth shut.

"Oh shit, Charley," he braced his hands on the dashboard, "When do you think they'll be there?"

"They left th' base at fower. Ye hae tae teel me whaur yer in-laws bide afair we gie tae th' city."

"Okay, it's Drury Lane—straight ahead for a bit, and I'll direct you from there. It will take about fifteen minutes if you drive this fast..." Willie held onto the leather strap handle above the door... "and we don't hit one of those stone walls..." Stone walls as high as the Austin's roof lined both sides of the narrow road.

Three reluctant messengers arrived at 4:30, and the housemaid directed them to chairs surrounding a low table. Gianna and James sat opposite them, with an empty chair beside Gianna reserved for her daughter. A fancy china pot of tea sat on a metal rack with a lit candle under it; matching china cups and saucers sat on little white doilies in front of the chairs. Despite the British government's attempts at rationing, a tray heaped with croissants and cookies covered the middle of the table.

James opened the conversation. "While we're waiting for Norma, Gianna and I want to know exactly what happened to William, and we would appreciate your unvarnished honesty."

Before John Leech could begin with the report he had rehearsed, Gianna said, "My husband wants honesty, and I agree, but I want you to be careful about what you tell Norma when she arrives. She is a strong woman, but it's only been a little over a year since she lost her husband, and her love for Willie is the kind that comes once in a lifetime!"

"We were hoping we could give you the details and leave before she arrived..." Steve's voice trailed off, still holding a note of faint hope.

Gianna smiled at his attempted getaway. "No, that won't do at all;

she will want to question all of you. I don't know what she will ask, but you must answer her questions truthfully and tactfully. In other words, do not kill her hope!" Gianna emphasized their obligation with a finger pointed at Steve.

Despite the danger of crashing into a stone wall or one of many large trees along the road, Willie tried to hurry Charley. It would be close to five o'clock before they arrived in Drury Lane. Steve and John Leech would tell Norma he was dead, and... "Jesus, Charley, can't you go faster?"

"Nae if ye want tae gie thaur in a body unbloody piece!" Charley slowed a little; the city approached, the road wandered, roads intersected, and traffic increased. Charley roared through a major intersection, and Willie yelled, "Stop! You should have turned left!" Charley braked hard—the little Austin stopped, and he reversed. The gears whined, a car blew its horn, and he turned the wheel the wrong way, stopping a couple of feet from a big tree. He cursed, drove forward, and snaked the car in fits and starts back through the intersection while a lorry waited with its horn proclaiming its dismay.

Straightened out and on the correct street, Charley slowed to a saner pace, and the Austin didn't miss the next turn. They pulled up outside a large, two-storey brick house—a thick brick wall topped with two feet of wrought iron separated the street from the front garden. Two storeys of bay windows on each side of a massive oak door dominated the town mansion's impressive front. To the right of the door, a wooden handle was connected to a chain. Willie ran to it and pulled hard. The chain tripped a hammer on a bell in the hallway. He heard the bell ring, and Charley caught up to him as the door opened. George, the chauffeur, now butler, stood stock-still in the doorway with his mouth open.

Steve began explaining Willie's death to Norma's parents by describing the turret, emphasizing the extreme danger that a rear gunner faced. "Willie was truly a perfectionist about doing everything right—he was the first rear gunner to take the perspex out of the turret so that he could see without any distortion. The wind blew through the turret, and he froze, but he saved our bacon twice, spotting and shooting down a night fighter before it could fire."

Gianna laughed nervously. "Yes, he is meticulous about everything he does. Norma says that if she lays something down and turns around, he puts it away. William even irons Nathan's diapers!" James, embarrassed, said, "Now, Gianna, they don't want to talk about William changing diapers."

Steve smiled and went on, "Over the last few operations, Willie wore his parachute in the turret—ever since he jumped out over France. I'm telling you this because there is a tiny possibility he got out and is a prisoner."

James interjected. "When Norma comes, please tell her of the possibility, but leave out the 'tiny.'"

Steve nodded and looked at Ronnie. "You saw what happened; you should take it from here."

◇◇◇◇◇◇◇◇◇◇◇◇◇◇◇◇◇◇◇◇◇◇◇◇◇◇◇◇◇◇◇◇◇◇

Ronnie began reluctantly. "When Willie spotted a night fighter stalking us, Steve swung the plane back and forth, weaving so we could see everything under us with each swing—most of the time, the night fighters attack us from below now—the Luftwaffe has mounted vertical cannons in the back of their night fighters' crew compartment so they can shoot into our fuel tanks. The fighter sneaks up under us where we can't see him, fires the cannons at our wing tanks, and, most of the time, the exploding tank blows the wing off. If the fighter doesn't get past the tail and the bomber swings back and forth, that tactic isn't as easy as it was."

"I don't like the sound of that!" said Gianna. "How do you find them before they fire... I mean, if it's dark...with clouds and no moon or stars?"

Ronnie looked at Wing Commander Leech. "Can I tell her about the fish pond?" John Leech nodded.

Ronnie said, "For a while now, we've had radar that picks up targets on the ground. We use it for navigation, as well as targeting our bombs. The technicians took that signal, changed its direction and range, added a second screen and an antenna, and now we can see planes behind and below us. We call it "fish pond" because, on the screen, the bogeys of so many bombers flying in formation look like fish in a green pond. The trick is picking out the fish that don't belong."

Gianna had enough detail for now; she waved Ronnie off. "Okay, I think I understand that. Now, tell me about how a fighter hit Willie's turret. With all this radar, why didn't you see him?"

Ronnie said, "We did see him, or we would all be dead. Willie and I spotted the fighter at the same moment; we both fired and hit his

326

wing and engine. He turned to face us, probably trying to save himself, and I couldn't get my guns down far enough to hit him, but Willie kept firing at him. The messerschmitt 110 has an armour plate and a thick windscreen in front of the pilot—the bullets from our puny guns bounce off, so we aim at the fuel tanks and engines."

Ronnie's voice became angry, "We use the same .303 ammunition used in a soldier's rifle, and firing head-on against an armoured German night fighter is like using a slingshot against a charging rhino!" Ronnie looked at his commanding officer. "If Willie had been firing cannon shells, we wouldn't be here!"

Commander Leech intercepted James' question. "But he wasn't firing a cannon, and we work with the tools we have."

Ronnie swore, not entirely under his breath, then said, "Yes, we damned well do, but we don't have to like it!" John ignored the added colour and waited.

After a short pause, Ronnie continued, "The German fired his cannons, hitting Willie's turret at the same instant Willie shot the fighter's left propeller off."

Gianna said, "So, William was still firing when his turret came off?"

Ronnie looked at Gianna with the respect he usually reserved for his commanding officer.

"Yes, until cannon shells exploded under the turret, blowing it away from the tail. When it separated, it flipped end over end and the fighter followed it. It looked like he was trying to kill Willie, but that doesn't make sense; I think he was just trying to get away." Ronnie's voice broke. "God, I hate the bastards who fly those fucking fighters!"

◇◇◇

Norma opened the door, looked around the room and gasped. She put her hand over her mouth. "Steve, Ronnie, why are you here?" She looked at John. "John Leech, you wouldn't be here if Willie weren't dead!" When no one said anything—she looked to the Wing Commander for an answer. "Is Willie dead?"

Steve took a deep breath and said, "Yes, we think he's dead, but there is a tiny chance that he survived." He looked at Norma's father and hung his head.

Norma fell into the empty chair at the table, grasped her head in her hands and spoke to the table.

327

"The night before last, I saw Willie in a dream. He was running...I was sure he had been shot down!" She looked at her mother. "The dream was so real I tried to touch him in my sleep. Even after I awoke, I could still see him..." She looked around the room... "And Willie was alive!"

Norma's father said, "A night fighter shot his turret off the plane, but he had his parachute on, and Commander Leech, Steve, and Ronnie are here to tell you exactly how it happened."

Norma turned to Steve.

"Tell me everything! I have to know every detail!" Her mother handed her a handkerchief, and Norma held it ready.

Fifteen minutes later, Norma had all the details she wanted, and everyone began trying to think of a survival scenario. When the discussion became more sombre, headed toward a dead end, Gianna poured the tea. Norma got up, went to the liquor cabinet, poured herself four ounces of Irish whiskey straight, and downed it in two tries.

◇◇◇◇◇◇◇◇◇◇◇◇◇◇◇◇◇◇◇◇◇◇◇◇◇◇◇◇◇◇◇◇◇◇◇◇◇◇◇

Willie pushed George out of the way and charged for the drawing room, shouting, "Norma!" as he ran through the doorway. She turned and tried to stand but fell back into the chair. He arrived beside her, lifted her, pulled her against him and said her name softly. She began to cry so hard she couldn't speak, and Willie held her, tears flowing down his cheeks.

Ronnie shook James's hand and said, "He's alive! He's alive! The little bugger's alive!" James laughed and turned to his wife, who sat with her hands on her face, laughing and crying. She stood, took him in her arms and hugged him. Finally, the commotion subsided, and Norma found her voice. Everyone stood silent, like children, during a prayer.

"I saw you running in my dream." Norma laughed, and everyone but Willie laughed with her.

"I did run! A bull chased me; I climbed a tree to escape him. I slept in the branches, and he waited all night under it!"

Norma, smiling, wiped away tears and asked, "What happened? How did you get here?"

Willie said, "Two guys from the Résistance found me there, and they thought my fear of the bull was a big joke! But he was big, and he looked mean to me. It turned out the bull just wanted me to pet him."

While everyone in the room laughed, Willie took Norma's hand

328

and pulled a chair over so he could sit facing her. "I wasn't afraid, but I was worried that you would hear that I was dead." Willie looked at their intertwined hands.

"I met a girl who lost her husband when the Gestapo caught him— they tortured and killed him." He rubbed her hand with his. "She is a singer like you…they were both singers. Later, the Gestapo caught her too, but our mosquitos bombed the prison, and, in the confusion, the Résistance rescued her."

Willie touched her hair. "She was so much like you; it's eerie. When I met her, I just wanted to get back here as fast as I could!"

He looked around the room, then took a breath.

"The rest is not so exciting. The Résistance took me to the Americans, who put me in one of their jeeps. A corporal with a slow drawl drove me to an airfield not far from the beaches where the Allies landed. He put me on an American plane, and they flew me to Dunholme Lodge." Willie spread his hands. "And here I am… And the most dangerous part of the story—well, after escaping from the falling turret—was the ride here from Dunholme Lodge with Charley."

Norma pushed down the rooster tail on Willie's head that perpetually refused to cooperate. It popped back up when she lifted her hand. She spit on her fingers and tried again.

"I've never dreamed about you before; I'm always the star in my dreams, but this time I was a bystander." She stopped and thought about it while the room waited for her to go on. She kissed Willie. "I hope I never have a dream like that again!"

John Leech crossed over to Willie and shook his hand. "Willie, I swear on my Victoria Cross that you will not fly another mission before the wedding and none for at least a week afterward." He grinned. "We can't take a chance on you falling out of the plane again!" Everyone laughed.

"I've still got a bunch of missions to go, sir, and I want to finish with the crew. I would rather fly whenever they do." Willie looked at Steve and Ronnie.

The wing commander shook his head. "They upgraded Mailly to a full mission, and bailout and returns are each worth a mission, so you have fewer than the others to go. I'll check with HQ, but I think you can skip a few and finish with the crew."

Willie looked at Norma. The hope in her eyes told him that Leech had better be right and that he had better not volunteer to fly if he didn't need to!

◇◇◇◇◇◇◇◇◇◇◇◇◇◇◇◇◇◇◇◇◇◇◇◇◇◇

On August 12th, Norma married Willie in the same white dress her mother had worn when she married James. The ceremony was mercifully short; at Norma's request, her father had negotiated the shortest vows ever heard in the Anglican Church. However, the priest had insisted on the 'and obey' for Norma. And she did indeed cross her fingers.

Norma insisted on sending a standing wedding invitation to all her fans at the Blue Bell, and they filled the church and overflowed outside, covering the sidewalks and lawn. They tried without success not to look bored during the Bach Wedding Cantata and broke into raucous applause when the priest pronounced Norma and Willie "husband and wife." The overflow heard the service through the open doors, and when the bride and groom finally exited to the waiting Bentley, it was through a gauntlet of rice and confetti.

At the Blue Bell, men danced in the barroom, in the party rooms, and outside. Norma had invited every girl whose name she could recall, and any man who wanted a dance partner eventually got one. Of course, most of the RAF crowd drank too much but were generally good-natured, and the few who became rowdy were whisked out the door by their less-drunk friends. Eventually, giving in to popular demand, Norma sang a few songs, avoiding "Lili Marlene" but doubling up on "The White Cliffs of Dover."

She sang the usual finale before saying goodnight to them, and they joined in, singing, "Praise the Lord and Pass the Ammunition," under her soaring descant. They put particular emphasis on the line, "...for a son-of-a-gun-of-a-gun-ner was he!"

Formalities and celebrations over, George drove Norma and Willie to the hotel where Norma's parents had arranged and paid for the Bridal Suite.

◇◇◇◇◇◇◇◇◇◇◇◇◇◇◇◇◇◇◇◇◇◇◇◇◇◇

Norma and Willie used room service for most of their meals and spent three days talking, cuddling, reading, and "making whoopee." Every morning, usually late—what society calls early afternoon—they went for a long walk on the beautiful medieval city streets, where Norma taught Willie some English history.

While walking down an ancient street, looking at Jewish shops, Norma said, "Medieval Lincoln Jews were persecuted much as Hitler's Jews are today. Thousands were killed during the plague. because it was thought Jewish heresy had caused it. Many Jews left for Eastern Europe."

Willie said, "Europe seems to have a bad habit when it comes to Jews—wherever they succeed, people persecute them."

"Oh, we English don't play favourites in the persecution business! Irish, Scots, Luddites, black slaves, white slaves, and Jews—we've persecuted them all!"

Willie stopped to look down the street, imagining people running on the rough cobblestones, chasing or running away from those separated from them by nothing more than beliefs—trying to eradicate those who believed they saw the truth in a different lie.

"Maybe this war will force the world to see how insane it is to believe in a lie—I know I have a new perspective since I heard the Mozart Requiem. The men I fight are not my enemies. The bomber I sit in drops bombs where General Harris tells us to drop them. The crew doesn't hate the people they kill. War is a devilish machine fuelled by lies, and we are the gears in the machine. There is no moral right for either side in a war, only suffering and death. Those responsible are never identified; both sides agree to that when the war begins."

Norma took Willie's arm. "If this war teaches humanity a perspective that will prevent such a catastrophe from happening again, it will be the first war to do that. I suppose we can hope that some benefit would come from such immense pain, but every day we live proves that we learn nothing from history. Both sides keep records so everyone can learn from them, but they hide them in archives and fail to heed the lessons."

Norma took Willie across the street to Lincoln Castle and showed him where the Lincoln copy of the Magna Carta was customarily kept for public viewing before the war.

"There are only four original copies left." Norma stroked the glass over the display. "The charter is the basis for British law as it pertains to the common people, guaranteeing basic freedom from the tyranny of the ruling class. Even the king is subject to the laws of the land. The English say that Thomas Jefferson, the father of the American Constitution, knew all 63 clauses by heart. That may not be true, but he based the American Declaration of Independence on that English document. That single piece of parchment changed the world when that seemed impossible, and its principal continues to mould the world's democracies. The ideas enshrined in that document are what was taken from the Germans by Hitler, and they are the ideas you are fighting for!"

Willie was surprised to find the case empty. "Okay, I believe you, but where is it?"

"When the war began, we loaned it to the U.S. to remind them of their country's origins. It's actually in Fort Knox for safekeeping at the moment." She laughed. "The Americans don't talk about it, but King John signed the Magna Carta, they based the U.S. Constitution on it, and George Washington actually descended from King John!" She spread her hands. "It's a small world, but because of tyrants like Hitler, its people are still far apart. Separating people is the first rule of tyranny. Bringing people together is the first rule of peace."

The cathedral was close by, and Willie became fascinated with the beautiful building's history, returning to it each day to discover something new. As he learned, he wanted to know more. The war, his turret, and his fear receded into the furthest recesses of his mind.

George picked them up on Wednesday morning, and as Willie walked with Norma along the stone path to her house, now his home, he wanted to laugh out loud but settled for smiling to himself. At that moment, he didn't believe he could climb into his turret again... Never... Not ever!

◇◇◇◇◇◇◇◇◇◇◇◇◇◇◇◇◇◇◇◇◇◇◇◇◇◇◇◇◇◇◇◇

Willie returned to No 44 squadron on August 20th. Since his previous mission, Bomber Command had fed the squadron a steady diet of mostly unopposed military targets, and the crew was in a buoyant mood when Willie stepped out of the limousine and said goodbye to George.

Ronnie slapped him on the back when he entered the Quonset hut, and the crew gathered around, using colourful language to describe his honeymoon. The obligatory banter lasted a few minutes, and then they returned to their cards.

"That's your mail, Willie." Steve plunked a letter in his hand. "It's from Meg Casey."

"I have a sister, Meg—she must have gotten married." Willie looked at the address. "That's my sister's handwriting…and yeah, it looks like she finally married her boyfriend."

Willie put the letter on a shelf above his steel frame bed and lay down, looking at the ceiling and thinking of his sister. The card games died, the crew began the bathroom rotation, and Willie and Ronnie decided to wait until the rush was over before brushing their teeth.

Willie swung his legs around to the floor and loosened the drawstring on his duffle bag. "I've been thinking about asking for a transfer to a desk…I have a problem with what we do."

"Yeah, dropping bombs…" Ronnie sat on his bed and watched Willie hang up his clothes… "We all have a problem with that, but no one has a solution."

Willie unfolded the blanket on the foot of the bed and spread it out, ready for him to get under it. He hammered his pillow, then lay on the blankets with his hands behind his head, looking up at the ceiling. "Well, I can't do it anymore. If they try to force me, I will go AWOL, and they can throw me in jail!"

"They don't do that to rear gunners with four missions to go."

"I think it's more than four, but okay, give me a reason why I should kill women and children."

"You shouldn't kill women and children—you should do your job." Willie waited, but Ronnie didn't explain.

"Isn't that my job?"

"No, it isn't. Your job, and my job, is to protect the bomber and crew by shooting down night fighters that attack the plane."

"Okay, but the crew's job is to drop bombs on women and children." Willie didn't want to split hairs or discuss semantics; "there isn't any difference."

"We are dropping our bombs where the generals tell us to drop them…most of the time, we can't even see the target. The way I look at it, the German government is using women and children as shields and as sacrificial lambs. They know we are coming, and they know that we will flatten all their cities if they don't stop supporting a leader who is slaughtering millions of people: women, children, babies, old people—it doesn't matter to Hitler! They could stop defending a maniac bent on destroying Germany, and, as a starter, they could evacuate the cities as we evacuated the children from London when they bombed us."

"That doesn't make it right."

Ronnie shook his head. "War is not right no matter what side you're on or what you do to fight it. Isn't the secretary who typed our orders as responsible for killing those people as we are? The secretary's job is to type; we shoot a gun at fighters. Jake's job is to flip the bomb release switches; Steve's is to fly the plane where Charley tells him the target is. Which of us has more or less blame?"

Willie tried to find an answer; he needed time.

"Don't try to figure it out; it's a trick question. The responsibility for how we fight the war lies with the politicians or perhaps with the people who vote for them. Someone has to make tactical and strategic decisions, and someone has to make political decisions. If everyone—and you and I are everyone—has a say, we might as well learn German now. Winning or losing is the only important thing about a war, but no one gets a trophy!"

Ronnie picked up Willie's letter. "Here, read the letter. I haven't gotten one in months, and I want to know why your sister has a new name."

✦✦✦✦✦✦✦✦✦✦✦✦✦✦✦✦✦✦✦✦✦✦✦✦✦✦✦✦✦✦✦✦✦✦

Willie pulled the flap open. It didn't take much effort because the censors hadn't sealed it after they read it.

He scanned the first sentence and said, "My mother fell down the cellar stairs again." Willie's voice rose as he read the following sentence. "Meg says, 'Mum's in the hospital with a broken back!'"

Ronnie waited, but Willie had stopped reading. And then he remembered, "You told me your house hasn't got a cellar."

"It hasn't. If Meg told the doctor that Dad broke her back, the RCMP, that's our police, would put him in jail. If Mum wanted him in jail, she would say that Dad beat her—not a word about the cellar stairs. The RCMP would take him to jail and throw away the key, and she would starve."

"What about the doctor? Doesn't he know what happened to her? Wouldn't he tell the truth?"

Willie spoke softly, "If Mum says she fell down the cellar stairs, the doctor knows what Mum is saying. His job is to do what Mum wants, and she wouldn't want him to ask questions she didn't want to answer. Mum isn't a good liar."

Ronnie opened his mouth, but Willie gave him a 'case closed!' look and returned to his reading.

"Meg says, 'A few days after Mum went to the hospital, Uncle Rowley and Jack helped Dad with his traps.'"

Willie looked at the wall. "I guess Dad's hired helper was sick."

"Why would they help your father?" Ronnie thought he had heard a name before. "Isn't Uncle Rowley your mother's brother?"

"Yes, and so is Jack. Uncle Jack is a lumberman, and he's a lot bigger and stronger than Uncle Rowley."

Willie looked off into the distance when he said, "Dad's funeral was two weeks ago, a few days after Mum got out of the hospital."

"What funeral? Your father died?"

"Yes, that's why my sister wrote. His foot got tangled in a trap line, and the trap dragged him over the side. Traps weigh about eighty pounds, and they sink fast!"

"That's awful!" said Ronnie. "Your father drowned!"

"They're not sure. The blow on the head may have killed him first." Willie read aloud, "Meg says, 'Dad hit his head on the washboard as he went over the side, and Uncle Rowley said he might have been dead when he hit the water.'" Willie looked up. "That's what she wrote, so it must be true."

Ronnie was quiet for a few minutes while Willie read silently.

Willie stopped reading and looked at Ronnie. "The coroner said his back was broken too."

"Jesus, Willie. Your uncles killed your father!"

Willie tapped the paper. "No, no, they tried to save him. The RCMP said the proof is in the rope burns on his legs. It's plain to see that the trap rope was tangled around his ankles when he and the trap went overboard—it happens to lobstermen all the time, and the coroner says that Jack and Rowley probably broke his legs when they pulled him back on board. They were trying to save him!"

"Tell me, Willie, did your father break your mother's legs?"

"Not both of them—he only broke her right leg."

"This is bullshit, Willie—they beat the shit out of him, tied a rope around his ankles, and dragged him behind the boat—they killed him!"

"I don't want to talk about it." Willie looked at the page, then at Ronnie. "The RCMP and the coroner ruled it was an accident, and they always do what's right." Willie read a little more and said, "Meg says they combined the funeral and the wedding so they wouldn't have to pay the preacher and the piano player twice."

"What? Your sister got married at the same time they buried your father?"

"No, that would be sacrilege. The preacher said a few words over the coffin..." Willie read a line for clarification. "It doesn't say why, but it was a closed coffin. Meg wanted to have Dad give her away, so, yes, it's right here... 'They wheeled the casket down the aisle behind her, and she got married with his coffin beside her.

Willie looked up at Ronnie. "You were almost right... They buried Dad right after the wedding, before the party."

"What about your sister's husband; do you know him?"

"Oh, sure, we're pals, eh... She's been sweet on him since they were twelve. Ian's got a lobster license and a scallop license, and Meg works in his father's fish plant. They won't have to worry about enough money for the baby."

"How old is your sister? ...Wait a second... What baby?"

"She's twenty-one; they're having a baby in October."

Ronnie perked up, smiling. "Shotgun wedding?"

"No, it wasn't a shotgun wedding—they planned to have a family. She told me about that over a year ago—before I enlisted." Willie held the letter up.

Ronnie said, "But… they had to get married. That's a shotgun wedding."

"Maybe in Rhodesia, but not in the Maritimes. Meg and Ian got married because they love one another, and they are having a baby because they want a family." Willie stood up and shook the letter in Ronnie's face. "And I will guarantee that Ian Casey will never hit my sister!"

Ronnie said, half under his breath, "I wouldn't advise any man in Digby to hit any woman, especially not his wife! Digby sounds like a tough place."

"Digby isn't so tough; we just take care of our problems. No big deal." Willie folded the letter and put it back in the envelope. "Sometimes, someone has to do something that breaks the rules, or the bad guys will win."

He grabbed his kit. "I'm going to brush my teeth." He stopped before he turned the corner. "Hitler is the bad guy, and someone has to stop him. If I don't go, someone else will have to, so I've decided to fly with you guys until we finish our tour." Willie disappeared.

CHAPTER THIRTY

3 September 1944

"If you have tears, prepare to shed them now."
William Shakespeare, from Julius Caesar, act two, scene three.

Erik arrived in Heilbronn on Sunday, September third; he had a week's leave, and the first day was almost gone. Marita, Walther, and Annalisa met him at the station, and although it was past Walther's bedtime, his exuberance boiled over. When his parents' reunion cooled, Walther squeezed between them and pulled on his father's hand to get his attention.

Erik tried to hug Walther, but he squirmed away, grabbed his father's suitcase and headed for the exit, leaving Erik no choice but to pick up his duffle bag and follow him.

When Erik caught up to Walther, he put his hand on the boy's shoulder. "Just a minute, son." Walther stopped, and Erik stooped to whisper in his son's ear, "I have something special for you later, but you must promise not to tell your mother." He winked, and Walther winked back.

"All right, you two, what's going on?" Marita stood with her hands on her hips.

"It's something between us men," Erik said, adding another wink.

"Yeah, it's just between us men!" Walther grinned and followed his grandmother as she passed them.

Annalisa led the way to the mercedes. Erik caught up and walked beside her; Marita followed with Walther. Erik smiled at his mother-in-law, examining her from toes to hair. Her thin frame had gained a few healthy pounds, and her eyes were bright.

"I see things are going well with the newlyweds," he said, though he decided not to mention the pounds.

She put her arm over his shoulder and squeezed. "I am so happy, Erik; I had given up hope that I could ever be this happy again!"

Annalisa fished for her keys in her handbag. "Jonas and I are very compatible. I love him more than I thought I would, and I like the feeling. He's the kindest man I've ever met."

"I'm glad for you, Annalisa, but what about Jonas? Marita tells me in her letters that he's working for you now!" He laughed, and she joined him—her eyes twinkled like Marita's.

Annalisa found the keys, picked out the car door key from a dozen on the ring and faced Erik. "The firm is still in Jonas's good hands, but he allows me to help him. I like working there, and Marita and I have everyone in town wanting to work for us. We have our pick of the best workers, and now that the Zwangsarbiter know that Jonas is putting money away for them, they have a sense of a future in their lives." Annalisa inserted the key, turned it, and the lock popped up. She opened the door and leaned against the side of the car. "Jonas is giving them a pledge that he will give them their back wages when the war is over. He has set up their fund in Swiss Francs, and we have all their personal information so that we don't lose track of them when this war is over. Their money is as safe as Jonas can make it."

Annalisa sat on the leather seat with her feet on the ground. "When this war is finally over, there will be a lot of debts to pay!"

Erik held the door while she swung her legs inside. "You and Jonas will have nothing to worry about—you haven't been killing people. I wish I could say the same."

The mercedes glided through the streets, purring smoother than Erik remembered. When Annalisa stopped at Wacksstrasse 21, Marita invited her for coffee, but Annalisa had left the girls with Jonas, and she was sure he would never put them to bed. She asked Walther to come home with her; she tried to bribe him with everything from Kuchen to sitting on her knee and steering the car, but he wanted to stay with his father.

"You can't say I didn't try!" Annalisa winked at Marita before driving off.

"Why did she wink at you?" Walther asked his mother as they climbed the steps.

"It's just between us women," she replied as she unlocked the door.

<hr>

When they were in the living room, Erik pointed to the small suitcase Walther had been carrying. "There's a package in there wrapped in white cloth—why don't you see what it is?"

Walther laid the suitcase on the sofa, eagerly opened it, and tried to hand the package to his father. Erik put up his hand.

"No, I want you to open it."

Walther unwrapped the package slowly, savouring the moment, and a Swiss Offiziersmesser with an inlaid Swiss coat of arms on the red handle slid onto his hand. He reverently opened the shiny knife blade, stared at it in awe, then folded it carefully back into its nest. Walther pulled open the scissors with a reverence not typical of a nine-year-old, then closed it again. He pulled out the tools one by one, opening and closing each one until he had seen them all. He reached up, Erik knelt down, and Walther put his arms around his father's neck and kissed him.

"I never get too big for that, Walther. Thank you, son." Walther pulled his father's head down and whispered in his ear, "Thank you, Vati. I love you."

"Now, what was that...more man talk?" Marita put her hands on her hips and grinned playfully.

"Yes, that was man talk!" Erik stood and kissed Marita on the cheek.

Marita opened her mouth to say something to Walther, but he was there first. "I don't want to go to bed now, Mutti. Can't I stay up for a few more minutes? Please?"

She shook her head. "I'm sorry, Walther, but you've got school tomorrow, and your father's tired. Now, brush your teeth, and we'll be in to say goodnight."

Walther hunched his shoulders and dragged his feet to the bathroom. Erik asked her, "Are you sure I'm tired?"

Marita kissed his cheek and whispered, "I certainly hope not!" She pointed at his suitcase and duffle bag. "Take those to the bedroom; I'll be along shortly."

Five minutes later, she sat on the bed beside him with two glasses of Eiswein in her hands. She handed one to him and said, "A toast to us," and they each took a sip.

Erik raised his glass, said, "A toast to the most beautiful woman in Germany!" and they drank another sip. She put her glass on the table, took the bottle and indicated with her finger that he should stay put. She left and returned with the bottle in a bowl of cold water.

"I'm ready!" Walther shouted from his room. "Come and tuck me in!"

Walther tried all the tricks he knew to keep them there but finally ran out of them. He let Erik hug him and kiss him on the cheek and said, "Oh yuck, whiskers!" as he laughed and pushed his father away.

Marita pointed to the bathroom. "Shave and a bath, and do a good job!" Laughing, she said, "No scratchy whiskers, please." Erik chuckled and left the room.

He sharpened his razor with a leather strap and paid particular attention to his shaving. When he finished, he sharpened the blade and shaved a second time, this time against the grain, until he couldn't feel any stubble. When he sat on the bed beside Marita, she felt his face and pronounced the job "satisfactory, so far, but you still need to bathe."

Erik got to his feet, removed his clothes, donned the bathrobe that hung in the closet and headed for the bathtub in the cellar.

"I'll be right back."

"Do a good job—we won't have any fun if you smell bad."

Erik put a hand under his arm, then removed and sniffed it. He screwed up his face. Forty minutes later, when he returned to the bedroom, Marita had two burning candles on the bedside table, and the flickering light reflected in two full glasses of red wine. Marita sat on the bed, naked except for a frilly nightdress that hid nothing. Erik's arousal showed before he took off his bathrobe.

"Remove the robe," Marita commanded, "and sit beside me while we drink a glass of wine." Erik obeyed, dropped his bathrobe in a heap on the floor and kicked it out of the way. Naked, his knees weak, he sat, and when he turned to her, she swung her right leg around him and opened the front of her nightdress—the wine stayed on the table.

Later, sitting in bed and drinking their glasses of wine, Marita said, "It's almost worth the absence."

"What is, Liebling?" Erik lifted the wine out of the cool water.

"The lovemaking... It's so good it's almost worth the wait." She smiled at him. "Almost, but not quite—I need you here, Erik."

He looked at the reflection of their naked bodies in the dressing mirror and said as he filled their glasses, "The war will soon be over." He filled their glasses, put the bottle back in the water and said, "The enemy will take over our country from top to bottom, and I don't know what our life will be like, but it will be better than this damned war." He looked into her sad eyes, seeing the same desperation he felt.

Ten minutes later, the bottle was empty, and they lay quietly in each other's arms.

◇◇◇

Erik and Marita spent five days making love, going for walks, and hurrying to the bomb shelter. On Friday, September eighth, the raid alarm started at quarter to two in the morning, and Marita and Erik gathered the family together as usual. They met Kriminaldirektor Richter and Frieda in the street and quietly walked to the General Wever Tower, as they always did.

The subdued social prattle stopped when Helmut and Frieda entered the shelter. Helmut and his wife seated themselves in their usual place, and the chatter gradually increased to a monotonic collection of whispers. No one sat within earshot of the Gestapo major and his wife except Erik, Marita, and their family. Helmut and Frieda spoke softly with the children, and Helmut gave them sweets, as always. Frieda usually brought a bag containing a folded board game and a pair of dice, but the children preferred to sleep.

There was no raid; the night was quiet when the all-clear siren pierced it, waking the children. Helmut and Erik walked together while the children walked ahead of them with Marita and Frieda.

Erik asked Helmut, "Have you heard anything regarding Matthias?"

"Yes, but I can't give you the names of the individuals who are responsible."

"But you do know who is responsible?"

"Yes, I do...as I know just about everything that goes on in this town. You do remember that I have big and little spies everywhere?"

"Yes, but Walther is no longer one of them..." Erik turned to Helmut... "Is he?"

"Not as far as I know, but in truth, I actually don't know everything." Helmut paused; Erik said nothing, so the Kriminaldirector said,. "There is a large element of people in this city, not the majority, but significant, who would kill me if they could, but not for the reason that others would have a year ago. Today, I am far too lenient for these 'New Nazis' tastes. They continually harass me, sending letters to the Führer's office that brand me as a communist, and worse." He smiled contemptuously and said, "They forget that I command the people who open and read all the mail…

"This element frequently takes the law into their own hands, and I have explicit orders from Himmler's office not to interfere. In other cities, there have been incidents where mobs murdered British and American flyers rather than turn them over as prisoners of war. And Goebbels has expressly forbidden the Gestapo to arrest or even look for those responsible."

Erik and Helmut stopped outside Wacksstrasse 21. Marita and Frieda looked at their stationary husbands and decided to follow the children into the house.

Erik said, "You know who did this, and even you can't do anything about it?"

Helmut nodded. "Yes, but I will tell you that those responsible are on a list I am compiling. Of course, it's for my protection, but I will arrange for you and others to have the list when the war is over, whether I survive or not. Their crimes are detailed, along with the evidence."

"And you will include a copy of the Führer's orders to leave these horrible people alone?"

Helmut shook his head. "No, the orders are verbal. I have written them down, but there is no official written order. Goebbels would never allow Hitler to put such things in writing!"

"I believe you. I don't know why, but I trust you. This group of thugs that you say killed Matthias—who are they in our society? Why would they kill the pastor of a church?"

Helmut looked down the street, then at Erik. "There is a new wing of the Nazi Party in this city that would rather sacrifice every resident than surrender, and only a few of us, and perhaps only for the moment, have the power to control them. Adolph Hitler is their God, and they will martyr their own children to save him."

Helmut nervously scanned the street. "The Reich Defence Commissar, Wilhelm Murr, intends to evacuate all the Württemburg cities, including Heilbronn and Stuttgart. That maniac will burn the cities to the ground and march the residents to Austria rather than surrender them to the Allies. His plan includes the execution of all Zwangsarbiter and war prisoners."

Erik, stunned, couldn't think of anything to say.

Helmut spoke so softly that Erik had to turn his ear toward him and bend his head down. "You are aware that I knew more than a year ago that your pastor was helping Jews, and I deliberately ignored it. You were with my wife when she witnessed him openly defy the laws forbidding anyone to comment negatively on the war or criticize the Führer. She told me, and I deliberately ignored it, but others—that element we are discussing—did not."

Helmut watched the street, keeping his words to a whisper. "There are officers like me who want this war to end with as little pain for the German people as possible. We try to avoid arresting those who openly kick the dying lion, but we can only go so far, and Matthias went beyond the point where I could protect him. The mob killed Matthias and his wife because I wouldn't. If I had known they would go so far...."

Erik could think of nothing to say as Frieda returned to her husband. He shook Helmut's free hand and, without saying a word, walked up the steps into the house with his head down and shoulders rounded.

CHAPTER THIRTY-ONE

9–10 September 1944

Yankee Doodle came to town, riding in a Boeing!

W HEN THE AMERICAN EIGHTH AIR FORCE found that cloud cover obscured their primary targets at Ulm and Günzburg, they diverted to their secondary target, Heilbronn. The B17 bombers, their vapour trails, the attacking fighters and the lace-like patterns their contrails drew were clearly visible in the cloudless sky.

Erik and his family were not quite to the shelter when the armada flew into sight, coming from the northwest. The sight motivated the flak batteries to begin firing, and the children sensed panic in the adults. The girls started to cry. Erik picked up Elke, and Helmut swept Brigitte into his arms as the rumble of hundreds of propellers turned by a million horsepower shook the ground.

As the group reached the shelter, bombs exploded in the railway marshalling yards across the river, and Erik took a last look at the rising cloud of dust and debris as he ran through the door. He could hear bombs exploding in the harbour area near the city center as they found their seats. They could have chosen from many empty ones, and Erik felt sick to his stomach as he thought of the hundreds, maybe thousands of people who wouldn't get to the shelter in time.

Erik said to Helmut, "This could be the big one," and then, almost hopefully: "The good news is that they are American bombers, and they will target the railway yards, the harbour and the industrial area."

"Is there anything we can do?" Frieda showed no sign of anxiety in her voice. She was calm, and her eyes showed no fear. "What about the people who didn't go to the shelters?"

Helmut took her hand. "We can't help them now; all we can do is wait. It's too late to help the people who haven't come to the shelter, and I fear there will be heavy casualties. When it's over, you should stay with Erik and Marita, if that is acceptable to them, and I will do what I can to control the inevitable chaos."

Erik answered quickly, "Of course… if our house is still standing. American planes will not purposely attack the civilian areas, but our house is between the railway yards and the port facilities. American bombers drop their ordnance in formation, and although they don't intentionally target civilians, many bombs still fall outside the target area."

◇◇◇◇◇◇◇◇◇◇◇◇◇◇◇◇◇◇◇◇◇◇◇◇◇◇◇◇◇◇◇◇

Bombs exploded for an hour without a gap, limiting conversation to yelling in one another's ears. The tower shook, and anxiety grew. Erik dreaded the devastation they would find when the doors opened, knowing that life for everyone in the city would change dramatically.

The explosions stopped at one o'clock, as though for Mittagspause, but the 'all clear' didn't sound. The rumble of the planes diminished minute by minute and finally disappeared. But still, the all-clear did not wail.

A strong smell of smoke invaded the shelter through the vents. Rumours spread of the city's total destruction, whispered from one person to another. An hour passed without explosions or the sound of approaching bombers, and an increasing number of people demanded that the veteran soldier guarding the door open it. They loudly reasoned that a bomb had destroyed the alarm or the power supply, and the 'all clear' would never sound. When the time since the last explosion neared two hours and smoke in the shelter was becoming unbearable, the soldier relented and opened the door just as the 'all clear' sounded.

Erik stood and took Elke's hand—Marita took care of Brigitte. Sensing the tension, Walther walked beside his father; Helmut and Frieda walked behind the family.

The smell of smoke was all-pervading before Erik was through the door. Outside, smoke covered the sky and filled the air. People spilled out of the shelter into an acrid fog that burned their eyes. The children coughed; Erik's eyes watered; he found breathing difficult. The tower was full of smoke; there was no alternative to walking away from it, so Erik guided his family toward home, dreading what he would find.

Once outside, the extent of the damage became progressively apparent. Buildings burned; fire had consumed entire blocks; rubble covered sections of the streets. As they walked, the smoke lessened, and before they reached Wacksstrasse, the wind was blowing it away from them. Blue sky appeared overhead—but three-quarters of the horizon was a wall of grey and black smoke.

The damage to Wacksstrasse was a single crater in the middle of the street, with no visible damage to the buildings. The children ran ahead for the last hundred metres, anxious to be in their home where toys and food waited. They hadn't eaten since breakfast.

A young officer driving Major Richter's Gestapo car intercepted Helmut before they reached the house, and he said his goodbyes to his wife and Erik's family.

◇◇◇◇◇◇◇◇◇◇◇◇◇◇◇◇◇◇◇◇◇◇◇◇◇◇◇◇◇◇

The south wind blew the smoke north, away from Wacksstrasse, and as soon as his family was inside, Erik changed into his uniform and went to see what he could do to help. The Bundesbahn had Erik's train scheduled to go to Gütersloh in the early evening, but he doubted he would leave Heilbronn today. Nevertheless, he had to check.

Erik walked toward the *Stadtmitte,* the centre of town, to what looked like the primary source of smoke. As he walked, flames rose above the buildings ahead, and the smoke worsened. He stretched one of the handkerchiefs he had brought with him over his face and tied it in a knot behind his head. His eyes burned, but he kept walking north, trying to pick streets that kept him upwind of the fires but led him in the general direction of the Bahnhof and the Stadtmitte, attempting to circle behind the fires.

As Erik neared St. Kilian church, the damage became more severe—rubble spilled into the streets, and everywhere he looked, buildings burned. Although several bombs had struck the church, it was still standing, but across the street, the priceless and irreplaceable Renaissance city hall was in flames, a total loss.

Erik's depression deepened as he walked across the Kaiserstrasse bridge to the railway station, and he said to himself, "So much for Americans not targeting civilians."

He expected to find a pile of rubble, but amazingly, the Bahnhof appeared undamaged. Inside, Erik spoke with a young man Erik would have bet was no more than sixteen, wearing a Bundeswehr uniform and searching for information about his train. There were others, most of whom looked lost, but no one had any helpful information. Some people were there because they had lost their homes and had nowhere else to go. He walked to the silent platform, stared at the tracks, clean and shiny in both directions and decided to return before his train was scheduled to leave.

Erik headed home, staying in the centre of the street, a safe distance from burning and unstable buildings. Emergency workers directed him to the side as the *Feuerwehr* pulled up in front of a burning block of houses and began to pour pitiful streams of water on the enormous blaze. The fire scoffed at their pathetic efforts, and the firefighters shifted their concentration to try and save a building downwind of the blaze.

A strong wind drove the flames ahead of it, lighting one building after another, making a mockery of the firefighters' efforts. As Erik looked on, the feeble attempt disheartened him, the damage shocked him, and his depression threatened to overwhelm him.

He had expected the Americans to target the railway, factories, and docks, but they had attacked the town's people as they walked home from church! This exhibition of naked brutality did not bode well for an American occupation.

An emergency officer crossed the street and walked up to him, throwing his right hand up in a perfect Wehrmacht salute to his superior officer.

The man said, "Sir, I respect your uniform and rank, but you must leave here immediately. It is forbidden for unauthorized persons to be in the area!" The uniformed civil defence sergeant pointed to the south, away from the fires.

Erik coughed, recovered, and saluted. *"Feldwebel,* I'm scheduled to return to my unit on the Bundesbahn tonight. Can you tell me anything about the trains?" Erik coughed again...and spit a glob of black goo onto the street.

The sergeant waited, then waved his hand in the general direction of the river. "The bombs destroyed the railway yards; it's the worst damage we've seen. I have heard that they hit the machines we need to repair the yards, and there isn't a straight piece of rail left on the ground! Your train would have to either leave or arrive on the track that passes through there." He hesitated, then decided to tell his superior everything. "The attack destroyed the rail lines north of the station as well. The wharves in the harbour and most of the buildings in the port are no more." He hesitated, then said, "This is a disaster! Many people have died!"

Erik hated to ask, dreading the answer, but he said, "Do you have an estimate of casualties?"

The sergeant shook his head. "I don't know… hundreds for sure." He gestured toward a burning block of houses. "Many didn't go to the shelters—so many bombers—no one thought the Americans would do this to our small city."

Erik could see that the man was in a hurry to return to work, so he asked, "Is there anything I can do to help? It looks like I will be here for a while longer."

"No, there is nothing you can do." He waved Erik away. "The hospital is undamaged, and most of the streets are passable. We are prepared for this; all we require from civilians is to stay away and let us work. There will be people with nowhere to go, and we will ask those who still have a home to help them."

Erik ignored the man's implication that he was a civilian and felt a surge of guilt as he thought of his undamaged house. But they had three children and…

The Feldwebel saluted, Erik returned it, and the sergeant walked to the emergency crews, looking back once to see that Erik was leaving.

Erik hurried back to his family and, as he walked, was surprised at his relief that the Americans had been the ones to bring the 'big one' to Heilbronn and not the British nightmare firebombing that he knew and feared. Fewer than half the bombed buildings burned and the city had been spared the dreaded 'Firestorm' that many German cities experienced. His spirits rose as he assessed the chances as good that the RAF would scratch Heilbronn off their schedule of cities to burn.

◇◇◇◇◇◇◇◇◇◇◇◇◇◇◇◇◇◇◇◇◇◇◇◇◇◇◇◇◇◇◇◇◇◇

The fires burned into the next day, and the area around city hall was still burning when, early Monday evening, Erik stepped onto the platform at the railway station. The children remained at home, and since the traffic ban was still in force for the city centre, Erik and Marita walked to the station and said their tearful goodbyes there. The repair crews had miraculously built a single track through the rubble that used to be the railway yards.

Erik said, intending to comfort Marita, "The war is near an end when they've got nothing more important than Heilbronn to bomb. I'll be home when the war ends in a few months, and we can begin rebuilding our country."

Marita pushed his hair back from his face. "God bless you, Erik, and please, don't take any chances!" Despite her efforts, a dark sense of foreboding resounded in her voice. She had tears in her eyes as she kissed him.

"I never take chances, Marita—that's why I'm still alive." Erik stepped on the train and waved goodbye.

CHAPTER THIRTY-TWO

14 September 1944

Aus gutem Eisen macht man keine Nägel, aus guten Männern keine Soldaten.
(You don't make nails from your best steel, and you don't make soldiers from your best men.)

Erik arrived in Gütersloh at midnight on Tuesday night, a day and fourteen hours late. The railway's priority was transporting war material, and passengers waited hours on platforms for scheduled trains that disappeared into thin air. Posted schedules that the Bundesbahn had meticulously kept just a few months ago now meant nothing.

"Major Fischer's orders are for you and me to report to him as soon as you can," Karl told Erik as they drove to the airfield.

"I can't do anything tonight—I need sleep. Tell Major Fischer we'll eat breakfast with him." Erik held onto the strap above the door as Karl missed a turn and yanked the car back on the road. The blackout headlights gave just enough light to drive safely at a fast walking pace.

When Karl had the car under control, Erik asked, "Have you had any flights since I left?" Karl would have been available to fly as a replacement for sick or injured navigators.

"No, I might as well have gone home." He looked across the seat at Erik and slowed the car noticeably. "Most nights, we don't have enough fuel for all the fighters, and mosquitos have raided us twice, taking out both of our fuel tankers on the first raid." He turned his attention back to his driving. "That's probably what the major wants to talk about."

◇◇◇◇◇◇◇◇◇◇◇◇◇◇◇◇◇◇◇◇◇◇◇◇◇◇◇◇◇◇◇◇◇◇◇◇◇◇

Erik and Karl entered Major Fischer's office at seven the following morning, where the major had ersatz coffee, Brötchen with cheese, wurst, and jam waiting for them. Erik loaded his plate; he hadn't eaten a meal in thirty-six hours. He sat in one of the plush leather chairs, set his coffee cup on the low table in front of him and spread jam on a piece of Brötchen before he took a big bite.

Major Fischer said, "I presume you were there on Sunday when the Americans bombed Heilbronn." He sipped his coffee as he waited for Erik to finish chewing.

Erik answered with his mouth full. "Yes, sir, and many buildings were still burning when I left. I was told that repair crews will have the railway yards and docks running by the end of the week. The Americans, who say they only bomb industry, destroyed over three hundred homes, and our beautiful city hall burned to the ground. Major Richter estimates three hundred deaths, and at least four hundred are in the hospital with serious injuries. So much for American accuracy, or perhaps they are learning from the British... Bomb whatever has a roof and hope there are people under it!"

While the major waited, Erik took another bite of Brötchen. "It was bad, but, to tell the truth, I am happy that the Allies have crossed Heilbronn off their list." Erik used his hand to corner the crumbs that had flown out of his mouth onto the table. He pinched them between his fingers and put them into his mouth. Then he bit off as much of the bun as his mouth could hold.

Major Fischer shook his head. "I don't share your optimism. The Allies have a surplus of bombs, aircraft, and men, and it looks as though the British intend to level every German city. Heilbronn should be at the bottom of the list, but at the pace the RAF is destroying cities, and considering General Harris's lust for German blood...."

Erik put what was left of his Brötchen down. "There is no industry in the centre of Heilbronn. The Americans who only bomb industry killed hundreds of people and burned whole city blocks a thousand metres from any industry. That should be enough German blood, even for Harris." He didn't want to talk about another attack on his home, particularly not one by the RAF.

"So, what do we do now?" Erik picked up the bun and took another big bite; it was almost gone.

The major set his coffee cup on the low table and leaned forward with his elbows on his knees. "The Allies control the skies. The only effective air force we have now is our night fighters, and our loss rate is climbing. Spare engines and ammunition are becoming scarce, and our fuel supply is limited. When I receive orders to intercept British bombers, I can only respond based on the fuel available. Sometimes, the British bomb our cities without a single fighter opposing them!"

Erik spread *Leberwurst* on another bun. "Where does that leave Karl and me?"

The major picked up his fake coffee, sipped it, and put down his cup before continuing.

"You are the best crew on the base, and I must utilize the best—I cannot waste fuel on unsuccessful crews. I want you to know I don't like doing it, but I must send you out on every mission. If there isn't enough fuel for all our planes, I will leave the less experienced crews on the ground."

Erik wolfed down the last of his second Brötchen, swallowed a long draft of coffee, and spoke while chewing. "I understand the situation, and Karl and I will do our best. I don't want to sit on the ground while others take the risk for me—and, of course, we have a much better chance of success and survival than the green crews."

"Thank you for your understanding." Major Fischer stood and extended his hand. Erik took the hint, wiped his hands with a napkin, and stood to shake it. Both men stepped back and saluted smartly.

◇◇◇◇◇◇◇◇◇◇◇◇◇◇◇◇◇◇◇◇◇◇◇◇◇◇◇◇◇◇◇◇◇◇◇

Erik and Karl flew an average of twice a week for the following twelve weeks, shooting down sixteen British aircraft, pushing Erik's record to over forty victories. But the shortage of fuel and ammunition kept the entire squadron on the ground many nights, leaving the British bombers to fly to their targets unmolested. British objectives designated as "must fly" for German night fighters were the synthetic fuel plants and major cities; otherwise, British bombers destroyed German assets with nothing to worry about except a lucky hit by a flak gunner.

mosquito bombers continued to strike at tactical military targets, effectively disrupting the rail system, the power system, and German citizens' sleep patterns. mosquito night fighter squadrons escorting British bombers created a significant distraction for nervous German night fighter pilots, shooting German messerschmitt and junkers night fighters down at a horrendous 'kill to loss' ratio.

◇◇◇◇◇◇◇◇◇◇◇◇◇◇◇◇◇◇◇◇◇◇◇◇◇◇◇◇◇◇◇◇◇◇◇

On December 4, 1944, Erik and Karl were in their barracks playing

353

chess when the siren announced the arrival of ground-attack fighters minutes before the full-throated roar of big thunderbolt radial engines reached their ears.

Karl knocked over the chessboard in his hurry to leave the room behind Erik. He followed on Erik's heels as they headed for a concrete bunker less than a hundred metres from the barracks. The roar of the engines and the wailing siren drove a dozen other men toward the same shelter.

Erik and Karl were still in the open when the centre aircraft of three side-by-side thunderbolts fired its load of ten rockets. His wingmen, fitted with two 500-pound bombs each, fired their fifty-calibre machine guns, leaving the high explosives for another purpose.

Erik yelled, "Down!" as he pulled Karl to the ground. The rockets passed over their heads, hitting the barracks and two neighbouring buildings. Pieces of walls and roof flew in the air, and the buildings burst into flames—the thunderbolts' machine guns dug up streaks of ground on both sides of Erik and Karl.

"Go! Go!" Erik pulled Karl to his feet, and they raced to the bunker, the first to arrive. Erik made it to a firing slit in time to watch the fighters turn for another run.

Karl said, "Did you know that those big round engines have two thousand horsepower?" as he watched through a slit on Erik's right.

Crossing the field in formation, the fat, stubby, short-winged aircraft strafed the parked aircraft with eight 12.7mm machine guns, firing six kilograms of armour-piercing steel tracers per second. They destroyed two Ju88 night fighters and both flak guns, killing the gun crews. Pulling up in formation and executing a smooth chandelle, they reversed course and began another pass.

"*Sheisse*, look at those bastards fly!" A newly arrived mechanic watched from the third slit. "Our piles of junk wouldn't last two min-utes in the air with those monsters!"

Erik corrected the mechanic. "The thunderbolt has a small wing, flies eight hundred kilometres per hour, dives like a polished crowbar, but climbs like a sloth. Me 109s and FW 190s can get away by climbing or turning. As a matter of fact, the FW 190 is better at everything except falling out of the sky. The thunderbolt turns like a truckload of bricks, and a 109 or an FW 190 can turn inside and get behind it. However, shooting one down takes all the ammunition our fighters carry. That's one tough aircraft, and the pilot is sitting in an armoured cockpit with a bullet-proof canopy!"

The two thunderbolts with bombs still hanging from their wings gracefully twisted out of formation in the chandelle and levelled off in tandem at two thousand feet. They dropped their bombs on the runway. Two of the four 500-pound bombs landed in the centre, blowing six-metre craters in the smooth surface—the remaining two bombs exploding on the runway's edges. The thunderbolts turned away from the field, still in tandem formation, then reversed their turns to make another strafing run.

"They'll fire every shell they've got!" Erik watched flame and tracers spit out of the wings, and two more night fighters became piles of junk. "Flying home without ammunition isn't risky for a thunderbolt—nothing we have can catch it!"

Karl said, "Ground defence flak on the field is useless at such low levels and high speeds, and the machine guns set up to defend the airfield can't damage one of those American thunderbolts, even if by some fluke they hit them. What's the damned point in resisting the inevitable?"

"Careful, or you'll become a cynic." Erik pointed at the exit. "And you shouldn't swear."

◇◇◇◇◇◇◇◇◇◇◇◇◇◇◇◇◇◇◇◇◇◇◇◇◇◇◇◇◇◇◇◇◇◇◇◇

The attack had lasted barely three minutes, and acrid smoke greeted Karl and Erik when they emerged from the bunker. Fire crews passed them, rushing to put out fires at the barracks and two nearby buildings, but their efforts were a hopeless cause; it was apparent the buildings would burn to their foundations.

As Erik watched the firefighters struggle with hoses, he said, "You know, I had you where I wanted you."

Karl shook his head. "I had your trap figured out, and when you moved your queen, I had a fork with my knight that would have forced you to sacrifice your rook to save her."

"I wanted you to think that, but that wasn't the move I had planned." Erik moved his imaginary piece and said, "I had your rook lined up with your king, and my bishop would have forced you to sacrifice it, leaving my queen to check the king when you took the bishop."

Karl thought for a minute. "Yes, that might have worked, but we'll never know."

Erik slapped Karl on the back. "Why don't we go over to HQ and see if Major Fischer will let us borrow his board to finish the game?" He began walking, confident that he would win.

"Okay, you're on!" Karl caught up. "I remember the position of everything, and it was your move."

Erik thought for a minute as they walked, then asked casually, "Where will we sleep tonight?"

"Fischer's office will do. I like those chairs, and the rug is thick and soft."

"Yeah, he'll find something for us. But I need a toothbrush."

A bulldozer pulling a grader behind it appeared on the runway, and two Lastwagen loaded with sand rounded the corner from the edge of the field and headed for the craters. The construction crew would repair the damage to the runway before darkness stopped the work.

Karl opened the door for Erik as he said, "We had no gas for the planes anyway," and they entered the major's office.

CHAPTER THIRTY-THREE

4 December 1944

"The Nazis entered this war under the rather childish delusion that they were going to bomb everyone else, and nobody was going to bomb them. At Rotterdam, London, Warsaw, and half a hundred other places, they put their rather naive theory into operation. They sowed the wind, and now they are going to reap the whirlwind."
Sir Arthur "Bomber" Harris, 1st Baronet.

No 44 squadron moved from Dunholme Lodge to Spilsby late in September, and the new digs delighted the crews. Steve's aircrew moved into a centrally heated barracks with hot water, showers they could use whenever they wanted to, and a lorry that drove them to and from their aircraft. The briefing room was spacious and bright, and the crews stowed their kit in lockers in an adjacent room. The geographical location was the best part—the base was only fourteen miles from the Blue Bell Inn.

On the fourth of December, Steve led his crew to the briefing room, where they took their usual places in a row of chairs halfway to the rear. The room buzzed with chatter that abruptly stopped when Wing Commander Leech stepped to the front of the room and held up his hand in a bid for silence.

"Good afternoon, gentlemen. The target tonight is Heilbronn, a small city between Nürnberg and Stuttgart. The city has some light industry and the bad luck to be a major river port and a railway-marshalling hub. These facilities have been bombed many times, with little or no permanent damage, and are always up and running a few days after we hit them. Most of the factories are now located deep in the salt mines nearby. Bomber Command thinks it is essential to send a message to the Germans, using Heilbronn as an example. The message is this: they can't hide from the RAF!"

Leech waited for applause, but the men sat on their hands, so he continued, "Heilbronn has seventy-thousand residents. Many of them work in the factories, the rail yard, and the port, and most will be home tonight. Bomber Command's rationale is that if we can't get their factories and they won't stop fixing the railway yard and the port, we will get the people who work in them! When we destroy the city, we destroy the lives of Nazi workers." The men didn't react; they sat sullenly looking at the map that hid the blackboard. Leech turned to a sergeant standing to one side. "Sergeant Weaver will explain the planned route."

A smartly dressed sergeant—his uniform with sharp creases where there should be and not a hint of a wrinkle anywhere else—lifted a pointer and aimed it at a large map at the front of the room. Lines connected four points, the first marking Spilsby, then two waypoints, and the last marking Heilbronn.

"The route is straightforward, as the navigators will see in their packages, with a planned diversionary raid on Karlsruhe." He pointed to the third point. "The force will consist of two hundred and eighty-two lancasters from Number Five Group and ten mosquitos from No 627 squadron acting as escorts and pathfinders. The master bomber is Wing Commander Maurice Smith, and he will fly the lead target-marking mosquito. Lieutenant Pereira's mosquito will mark the target area with flashlight bombs set to detonate two thousand feet above the city. Smith's pathfinder will fly under the expected cloud cover to drop red markers on the city center, and a third mosquito will drop yellow markers on the railway yards and Neckar River Port. The marker assigned to your aircraft is in your package." He looked around the room. "Are there any questions?"

There were no questions.

The briefing lasted an hour: First, the met forecast, then intelligence with flak and night fighter predictions, and finally, the navigation officer with 'no-wind' courses and distances for the legs to and from the target.

The intelligence officer, usually the purveyor of bad news, was uncharacteristically optimistic regarding both flak and night fighters. "German night fighters have been staying on the ground most of the time lately...likely because we destroyed their fuel plants. There will be some fighter activity, but we don't expect them to be out in force. The mosquitos from 627 will escort you there and back, mingling in the bomber stream to root out any Nazi vultures. Try not to shoot them down."

He added as he gathered his papers, "The city is lightly defended as far as flak is concerned—I assume the Germans don't believe we would waste bombs on it. It is also possible that the Luftwaffe doesn't think the city is worth the fuel it would take to defend it. Heilbronn is a target that could, in fact, be a piece of cake!"

The aircrews collected their kits and parachutes from the dispersal next door and gathered outside to wait for the transport lorries. It was cold, and the gunners stood quietly in their extra clothing and watched their comrades stamp their feet and complain.

Ronnie remarked, "This is the only time I feel happy to be a gunner," as a lorry stopped rolling in front of him and Willie. They climbed into the back, and Willie wanted to say, "Only one more mission," but superstition stopped him.

When Steve finished his 'Rah-Rah' speech, Willie tried to piss on the left wheel but, as usual, couldn't.

Ronnie cheerfully said, "The last time you couldn't piss was the night you got your turret shot off." He drenched the wheel and laughed at Willie, still squeezing his dry implement. "Don't worry; I've pissed enough for both of us." Ronnie pulled himself up through the rear hatch, and Willie reluctantly followed, taking a last look at the wet tire before he closed it.

One after another, four big twelve-cylinder engines belched black smoke as their over-rich cylinders fired. The exhausts cleared the excess fuel, and the Merlin '24' engines smoothed out. Willie fiddled with his ammunition belts, checked the feeds, and then opened and closed the breeches. He blew imaginary dust out of them, waiting while Steve and the flight engineer went through the complicated checklist. Finally, Steve released the brakes, and Willie bounced along on the lancaster's tail as 'C for Charley' taxied to position in its slot on the runway. The green light flashed; Willie let out his breath as the Merlins smoothly spooled up to maximum power. The aircraft shook and rattled as it slowly accelerated; the tail lifted, Willie stopped bouncing, and his eyes, now ten feet above the runway, watched it slide out from under his feet. If a tire didn't blow out, if an engine didn't cough, if every bolt was tight, and if no one had made a mistake fastening the bombs in the racks, Willie had a good chance of living for at least a few more hours.

In the cockpit, Flight engineer Phillip Carpenter read out the numbers as the airspeed built. Just before the "go/no-go" point, Phillip said, "all green." He double-checked the fuel tank readings and called out "rotate" as the airspeed passed a hundred and fifteen miles per hour and sixty-five thousand pounds of aircraft, fuel, and bombs slowly lifted off the runway. Phillip pulled the gear lever, the lancaster surged slightly, and Steve trimmed to cruise-climb at 160 mph. Behind them, a four thousand pound "blockbuster" and eighteen hundred incendiary bombs filled every fastening in the bomb bay—their target—the red markers in the center of Heilbronn.

The fourth of December 1944, 18:50h: German radar reported a 'significant' bomber formation north of Saarbrücken, target unknown, and the alarm sounded to scramble the fighters. Karl and Erik played chess on a chessboard wheedled out of Major Fischer, comfortable in their new room in a building that had been a hangar.

The adjutant stuck his head in the room, said, "Bombers up! Time to fly!" and disappeared.

Erik tipped a pawn; they picked up their gear and jogged to the plane. Fuelled and ready, their Bf 110G, both props turning, rocked gently on its soft landing gear. When Fritz saw them, he shut the engines down, stopping the propellers before Erik and Karl got close. Every aircraft pilot and mechanic has nightmares about someone walking into a turning propeller, and the paranoid ones shut off the engines if anyone comes within ten metres of them. Fritz climbed down from the cockpit, and Erik met him at the bottom of the ladder.

Erik pointed at Fritz and said sternly, "It is verboten to warm the engines—the orders from the Führer are clear! Engines must not be run on the ground except to taxi the aircraft!" He whacked Fritz on the back. "Thank you, my friend; I will bring you cigarettes if they take you to jail."

Fritz grinned. "Should I expect the Gestapo or the SS at my door?" The grin disappeared. "They can all go to hell! My airplane will not move until the engines are warm; in this cold weather, that takes ten minutes. Otherwise, they can find another mechanic!" He stamped his feet, turned and stepped back from the propellers. Erik searched for something a propeller might hit, yelled "Clear," and hit the port engine's starter. It fired on the first cylinder and ran perfectly. Erik repeated the process on the starboard engine with the same result.

Fritz waited to watch his aircraft take off. Erik waved at him from the cockpit, and Fritz gave him a 'thumbs up.'

<hr>

The takeoff on the repaired runway was smooth and short against a forty-kilometre-per-hour wind dead on the nose. Erik took off without the flaps, smoothly transitioning to a slow climb at cruise speed. The British jammed Deelen, but Karl quickly found the bombers on the fighter's radar as they passed through two thousand metres. Despite the technicians' guarantees that the British could not locate the new sets, Erik and Karl agreed that they should switch the radar off as soon as he had a course to the target. If the bombers changed direction, Karl would find them and calculate a new intercept course from the following radar picture—better the extra calculations than a mosquito following the radar signal to its source in the black box in front of Karl.

He left the set switched off until they reached six thousand metres. The radar warmed up in thirty seconds; he asked Erik to turn right, then left, and then announced that the bombers had changed course to the south.

"The main body is not going to Karlsruhe... Their course is more south, toward Stuttgart or Nürnberg," Karl switched off and gave Erik a new course.

Erik said, "We are behind them and trying to catch up. Is that correct?" His frustration showed.

"Yes," Karl confirmed, "our closing angle is less than ten degrees, and we are a hundred kilometres behind the main bomber stream—it will take two hours to catch them."

"*Scheisse,*" said Erik. He worried about the target; Heilbronn was on the same course as Stuttgart.

CHAPTER THIRTY-FOUR

4 December 1944

Vorsicht! Wer anderen eine Grube gräbt, fällt selbst hinein.
(Be careful! If you dig another's grave, you might fall in it yourself.)

Larry Inman set the mosquito's throttles to match the speed of the bomber stream cruising five miles ahead of him. Danny Powell, his navigator, his HF radio set to the bomber frequency and his radar tuned, searched ahead of the mosquito for bogeys that didn't belong. Danny was good at this game; the mosquito had accumulated nine air-to-air kills, all but one against night fighters. They had also killed a focke wulf 190 during the daylight raid on the Amiens prison but got no credit for it since, officially, the mission didn't happen.

Daniel announced, "Two bogeys coming in on our left, headed for the bombers."

"Take me to them, on their six o'clock if you can."

"Left twenty degrees will put us directly behind them. And it looks like they're at about angels twelve…the same as the bombers. You can turn left anytime."

Larry's mosquito was at twenty-two thousand feet, ten thousand above the bomber stream. He swung left twenty degrees, opened the throttles, and dropped the nose. Following the bombers at their pace, the mosquito's cruise was at a hundred miles per hour under its top speed, and it jumped ahead as Larry called on more horses and gravity to join in the game. The negative gravity generated when he dropped the nose momentarily lifted Larry off the seat into his belts.

The bomber stream and the German night fighter vultures were at twelve thousand feet, and Larry descended in a shallow dive, pushing the indicated airspeed to the 'never-exceed' red line of four hundred-and-fifty mph. The mosquito closed on the fighters quickly, and Larry backed the throttles.

Daniel said, "We're going to overshoot; I'm moving us to the left… turn ten degrees…now." Larry adjusted the directional gyro with a gentle nudge on the rudder and ailerons as his mind estimated that the new course would intersect the night fighters' course at least a couple of miles behind the bogeys, using up altitude and adding distance when he turned right for the attack. Danny would time a right turn so they would close on them from their right rear quarter.

"Turn right forty degrees... Now!" Larry turned right.

"I've got them, Danny... Thanks; it's a perfect setup."

Above the low winter cloud deck, two night fighters, sharply silhouetted in the starlight, sat like stupified partridge in a leafless apple tree on a sunny, frosty morning, their tails pointed at Larry's mosquito.

Larry lined up behind what he recognized as a Ju88, pulled off half the power, and pressed the buttons on the cannons and the browning machine guns when the range was three hundred yards. Despite the darkness, Larry saw pieces of the night fighter flying off into the void as his shells raked the back of its fuselage. He touched the left rudder... his tracers sliced into the fuel tanks in the junkers' wing, and the Ju88 exploded. The mosquito's tremendous speed advantage carried it straight at the fire and debris—Larry pulled the stick back, and the mosquito zoomed through the top of a ball of fire rising over the wreckage.

"I lost the other one..." Daniel sounded frustrated. "It will hide among the bombers."

"Okay, we'll look for him under the stream."

The trailing bombers' black shadows blotted out sections of the stars in the clear sky ahead, making them easy to find. Larry imagined how simple it would be to creep under one of them, and he felt pity for the crews who had to get in their lancasters. Life in a mosquito was a lark compared to the fragile life of the men locked up in an aircraft with seven tons of armed bombs; Larry loved every minute he spent in his mosquito.

A lancaster flying a mile ahead and to the right exploded, and Larry instinctively turned toward it. Daniel shouted, "I've got him!"

"Take me to the bastard." Larry lowered the nose a little and opened the throttles to their stops.

Daniel said, "He's turning away and diving! Turn right ten degrees!"

Larry did as Daniel instructed. Daniel said, "His speed is increasing fast... He's headed for the deck!"

Larry pulled the nose up. "There's no use chasing him into the clouds. He knows where we are now, and he'll probably go home—for sure, he'll never catch the bombers again."

Larry set his climb and speed to cruise on station above and behind the bombers while Daniel looked on his radar screen for intruder bogeys.

Jeffrey announced, "Two bogeys in the fish pond—one bogey is closing fast on the other." Seconds later, Willie said into the intercom, "There was an explosion behind the bomber stream—I'm betting a mosquito just scratched a German night fighter!"

A minute later, Jeffrey said, "I have what looks like a night fighter, about a mile behind and well to the right. He's off my radar now, but I think he's sneaking under a bomber."

Steve keyed the bomber frequency and announced in the clear, "Bomber on the starboard edge opposite 'C for Charley'; a fighter is approaching you."

Two bombers responded, but minutes later, a lancaster ahead and to the right of 'Charley' exploded and plunged to the ground.

Willie announced, "Another lancaster down! Why didn't we see the fighter on our radar?"

Jeffrey's voice rose in volume and pitch, "We did until he passed us! That was the bomber we tried to warn! The shooter is back in the pond, and the mosquito is chasing him." Thirty seconds later, his voice lowered and grew softer, "Son-of-a-seacook, the bastard got away. Our guy is coming back."

Above the clouds, the night was clear and cold, and the winds at their twelve thousand foot altitude pushed them 40 mph faster over the ground than they were flying through the air.

"Sixty minutes tae th' targit wee jimmies." Charley's Scottish brogue was becoming understandable most of the time—probably because the crew was getting used to it.

"That's a few minutes ahead of schedule." Steve felt the beginning of his adrenalin rush. "Everyone, sit up straight and pay attention. And Jeffrey, try to be more specific when you warn a bomber!"

A lancaster blew up half a mile ahead, and the debris went underneath them. Jeffrey said, "I don't have a bomber identification on my screen, and I can only see what's behind us. There are two more Lancs' with fish ponds at the front—I don't know why they didn't pick up that fighter!"

Willie watched pieces of airplane fall to the earth under his feet, followed by the familiar white ball and a red glow. He felt his stomach knot, checked the straps on his parachute and strained his eyes in the weak starlight, trying to find a black shadow in the black sky before it killed him.

Eight hours earlier:

Walther pulled a chair to the living room window so he could sit while watching the street in front of his house. Tonight, Walther would satisfy the requirement for his 'winter camping' badge; he would sleep in a tent on the Wartberg, a hill overlooking Heilbronn. His Pimpfe group had camped overnight twice before, but not in winter.

Marita had found everything on the list the Pimpfe leaders had sent home with Walther but decided he would need more to keep him warm. She brought two sweaters, a pair of wool socks and a blanket from Walther's bedroom, just in case, and was stuffing them into his duffle bag when Walther intercepted her.

"No, Mutti!" He said, shaking his head as he pulled at the sweaters and blanket. "We are not allowed to take anything that isn't on the list!" Marita stepped back and let him throw them on the floor. He tightened the drawstring on his bag and looked up at his mother. "Don't worry about me, Mutti; I'll be alright." He stood up straight and smiled at her. "I've got the knife Vati gave me, and I'll use it if an animal tries to eat me!" He pulled the Swiss Offiziersmesser out of his pocket and showed it to her. She laughed and pulled him against her leg, rubbing his hair with her hand.

She said, "Okay, I won't worry, but I will need you back here in the morning. Promise me that you will come back to protect me!"

Walther looked at her strangely. "Of course, I'll come back to protect you, Mutti—I will always come back!"

A Wehrmacht Lastwagen pulled up to the curb with a squeal of brakes, and Walther ran to the door before his mother could catch him. He opened it as his group leader, Ingrid, was about to climb the steps. He was so excited he bounced down the steps with his duffle bag without saying goodbye.

Marita reached the door too late. She yelled to him, "Goodbye, Walther! Don't give Ingrid any trouble!" waving her hand until Ingrid forced him to look at his mother and wave back. Marita watched the young leader help him over the tailgate into the canvas-covered back of the Lastwagen, where ten screaming nine-and-ten-year-old boys enthusiastically greeted him. The Lastwagen roared away, and Marita waited on the step until it was out of sight. She felt a little bit guilty—she was happy to be alone. Annalisa had taken the girls to her home in Weinsberg, and Marita looked forward to stretching out on the sofa, listening to the radio, and later, soaking in the bathtub with a glass—perhaps a bottle—of sweet wine.

Deutscherundfunk listed a Berlin Philharmonic performance of Beethoven's Sixth Symphony beginning at 17:00h, part of a concert conducted by Wilhelm Furtwängler. Marita planned to spend two hours listening to beautiful pastoral music and leisurely eating a quiche, followed by Belgian chocolates that Erik had sent. She had shamelessly hidden them from the children, telling herself she would save some for them. The plan included a soak in the bathtub and a glass of wine following the symphony—she would take the bottle to the bathing room with her. Marita headed for the kitchen to warm up the quiche.

⬦⬦⬦⬦⬦⬦⬦⬦⬦⬦⬦⬦⬦⬦⬦⬦⬦⬦⬦⬦⬦⬦⬦⬦

As he scanned the green tube for strangers, Jeffrey kept his eye on a bogey he was certain represented a mosquito. His eyes caught a new flash on his screen—an unfamiliar blip slowly gaining on the mosquito. He waited for another sweep, then spoke to Steve through the intercom.

"I've been keeping an eye on our friendly bogey behind us. There is another aircraft gaining on him, probably not friendly. Right now, it's about a mile behind and closing. If it's at the same altitude, it means trouble."

Without answering Jeffrey and against formation protocol, Steve immediately broke radio silence on the HF bomber frequency.

"Friendly mosquito above and behind the formation—'C for Charley' here—we have a bad guy coming up on your six, now less than a mile behind you, over."

"Thanks, 'C for Charley,' we'll take care of it. Keep us informed—out." Danny turned to Larry; they were listening to the same frequency.

Danny said, "Maybe we should get out of here."

⬦⬦⬦⬦⬦⬦⬦⬦⬦⬦⬦⬦⬦⬦⬦⬦⬦⬦⬦⬦⬦⬦⬦⬦

Karl had seen the spot on his radar as soon as it pulled in behind the bombers. The blip was maintaining a constant distance behind the formation.

"Erik, I've got something two kilometres dead ahead, and I assume at our flight level. It's not a bomber because it isn't in the stream, but it's stationary with respect to the bombers."

He waited for Erik's reply, and when he didn't, Karl said, "It's probably a mosquito escort waiting for us to move on the bombers." He waited for an answer, but none came. He knew Erik was thinking, so he stayed silent for as long as his curiosity let him, then asked, "What are we going to do?"

When Erik had turned over all of his options, he finally said, "We're going to have to kill him... If we don't, we will have to stay behind him, and in that case, we might as well go home."

Karl wasn't sure what Erik was going to do. "Should I leave the set on? A bomber might be tracking us...."

Erik checked the throttles. "Yes, but only until I have him visually." The throttles on the Bf 110 were open. Erik put the nose down a little to gain speed, hoping he was above the fighter and could slip under it. mosquito crews and their radar faced forward—there was no chance they could see Erik's messerschmitt, making the mosquito a sitting duck if the altitude worked out. He thought for a moment of firing from behind with his nose cannons, but with no tracer ammunition, he might miss, and that would be suicide.

Jeffrey reported to Steve. "The bogey is gaining speed; I think he's descending. My guess is he will try and kill the mosquito with the up-firing guns."

Steve keyed his mike, still connected to the squadron frequency. "mosquito, it looks like the bad bogey is descending and increasing speed, closing fast. He probably has the upward-firing guns and intends to use them on you—be careful, over." Steve's hands squeezed the column so hard his knuckles whitened.

"Thanks, 'C for Charley.' Keep watching and tell me when he's within a hundred yards, out."

<hr>

"Okay, Karl, I've got him in sight... You will shoot... Get ready!" Erik pulled the throttles back a little as he approached the mosquito, slowing the 110 so there was only a small difference in their speeds. His messerschmitt was two hundred metres behind and forty metres below the mosquito.

As he approached, even the bottom of the mosquito was beautiful, and Erik felt a twinge of guilt at what he was about to do. He let his mind wander as his fighter crept under the beautiful machine. Erik imagined there was no war... He put himself in the mosquito with the British pilot.

They talked about flying, compared the mosquito with other fighters, did a few steep turns...

Erik raised his eyes to the gunsight in the canopy over his head, dreading the deed that duty demanded.

"Now!" Jeffrey yelled into the intercom. Steve keyed his mic...

Larry heard, "Now! He's there now, over!" and without answering pulled the throttles back to idle, yanked the stick into his stomach, kicked the rudder and stick hard left, then right. The mosquito zoomed up two hundred feet, wobbled, stopped, and the messerschmitt passed under it without firing.

Larry opened the throttles and pushed the stick ahead as the wings stalled—the engines responded instantly, the propellers bit the air, and Larry thanked God for the 'negative g' carburetors on the new Merlin engines. As the mosquito's nose dropped, it accelerated, and the ME 110 appeared in the windscreen, barely a hundred yards in front of Larry's guns. He guided a stream of bullets into the night fighter, holding the firing button, steering the orange tracer necklace with the flying controls until the German fighter exploded in a ball of fire, breaking up as it fell away from him.

The mosquito disappeared behind Erik just before the sight reached it. With a sickening knot in his stomach, he pushed the stick ahead in a desperate effort to save himself, knowing it was too late. Tracers arced over the canopy and fell in a long curve in front of him, descending until the cannon shells and bullets from the mosquito's guns found their target.

Erik didn't hear his fighter explode, and Larry and Daniel notched their eleventh night-fighter kill.

Larry said, "Danny, check the ammunition," more to slow his senses and heart rate back to normal than anything else.

Danny answered, "We've got enough in the cannons for another ten seconds and maybe a few more seconds than that in the brownings." Danny's voice shook.

"Okay, Danny, we're going to stay with the stream, but we will only attack a fighter if he is in a position to take out a bomber. He took his hand from the stick, tried to keep it from shaking, then grabbed the controls again.

Danny said, "Nice work, Larry—I don't mind saying you scared me shitless." Larry had never heard Danny admit to being scared before.

"Without the guys in the bomber, we would be the ones burning on the ground." Larry wanted to thank them, but radio silence was more important. He opened the throttles a little and began a sweep across the rear of the bomber group while Danny searched the radar screen for fighters. They were quiet, their nerves strung as tight as the 'E' string on Danny's fiddle.

CHAPTER THIRTY-FIVE

4 December 1944

"If you are going through hell, keep going."
Winston Churchill

THE SIREN SOUNDED AT TEN MINUTES TO SEVEN, at the precise moment Marita slid down the sloped back of the large porcelain bathtub into the hot water. The candles' flickering light played in a glass of wine on a small table beside the tub. She had put a handful of Belgian chocolates beside the wine and the open bottle on the cold floor within easy reach.

Marita considered staying where she was but felt Erik's presence declaring his 'no exceptions' rule. She sighed, grabbed the sides and lifted herself to a standing position.

A sudden, strange moment of grief gripped her, and a sense of urgency drove her to move fast. She dried herself, extinguished the fire in the heater, blew out the candles, and hurried upstairs in her bathrobe. She dressed and ran outside, where Major Richter and Frieda waited for her on the street. They began walking with the same sense of urgency Marita felt, increasing their pace until, a hundred metres before reaching the General Wever Turm, they were close to running. People entered the tower in a silent, orderly stream, and the room was half full when they found their seats.

Frieda held Marita's hand. "I don't understand why I'm so afraid tonight—do you think that means something?" Frieda pushed closer to Marita, pulling her friend's arm against her side and holding it tightly. She shivered and looked into the distance.

Marita slid closer, put her arm around Frieda's shoulders and brought her mouth close to Frieda's ear, "I'm nervous too, and I feel sad. It started while I was in the bathtub. I can't explain it, but…" And suddenly she knew… "Oh God, I'm afraid something has happened to Erik!" Tears filled Marita's eyes, flowed down her cheeks, and she sobbed.

Frieda affectionately pushed Marita's hair back. "It's the war and the tension of so many raids. Helmut thinks it will all be over soon, and we'll be able to live normal lives again." Frieda put Marita's hand on her lap and held it in hers. "I've had strange feelings all day—it must be *Föhnkrankheit*; when the *Föhn* winds come out of the mountains, it always makes me crazy. Sometimes Helmut has to get out of the house!"

The room became silent as the sound of a single, low-flying aircraft, then a barely discernible explosion penetrated the thick walls. A few seconds later, a bright white light shone through the open door as though it were suddenly daytime. The light was still bright when the guard closed the door.

Marita, startled, looked at Helmut, whose face suddenly darkened. He said, "I don't like the look of that—they've never dropped that type of flare before."

Erik had explained the usual target marking routine to Marita, how the British used *Fallschirmfackeln*, flares suspended under a tiny parachute, to light the objective before the target aircraft dropped their coloured markers.

Five minutes later, the din of people talking paused again when another low-flying airplane flew over the shelter, setting off another round of speculation.

Helmut answered Marita's question before she asked it. "That's likely a mosquito dropping the target markers. Your husband described the routine, and if this is an RAF attack like he described, the bombers will be here in a few minutes."

The people close to them heard his remarks and stopped talking. Everyone had heard and read enough about bomb markers to be terrified, and they knew Marita's husband and the head of the Gestapo would understand what they were talking about. The rumour of an impending full-force British bomber attack flew through the room in whispers, and many of the trapped people quietly prayed the rumour was wrong.

Suddenly cold, Marita shivered as she said to Frieda, "Thank God the children are safe. Walther is camping at the Wartberg Tower, and the girls are in Weinsberg with Annalisa and Jonas."

Marita held Frieda's cold, shaking hands, fighting the intuition that told her to get out of the shelter—run away—go to the river! She looked at the soldier guarding the door. Marita knew him to be a sixty-year-old veteran and a fierce Nazi, and she knew he wouldn't let anyone past him.

A distinct rumble came from nowhere, and then, as it grew, from everywhere. The tower was surrounded by the sound…its intensity increased until, in minutes, it found the tower's frequency and shook it, rattling the metal air vents.

A flak shell exploded—Marita knew the sound from previous raids—at first distant…then closer, rising in volume and frequency as the purveyors of death came closer and the rumble became a horrifying roar. The floor vibrated, the steel door rattled on its hinges, and the concrete walls shook.

Marita's instincts screamed, "We must get out!" She touched Helmuth's arm and looked into his face—there was no fear, but the resignation she saw terrified her more.

Helmut grasped the edge of the bench with both hands. "I'm afraid the war may not have ended soon enough for us." The shaking building and the rumble of two million horsepower drowned out Helmut's foreboding to everyone's ears but Marita's and Frieda's.

Marita put her mouth close to Helmut's ear. "I have a terrible feeling! Something compelling is telling me we should get out of here and go to the river! Now!"

He shook his head. "The door is closed and guarded—it's too late; that man won't open it for anyone, not even for me!" Marita looked at the old soldier standing at the door, sweeping the room with his eyes, looking for something. She thought he looked as though he were looking for traitors against the Reich; he held his MP40 machine pistol ready to fire.

No 83 squadron under Lieutenant Pereira followed the 'dash' signal of Oboe at twelve thousand feet while his navigator listened intently for the 'dot' string. Gradually, the dot signal strengthened until it crossed and mingled with the dash. Pereira said, "Time," and the bomb-aimer released the Parachute flares. They fell to two thousand feet above the ground, where barometric fuses ignited them. The burning flares, still in clouds, lit up the city below and the sky above as though it were midday.

Seven minutes later, master bomber Maurice A. Smith flew his mosquito over the city, under the clouds in the bright light of the flares.

He dropped his red markers in the town square a few metres in front of the burned-out city hall. Another mosquito from No 627 squadron marked the railway yards and the docks with yellow markers. Three minutes later, the armada of two hundred and eighty-two lancaster bombers began dropping the one-thousand-two-hundred-and-fifty-four tons of bombs they were carrying. Four hundred and fifty tons of them were incendiaries designed to burn the city to the ground.

As 'C for Charley' approached the target area, Willie searched for shadows or reflections off perspex and whirling propellors while Jeffrey stared at the blips on his fishpond display. It was Jeffrey's job to report unusual activity on his screen to Steve, but no night fighters approached their aircraft or any aircraft near them. The mosquito escorts continued to crisscross above the formation, and occasionally, German night fighters shot down a lancaster or lost one of their own. But for Steve and his crew, the mission was going as planned.

Jake Collier, the bomb-aimer, guided Steve to the red marker in the now-burning city's center. The red flares still burned brightly in the middle of an enormous orange fire as he flipped the guards off the release switches and dropped the load in the prescribed sequence. Jake announced, "Bombs gone!" and Steve stayed on the bombing course until after the flash of the cameras that would record the damage. The fire's heat burned away the clouds, making the burning city clearly visible below. The cameras flashed, and Steve immediately turned right as ordered in the briefing. Jake got up from the bomb aimer's position on the floor, uncomfortably warm from the heat radiating upward from the ground.

The bomber shook at the same instant Willie heard an explosion in the forward section, followed by the sound of shrapnel rattling along the side of the fuselage, remarkably like hail on a tin roof. Pieces of shrapnel and aluminum hit the rear stabilizer and rudder, peeling off chunks of aluminum skin to reveal the ribs underneath.

"The controls are fucked." Steve yelled at Phillip as he fought to keep the plane in the air. "Get those engine fires out before a tank blows!"

Phillip Carpenter, the flight engineer, cut off the fuel, hit the fire extinguishers and feathered the propellers on the inboard engines. The propellers stopped—the fire in the engines died. Phillip opened his mouth to report the fires out, and the starboard engine reignited, setting fire to fuel flowing out of the ruptured wing tank.

Steve said, "We've got to abandon ship—the tank is going to blow!" Phillip flipped his jump seat to the side as Steve shouted into the intercom, "Abracadabra, abracadabra, jump, jump!"

Following Willie and Ronnie's premature exit at Mailly, Steve had decided there was indeed merit in the official method of announcing the need to evacuate the aircraft. In the RAF, the only phrase that officially qualified to tell the crew to get out of the plane was the one Steve had just used.

Charley had the hatch open when Jeffrey knelt with his parachute ready. He slid easily out of the opening and disappeared, followed by Jake. Phillip clipped his parachute on the harness and held the bundle over his head, following the procedure set in their rehearsals. He slid out of the hatch and disappeared. Steve was the last to leave. His parachute opened when he pulled the handle, and he counted six parachutes scattered around him—everyone was out—and the enemy waited on the ground.

When Willie heard the jump order, he checked the clips, turned the release on his belts, swung his turret 90 degrees, opened the door, heaved himself backwards, and a two-hundred-mile-per-hour wind blew him into space. The last thing he saw before he pulled the 'D' handle was Heilbronn, a sea of flames stark against the black earth and sky. The parachute blossomed, yanking him to a stop facing the burning city. Willie stared at the horrifying scene, mesmerized. He imagined he could feel the heat, thought he could hear screams. He heard Mozart's 'Dies Irae,' the 'Day of Judgment,' ringing in his head.

Willie twisted in his shrouds, grabbed a handful on one side and pulled. The parachute slowly turned until he could see six parachutes bunched together. Only one chute was not falling away from him, and he surmised that Ronnie was the maverick. They were about two hundred yards apart—and Ronnie was below him. Willie was small and had the same standard-issue parachute as the others. Suspended in space, he watched the rest of the crew fall away from him. They would be more than a mile from him when Willie reached the ground at least five minutes after they did. He could see he was drifting south, away from the fires, although he was almost two miles above them.

The fire reflected from the iridescent white parachutes, and Willie assumed they would be visible for miles. Someone would be waiting for them when their feet hit the ground, and they would be the enemy. He reminded himself that he had the Geneva Convention to protect him and prayed the Germans agreed.

◇◇◇◇◇◇◇◇◇◇◇◇◇◇◇◇◇◇◇◇◇◇◇◇◇◇◇◇◇◇◇

The temperature in the tower rapidly increased to an unbearable level. Marita put on her wool coat, lifted the collar to shield her neck and face from the intense heat and pulled the brim of her hat down to meet it.

Helmut removed his uniform coat, and Frieda was down to a thin blouse and skirt. Marita tried but couldn't convince them to do the opposite. She and Erik had discussed this scenario, and she could hear his voice, "Marita, you must protect your skin from intense heat; it is the same as extreme cold. Do not take clothing off; put it on!"

Smoke filled the room through the ventilation system, and the temperature climbed. Marita's eyes watered, and she closed them; she pressed her mouth and nose against her collar, breathing through the fabric. Some of her neighbours began to cough uncontrollably—children cried and screamed in frustration as they rubbed their eyes. Helmut pulled Marita and Frieda off the bench. "We must get on the floor!"

The air was better but worsened quickly. Within minutes, Marita gasped, trying to find oxygen in the thickening smoke. An older woman fell off a bench and lay on the floor without moving. A child went to her hands and knees, gasping. She vomited everything in her stomach, then fell on her side, squeezing her eyes shut and crying.

Helmut struggled to his feet, shouting over the steady crash of bombs, "There's no oxygen here; we've got to get out; we'll suffocate if we stay! We must get to the river!" He pushed Frieda toward the door, reached behind to pull Marita. The door was open, the guard was gone, and people streamed from the tower exits into what was becoming an inferno. Helmut found an opening in the flow of crying, gasping, desperate people.

Their eyes filled with smoke and tears, people bumped into one another, and Marita struggled to stay on her feet as she descended the sloping ground toward the river. The heat seared exposed skin, wisps of smoke rose from her clothes; sharp, unbearable pain stabbed her scorched face.

376

The air alternated between waving clouds of gray smoke and tongues of red flames devouring the oxygen. A pyre of flames disappeared and then, fed by the ferocious wind, returned to consume what it had missed. Choking smoke limited visibility to a few feet, then whirled upward. Marita's instincts told her to go downhill; she must go to the river. Her eyes burned, she closed them to slits, saw people stagger and fall down the hill, some with their clothes on fire. Marita hesitated and Helmut pushed her past them, saying, "Go to the river!"

She pulled her coat tight against the scorching wind and hid her gloved hands in the sleeves. Hot sand and small stones picked up by small, superheated whirlwinds embedded themselves in the exposed skin of her face. Leaves on the trees turned black, shrivelled and dis-integrated without a visible flame. Marita held the fabric of her coat's collar against her mouth so she could breathe through it—she feared the hot gases would cook her lungs and windpipe. People fell, gasping; most died silently.

"The river! We must get in the river!" Helmut gasped as he pulled the women, one on each arm. There were only a few people still standing. Marita staggered forward, but Frieda screamed and fell, her hair and blouse on fire. She took her hands away from her face to beat at the flames, and Marita could see that heat had shrivelled black wrinkles across her face. Marita and Helmut beat at the fire with their hands until Marita's gloves smouldered and began to burn her hands. Helmut's gloveless hands were scorched black. Frieda's skirt burst into flames, and her hoarse screams became a whimper. They died and she lay still. Marita stared at the fire eating Frieda's body.

Helmut pushed Marita down the hill, yelling, "Go! There's nothing to do!"

Marita stumbled thirty metres farther, fell to her knees, tried to get up but couldn't. Helmut put his burnt hands under her armpits, lifted her and shouted, "Walk! Go!" but she couldn't. He bent down, folded her body over his shoulder and back and staggered toward the water, now only twenty metres farther. His pants smoked, a piece of phosphorous burned his hair, his scalp. Helmut gasped, and Marita beat at the flames with her hand, trying to sweep them away. Burning phosphorous landed on Marita's back and arm, burning through her coat into her muscles—she could smell the burnt flesh—the pain was unbearable. Helmut held her tight and staggered forward. When she struggled, he tightened his grip.

Helmut reached the river with his clothes on fire, threw Marita in the water and collapsed on the muddy bank.

The cold water shocked every nerve in Marita's body. She rolled in the shallow water, the pain lessening. She gasped, rolled onto her back, breathed, turned over and lifted herself to her hands and knees. She looked to where Helmut lay on the bank, a metre from the water's edge, his body burning.

◇◇◇◇◇◇◇◇◇◇◇◇◇◇◇◇◇◇◇◇◇◇◇◇◇◇◇◇◇◇◇◇

The low, almost indiscernible rumble seemed to come from everywhere—Ingrid noticed it before the boys.

"Hush, boys; I think I hear thunder."

The boys stood still, listening—the steady rumble was too persistent to be thunder—Ingrid knew it wasn't. She switched her mind to danger, and her protective instincts kicked in.

"I want you to listen to me. Those may be British bombers on their way to bomb our city, and we might have to hide in the woods." Ingrid looked at the curious children. "First, I want two of you to scout out a place where we can go. Walther and Peter, you are the scouts. Report back in five minutes!"

Walther ran, anxious to play the game. He checked over his shoulder; Peter was behind him and gaining.

The sound of a single bomber flying overhead stopped the boys in their tracks, and as Walther turned around, night became day.

"Wait, boys! Stop!" Ingrid yelled and beckoned to the rest of the Pimpfe group. "We'll go with you."

A ball of fire burst in the distance and fell out of the bottom of the clouds. The boys, mesmerized, stared as it became a massive splash of light on the black horizon, then glowed red. Walther pointed at the burning bomber, now a glow dying on the horizon. "I'll bet my Vati shot that Englander down! He flies a night fighter, and he will shoot down all the bombers! Vati told me he would protect us!"

"Yeah!" Peter looked at Walther, his face glowing with pride to have a famous friend. Another bomber burst into flames, plummeting through the clouds and dragging a tail of fire. Peter said, "I wish my father was a fighter pilot!" He looked at Walther. "My father is a prisoner in Russia.

He can't even fight anymore!" Walther said, "Maybe he can escape; then he can fight like my father!"

Ingrid gathered the excited boys around her at the edge of the woods. They jumped and cheered when another bomber fell.

"Your Vati got another one!" shouted Peter. Walther was fast becoming a celebrity.

The excited boys pointed at their houses, lit by the *Fallshirmfackeln* floating down through the clouds. A plane flew low over the city and dropped a red flare in the town square. Another dropped yellow flares over the *Industriegebiet*, the docks and the railway yards.

Ingrid covered her face and screamed, *"Gott in Himmel, nein!"* She repeated the phrase over and over. The rumble of a thousand engines shook the ground; yellow and orange flak burst above the clouds, and the sound overwhelmed the boys' cheers until they stared, silent, gathering around Ingrid as she faced the oncoming terror. She was eighteen, a leader in the *Bund Deutsche Madel,* and this was not supposed to happen.

Walther tapped Ingrid's elbow. "What's happening? Will people die?"

Ingrid lowered her tear-filled eyes and said, "I don't know, Walther, but I think we should pray." She beckoned the children close to her and began reciting, "Our Father who art in Heaven, hallowed be Thy name...." Walther closed his eyes as his mother had taught him and said the prayer with her. Twenty little boys were no match for over a million straining horsepower, and as the noise increased, Walther could barely hear himself. He lost track of the prayer and opened his eyes, found Wacksstrasse 21 and searched the sky for bombers; he could hear them above the clouds. The sound moved over his house.

<hr>

Five hundred phosphorous incendiary bombs landed on the flare in the town square—fire splashed outward; a building instantly burst into flames, then another. Minutes later, clouds of bombs fell, widening the inferno over all of Heilbronn, and still, the bombers kept coming. The sound at the Wartberg watchtower made it impossible to talk. Thousands of explosions started fires—orange tongues, then walls of flames rose above the houses and spread throughout the city—Wacksstrasse 21 disappeared in the smoke and flames. Walther fell to his knees, his mouth open in a scream no one heard.

Walther looked for the General Wever Turm and found it isolated, alone in a pool of darkness. He stopped crying; his mother was safe. But then flames leapt toward it as bombs exploded in the dark pool. In seconds, a sea of fire surrounded the tower.

Only Walther heard his screams. "Mutti! Mutti, I'm sorry!" He tried to stand but gave up, knelt, and sobbed at the ground. He cried, *"Mutti! Bitte, Verzeih' mir!"* Ingrid knelt beside him, pulling his head to her breast and crying soundlessly, her tears falling into his thick hair.

Twenty boys stared at the conflagration, awestruck as fire devoured the city. The inferno reached into the sky above the Wartberg; heat followed the ground up the hill to where the terrified boys watched their homes disappear in an orange and black sea. A wave of burning gas engulfed the General Wever Turm, and Walther shouted, *"Mutti! Mutti! Nein!"* and pounded his small fists on Ingrid's chest.

The disaster unfolding before them became too much for innocent minds—the boys sobbed hysterically—Walther screamed, *"Mutti! Mutti!"* over and over. But the roar of exploding bombs, fire moaning its satisfaction as it devoured the city, and the roar of a thousand unmuffled engines overwhelmed his cries of grief.

Ingrid tried to control the children, herding them into a circle around her, but the words she intended to comfort them died when they left her mouth. Finally, she sat on the ground with them, putting her arms around one, then another as they voiced their agony and grief to the burning heavens.

⋄⋄⋄⋄⋄⋄⋄⋄⋄⋄⋄⋄⋄⋄⋄⋄⋄⋄⋄⋄⋄⋄⋄⋄⋄⋄⋄⋄⋄⋄⋄

Marita breathed, sobbed, and breathed again. She removed her heavy, soaked, charred coat and sucked cooler air into her burned lungs. She crawled into deeper water until she was swimming away from the tower, away from the fire. The frigid water cooled the air close to it and the heavy, cold air was full of oxygen. Marita filled her lungs, giving her the strength to pull water to her body with her hands and kick it behind her with her feet, propelling her toward the opposite shore.

She put her burned face in the frigid water, lifted her head, gasped, swam, immersed her face again, and the pain eased.

Marita swam desperately. The freezing water triggered every nerve in her body to scream at her brain, and her body became numb as her nervous system shut them down, one by one. She coughed relentlessly as she mechanically moved her arms and legs in the familiar breaststroke she had learned as a child in school. As she swam across the Neckar River, away from the flames, Marita felt an inexorable weakness slowly crushing her will as she looked at the dark shore, knowing she couldn't make it—her brain was shutting her body down. Her movements slowed, her mind drifted to her children...safe...no need to go on....

"Ein Boot! Dreh dich um!" Marita woke, saw people running up and down the riverbanks, heard shouts. A woman pointed. "Ein Boot!" Marita twisted. A boat, beside her; a hand...she reached out, sank, swallowed water. Hands grabbed her wrists, arms lifted her and laid her on a blanket on a flat deck. She coughed, spit, and gasped. Someone's gentle hands rolled her on her side. She saw a face, heard it say, "You're lucky—you may live," and then surrendered to pain and exhaustion.

<hr>

Willie lost sight of the other parachutes as they pushed into the scattered clouds, but Ronnie was closer and dropped almost as slowly as Willie. He was close enough, and enough starlight combined with orange light from the burning city glowing through the clouds, that Willie could recognize his friend's small form dangling below the white silk mushroom. Willie considered shouting to him but immediately dropped the idea.

"Is that you, Willie?" Ronnie raised his voice, a little too loud for Willie's liking.

"Yes, I'll see you on the ground." Willie strained to whisper loud enough that Ronnie could hear him. "Remember where we are!"

Ronnie said, "Yeah, we're in the land of Oktoberfest." He chuckled loud enough for Willie to hear him clearly. His form and then the white dome of his parachute dropped into a hole in an orange cloud, dug by the air compressed under the white silk. The mushroom disappeared entirely when the fluffy cloud folded back into the hole, leaving a dent in the flat orange top.

Another half-minute passed before Willie watched the air around his feet push the clouds aside. He looked up; he was passing through frozen water vapour flowing like tainted milk, coloured by the burning city's light. It poured into the centre of the white canopy, boiled outward, then disappeared into the darkness.

Willie spent two strange minutes in the flame-coloured cloud— enough to lose all sense of direction. Even up and down became a problem. His inner ears told him he was falling crooked, but his brain told him he couldn't be. He imagined all the bad things that could face him when he came out in clear air. But the ground was still almost half a mile below him when a wave of orange fluff spilled outward, and the fire devouring Heilbronn burst into view. The inferno's reflection off the clouds lit the ground below in an unnatural light.

◇◇

As Willie fell, it became evident that he would drift into a field behind a large barn built on the end of a house with a thatched roof. People lined the road on the other side of the buildings, standing with their backs to Willie, riveted by the fire burning where an hour ago Heilbronn had been.

Willie watched Ronnie land on his feet a few hundred feet in front of the observers, and he saw arms extend toward the fallen airman, pointing him out. Voices rose, loud enough for Willie to hear their anger. They were running toward Ronnie when the house and barn came between Willie and the unfolding drama.

He landed softly in the field behind the barn, rolled, and immediately released his chute. Running along the back of the barn, he rounded the corner, and spotted a big man standing in front of the house. He raced past him intending to cross the road to where Ronnie was running away from a mob, and the big man started on an intercept course.

Ronnie ran away from the people on the road, but they chased him, some carrying farm tools. A man with a rifle stopped to fire, and Ronnie fell. In seconds, his pursuers were on him, flailing at him. Ronnie screamed; men yelled.

Willie shouted, "No, don't...." but a hard blow from behind knocked him to the ground. He struggled to face his attacker, but strong hands pressed his face into dirt that filled his mouth so he couldn't cry out. A heavy body pressed him flat, and a deep voice spoke in his ear, *"Ruhe! Mach kein Geräusch!"* Something in the sound made Willie lie still. Ronnie's screams stopped, and Willie began to shake. A tightness constricted his throat, his eyes watered, and he gave up his struggle.

The weight released him; a pair of strong hands turned him over, and he looked into a kind, bearded face.

The man was old, his beard thick and gray. He picked Willie up in his arms as he would a small child and trotted to the house. He opened

382

the door, put Willie on his feet inside a room that could only be a kitchen, yelled something, closed the door and disappeared.

Willie stayed where the man had placed him until an old woman took his hand and, speaking softly and continuously, led him past the kitchen and down stone stairs to a storage room in the cellar. She pulled a barrel aside and, pointing and babbling urgently, left no doubt she wanted him to get into a wooden bin behind it. He did as she directed, and the old woman covered him with a blanket, then arranged potatoes, turnips, and carrots on top of him. Lying on his side, curled into a fetal position, he tried not to make a sound when he breathed. He heard her whisper something, then turn out the light and close the door.

Willie could hear the angry crowd, even through the cellar's thick stone wall. They banged on the door; he heard loud voices, shouting in tones filled with anger and threats. The old man and woman shouted at the mob but appeared to be losing the argument as the revenge-crazed pack pushed their way inside. They upended furniture and opened and slammed doors until finally, they were on the cellar stairs and headed for the storage room.

Someone opened the door; Willie heard two men instructing one another. They upset barrels and boxes, banged against storage bins, including Willie's hiding place, then left the room. The outside door slammed shut and the shouting faded.

For another ten minutes, Willie listened to the sounds of the old couple righting furniture and talking in subdued tones and waited for them to come to the cellar.

Five minutes later, the outside door opened again, and the shouting began as before. Willie guessed that the crowd had returned, hoping to catch him when he came out of hiding, but after another bout of shouting, they slammed the door, and all was quiet.

Another fifteen minutes passed before the old man pulled the vegetables off Willie. He stood up, handed the blanket to the old man, and said, "Thank you, sir." He tried a barely identifiable *"Danke schön,"* and the man gave a short nod.

The old man led Willie to the kitchen where the woman worked at a massive table that must have been built in the room. She sliced cheese and bread and piled it on a white cloth. When it contained all it would hold, she gathered the corners together and tied them. Her bearded husband sat opposite her, drawing a crude map on a piece of paper. He gave it to Willie. Willie pulled out his survival kit, unfolded the silk map supplied in every kit and laid it on the table. The man put his finger on a spot southwest of Heilbronn and then traced his finger to the Swiss border. The farmer then lifted his calloused hand and wagged his index finger in a contrary motion. He said, *"Keine Strassen!"* put his hands in front of him as though holding onto a steering wheel, made a motor sound with his lips, and shook his head. Willie nodded. He would not use the roads.

Willie took the man's arm and pulled him toward the door from the kitchen into the barn, but the old man resisted.

"We need to take care of the parachute!" Willie was frustrated by the blank look on the man's face.

"Fallschirm?" The old man imitated hanging from a parachute, and 'fall...' was another clue. *"Ja,"* said Willie, excited at the progress.

"Fertig schon—okay!" The old man waved his hands horizontally in the international sign for "Already taken care of."

"Yes, of course you did!" Willie nodded. He guessed that the man must have taken care of it while his wife hid him under the vegetables. He wanted to ask about Ronnie and was searching for a way to do it when the old man spoke.

"Leider ist ihr Freund Tod." The man pointed to where Ronnie had fallen and made a throat-cutting gesture. Willie got the point when his rescuer put a sympathetic hand on Willie's shoulder.

Willie went to the door, opened it and took a compass bearing, pointing with his arm. The old man nodded, and the old woman gave Willie the food. Willie kissed and hugged the old woman, shook the old man's hand and walked through the field, downhill toward a stand of trees.

The fires in Heilbronn burned fiercely, and the light reflecting down from the clouds showed every blade of grass, even though Willie was over ten kilometres from Heilbronn.

CHAPTER THIRTY-SIX

4–5 December 1944

"When you're at the end of your rope, tie a knot and hold on."
Theodore Roosevelt

MARITA FORCED HER EYES OPEN, and the light exploded, blinding her brain, then slowly dimmed until Walther's face smiled out of a bright haze. She tried unsuccessfully to return the smile, and he leaned over and kissed her. There were tears in his eyes, and, for a moment, Marita thought that she had died. But Walther spoke, and her heart soared.

"Mutti, es tut mir so leid." She tried to lift her right arm, but something held it down. She tried to talk, to tell her son he needn't be sorry, but couldn't form a word. Then Annalisa's voice came out of the haze.

"Yes, you can kiss Mutti, but don't touch her…she's very sick, but she's going to be fine."

Marita focused on the sound and found her Mother; Elke held one hand and Brigitte the other. Annalisa whispered to each girl, then released them. They stepped cautiously to the bed and kissed Marita's cheek. Annalisa moved to the side of the bed, and the girls stepped back to give her room. Tears glazed Marita's eyes, blurring her Mother's face as she spoke.

"Liebling, you've been asleep for two days. You are in the Wehrmacht hospital in Weinsberg, the children are fine, and you will be well again. Liebling—what you need now is rest."

Marita tried to talk—she had an urgent question but couldn't move her lips and tongue without unbearable pain. Tears filled her eyes, and her Mother's face became an unrecognizable muddle.

Annalisa gently touched Marita's shoulder. "Please, don't try to talk, Liebling." She sat on a chair beside the bed, cooing quietly as she gently rubbed a small piece of her daughter's exposed forehead.

A nurse pushed a needle into Marita's arm, and gradually, the muddle faded, and the haze returned. Marita tried with all her will to keep her Mother there, but everything disappeared. There was a question... she wanted to ask the question...

◇◇◇◇◇◇◇◇◇◇◇◇◇◇◇◇◇◇◇◇◇◇◇◇◇

When Marita next woke, her hands could move. There was pain, but it was bearable. The sun shone in the room, spilling over her bed. Annalisa sat on a chair beside her, hands in her lap, her chin against her chest, breathing deeply.

"Erik?" Marita whispered through her burned vocal cords.

Annalisa awoke, and Marita asked, "Where is Erik?"

Annalisa sat on the edge of the bed and put her hand on Marita's shoulder. "He didn't return from the mission the night they attacked Heilbronn. Officially, he's missing, but..." She squeezed her eyes shut, looked at the ceiling, and then returned to Marita. Marita saw her Mother's sadness and knew that Erik was dead. Annalisa's tears fell on Marita's pillow, and tears poured sideways out of Marita's eyes into the bandages covering her face, soaking them. She looked at her Mother, whispered, "I think I knew," and Annalisa smiled.

"Walther and the girls are outside, waiting for me to tell them they can come in. Do you feel up to it... Just for a minute?"

Marita said, "Yes, I want to see them. Do the children know?"

"Walther knows Erik is missing, but he still has hope." Annalisa left the room and returned a minute later with the children. They lined up on the side of the bed, touching the sheets, restraining themselves from hugging their Mother. Marita's eyes shifted to Walther and the girls, then to Annalisa.

"I want to live..." She tried to smile, "I need to know the truth…am I going to live?" The struggle to speak was immense—Marita began to cough, ripping her partially healed vocal cords. A nurse appeared and herded Annalisa and the children away from the bed. Annalisa looked around the nurse and said, "Yes, Liebling, you are going to live!"

Marita lost track of time—day and night were only the light and the dark that came and went—there was no pattern, only pain, and sometimes, merciful oblivion.

◇◇◇◇◇◇◇◇◇◇◇◇◇◇◇◇◇◇◇◇◇◇◇◇◇

The nurse pulled the bandage off her back in one short, hard pull. Marita yelled, then sucked in her breath; the nurse had told her the hospital had nothing for her pain. She had been in agony so long she had learned to

386

defeat it by pulling her mind into a room where visions were stronger than despair. She despised pain's ability to overwhelm her if she left the room, especially when her Mother and children were with her.

The nurse talked as she applied another bandage… She knew the value of distraction.

"They removed some muscle from your back and right arm. It was impossible to get the phosphorous out without taking some of the flesh, but the doctor says you will be fine—most of it will grow back. Your face is okay on one side, but the other side is not good. It will heal, and it may be possible to repair some of the damage later…" She leaned over and looked into Marita's eyes. "You are one of the lucky ones. Don't lose hope—the pain will end!"

Annalisa and the children stepped through the door and lined up against the wall. The nurse motioned for Annalisa to help Marita through the agony of turning over.

Marita gritted her teeth. She would not scream in front of the children. They accomplished the feat in seconds, and Marita successfully swallowed her agony. Annalisa and the children stepped aside to let the nurse go to her next patient. She stopped at the door, smiled at Marita, winked, then disappeared, her heavy leather shoes slapping the hallway floor.

Marita tried to smile at Annalisa without appearing pitiful. "I don't care about my face as long as you and the children can stand to look at me!"

Annalisa said, "We think you're beautiful," and Walther said, "I love you, Mutti." He put his head beside Marita's and kissed her undamaged cheek. The girls looked to Annalisa for permission, and she nodded. They climbed on the edge of the bed and gently hugged Marita, holding her as long as they could, given the awkward position.

Annalisa guided the girls away. "All right, children, it's time to go. Say goodnight to Mutti." She herded them out the door.

Five days after the bombing, the hospital had to release Marita to the care of Annalisa and Jonas. The hospital in Heilbronn no longer existed, and there was a desperate need for the beds jammed into the Weinsberg military hospital. Two nurses helped Marita into the car, and despite the terrible pain, she didn't make a sound. Jonas drove home very carefully, and Marita gritted her teeth and sucked in her breath with every move the car made.

Once inside the beautiful stone and stucco house, Annalisa and Jonas helped Marita to her bedroom and into a soft bed. Annalisa poked her with a needle, and she fell asleep again.

◇◇◇◇◇◇◇◇◇◇◇◇◇◇◇◇◇◇◇◇◇◇◇◇◇◇◇

Willie waited at the tree line until he was satisfied no one had followed him, then walked through the forest at a furious pace, dodging around trees and most of their branches. The Swiss border was a hundred miles away, and Willie had RAF food for a week and enough for another four days wrapped in the cloth.

Walking at night and assuming the clouds persisted, progress would be slow in the almost total darkness, but the winter solstice was not far off; the nights were long; he could walk sixteen hours every night. Willie wore enough clothing layers to survive in his turret, and, even considering the winter weather, he was confident he would be comfortable. He decided his chances were good.

Willie spent the rest of the long winter night walking due south, using a new non-military compass with fluorescent tips that Norma's father had given him, "just in case he fell out of the plane." James had intended the gift as an expensive joke, but Willie had packed it in his kit.

Morning dawned on his left, bright and clear, with frost on the ground and a crispness that Willie found exhilarating. He ate one of the old lady's pieces of black bread and cheese and drank from a brook crossing his path. While sitting beside the bubbling water, the sun broke through the trees, warming him.

Although Willie tried to avoid thinking of Ronnie's death, the vision haunted him, tempting him to continue walking in the daylight just to clear his mind. Instead, sticking to his plan, he picked a thicket of small trees to use as shelter for the day. It took him fifteen minutes to make a comfortable bed of spruce branches woven together so that the soft tips supported his weight. This time of year, the day would be short, and without using all of it for sleep, he would lose his edge. As he slept, the sunlight found its way through the thick branches but stayed low in the winter sky.

He woke late in the afternoon, knelt at the brook, splashed water on his face and unfolded the silk map. He had marked a line to the Swiss border, ending where Switzerland bulged into Germany north of Schaffhausen. It was possible to enter Switzerland there without crossing

388

the Rhine, and the stretch of the border where he planned to cross had no villages marked. By avoiding Stuttgart to the west, the map indicated that Willie could use forests for cover with only short stretches of open countryside to his destination. Satisfied that he could be at the Swiss border in seven days, Willie folded the map, untied the cloth and ate a little more of the cheese and black bread, ignoring his still persistent hunger and waiting for darkness.

⋄⋄⋄⋄⋄⋄⋄⋄⋄⋄⋄⋄⋄⋄⋄⋄⋄⋄⋄⋄⋄⋄⋄⋄⋄⋄⋄⋄

Wing Commander John Leech truly hated this part of his job, but it was his obligation as squadron commander to inform loved ones of their loss. Willie was now married to a British citizen who lived within thirty-five miles of Spilsby base, and Norma deserved to hear the news from his commanding officer face-to-face. Leech had called her parents, and they agreed to meet in the drawing room where Willie had made his dramatic entrance the last time John had assumed he was dead. This time, John was more certain of Willie's fate, but he decided to leave the door of hope open a crack until he heard from the Red Cross.

He pulled his borrowed Austin to the curb in front of the Stanfield home, having spent the forty-five minutes driving there trying to decide how to do the least damage. John settled on the Hippocratic Oath— 'do no harm' —which led to his decision to lie if necessary. His plan and his resolve were solid as he reached for the doorbell chain.

George opened the door before John could pull the chain, stepping aside as the Wing Commander stepped into the foyer. He took Leech's heavy wool coat and escorted him into the drawing room. The family had already gathered around the table, leaving John no choice of places. He shook hands with everyone and sat down in the only empty chair.

Norma was on his right, and he couldn't shake the feeling he was about to be shot by a firing squad. He hesitated, finding it difficult to say what he had planned to, and almost jumped up to kiss James when he stepped into the breach for him.

"We have been discussing the possibilities for this visit, and none seem pleasant—I take it this is not a social visit."

"No, sir, I regret to say that I do not bring good news. As you probably guessed, Willie is missing again." The wing commander began fiddling with his cup, rattling it on the saucer. Norma, sitting within easy reach, put her hand on his.

389

She said, holding his hand tightly, "He is missing, but not dead or captured? Again?" She didn't seem worried—she almost smiled.

Leech looked around the table, head bobbing like a chicken. "Yes, exactly, but let me explain everything before you come to any conclusions." Taking his hand off his cup, he leaned back in his chair, looked down at his little plate and began fiddling with his spoon. He could feel Norma looking at him and put it down before she could take it from him.

John put his hands in his lap, lifted his eyes and began the speech he had rehearsed in the car. "The night before last, Willie's lancaster left on a mission to bomb Heilbronn, a small city near Stuttgart and Nürnberg. Everything went as expected, and the operation was a success from Bomber Command's point of view. The destruction of the target exceeded expectations, with relatively few losses on our side. Unfortunately, 'C for Charley' was one of the eleven bombers we lost.

Witnesses in another lancaster saw Willie's aircraft hit by flak, then parachutes exiting the plane, probably all seven crew members, but we don't know for sure." He looked down at his hands, still folded in his lap. He waited a few seconds, letting his mind work out the next sentence. So far, he was on script.

He looked up, concentrating his gaze on Norma. His right hand headed for the spoon, but he stopped it just in time.

"We have information from the Red Cross that the forward crew members are in German hands as prisoners of war. We have a report from the Germans, confirmed by the Red Cross, that the mid-gunner, Ronald Cummins, parachuted successfully, but German soldiers killed him when he tried to escape. There is no report of Willie, nor his parachute or equipment." He put both hands on the table and resisted fiddling with his spoon again. "Unfortunately, I have no other information for you. We are waiting for news from the Red Cross, but if he were a prisoner, we should have heard something by now."

Norma reacted instantly. "He isn't dead! I would know if he were dead!" She looked straight into Leech's eyes, and he shifted his gaze to look at her father but saw only hope.

John spread his hands. "I can't, with a clear conscience, give you any encouragement that he may still be alive. We believe that the local people murdered Ronald, not German soldiers. Unfortunately, that is a common occurrence these days, and we believe they probably killed Willie as well, but we have no proof either way. They would have bailed out at the same time, and they likely landed close together. They were not far from Heilbronn, and the locals..." He looked at Norma. The hope he saw in her eyes would make the reality worse when it came, multiplying the shock. He changed his tactic to the cold truth as he saw it.

"I don't hold out any hope for Willie, and I don't think you should either. Without notification or proof of his death, I admit that a small chance of survival still exists, but the odds against it are astronomical. I believe that hope is the enemy of reason, and the stronger you hope when there is no possibility, the worse will be the fall when reason returns."

Norma spoke up confidently. "He is walking!" She looked defiantly at the Wing Commander. "Where would he go to escape from that part of Germany?"

"I admit, I have looked at it, and he would try to get to Switzerland. The nearest border point is about a hundred and twenty miles, and the border is lightly guarded. The German government permits German and Swiss citizens to cross at checkpoints, but the border on the German side is fenced and patrolled with armed soldiers everywhere else. He would need to avoid those soldiers and get through the barbed wire."

John didn't like how this was going. Willie had proved himself very resilient, but three escapes in nine months—not a chance!

"I went through that exercise because I knew you would ask the question, not because I think that is a possibility. There is so little chance that I would call it no chance that Willie is alive, and you should accept that."

James spoke, "You will excuse our skepticism, Wing Commander. You don't have a sterling record on that account, and to me, this is the most likely survival scenario of the three."

John opened his mouth to defend himself, but James cut him off with an edge to his voice. "This escape doesn't sound too difficult for someone as resourceful as Willie. I even gave him an excellent compass for a wedding present; I told him he should have a good compass if he kept insisting on walking around Europe in the dark." James laughed, and everyone but John joined in. Standing outside the door listening to the conversation, George poked his head around the corner.

"Shall I see if Willie is coming up the walk, sir?" He laughed weakly at his joke.

James laughed nervously and motioned for George to come into the room.

"Come in and have tea with us, George. He's your friend as well."

George pulled another chair to the table, and Gianna fetched a cup and a small plate. George picked up the pot and poured tea all around.

John left after tea, frustrated that the family's expectations weren't realistic. He had seen this before, and it never ended well. Despite his efforts to avoid giving them false hope, they had chosen to grasp at a single straw. But he knew from bitter experience that they were building a high platform from which to fall.

CHAPTER THIRTY-SEVEN

10 December 1944

"When a tree falls, it resounds with a thundering crash; and yet a whole forest grows in silence."
Jocelyn Murray

MARITA SLEPT UNTIL DAYLIGHT when Annalisa came into her room and said, "Everyone else has gone for a walk, and it's time we had a mother-daughter talk." She crossed the room with a breakfast tray of cold meat, cheese, and buns.

"That sounds ominous." Marita pushed down on the bed with her hands, raising herself to a sitting position. Despite excruciating pain, she smiled when her mother put a tray on a small table and sat next to her.

Annalisa took a deep breath, then delivered the message both had been dreading.

"I have bad news about Erik." She stroked the only strip of hair on Marita's head not covered by a bandage. "I'm afraid the Luftwaffe called last night and confirmed that he died in the raid."

Marita kept her head down and twisted the wedding ring on her right hand. "Are they certain?"

"Yes, they found Erik and Karl in their plane near Karlsruhe."

Annalisa took Marita's hand. As her eyes filled with tears, Marita said softly, "Mutti, what am I going to do? I can't imagine my life without him!"

Annalisa bowed her head, losing the battle against her own tears. "He was such a good man that I didn't think God would allow him to die. I suppose I thought He had destined Erik for some higher purpose." She lifted her head and looked past Marita. "What kind of world has God given us? Why would He allow so many good men to kill other good men? Doesn't He care about us?"

Marita and her mother wept silently, holding hands. After what seemed like a long time, Annalisa lifted her head, wiped the tears and said resolutely, "But there is no time for mourning right now...Erik is gone, and we are in a dangerous situation." She stood up. "And that is the second part of what I wanted you to hear. I had planned to tell you later, but I think we should get it over with now."

Marita wiped her eyes with her sleeve. "I'm ready to do whatever you need me to do. I have no more to lose." She lifted her chin, ashamed of what she had said. She looked at her mother and replicated her decisive tone as she said, "I'm sorry, that's not true! Many thousands are worse off than I am—I'm alive, and I have my children. We must find a way to survive!" Marita reached for her mother's hand. "I'm so sorry, Mutti... I'm acting like a spoiled child. I understand now what you went through when Vati died. At the time, I was so wrapped up in my own family, I'm afraid I ignored your pain."

Annalisa turned to the tray but seemed to decide against eating anything. "I was just now thinking about your father, but you knew that, didn't you?" Marita nodded, and Annalisa became more serious, "I know how you feel because I've felt it too, but we have to go on. I had time to grieve—something we can't give you."

Marita wasn't ready to eat either. She looked into the distance, although the wall was only four metres away.

"I've known that Erik was dead, but Walther talks incessantly about his father coming home to us and making everything right again. How am I going to tell him?"

"Do you want me to talk to him?" Annalisa touched her hand.

"No..." Marita shook her head... "I should do it, but I think it would be easier if you were here." She hesitated a moment, then went on. "Could I have a little time alone? Maybe we could have breakfast later?"

An hour later, Annalisa returned. She poured two cups of coffee and handed a tray to Marita. She peeled a cold egg for each of them, tore two Brötchen in half, and spread apple jelly on them.

"How are you feeling, dear?" Annalisa lifted her steaming cup.

Marita held hers in her hands. "I already knew in my heart that Erik was dead, but the certainty is harder than I expected. I will need time." She sipped her coffee and looked down at the pattern on the blanket covering the Federbett. She thought of the night of the raid when she felt Erik telling her to go to the shelter—and then, in the tower, he told her to run to the river. She turned to her mother and said, "Tell me about the damage to the city. How bad is it?"

Annalisa lifted her head and stared out the window. Her eyes glistened, and she wiped them with her napkin.

"The bombs and the fire destroyed the city. Countless people died… there are thousands of bodies to bury." Annalisa looked at her daughter, her face cloaked in grief. "Many of them are our friends, but there is no casualty list so we can find out, and there is no telephone number to call someone who knows."

Annalisa took the coffee cup from Marita, who had lost interest in it and was looking for a place to put it. She set it on the bedside table as she said, "The city has dug a mass grave at Kupfer… Marita, the city's centre, the entire Stadtmitte, is a pile of rubble, and the industrial area doesn't have one brick still on top of another. There was so much heat the people in the shelters suffocated and burned. I don't know how you survived!"

Marita touched her burned face. Until now, she hadn't found the courage to tell Annalisa about Helmut and Frieda and her escape to the river, and her mother tactfully hadn't asked. A shiver went through her body as she and Annalisa looked into one another's eyes. Her mother patiently waited while Marita struggled to find words.

◇◇◇◇◇◇◇◇◇◇◇◇◇◇◇◇◇◇◇◇◇◇◇◇◇◇◇◇◇◇◇◇◇

Marita began in a flat monotone, looking at the edge of the blanket she was twisting with her fingers. "When the fires started, our shelter became unbearably hot. People collapsed, weak and dying of suffocation. Helmut pushed Frieda and me down to the floor to find cooler air, but it was still too hot, and there wasn't enough oxygen. Helmut took us outside, but… Mother, the heat was unbearable! It hurt to breathe!" Marita's voice rose, the tone desperate. "The wind was so strong it was hard to stand... Trees burst into flames, burning leaves and pieces of wood landed on our clothes—and phosphorous from the bombs—my God, it was terrible! We had to get to the river, but the air was so hot! Mutti…I could feel my face burning. I couldn't breathe; there wasn't anything in the air, and I kept getting weaker. I tried to keep going but couldn't move my legs! People ran with their clothes on fire, then fell, screaming. Oh God, Mutti; the sound wakes me every night!"

She looked into Annalisa's eyes. "Helmut pushed us down the path toward the river, but Frieda's clothes burst into flames, and we stopped and tried to put them out. I saw her flesh burning…." Marita looked into the distance. "My God, poor Frieda…."

395

She paused, head down, sobbing, coughing, and Annalisa waited. Finally, Marita lifted her eyes and looked at nothing.

"Frieda died, and Helmut tried to force me to go on, but I couldn't stand. I fell—I wanted to die, but Helmut picked me up. He carried me to the river on his back." Marita sobbed, coughing, unable to speak.

Annalisa sat on the bed and put her arms around Marita's shoulders, but Marita pushed her away, rocking herself back and forth, looking at the foot of the bed.

"I remember him lifting me, the terrible pain in my back and arm... And then the cold water, but I don't remember...."

She sobbed, then coughed again until she thought her vocal cords would shred. Her voice was hoarse and weak when she said, "I saw him burning on the riverbank, only a step from the water. Helmut saved my life when he could have saved his own!" She wiped her face with her sleeve, a hopeless cause. "Did you know he promised Erik he would protect me with his life?"

Annalisa couldn't answer. Marita looked at her hands, twisting her wedding ring around on her finger.

"I tried to swim across the river, but I couldn't make it. When I couldn't swim another stroke, hands lifted me into a boat, and someone said, 'She may live.' I didn't know anything else until I saw you and the children."

◇◇◇◇◇◇◇◇◇◇◇◇◇◇◇◇◇◇◇◇◇◇◇◇◇◇◇◇◇◇

For more than a minute, neither Marita nor her mother spoke, and when Annalisa finally began, her voice broke.

"Marita, how horrible...I am so sorry I asked you to tell me." She held Marita's hand, waited momentarily, and took a deep breath.

"Jonas says we must leave Germany. He believes this area could be in the middle of a battle in a few weeks, and he wants to take us to his house in Switzerland."

Marita jolted herself back. "But what about the factory? Who will run the factory?"

"There is no factory; it burned to the ground and will take months to rebuild. The SS has ordered Jonas to set up a new factory in the salt mine, but there are no workers, and Jonas wants no part of working for the Nazis anymore. He has put money aside over the past years, and it's in a bank in Schaffhausen, near where he has a holiday house.

Switzerland welcomes Germans with money deposited there, and everyone who can afford to is getting out of Germany. Jonas wants us to live in Switzerland until the war is over."

Annalisa looked sympathetically into Marita's eyes.

"I'm afraid we must leave tomorrow afternoon. The trip will take about four hours and will be difficult for you, but we must go. Do you think you can do it?"

Marita wasn't worried about the pain. Determined that her life would go on for Walther and the girls, she said, "I'll be okay, and you mustn't worry about me; I come from a line of tough women." She managed a crooked smile. "Maybe it would be good to have a big glass of Schnapps before we leave?"

Annalisa laughed. "I will take the bottle with us!"

Marita held up two fingers. "If you leave it here, someone will steal it."

◇◇◇◇◇◇◇◇◇◇◇◇◇◇◇◇◇◇◇◇◇◇◇◇◇◇◇◇◇◇◇◇◇◇

Marita and Annalisa talked about the details of their move as they finished their breakfast. When they ran out of words and food, Annalisa took the tray and walked to the door, where she turned, and Marita knew what her mother would say.

"If it's all right with you, I will get Walther now."

"Yes, that's all right," Marita answered. "What about the girls?"

"I can handle that. I'm afraid we haven't much time. You should sleep after you see Walther."

Marita returned the smile, and her mother disappeared, closing the door behind her.

Five minutes later, Walther ran to his mother and sat on the bed beside her. "What do you want, Mutti? Oma said I should come to see you."

"I don't need you to do anything for me right now, Walther; you take such good care of me—I am so proud of you." She kissed him on the forehead and took both his hands in hers. "I want to talk to you about your father."

Walther lowered his head, his eyes wet with tears that threatened to flow. He spoke into his chest, "Is Vati dead?" He lifted his head and looked at his mother. Her heart broke as she looked at her son, holding back his tears, trying to be a man. She knew that he knew what she had to say.

"Yes, they found him and Karl in their crashed plane. He was shot down in the raid on Heilbronn, trying to protect us."

397

Walther struggled to keep his head up without crying, but he finally gave in to his grief and fell on his mother's lap, crying his heart out. She stroked his head and waited, silently weeping with him.

Walther sobbed for a few minutes, then fought to regain control. He forced himself up from his mother's lap and announced, his voice filled with determination, "I am the man of the family now, and I will take care of you and my sisters. Vati told me to take care of our family, and I promised I would, so you don't need to cry anymore." He caught a sob by holding his breath, then wiped his face with his sleeve.

"I'm going to my room now, but I will return if you need me to help you. I love you, Mutti!" He kissed his mother, ran to Annalisa and wrapped his arms around her, sobbing. She stroked his hair and kissed the top of his head. He let her go, swallowed his sobs, and, holding his breath, looked back at his mother and smiled. Marita could hear his muffled cries as he went down the hall, and her heart broke again.

Half an hour later, Walther returned, red-eyed but under control. He went to his mother and put the Swiss Offiziersmesser in her hand. "I want you to keep this until there is no more war. I will borrow it if I need to." He turned and ran back to his room. Marita looked at the red-handled knife with the white cross and remembered the day Erik had given it to Walther. She tightened her grip on it for a few minutes, then laid it on the bedside table.

CHAPTER THIRTY-EIGHT

12 December 1944

Glücklich allein ist die Seele, die liebt.
(Only the soul that loves is happy.)
Johann Wolfgang von Goethe

WILLIE CHECKED ROAD SIGNPOSTS and route numbers whenever he could find them and adjusted his course when he needed to. Picking his way through the woods using his compass, he was fortunate to have clear nights with starlight and sometimes the sliver of a new moon. With his excellent night vision, the light was enough that Willie could hurry across roads and fields and make relatively good time through the trees.

On the seventh day, Willie found himself in a forest looking at the Swiss border in the pre-dawn light. But first, he would need to cross a road, a narrow strip of trees, and a cleared area a hundred feet wide. Willie couldn't see the fence he expected at the border, and there would be guards… He decided to leave the road crossing and the final open space until complete darkness, still eight hours into the future. He walked uphill, deeper into the woods where he couldn't see the road, and anyone on it couldn't see him, made a bed of small boughs, something he was getting good at, and went to sleep.

◇◇◇◇◇◇◇◇◇◇◇◇◇◇◇◇◇◇◇◇◇◇◇◇◇◇◇◇◇◇◇◇

Private Schultz Schliederer worked his way down the hill toward the road, close to panic, dreading his sergeant's reaction when he returned to base. It was still three kilometres to where he was already supposed to be—his unit would be lining up for roll call.

Schliederer had spent the night in a barn with his girlfriend, and they had fallen asleep after consummating the proverbial 'roll in the hay.' His friends had agreed to cover for him as usual, but this time, he was too late for them to help, and the jig would be up at roll call. In the simple logic of his child's mind, he would automatically become a deserter—a *Verweigerer*—and the Wehrmacht, without exception, punished desertion with death.

His feet made no sound on the forest floor, damp with the morning dew, as he made his way around a thicket. He looked past it, searching for the best route between the trees and, out of the corner of his eye, spotted a British airman's uniform. He nervously unslung his rifle and cautiously moved toward the sleeping figure. Twenty feet from his helpless enemy, he aimed his gun and shouted, "Hände Hoch!" just like in American Western movies.

Willie sat up, put his feet under him and slowly raised his hands as he stood, carefully watching Schultz.

Schultz suddenly realized the barrel wasn't loaded and slid the bolt back and ahead, levering a bullet into it, but then, confused, put the safety on. The rifle was heavy; he was nervous and couldn't steady the barrel.

Willie's antagonist was young—pimples and craters scarred his boyish face, awakening a twinge of sympathy as Willie remembered those awful days. The boy's hands shook, the rifle's safety was on, and Willie considered running, suspecting that if the boy hit a moving target, it would fall in the 'accident' category. But the noise the shot would make in the still, quiet morning would no doubt attract unwanted attention, so Willie opted to await an opportunity to disarm the boy.

The young soldier waved his rifle toward the road, and Willie walked in that direction. It took two minutes to reach the trees beside it. The sound of a Lastwagen approaching obviously frightened the soldier, and instead of pushing Willie to the road, he motioned him to move deeper into the trees and duck into cover. The canvas-covered Wehrmacht truck drove past. The young man waited until he could no longer hear it, then looked both ways and listened for a few seconds before he waved Willie forward. Willie obeyed but slowly lowered his hands as the boy lowered his rifle. The boy was more interested in the threat from the road than in his prisoner.

When they reached the road, Willie said, "You're more afraid of the German army than I am!" The confused boy aimed the rifle at Willie. He was too close to his prisoner, and the safety was still on. Willie could have taken the gun out of the boy's hands, but instead pulled out cigarettes that had been part of his survival pack. He offered them to the young soldier, but the boy shook his head, and Willie stuffed them into his pocket. The boy relaxed and let the gun hang loosely at the end of his limp arms, its barrel almost touching the ground.

◇◇◇◇◇◇◇◇◇◇◇◇◇◇◇◇◇◇◇◇◇◇◇◇◇◇◇◇◇◇◇◇

A quiet mercedes rounded the corner before Willie or the boy heard it. There was no use running, and they stood on the side of the road. It stopped beside them. The boy had to step back from Willie so he could raise his rifle and point it in his general direction—but his prisoner didn't raise his hands.

A voice from the open driver's window asked the boy a question that made him suddenly nervous. He forgot about the gun and lowered the barrel as he gave a long answer to the question.

The young soldier didn't seem to be sure what the car represented. He tried to look and sound as mature as he could, but the effort ruined the result. He had his rifle's barrel jammed between himself and the mercedes' door and didn't look at Willie the entire time he spoke.

The gentle, fatherly voice in the car suggested something to the young soldier, and the boy responded in a child's whiny, almost tearful voice. He put the butt of the gun on the ground and pointed vaguely down the road, forgetting about Willie.

The man got out of the car, took the gun, opened the breech with a familiarity born of experience, ejected the shell from the barrel, removed the magazine and threw the rifle into the woods beyond the shallow ditch. He turned to Willie.

He was a middle-aged man, a good eight inches taller than Willie, with a kind face. He wore a dark suit and tie, not unlike the Gestapo wore while in Germany, but the car had two women and three children in it, ruling out that possibility. Willie was amazed when the man said, in near-perfect English, "My name is Jonas Schneider—I will help you and the boy get into Switzerland."

"Um...uh...thank you...sir..." Willie stammered, "I...I...would appreciate that."

The man turned his head to listen, looked toward the sound of another Lastwagen and said to Willie, "Take him to the trees! Quickly!" Willie grabbed the young soldier's arm, pulled him to the woods and pushed him down. Jonas Schneider stepped to the open door of his mercedes and unbuttoned his fly.

The stream of pee started just as the Lastwagen rounded the corner.

401

The soldiers in the back waved and hooted as they drove past, disappearing as Jonas finished relieving himself. Willie and the boy waited for Jonas to button his fly, then returned to the mercedes.

Jonas pointed at freedom in Switzerland. "Can you take the boy? There will be greater risk, but it will be possible if you do as I say. Will you take him with you?"

Willie nodded, "Yes, sir, you can trust me to look after him."

Jonas turned to the boy and spoke in German. When he finished, the young soldier nodded and bowed his head.

"I told the boy that you would take him across the border. I will find you and take you both to my house when you are in Switzerland. The boy is terrified; he thinks his commanding officer will shoot him if he returns to his unit, so he will not likely trouble you."

Jonas asked, "Do you have a compass?" and Willie said, "Yes, sir," as he dug it out of his breast pocket to show him.

"That's a better compass than the RAF would put in an emergency kit!" He pointed across the Swiss border. "Once over the border, walk to the south for thirty minutes—let us say a kilometre—for you, almost what you call a mile—then go precisely to the east. In about another thirty minutes, you will find a paved road. I will drive slowly back and forth on that road until we find one another. It will be dark, and I will turn on the interior light so you will know my car."

Jonas looked back at the mercedes. "First, I must drive my wife and family to my house, but I will come to find you two hours after dark. You must trust no one until I find you! German headhunters watch the roads and roam the woods. They look for Verweigerer, what you call deserters, and when they find them..." He made a slashing motion across his throat. "But if you walk a kilometre away from the border before you turn to the east, you will be okay." His expression was kind despite the drama in his voice. "Are all those things clear? My English is not so good, I am afraid."

Willie nodded as the sound of another approaching vehicle reached his ears. Jonas got into the mercedes, closed the door and drove smoothly away. Willie led his charge into the woods and pulled him down behind a fallen tree. A Kubelwagen sped noisily past with only a driver in it, and the driver kept his eyes straight ahead.

◇◇◇◇◇◇◇◇◇◇◇◇◇◇◇◇◇◇◇◇◇◇◇◇◇◇◇◇◇◇◇◇◇◇

It was not yet dark when Willie led the boy a hundred metres through woods toward the border and stopped at the edge of a wide opening. A path skirted the woods on the other side, and Willie assumed that guards used the well-worn trail to patrol the border.

Willie sat behind a small thicket of short bushes, watching the boy soldier without speaking. He tried the cigarettes again, but again, the boy refused them. Finally, Willie pointed at his chest and introduced himself. "Willie," he pronounced carefully, almost whispering.

"Schultz." The boy pointed at his narrow chest.

Willie tried to shake the young soldier's hand, but the boy bypassed it and embraced him. Willie nervously put his arms around him, and they remained in the hug for what seemed a long time.

Schultz pulled back with an embarrassed grin. He said, *Es tut mir leid.*"

Willie grinned and put his hand on the would-be soldier's shoulder. "It's going to be okay, Schultz." The boy said, "All okay!" They smiled at one another and sat down to wait for darkness.

◇◇◇◇◇◇◇◇◇◇◇◇◇◇◇◇◇◇◇◇◇◇◇◇◇◇◇◇◇◇◇◇◇

As Jonas drove the mercedes away, he watched the men in the mirror until they disappeared into the woods. A Kubelwagen rounded the bend as Jonas accelerated to cruising speed, and he kept one eye on the mirror until the vehicle passed where the fugitives had left the road.

Annalisa touched Jonas's arm. "I'm so proud of you, Jonas—I wonder just how far you would go to help another human being." She pulled on his arm and leaned over to kiss him.

Jonas said, "That flyer is the enemy, but I pray he makes it."

Marita called from the back seat, "Pray? Jonas, you disappoint me—I thought you didn't believe in God!"

"I am not an atheist, but I do have a bone to pick with God. This war has made me question His existence, or, if He does exist, either His motives or His ability to control anything. However, just in case, I will pray that they make it to safety because they will need all the help they can get." He smiled in the darkness and looked at Marita in the mirror. "Just in case." She winked the eye that a bandage didn't cover.

The border crossing went well for Jonas and his family—they were in Switzerland and driving to their new home within fifteen minutes. As the car climbed a long, steep hill south of Schaffhausen, the low sun, shining through a thin haze of oncoming clouds, added a glow to the stunning alpine scene, and, despite her pain, Marita felt a surge of hope.

403

As they climbed, clouds moved over the sun, surrounding the towering mountains, and the growing dusk washed out the colour until the mountains disappeared into darkness. The valley slowly disappeared in softly-falling snow, even though the clock gave them another half-hour of daylight.

Jonas turned off the road onto a gravel lane with a two-storey house at the end of it. Lights shone out of every window and a wide, lighted porch swept around two sides. Jonas stopped the car in front of wooden stairs four metres wide, leading to a veranda and an open door. A smiling white-haired man walked down the stairs to meet the car. He took two suitcases and led the party into the house. Jonas carried the final two while Annalisa helped Marita exit the car and negotiate the stone pathway. The children ran ahead, squeezing past the caretaker at the door. Jonas put the bags inside, then returned to help Annalisa get Marita up the stairs and over the threshold.

The friendly caretaker picked up the suitcases Jonas had been carrying and disappeared behind the children. When Marita was safely in the house, Jonas said to Annalisa, "Marcus will see that you get settled—I'm going back; hopefully, I will return with the fugitives."

The mercedes roared out of the yard in a cloud of soft snow. Annalisa stood on the verandah, watching the car round the sharp corner at the driveway intersection and drive onto the road and into the wall of falling snow. She said, "Be careful, my darling," softly to herself, feeling blessed but afraid. Why had God given her so much joy amid so much sorrow? Surely, at some point, He would want something in return.

◇◇◇◇◇◇◇◇◇◇◇◇◇◇◇◇◇◇◇◇◇◇◇◇◇◇◇◇◇◇◇◇◇◇

Willie and Schultz approached the border in almost total darkness. There were no trees for a hundred feet between them and the path, but clumps of thick, low bushes had grown on both sides since the area had been cut. A high barbed-wire fence marked the edge of freedom on the other side; a few shrubs grew between the path and the barbed wire. Once past the wire, there was nothing but miles of Swiss trees.

Schultz crouched beside Willie; a cluster of thick shrubs hid them from anyone on the trail five metres in front of them. During the daylight, Willie had watched patrols going both ways on the path and timed their appearance. The most he could hope for was fifteen minutes to get past the fence, which could be as little as ten. He would wait for the next patrol to pass before figuring out what he could do about the wire.

Schultz leaned against Willie, looking for protection from the damp wind. He was almost a head taller but thin, his youthful chest not much larger than Willie's. His face was so close that Willie could see Schultz's blue lips, and despite the boy's effort to control it, he shivered violently, his thin, damp Wehrmacht uniform providing little warmth. Using the proven 'point and grunt' language, Willie offered his insulated coveralls, but Schultz shook his head and laughed self-consciously.

Willie ignored him, opened the coveralls and stepped out of them, still protected by his heavy wool winter uniform. When he passed them to Schultz, the boy held the coveralls even with his shoulders and showed Willie that a foot of feet was still uncovered. He used a grateful smile to thank Willie for the offer and handed them back. Willie took the knife out of his survival kit and slit the legs up to where his knees would be, compared the coverall's arms to Schultz's, and gave them the same treatment. Schultz's expression went from hopeless to the opposite as he pulled them on. The extremities left a fair bit of his legs and arms sticking out, but the front closed completely, covering his narrow adolescent chest. Schultz whispered, *"Danke...Danke schön,"* as he stretched to test whether he could move freely.

◇◇◇◇◇◇◇◇◇◇◇◇◇◇◇◇◇◇◇◇◇◇◇◇◇◇◇◇◇◇◇◇◇◇◇◇

The sky had become a solid overcast suspended a few feet above the ground, and a light, cold rain started to fall, limiting visibility to a couple of metres. Willie looked toward the border—the beginning of safety—and thought of Norma and Nathan. He had done his share; he longed to work at a job where no one would shoot at him, and he ached to spend his nights with his new family.

It was as dark as night could get when Willie heard voices approaching them from the east—the patrol was coming down the path. He put his hand on Schultz's shoulder, and Schultz nodded. Willie shifted his position so he could see whoever was coming.

A lantern flickered through gaps in the trees a half-dozen times, then broke out into the open. Two Wehrmacht soldiers sauntered down the trail and stopped directly before the prospective escapees. The guards carelessly leaned their rifles against a tree and lit cigarettes. They smoked and talked, and Willie couldn't understand anything they said, but Schultz moved his fingers apart and together in a "yapping" motion.

The soldiers talked and laughed until their cigarettes were too short to hold between their fingers. One of them let out a long burst of wind, and the other said something that, to Willie, sounded congratulatory. The soldiers roared with laughter. Schultz held his nose, and Willie laughed silently. The soldiers ground their cigarette butts into a stump, picked up their rifles and continued down the trail, still talking.

Willie waited until the sound of their voices and the flicker of the lantern disappeared, then motioned Schultz to follow him, glancing down the path as he carefully stepped over a root. The boy tripped on it and fell flat on his face with a grunt. Willie froze and looked down the path, but there was no other sound or light. He took Schultz's arm and guided him to the bushes as he would a blind man.

They were next to the fence, and Willie was trying to find a way through it when the border guards' light flickered through gaps in the trees. The patrol was early. He steered Schultz behind the bushes on the Swiss side of the path; the boy stumbled, but Willie caught him. They were barely behind cover, and the land of mountains and chocolate was only six feet away when Willie pushed Schultz to the ground.

The soldiers stopped at the stump they had left ten minutes before, leaned their rifles against the same tree, and lit their cigarettes. Nothing stood between Willie and their guns, less than ten feet away. He estimated his chances of crawling to the rifles undetected were good but decided against it. If they lifted the lantern and looked directly at Willie and Schultz, the race to the guns would be on, but Willie resolved that the chance of winning that race would be slim. Even if he won the race, there was still a question in Willie's mind whether he could shoot the men. Despite that, Willie would have felt better if the man in the mercedes hadn't thrown away Schultz's rifle.

The soldiers smoked, laughed and joked for another ten minutes, as they had on the outbound leg, but no wind was broken this time. Willie took the time to examine the fence in the yellow light thrown by the kerosene patrol lantern. When they ground out their butts, picked up their rifles and moved on, Willie had a plan. He waited until the last flicker of the swinging lantern vanished, then pulled Schultz to his feet.

The fence consisted of four rolls of loosely coiled razor wire fastened to posts—enough to slow down a man in a hurry, but Willie reckoned that he and Schultz could get through without a scratch. He searched until his foot kicked a heavy branch he had seen in the lantern's light, probably cut from a felled tree when the Germans cleared the area. Willie pushed it under the bottom coil of wire where it went over a depression and lifted, angling it so Schultz could crawl under the fence. Schultz did the same for him from the Swiss side. When Willie was safely in the Swiss forest, Schultz joyfully threw the branch away and grinned. The reflection from his white teeth cut through the black night.

◇◇◇◇◇◇◇◇◇◇◇◇◇◇◇◇◇◇◇◇◇◇◇◇◇◇◇◇◇◇◇◇◇◇

The faint light that penetrated a five-thousand-foot layer of clouds and Willie's keen night vision allowed him to negotiate his way through the trees. Although most of the time he led Schultz by the hand, the boy still repeatedly tripped and fell. Willie compensated for the slow pace by walking south for close to an hour before turning east to intercept the road that Jonas had promised would be there. No marauding German deserter hunters crossed their path, perhaps because the light rain was now a steady downpour, and every branch they touched dumped water on them.

Soaking wet and cold, they reached the road in an hour and waited in the trees on a three-hundred-metre straight stretch. A dozen cars passed them, their bright headlights lighting up the pavement for a hundred metres in front of them. It seemed longer but had only been thirty minutes when a car approached with its interior lit. Willie pulled Schultz out of the darkness and stood on the edge of the road where the orange light of the car's headlights splashed on them. It stopped beside them, and Jonas said through the open window, "I'm glad you made it."

Willie grinned. "I don't have words to tell you how happy I am to see you!" He opened the back door, and the soggy pair climbed into the back seat.

Willie chuckled when he suddenly thought about the reunion he would have with Norma, then laughed out loud. He laughed so hard he infected Schultz and his saviour. They sat there and laughed until a car approached from the opposite direction. They had themselves under control when it passed.

Jonas waited until the car's taillights were out of sight, then turned the mercedes around. Three times on the way to the house, Willie chuckled loud enough that Schultz poked him in the ribs. He pushed on Schultz's shoulder and yelled, "We made it! I'm going home!" Schultz laughed and pushed back.

Jonas talked to Schultz from the front seat, and Schultz answered. They talked back and forth for a few minutes before Jonas said in English, "I asked the boy about his parents and how he got into the Wehrmacht.

"Schultz's father has been in Russia since Germany invaded in 'forty-one.' He doesn't know for sure whether his father is still alive. The British killed his mother and sister when they bombed their home in Köln in May of 'forty-two.' At the time, he was thirteen and a member of the Hitler Jugend, and the boys were in the forest playing soldier when the British levelled the city. Schultz's grandparents were also killed, so he had nowhere to go. The *Sozialamt*, I think you call it social services, put him in an orphanage until the Wehrmacht took all the fifteen-year-old Hitler Jugend boys in May of this year."

"I wasn't on that raid," said Willie, relieved. "I was still training in Canada." Jonas translated to Schultz.

Willie half-smiled at Schultz because he couldn't think of anything to say. His elation had died.

<hr>

Two-and-a-half hours later, the mercedes ploughed through six inches of snow, pulled up in the yard in front of a beautiful two-storey alpine house, and everyone got out of the car. Willie looked up, laughed, spun around, and held his hands out to catch the snowflakes. Schultz began to sing, "Oh Tannenbaum, oh Tannenbaum…" in a beautiful tenor voice as he danced with Willie.

They stopped, breathless, and Willie turned to his rescuer. "Sir, do you have a telephone? I have some money, and I will pay for the call."

Jonas said, "Yes, I have a telephone, and the Swiss system is the best in the world, according to the Swiss. As a matter of fact, the connection to England is excellent!" Willie danced into the house, chuckling to himself.

Jonas pointed at a telephone on a small table. "You can call anywhere you like for as long as you want to talk. I don't care what it costs, and I won't take your money." He suddenly asked, "Do you need money to get home?"

"No, sir," Willie couldn't get the smile off his face, "I have Swiss francs that I carry on missions, and you have already been generous enough."

Jonas turned to Schultz. He asked in German, *"Wie alt bist du, Junge?"*

"Fünfzehn, mein Herr, aber ende Januar bin ich sechzehn." The boy straightened his shoulders.

Jonas turned to Willie and said in English, "I just asked Schultz his age... He said fifteen, almost sixteen. Now, about that phone call..." Willie was having difficulty standing still. "But you must be famished, and you're soaking wet; wouldn't you rather change your clothes and eat first? I'll find something for you to wear...I never throw anything away."

Willie looked down at a small puddle growing around his wet feet and said, "No, sir, I can't eat until I talk to Norma's parents." as emphatically as he could.

Jonas relented. "Okay, I'll dial the number and get you connected. Write it down on the pad beside the phone."

Willie wrote the number down, and Jonas called the international operator. When the phone in England began ringing, he handed the receiver to Willie.

"Stanfield residence," George answered, clear as a bell.

"Good evening, George—it's Willie. Can I speak with James or Gianna?"

There was no answer, just heavy breathing. Willie took the receiver from his ear, looked at it, then tried again.

"George? Are you there, George?"

George sounded uncertain and hesitant.

"Willie? Is that you, Willie?" Then he said a bit louder, "I can't believe it's you! You're alive! My God, you're alive!"

Willie laughed. "Yes, I'm alive, and I'm in Switzerland. I want to tell James or Gianna so they can tell Norma. She must be worried."

"Willie," said George, in a conspiratorial tone, "You are not going to believe this, but Wing Commander Leech is sitting in the drawing room with Norma and her parents at this very minute. I was with them when the phone rang. My God, Willie, it's been eight days! Wing Commander Leech is trying to convince Norma to accept that you are dead, but she won't believe him. What do you want to do... Do you want to speak with Norma first? It might be more fun to speak to

Commander Leech first…" He kept his voice down. "You can't miss a chance like this…can you?"

Willie thought for a few seconds, then replied, "You're right, George; I think I should talk to John first; a chance like this only comes once in a lifetime, and only if you're lucky."

George said, chuckling, "Yes, William, I am very much looking forward to this." Willie could see George smiling.

There was a clunk in Willie's ear as George dropped the phone on the hall table.

Two minutes passed; John Leech picked up the phone and, irritated, said, "Wing Commander John Leech here. Who wants to speak with me? This had better be important, and you had better be able to explain where you got this number!"

Willie had worked out a plan and aimed for authority when he said, "Wing Commander Leech, I hear that yet again you've been telling certain people dear to me that I'm dead, and I'm calling to tell you that this deviant behaviour has got to stop!" Willie paused—there was a series of clunks in his ear, a string of curses, and then John said, "Willie? Is that really you?"

Willie continued, "This is the second time you've scared my wife out of her wits, and it can't happen again!" He tried hard not to laugh, but a snort came out.

"Willie, you little bastard…I can't believe you've done it again! Where in hell are you?" John laughed so loud that everyone in the adjacent room heard him. Sitting at the table with Norma and Gianna, James looked at George, and the look on his butler's face made James laugh.

"What's going on, Daddy? What's so funny? Her face lit up. She screamed, "It's Willie. It's Willie, isn't it?"

George couldn't stand it any longer. He took Norma's hand and pulled her gently out of the chair.

"Yes, it's Willie! He's in Switzerland!" He laughed, stepping from one foot to the other like a nervous little boy.

Norma screamed, "Willie!" and ran to the hall. She yanked the receiver from John Leech's hand and shouted, "Willie? Is that you?" She sat down hard on the chair next to the small table.

"Yes, darling, it's me, and I'm fine. John thinks he can have me home for Christmas."

"Oh, Willie, I love you so much!"

"I love you too," said Willie, tears of joy running down his cheeks.

They whispered sweet things to one another for five minutes, and when Willie hung up the phone, he found Jonas behind him, grinning from ear to ear.

"That sounded like it went well!"

"Yes, sir, it did. My commanding officer had just told her that I was dead, that she should give up hope that I would return." He laughed, enjoying himself. "I'm afraid I couldn't resist having a little fun with him."

"The war will soon be over, and surely he will keep you on the ground. Perhaps you will have a more normal life." Jonas swept his arm toward a large room with comfortable chairs. "We will go and meet my family." He looked at the puddle on the floor and steered Willie toward the stairs. "But first, you will stop ruining my wood floors. Both of you, come. We will find dry clothes for you." Willie and Schultz followed Jonas up the stairs.

◇◇◇

Dry and warm, dressed loosely in Jonas's clothes, Willie and Schultz followed Jonas into a spacious room full of windows facing a wall of mountains they couldn't see in the snowy darkness. The introduction began with two girls, Elke and Brigitte, then Walther, who shook hands wordlessly. Marita, his mother, and finally, Annalisa, Marita's mother. Willie ran it past his memory a couple of times.

When the introductions were over, Schultz sat in a chair beside Annalisa. Willie and Jonas remained standing.

In the way of little girls, Brigitte asked, *"Bist Du Pilot?"* Jonas translated, "Are you a pilot?"

"No, but I fly in airplanes." The little girl looked up at Jonas, and he translated Willie's answer.

"Unser Vati war Pilot. Jemand hat ihn getötet als er versuchte uns to beschützen. Hast Du unseren Vati gesehen?"

"I think you should meet their mother next." Jonas took Willie's arm.

"No, please, tell me what she said." Willie stood his ground. Brigitte and now Elke looked up at him expectantly.

Jonas let go of Willie's arm. "There is no need to hear that. She's only a little girl. She's six years old."

Willie stood still and stared at Jonas until he shrugged his shoulders and reluctantly translated what the little girl had said.

"Erik, their father, was a night fighter pilot and a fine man, the finest I've known. He died defending Heilbronn, and the children don't understand war. They don't know why anyone would kill their father, and they want you to tell them whether you saw him."

Willie looked at the little girls. They looked at him, then Jonas. Before Willie could speak, Walther, sitting with his mother, left the sofa and stood before him, his back ramrod straight.

"*Du bist RAF Flieger…*" The little boy looked straight at Willie. "*Mein Vater war ein Nachtjägerpilot, und ist abgeshossen worden. Fliegst du in einem Bomber?*" No one in the room made a sound.

"He asks if you fly in a bomber," said Jonas softly.

"Yes, I am a rear gunner," said Willie.

Jonas used many more words than Willie thought necessary to explain Willie's job in the lancaster, and Walther nodded.

"*Bist du abgeschossen worden?*" asked Walther, looking at Willie with satisfaction.

Jonas had briefed Willie on the family as they drove to the house but intentionally hadn't mentioned that Walther's father had died in the raid.

"He asks if you were shot down." Jonas, uncomfortable, looked at Marita. She looked at Willie and said, "Perhaps it's time for the children to go to bed."

Willie said, "Please let the children ask questions until they are done."

Jonas translated, and Marita nodded.

Willie looked at Walther. "Yes, the flak guns shot our lancaster down. We jumped out with our parachutes."

Walther and Brigitte waited patiently for the translation, and then Walther turned back to Willie, his hands balled into tiny fists.

"*Hast du unsere Stadt zerstört und meinen Vater getötet?*" Walther fought tears.

Willie wanted to hug the little boy, but when he looked at his mother, he caught a look that told him not to do it. Jonas hesitated, then translated.

"He asked: 'Did you kill his father?'" Jonas added, "Please be careful; it's only been a few days since he learned his father was shot down."

Willie shifted his gaze back to the little boy and kept it there as he said, "Walther, our bomber was one of the planes that dropped bombs on Heilbronn. Our target was the centre of the city, and if your house was there, then we may have been one of the planes that dropped bombs on it." He blinked back tears. "But Walther, I wouldn't know your father's plane; there are hundreds of them in a bombing raid."

Jonas translated again, using far more words than Willie had.

Walther said, through a flood of tears, *"Meine Fussballfreunde waren im Luftschutzraum, und sie wurden verbrannt!"* Walther sobbed, *"Mein Vater ist abgeschossen worden weil er versuchte die Englishe Bomber abzuschiessen. Die Nummer seines Flugzeugs ist einhundertvierundsechzig."*

Willie hung his head and tried not to cry as Jonas translated. Marita watched her son through tears, and Annalisa sobbed. Schultz kept his eyes on the floor in front of his chair. Willie guessed that Schultz was thinking of his mother and sister.

Jonas said, "Walther's football friends burned in the shelter, and his father was shot down while trying to shoot down the bombers. He said the number on his father's plane was one-hundred-and-sixty-four."

Willie, losing his battle with tears, said, "I didn't shoot down any fighters. We didn't see any except on our radar."

Suddenly, the number of Walther's father's aircraft, one hundred sixty-four, hit him. Mailly de Camp. He had seen Walther's father.

Willie blurted out, "Walther, I did see your father a few months ago...I recognize the number. Would you like to hear the story?" Willie looked from Walther to his mother and back while Jonas translated. Brigitte had given up and was playing a hand game with Elke. When she heard about a possible story, she stopped and listened carefully. Schultz lifted his head and sat back in his chair.

Willie began his tale: "We were flying over France, and it was dark. I didn't see your father's plane until it almost ran into my turret! He was so close I could see his face clearly, and he stared back at me. We didn't have time to fire our guns as your father dove his plane away from me, but I saw the number as he turned. The mid-gunner and I did fire a few seconds later, but we didn't shoot him down."

When Willie finished, Walther's tears had slowed.

Marita said, *"Erik hat mir die Geschichte erzählt. Er meinte dass irgendwie wäre der junge Mann im lancaster etwas besonderes."*

Jonas translated, "Erik wrote Marita about the incident. Apparently, you made as good an impression on her husband as he did on you!"

"I was afraid I had killed his navigator," said Willie.

"She showed me the letter," said Jonas, "and, by some miracle, Karl wasn't injured."

Willie bent his knees so that his face was level with Walther's. He took his compass out of his pocket and gave it to the little boy. "Take this, Walther, and you will always know where home is, even in the dark."

Jonas again used too many words, and before he finished, Walther put his arms around Willie's neck and hugged him so hard it hurt. Willie buried his face in Walther's shoulder to hide his tears.

THE END

From the Author

Write a Review and Join my Email

I hope you enjoyed the book, and I invite you to read the third one in the series, *Reap the Whirlwind*. But before you do, I have a favour to ask.

Most people pick books by looking at the cover, reading the blurb, and checking the reviews. I can control the first two, but the third is up to you, and your honest review will help others decide whether the book is for them. Most importantly, a good review, honestly written, is a justification for my writing. If you don't tell me whether you liked it or, shudders and shivers, not, I might assume you didn't, and that would be depressing.

If you are on Amazon, you can leave a review. Tell everyone what you liked or didn't like about the story or my writing.

Alternatively, if you aren't on Amazon or your review is rejected, use the links or the QR code to reach me and tell me whether you liked the book. Please give a rating, 1 to 5, and any comments you want to share, and I will submit an Editorial Review in your name.

Web site: *thesongsofwar.com.*
Facebook: *Robert Faulk, Author*
Email: *robertfaulk@thesongsofwar.com*

Join my newsletter on the website, by email, or on my Facebook page, and I promise to keep you updated on what I am doing. I will send you tidbits I cut from the books, historical context, and previews of new books I am writing.

Epilogue

Fanatics never Surrender

Working from our Canadian office, Bob sold earth-moving machines I bought in Europe, usually a simple business transaction. I purchased a machine…and he sold it…except when it wasn't simple, like when he sold a machine I didn't own.

In my daily telephone report, I told him I was negotiating for a Cat 215 excavator, S/N 1204, and the deal should close in a day or two. A few hours later, a customer called him looking for precisely that year and model, and Bob sold him the machine, taking a generous deposit. And the following morning, Bob called to give me the good news. Unfortunately, I had to tell him someone had outbid me—and he said I simply had to find a machine that would fit the description of the one he had sold.

I was looking for a Caterpillar 215 excavator with a serial number close to 1200, with 1,400 hours on it. I found one in the European Caterpillar system that was close enough; if I could talk the owner into selling it to me for a price that would work.

I drove from my base in Köln to Stuttgart to meet the contractor who owned S/N 1214, close enough to 1204 for my purposes. When I looked at the machine, it had 1,298 hours on it, almost a perfect fit with the contract my partner had signed to supply said machine.

Since the machine was already sold, the price of the Stuttgart machine would be the sticking point, so the contractor and I went to a pub, a Gastätte, where civilized German businessmen go to negotiate contracts over a beer or a game of chess. We drank beer while we played chess and, for an hour, talked about everything but the price of the Cat 215 excavator.

As happened to me frequently in such situations, the conversation turned to the war, still fresh in the minds of most Germans. It certainly was fresh in Walther Stephanie's mind, and the story he told me was of standing on the Wartberg as a nine-year-old boy, watching British lancaster bombers destroy his city, his home, and the air raid shelter where his mother would be sheltering from the bombs.

As he told me the story, his chess became clumsy, his hand began to shake, and finally, he had to tip his king. We finished our beer in silence, and he invited me to his home for Abendessen, where his mother would tell me the rest of the story.

The evening meal was typical for Germans... Grünes Hering, Zwiebeln, und Schwarzbrot...raw herring with sour cream, raw onions, and black bread...and, of course, an outstanding Pils.

Marita, now close to seventy, told me how she had survived by jumping in the river and showed me her scarred face, arm, and back. They told me their memories of Erik and the war from their unique perspectives.

Sixty percent of the city had been totally destroyed, and seven thousand people were dead or missing. There weren't enough gravesites, so a mass grave (Ehrenfriedhof Heilbronn) was dug near Köpfertal, where every year a remembrance ceremony is held for the victims.

◇◇◇◇◇◇◇◇◇◇◇◇◇◇◇◇◇◇◇◇◇◇◇◇◇◇◇◇◇◇

On their sweep through southeastern Germany, American forces attacked Heilbronn on the fourth of April 1945, expecting the same light resistance they had met since they had entered the country. But a fanatical Nazi loyalist, General Foertsch, had taken control of the city's defence and organized every able-bodied soldier he could find, including a platoon of Hitler Jugend. The boys were all sixteen or younger, but their training had included army discipline.

The battle was fierce, and, as expected, the Americans prevailed, but their casualties were higher than the total since they had entered the country. German losses remain undefined, except for fifteen hundred prisoners. Those 'unclear' losses include most of the Hitler youth platoon—their officers shot them in the back when they attempted to surrender to a company of horrified American soldiers.

The French arrested Wilhelm Murr, the Reich defence commissar for the region, in Egg, Austria. On the thirteenth of May, 1945, a week after the war officially ended, he and his wife took poison rather than face a conviction that would result from a war crimes trial.

LIKE ANTS UNDER THE DOOR

LIKE ANTS UNDER THE DOOR is the story of the Russian Front, told through a German Wehrmacht soldier, Johann Finke. When Johann received the dreaded letter demanding he report to the German Army, he had just become the new first violin in the Bielefeld opera orchestra. It was March of 1941, Hitler had Western Europe on its knees, and popular opinion was that the war would end in a few months; Churchill surely had no choice but to make a deal with Hitler.

Hitler could not leave Russia on his eastern flank, led by a man as power-centred as Stalin was. Hitler and Stalin were competitors for Eastern Europe—and Hitler knew surprise was the key to victory.

Johann was a concert violinist, not a soldier, but his grandfather, a hero of the Great War, had taught his grandson the skills of war disguised as 'sport.' When Johann arrived at the German Army's training camp, he was ready for the nightmare his grandfather had predicted.

Johann Finke had been a soldier for three months when Hitler attacked Stalin's Russia without warning. A Jäger scout with the Sixth Army, Johann began a journey through hell as one of over three million men who crossed the Russian border, and it would be four bitter years before he saw his family again.

Eighteen months after Germany's finest soldiers entered Russia, the German Sixth Army had been reduced from three hundred thousand of Germany's best to a ragtag group of fifty thousand starving wretches who finally surrendered to the Russian Army in Stalingrad. Johann and his men escaped, but any hope of victory disappeared, and Johann began a race to reach his family before the Russian Army.

While Johann's wife, Barbara, struggled in Germany to save her children from Allied forces coming from the west, Johann fought desperately to slow the Russian advance, knowing the relentless Russian juggernaut would not stop at the German border or the door to his home. The Russians had tasted German blood at Stalingrad and Kursk and wanted more. Hitler had violated Russia, and Stalin vowed that all of Germany would pay the bill!

About the Author

Robert Faulk, a Canadian born on a farm and educated in a small rural school, grew up in a world of hard workers—men and women who farmed the land and harvested the forests and the sea with their hands. He studied engineering at university and worked in construction before taking his family to Germany to pursue a career as an opera singer. Over the next ten years, Robert met many Europeans willing to share still-fresh memories of the Second World War. He used their stories, often traumatic and deeply personal, to write a series of five books of historical fiction, "The Songs of War." The books expose the most contemptible cost of any war—the human cost..